# VILLAIN OF SECRETS

a VERONA LEGACY story

# VILLAIN OF SECRETS

## A VERONA LEGACY STORY

## L A COTTON

Published by Delesty Books



Edited by Andrea M Long
Proofread by Sisters Get Lit(erary) Author Services
Cover Artwork by Dily Iola Designs
Cover Designed by Lianne Cotton

# VERONA LEGACY

Angel of Tears
*A Verona Legacy Short Story*

Prince of Hearts
*Nicco & Arianne's Duet Book #1*

King of Souls
*Nicco & Arianne's Duet Book #2*

Villain of Secrets
*A Verona Legacy Story*

Savior of Regrets
*A Verona Legacy Story*

*True love cannot be found where it does not exist, nor can it be denied where it does.*

Unknown

# PROLOGUE

"*L*orenzo, get over here," my dad yelled, waving his hunting knife in the air.

I dropped the ball and jogged over to him and Uncle Toni. "What's up, Papà?"

"You ever skin a rabbit, kid?"

My brows crinkled as I leaned over his shoulder and saw the bloodied fur. "No, I didn't ever skin a rabbit." The words got stuck in my throat. Poor little thing looked like it had been skewered wide open. But there was something fascinating about the way its eyes stared back at me. Empty. Lifeless.

When our Nono died, Aunt Lucia said it was only the physical body that was gone. That the eternal part of a person, their soul, would go on to the afterlife.

Was there an afterlife for rabbits?

"You want to learn?" My father's gruff voice yanked me from my thoughts.

Uncle Toni tsked. "Vin, leave the kid alone. He's nine."

"Ten," I said, proudly. "I'll be ten in a few days."

"Nothing wrong with toughening him up, mio fratello. He might be nine now, but he won't stay that way for long. Here, Son." He thrust the blood-stained knife at me. My hand trembled as it curled around the hilt. Sunlight bounced off the blade, making the drops of blood shimmer.

It was the holidays, and me and my dad were out at one of our family's cabins in the Blackstone Reserve. We came every year—me and my dad, Uncle Toni and Uncle Michele, and my cousins, Nicco, and Matteo—while the women stayed at home and prepared for the holidays.

My dad said shit like that was for women to take care of. He said that it was better to get out of the way while they were doing their thing. Whatever that meant.

He didn't seem to like my aunts very much. My dad didn't really like anyone much. I liked them though. I liked how they always made a fuss over the kids, over me. Growing up without a mom, I'd craved their warm smiles and gentle touch. They were so warm and touchy feely compared to my father. But I was growing now, and I wanted to be tough like him, like my uncles.

I didn't like my girl cousins so much either. They were annoying: always laughing and giggling and talking about stupid girl stuff. I was glad I didn't have a sister like Nicco and Matteo, but a brother would have been nice. Someone to talk to when my dad was out, which was a lot.

My dad didn't like to show his feelings. I often wondered if it was because my mom died when I was born, and he was left with me. Sometimes he acted like I was nothing more than a burden. But then there were other times, like right now, when he looked at me with so much intensity, I knew without doubt that he loved me.

"Come on, figlio mio. Hunting is a rite of passage. It

makes you a man. Besides, what's a little blood on your hands." He chuckled darkly, sending a shiver racing down my spine.

Frozen in place, my hand trembled as I stared down at the lifeless animal. I didn't want to skin the poor thing—it sounded messy and disgusting—but I wanted to please my dad. I wanted him to look at me with pride in his eyes, the way Uncle Toni always looked at Nicco.

"What do I have to do?" I asked, trying to disguise the quiver in my voice.

"Vincenzo," Uncle Michele muttered, but my dad ignored him.

I glanced back at my cousins playing in the snow. It was only a thin layer right now, enough to make them slip and slide as they ducked and dodged snowballs.

Sometimes I wondered why their dads didn't want them to learn this stuff. Michele, not so much. He was different to Uncle Toni and my dad. Softer. Calmer. He rarely raised his voice or hand to anyone. But he was always watching. Always taking everything in.

Uncle Toni was the eldest, the head of the family. After our Nono died a few years ago, he had stepped into his role. I was used to being over at Nicco's house. He was my best friend. But something was different about it now.

We weren't supposed to talk about it, but I knew who my family were. I knew what they did. Me, Matteo, and Nicco often snooped on their *business talks* at Nicco's house.

"Lorenzo," my father snapped, jolting me from my thoughts. "We don't got all day, ragazzino."

*Ragazzino.*

I hated that word. I might have only been ten minus a few days, but I wasn't a kid. I'd practically raised myself. I didn't have a mom around to fuss over me, and Dad's constant string of women never stayed more than one night. We had a housekeeper, Greta, but she barely spoke a word of English. She made good cannoli though.

"What do I do?" I repeated, my stomach a tight ball of nerves.

"Get down here." He grabbed me by the arm and yanked me down onto the overturned log, right at the same time as Uncle Michele got up.

"I'm going to warm up."

"Pussy," my father grumbled, and something passed between them.

"Bloodthirsty coglioni." Uncle Toni got up too, squeezing my father on the shoulder. "Go easy on the boy."

My brows crinkled. I didn't understand what they were talking about. But I still had the knife in my hand and my father's icy stare drilling holes into the side of my head.

"Pinch its hide and cut it near the base of the neck."

My fingers trembled as I reached for the dead animal. The blood was cold and sticky as my hand slid into the wet fur.

"Good, now make the cut," my father barked at my hesitation. I dry heaved as the blade slid into it like butter, but no more blood spilled.

"That's it. Now turn the knife edge facing up and cut from the stomach to the neck." I did as he instructed. "Okay, use your fingers to pry the skin apart. It'll be a little tough, so you'll really need to pull."

Puke rushed up my throat, but I swallowed it down as I began unwrapping the rabbit like a candy sucker. It was all kinds of messed up seeing the flesh and bone underneath, but I couldn't tear my eyes away from the helpless thing.

"Good, Lorenzo, good." My dad gripped my shoulder. "Now we make little cuts around the feet here," he sliced the fur, "and here, see. Then we can pull out the legs."

"Holy crap," I breathed as he helped me.

"What do you think?"

"It's… gross but kinda cool."

Laughter rumbled deep in his chest. "You are more my son than I give you credit for." He stared at me in that intense way of his. I didn't know what he meant, but I liked hearing him say it. All I ever wanted was to make my dad proud. To get him to pay attention to me the way Uncles Toni and Michele doted on my cousins.

"Good, Lorenzo, good. Now we can remove the guts."

"Th-the guts?" I dry heaved, and he chuckled.

"But of course. We can't eat the guts, Son."

"It'll be bloody?" My eyes were fixated on the animal's rounded stomach.

"There will be some blood, but it's small. It won't be as bad as something bigger."

"Like a deer?"

"Exactly." He gently gripped my wrist and guided my hand—and the knife—back toward the rabbit. "You'll have to cut through the membrane and scoop out the entrails with your fingers." He continued forcing my hand until the knife slid into the rabbit's stomach. Blood gurgled around the blade and I squirmed.

"Surely you're not scared of a little blood?"

"N-no," I said, breathing through my nose, hating the way it made my stomach roll. I wanted to be strong like my dad. Like Uncles Toni and Michele.

I didn't want to get all squeamish at a little blood.

Animal blood, no less.

Pushing past the urge to puke all over myself, I pulled the rabbit's insides out. The snow around our feet ran red with the splatters of entrails.

"I did it," I said, puffing out my chest, feeling a lick of satisfaction zip up my spine.

When my father had handed me the hunting knife, I hadn't wanted to do it. Nicco and Matteo weren't expected to do such grim things. They were here enjoying the cabin and the snow and hunting, but then they were left to goof around because their fathers weren't like mine. They didn't push and push and push.

"I'm proud of you, Lorenzo, you did good."

"Yeah?" I grinned. I couldn't help it. Praise from my father was rare. You had to enjoy it while it lasted.

"Yes." He gave me a stiff nod, gripping my jaw, smearing his bloody fingers all over my face. "You have so much to learn about the world, about this life…" he trailed off.

"About what you and my uncles do?" The words spilled out before I could stop them.

His eyes narrowed, a flash of surprise there. "What do you know about what me and your uncles do?"

"I know some things…" My voice wobbled.

"So eager to grow up." He smirked. "There is time. One day soon, Lorenzo. Soon."

I knew we were done here. This rare father-son moment was over, and I'd go back to being nothing more than a pain in his ass.

"Go on. Go clean up and play with your cousins."

"Okay." My head hung low as I moved around him. But at the last second, he snagged my wrist and hope swelled in my chest.

Maybe he wanted to hang out some more. Even if we

were skinning rabbits, it was better than him pretending I didn't exist.

I waited, my mouth hanging open like a dog waiting for scraps. "P-Papà?" I said, filling the heavy silence.

And then he said seven little words that would one day mean everything to me.

"Blood is life, Lorenzo. Never forget that."

# CHAPTER 1

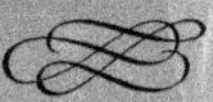

ENZO

"*E*, that's enough." My cousin Matteo's voice barely penetrated the roar of adrenaline in my ears as I drove my brass knuckles into the guy's face. The skin along his cheekbone split wide open, blood spraying into the air like a fine mist.

"Stop," he whimpered, trying desperately to clutch at my arm. "Please, stop."

"I'll stop when you tell us what we need to know, stronzo."

"I-I already told you… I don't know nothing."

Whack.

I hit him again.

His face was a mangled mess, but I didn't care. The asshole was a rat, the lowest of the low. He could rot in hell for all I cared. I was only here to get answers.

"I'm gonna ask you again, tell me what the fuck you know?"

He trembled like a pussy, a wet patch staining his pants, the smell of piss permeating the already stale air. "I-I… please…" His right eye was swollen shut, his lips puffy and sore.

I raised my fist, ready to lay into him again, but Matteo snagged my wrist. "Enough," he snapped. Our eyes met, and I saw the disapproval shining there.

My cousin never did like getting his hands dirty. He was a lover, not a fighter. But love didn't get you anywhere, especially not in our business.

"I suggest you let me the fuck go, *cousin*," I seethed.

"I'm not going to let you do this, E. Uncle Toni's orders were to feel the guy out, not leave his eyeball hanging out of its socket."

"He knows who pulled that shit at Johnny Morello's."

"Maybe, maybe not." He lowered his voice as if the guy currently tied to the chair could think about anything besides the pain he was in. "But I'm not about to let you kill the guy because you're looking for something to take your anger out on."

"It's not your call to make," I gritted out, feeling a lick of irritation.

Matt didn't get it.

Nobody did.

I needed this.

I needed to feel the crunch of flesh under my brass knuckles. I needed to hear the grunts of pain. I needed the cloying stench of blood.

I needed it all.

"No," he yanked out his cell phone, "but it's not yours either."

Fuck.

*Fuck!*

"I won't let you do this, E. You want to go into self-destruct mode, fine. I get it. But I won't stand by and watch you lose yourself. So you can either back the fuck up, or I can call for back up." He pinned me with a look that said he wasn't going to give me a choice.

"You never did have the balls for this life, coglioni." I spat the words out, tearing off my brass knuckles and shouldering past him.

I heard his long exhale of relief, but it didn't tamper the anger vibrating inside me.

The guy tied to the chair, bleeding out, was a rat.

A traitor.

He deserved everything he had coming to him and more.

Barreling through the back door of the club where we sometimes handled business, I spilled out into the inky night. It was New Year's Eve, and it was fucking freezing. When I inhaled a ragged breath, it burned my lungs, but no more than the smoke I was about to light up.

Matteo found me a few minutes later, sucking on the cigarette as if my life depended on it. "Those fucking things will kill you," he grumbled, wafting the tendrils of smoke away.

"It's this or I go back in there and finish what I started."

"What the fuck has gotten into you?" His expression softened with concern.

"Like you really have to ask."

He knew.

The entire Family knew.

"Look," he let out a sigh, "I know it was a shock, but it's been weeks. Vincen—"

"Don't. Just don't." I clipped out.

You couldn't put a timeline on discovering your father, the man who raised you, the man who pledged his entire life to the Family was a traitorous piece of shit who had betrayed us.

Betrayed me.

There were days when I still couldn't believe it. Vincenzo Marchetti was the boss' right-hand man. His brother and confidant...

And he'd screwed us over.

But it was worse than that.

So much worse.

My father had killed my aunt. When she'd discovered proof of his betrayal, he'd killed Aunt Lucia, leaving Uncle Toni a widow, and my cousins, Nicco and Alessia, motherless. He'd made it look like she had up and left because she couldn't handle being in this life.

Motherfucker.

I flicked the end of my smoke and dragged my boot across it.

"Better?" Matteo asked.

"What do you think?"

"I think you need to find a better way to relax than with your fists." His eyes dropped to my tender knuckles, but I barely felt the sting. "There's that party at The Diamond. We could swing by and check it out?"

Pushing off the wall, I pulled the collar on my leather jacket up and headed for Matteo's truck. "Let's go," I said.

Liquor *and* pussy?

I didn't need asking twice.

~

THE DIAMOND WAS A POPULAR PLACE ON THE EDGE OF LA RIVA and Romany Square. One of our guys, Jonah, owned it, and always threw invite-only New Year's Eve parties for the Family's most trusted associates, and a few non-associates if the line of barely-dressed women lining the street was anything to go by.

"Jonah sure knows where to find them." Matteo let out a low whistle.

"See something you like?" I taunted.

"Fuck off." He flipped me off. "I'm just saying, that's a lot of skin on display for winter. I'm pretty sure my balls have crawled back into my body."

He wasn't wrong. The wind had an icy bite that was like a thousand tiny blades over my face as we approached the entrance.

"Enzo, my man," the security guy extended his fist. "Wondered if you'd stop by. Matteo." He nodded at my cousin. "Jonah is inside, already draped in pussy."

"Wouldn't expect anything less." I smirked. Jonah was always down for a good time.

"Hey, you good?" He pressed a hand to my chest, his eyes going to my tender knuckles.

"Nothing I couldn't handle." It came out tight. Giving me a stiff nod, he dropped his hand. "Enjoy your night. Don't do anything I wouldn't." His gruff laughter followed me inside.

The heat instantly hit me, and I shucked out of my jacket and handed it to the attendant in exchange for a ticket. Matteo did the same, rolling up the sleeves on his fitted black shirt.

"It feels weird without Nicco," he said.

"Yeah."

Nicco wasn't only our cousin, he was our best friend, and our capo. Usually where he went, we followed, but we couldn't exactly follow him and his wife—fuck me, we were too young to be wifed up—to New York on their honeymoon.

"Are you… pouting?" Matteo snickered.

"Fuck off. I don't pout."

"Cous, that's a pout if ever I saw one." He grabbed my cheeks and smushed them together. "You're missing him, aren't you?"

"I'm not… oh, fuck off." Shirking him off, I made a beeline for the bar. Sleek, black, and chrome, the counter ran along one length of the room. I dropped onto a stool at the end and rapped my knuckles on the counter.

"Enzo, my man," the bartender said. "What'll it be?"

"The strongest thing you've got."

"Shit, man. Bad day?"

"Try bad fucking year."

"I'll make it a double." He chuckled. "Matteo?"

"I'll take a beer, thanks."

"You should probably wrap those." Matt motioned to my hand.

"Nah, I like the pain."

"Of course you do," he mumbled. "You know, I wasn't trying to be a jerk back there."

"I know." My jaw clenched, remembering how good it had felt to put my fists through that asshole's face. "What did you do with him?"

"Called clean up and told them to turn him over to the cops."

"Shit, Matt, that isn't—"

"He's not going to talk, not to us. But he might if he thinks he's going to spend the next six years getting ass raped in the State Pen. Dante and Craddick will work him over."

Dante and Craddick were two of the local police officers in our pocket.

"Someone tried to move in on our territory, we need to find out who." My hand trembled as I made a tight fist.

Morello's was one of the Family's businesses up in Providence. It had been broken into last week and trashed. They hadn't gotten the contents of the safe, but they had left a nice little message in the way of a barely recognizable Johnny Morello. The guy was lucky to be alive.

It was a bold move, hurting one of our own.

"And we will," Matteo said, eyeing me with caution. "But some decisions aren't our call to make."

The bartender slid our drinks in front of us but didn't hang around. I grabbed mine, taking a big mouthful. As promised, the double measure of scotch was strong, but I welcomed the burn.

"He's a rat, Matt. And you want to just hand him over to the cops?"

The tip-off had come from our friends down in Providence about a guy who had been running his mouth about Johnny Morello's. We'd caught up to him just outside Verona County and lifted his ass to see what we could find out.

"Not me. Uncle Toni. And it's different, you know it is." His expression faltered. "He's not our rat to exterminate."

Silence descended over us, thick and heavy. It was like a fucking noose around my neck. How was I supposed to just accept what my old man had done?

*A traitor.*

He'd betrayed us right under our noses. I couldn't just let that go.

I wouldn't.

"Hey, Enzo, looking good." A tall blonde approached us, running her hand up my arm. "I was hoping to see you here."

"Yeah?" I tried to place her but came up blank.

"Mari," she reminded me, "we hooked up last month."

"Marielle, right? I remember."

Matteo smothered a snicker, and I shot him a hard look.

"You got any friends for my cousin?" I said around a smirk. "He's going through a bit of a dry spell, if you know what I mean."

"Fuck you," he mouthed, fighting a smile. "I'm going to take a leak." He gripped my shoulder and leaned in, whispering, "Don't do anything I wouldn't."

"What, you mean cuddle and talk about the weather?"

"Don't worry, Matteo, I'll keep him company." Marielle moved closer, tucking her tight little body against mine. She was wearing a sparkly halter top that left nothing to the imagination. Her long hair hung down her back and her pouty lips were painted blood red.

My favorite color.

I could imagine them wrapped around my dick while I fucked her mouth, my hand fisting her silky blonde locks.

"I'm down, if you are." She flashed me a knowing smirk.

"You read minds, hot stuff?" My brow quirked. "What other special skills do you have?"

"Take me around back and I'll refresh your memory."

"Let's go." I nudged her forward so I could climb off the stool. She slipped her hand into mine, and for a second, I wanted to shove her away. I wasn't looking to play games or let some bitch think she had ownership of me. But everyone was too wrapped up in the party to notice me and Marielle slip out the back exit.

Without a word, I pulled her into the wall and gripped her shoulder, forcing her to her knees. Her giggles grated on me, but I tried to block it all out as she popped my belt and the button on my jeans like a pro. Wrapping my hand around her luscious locks, I yanked Mari's head back, forcing her to look at me. She licked her lips, staring up at me with lust-drunk eyes and an overeager smile. "I can't wait to taste you again."

Right. Because we'd danced this dance before… only I had zero recollection of it because I'd been too out of it to remember.

She dipped her hand into my jeans and stroked my dick, pulling it free until it bobbed between us. "Maybe later, I'll get another ride." Her brow lifted.

"Suck me good, and perhaps I'll reward you."

She didn't waste any time, taking me into her mouth and sucking me hard.

"Fuuuuuck," I hissed, my head dropping back against the wall with a *thud*. She felt good, hoovering me down until I hit the back of her throat. I tightened my fist in her hair, forcing her to take me deeper. Her hand went to my hip, trying to steady herself as I fucked her mouth without restraint.

"E-Enzo," she garbled, tearing off me, "what the fuck? I can't breathe."

Her words were like a bucket of ice-cold water and I released her. "I thought you wanted to get me off?" I growled.

"I-I do." She pouted, reaching back for me and jacking me slowly. "But let me take control, yeah?"

"That's not how this works, dolcezza, and you know it."

I didn't want her controlling shit. I wanted to get off, go

back to the party, and drown my demons in the strongest liquor Jonah had lining his top shelf.

"Enzo, I can make you feel good. Just relax, let me take care of you."

Her words were like a knife to the fucking stomach.

*Let me take care of you.*

Only one girl had ever whispered that to me... and I'd almost let her.

I'd almost handed her the power to completely ruin me.

Nora Abato.

Fuck.

Just thinking her name gutted me in a way I hadn't expected.

If my piece of shit father taught me anything, it was that pussy was the enemy. Before you knew what was happening, it lured you in with promises of a good time. You grew attached, you wanted more... you wanted *her*.

But love didn't make you strong, it made you weak.

And I had no desire to find myself wifed up like Nicco, risking everything for something as fickle as love.

"Enzo?" Marielle's shrill voice yanked me back into the moment.

"We're done here." I pulled my dick away and tucked him back inside my jeans.

"Done? But we only just—"

"You should go on back into the party."

"But—"

"Ma sparisci!" I barked and she hurried inside, her gasp of surprise barely thawing the ice around my heart.

I pulled out a smoke and lit it up, dragging in a deep lungful of tobacco. When the back door opened again, I was hardly surprised to find Matteo.

"Thought I'd find you out here," he said. "What did you do? Your little friend looked pissed."

"Told her to fuck off mid-blow job."

"Shit, man," his chuckle came out thin, "that's cold, even for you."

"She was getting clingy."

"And God forbid anyone try to get close to you, right?"

"Don't." I bristled.

"You and Nor—"

"I said don't."

I didn't want to talk about me and Nora, or the way she'd started to soften my hard exterior.

It had been a few good fucks, nothing else.

So what if she was my best friend's wife's best friend? I'd done a pretty good job of avoiding her the past few weeks. I was confident I could keep it up. Especially since I had no plans to return to Montague University next week.

Nicco, Matteo, and I had enrolled eighteen months ago to gather intel about Roberto Capizola, the Family's biggest threat in the last decade. But he was no longer an issue. The job was done, and we didn't need to keep up pretenses anymore.

I no longer had to tolerate college classes or any of the bullshit that came with being a student.

"Whatever, man. I'm heading back inside. Jonah was just about to break out the snacks."

"Snacks? Seriously?"

"What? I'm hungry." He shrugged.

"You're a fucking idiot. It isn't any wonder you can't get regular pussy."

"Hey, I can get regular pussy. I just choose not to."

"Don't tell me you're going to pull a Nicco on me?" It was

bad enough I'd lost one best friend to a woman; I didn't need to lose Matteo too.

"Ah, don't worry, cous. Even if I did meet the woman of my dreams, I'd never abandon your cranky ass."

I flipped him off, shouldering past him to go inside. Tension rippled through me and since Marielle had ruined what could have been a perfectly good blow job, I'd have to settle for finding peace at the bottom of a bottle of expensive scotch.

Something strong enough to drown out the demons.

# CHAPTER 2

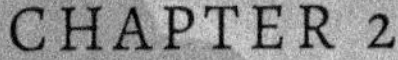
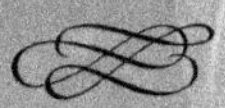

NORA

There was something inspiring about the first day of a brand new year. It wasn't so much any one thing, it was the possibilities. The ifs, whats, and maybes.

Being a college freshman, I might have expected to wake up this morning with a killer headache and last night's makeup smeared across my face. As it was, I felt as fresh as a daisy and my skin was silky smooth thanks to the nourishing mask I'd applied last night.

There was something to be said for staying in on New Year's Eve.

"Nora," my mom called. "Breakfast."

My stomach grumbled at the mention of food, and I smiled to myself. Apparently, I wasn't the only one happy that I didn't feel hungover.

Pushing the covers off my body, I sat up and swung my legs over the side of my bed, taming my wild curls out of my face. Hangover or no hangover I never escaped a bad case of bed hair.

A yawn escaped my lips as I leaned over and snatched up my cell phone, checking for messages. I smiled at the two from my best friend Arianne. The first was a picture of her and her husband, Nicco as they posed in front of Times Square. The second was a message.

**HAPPY NEW YEAR, NORA. YOU'RE THE BEST FRIEND A GIRL could ever wish for and I love you more than anything. Except Nicco (he made me type that).**

I CHUCKLED, SCROLLING DOWN THE MESSAGE.

**NEW YORK IS AMAZING. WE HAVE TO COME ONE TIME. JUST the two of us. I'll see you when we get back to Verona. Nicco says hi. xo**

SMILING, I TEXTED HER BACK.

**ENJOY YOUR LAST COUPLE OF DAYS. YOU DESERVE IT, ARI. xo**

AFTER THE SHITSHOW THAT WAS OUR FIRST SEMESTER AT college, my best friend deserved all her dreams to come true. It was hard to believe that she was married to Niccolò Marchetti, son of mafia boss Antonio Marchetti. But having witnessed them fall headfirst in love with one another, who was I to judge?

They were young, yes. But when you knew, you knew. Besides, they had that written-in-the-stars thing working for them.

My heart cinched, but I shook it off, pushing my feet into my fluffy, pink slippers.

"Nora, cucci—"

"I'm coming, Mom," I yelled. Grabbing my Montague University hoodie, I slipped it on and followed the smell of pancakes down the stairs.

"Happy New Year, baby," she sing-songed as I entered the room.

"Happy New Year, Mom." I helped myself to coffee before perching on a stool at the breakfast counter. "Something smells good."

She grinned. "It's almost done."

"Where's Dad?"

"You know your father, Nora, he's out jogging."

My mother and father worked for Arianne's parents, Roberto and Gabriella Capizola, they had for my entire life. We lived on their estate in a separate cottage nestled on the west perimeter. It was modest, but it had the best views of the Blackstone River. I'd grown up here, exploring the grounds, playing with my brother Gio, Ari, and her older cousin Tristan. But as I got older, I dreamed of more. Of life beyond the gated perimeter and guards posted on every way in and out.

"When are you headed back?" Mom placed a stack of pancakes in front of me. I added a handful of blueberries and a drizzle of syrup and dived in.

"I was thinking I might head back later."

Her brows knitted. "I'm not sure I like the idea of you staying there all alone now Ari is—"

"Ari is married, Mom. *Married.* Of course she's going to live with Nicco. I'm safe, I promise. La Stella is one of Roberto's buildings. It has excellent security and Maurice is still around."

He wasn't, not really.

But she didn't need to know that.

I didn't need close protection now. The threat to the Marchetti, to Arianne, was gone. But Maurice, my assigned bodyguard, did show up now and again to check in. I think it was Arianne's way of letting me know she still cared.

I knew she did. But she was married. *Freakin' married.* Our friendship was going to change whether we wanted it to or not.

"What's the matter with your pancakes, cucciola?"

"They're great, Mama, I'm just…" I swallowed the words. It was New Year's Day. I didn't want to be all mopey on the first day of a brand new year.

Giving my head a little shake, I inhaled a deep breath and forked another piece of pancake into my mouth. So what if Arianne no longer lived in our apartment and was married? It didn't mean life was over. She was still going to attend classes at MU. We'd still see each other all the time.

"Love changes people," my mom whispered.

My eyes slid to hers, and a weak smile tugged at the corner of my mouth.

*Oh, Mama, you don't know the half of it.*

I didn't hang around at the cottage. After eating my mom's famous risotto with my parents, Maurice gave me a ride back to University Hill.

"I'll do a quick sweep," he said, producing his key.

"You still have that?" My brow lifted, and he chuckled.

"I'll just be a second." Hand secured on his gun holster, he slipped inside.

I wasn't even a little bit worried.

The bad guys were gone, and everything was fine. But as I waited for Maurice to do his thing, a shudder ran down my spine as the memories tried to push themselves to the surface.

Less than two months ago, I'd been kidnapped and used as bait to lure Nicco and Arianne to their bloody end. Nicco had been shot, and my best friend had stabbed Scott Fascini, the guy working with his father to bring down the Marchetti with a knife until the life drained from his eyes.

He was gone, and his father was locked away with no chance of parole for a long time.

Nicco and Ari were safe.

I was safe.

Everything was—

"All clear." Maurice yanked the door open and I went inside.

We'd barely had time to make ourselves at home here before Arianne and Nicco got engaged. Swallowing the pinch of loneliness, I walked over to the window and pulled the blinds, letting the winter sun pour into the room.

"You don't have to stay," I said to Maurice when I noticed him hovering.

"Mr. and Mrs. Marchetti—"

"Asked you to stick around?" The words caught over the lump in my throat.

"They thought you might like the company." He gave me a stiff nod.

"Maurice, I'm fine."

*Fine.*

The word was cotton in my mouth.

I needed to do this—I needed to be here alone, without Maurice standing watch.

"Miss Ab—"

"Maurice," I snapped. "I said I've got this."

His expression softened. "Very well, Miss—"

"And for the love of God, stop calling me Miss Abato. I'm Nora, just Nora."

"Very well, Nora." His mouth quirked. "I'll be right outside."

"That wasn't what I… yeah, okay."

I knew Maurice wasn't going to defy Nicco's orders, so he could stand guard outside for all he liked, and I could go on pretending my life was normal.

I set to unpacking my case. Mom had insisted on doing all my laundry, so all I had to do was hang things back in my closet. Halfway into it, a knock at the door startled me. My brows furrowed wondering what Maurice could possibly want already.

Stomping to the door, I pulled it open. "Yes—you're not Maurice."

"No, I'm Luca." The guy smiled, and I swear my knees went a little weak. He was handsome. Tall with thick dark hair that fell over his eyes a little. Hazel eyes sparkled with humor as he took me in.

"What the hell do you think you're doing?" I snapped, feeling my anger levels rise as he blatantly ogled my chest.

"Uh, your shirt." His gaze lifted to mine.

"My shirt?" I balked.

"Yeah, I like it…"

I looked down, my cheeks burning when I realized I was wearing my boo bees t-shirt.

"Oh my God," I breathed, clapping a hand over my mouth. "I didn't… I wasn't expecting visitors." And humorous shirts were my favorite thing, I had an entire collection.

"Relax, I dig it."

"I… really don't know what to say to that." I forced a smile, slightly mortified that he'd caught me wearing my little ghost-bee motif t-shirt. "What can I do for you, Luca?"

"I just moved in across the hall, and it would seem I forgot all the important things like coffee, cream, and sugar."

"There's a coffee shop right along the street." My brow lifted, and he chuckled.

"Okay, you got me. I'm just trying to introduce myself to the neighbors and asking for some coffee sounds way better than being all creepy."

"Are you… a creep?" A smile played on my lips.

"Depends on your definition, I guess."

Our mutual laughter filled the space between us. "Well, since you're here, do you want to come in for coffee?"

"Yeah?" His whole face lit up. "That would be great… I mean, in a totally non-creepy way."

I glanced down the hall and noticed Maurice trying to make himself inconspicuous. He caught my eye and shook his head.

"Relax, Maurice," I called. "Luca is my new neighbor. I'm sure you know all about him." Nicco's team probably ran background checks on everyone living in the building since Arianne spent time over here.

"Uh, do I need to be worried about the fact you have armed security standing out in the hall?" Luca's brows crinkled as he followed me into the kitchen.

"Who, Maurice? He's nobody. How do you take your coffee?"

"Extra cream, one sugar please."

I switched on the coffee machine, suddenly feeling out of my depth. Here I was, dressed in my lounge pants and my oversized boo bees t-shirt, with a hot guy waiting for me to make coffee.

It wasn't exactly the New Year's Day I'd imagined.

"So Luca from across the hall, what's your story?" I asked as I poured us both a mug of coffee, adding sugar to his and creamer to mine.

"I just moved from Pawtucket. I work for a marketing company and they had a promotion opportunity… and here I am." He pushed his hair out of his eyes, smiling. "What about you?"

"Well, I didn't just move, as you can tell." I glanced around the apartment. "Born and raised in Verona County. I'm a freshman at Montague University."

"A freshman, wow, I thought you were older. Now, I do feel all kinds of creeper for being here."

"How old are you?"

"Twenty-three. I graduated a year ago."

"So old." I rolled my eyes. "Well, you picked a good neighborhood. It's a busy student area so there are plenty of bars and restaurants and good takeout. There's a gym downstairs too, if that's your thing."

From his muscular biceps I assumed it was.

"I work out occasionally, but I prefer to run."

"There's a park one block over that's popular with the jogging crowd."

"Sounds good." He sipped his coffee.

"So didn't anyone else on the floor answer? Or have you been drinking coffee, making small talk with the neighbors all morning?"

"Yours is the first door I tried."

"I see. Well lucky for you I was feeling neighborly then."

"Indeed." His eyes glided down to my chest again, and heat flashed through me.

"Maybe I should change my t-shirt," I suggested with a playful lilt.

"It's very… eye-catching." He chuckled.

"Men," I mumbled to myself as I drained the rest of my coffee and rinsed the mug under the faucet.

"Strange time to move, on New Year's?"

He shrugged. "As good a time as any. Besides, I'm not a fan."

"You're not a fan of New Year's?"

"Bad break up a couple of years ago. Kind of ruined it for me."

"Say no more." My stomach knotted thinking of a certain blue-eyed mafioso who had been avoiding me ever since I'd found him in bed with a busty blonde.

Of course, the first guy I set my sights on after arriving at MU had to be broody and dark and a total asshole.

Enzo Marchetti was as ruthless as he was cold. And now he was my best friend's family. Talk about a stroke of bad luck.

"Nora?" Luca's voice yanked me from memories I'd rather forget.

"Sorry, you were saying?"

"Actually," he stood, "I should be heading out. But thanks for the coffee. It was nice meeting you."

"Oh, okay." His departure seemed a little abrupt, but I wasn't about to beg him to stay. He was a stranger, and I wasn't desperate.

"I'll see myself out," Luca added. "Maybe I can repay the favor soon?"

"Sure." I smiled. Why did things feel awkward all of a sudden?

Luca gave me a small nod and headed for the door. When he reached it, he glanced back. "It really was nice to meet you, Nora. Shirt and all." He smirked.

Then he ducked into the hall and was gone.

"HE JUST INVITED HIMSELF INTO YOUR APARTMENT?" ARIANNE shrieked down the line.

"Babe, relax. Maurice was right down the hall. Besides, I thought everyone who moves into La Stella was vetted."

"They are," I heard Nicco grumble in the background.

"*Not* the point," Ari hissed. "He was a total stranger and you let him into our—your home. Sorry." Regret coated her voice.

"Don't be. I could have moved back into dorms, but I didn't want to. Besides, it's nice having my own space." The lie rolled off my tongue. "And now I have a new friend who lives across the hall."

"You met him once," she pointed out.

"And he offered to repay the favor next time." I chuckled,

but she didn't join me. "Ari," I added, "I'm going to be okay, you know?"

So she was married now. It wasn't like I didn't have other friends, and we'd still hang out. Nicco would have mafia business to take care of, and me and Ari would have girl's time.

Things wouldn't change that much.

"I know," she finally said, breaking the beat of silence. "I really miss you, Nor. I want you to know that."

"But you're happy, right?"

She hesitated and then let out a dreamy sigh. "I am, I really, really am."

"Well, that's all that matters, babe. Friendship doesn't die just because you went and got yourself a husband." My laughter almost sounded convincing. "When do you get back?"

"Tomorrow. Nicco has to go see his father so I was thinking we could have girl's night at our apartment."

"Sounds good. Just let me know what time."

"I will. I should probably go. Nicco is taking me on a private river cruise to Ellis Island."

"Have fun. I'll speak to you tomorrow."

"And Nora?"

"Yeah, babe?"

"No more inviting strange guys into the apartment."

"Yes, *Mom*," I hung up, smiling.

But it quickly fell when I realized this was my reality now. Arianne was gone. She had a new life, a husband, and a whole new family.

And what did I have?

I had a t-shirt with boo bees on it.

# CHAPTER 3

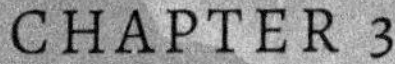

ENZO

"*A*ri," I said thinly as she opened the door to her and Nicco's place in Romany Square.

"Hello, Enzo." She smiled and dammit if it didn't soften something inside me. This petite, shy girl had stood up for the Family, she'd stood up for Nicco... I would never forget that. If it ever came to it, I would lay down my life for her. Because like it or not, she was family now, and despite my reservations about their marriage, family was everything to me.

Every-fucking-thing.

"Nic around?"

"He's just in the shower. We only got back an hour ago and we... uh... we were hungry." She flushed from head to toe and I chuckled.

"Hungry, is that what we're calling it these days?"

33

"Oh God," she murmured, spinning on her heel and disappearing into their apartment.

"This place is really starting to look like home," I said, admiring the living room. It was a big open plan space with a state-of-the-art kitchen set in one corner. They had a huge sectional that was big enough to sleep on, but it was littered in pale pink girly throw cushions.

My cousin was whipped good. It was warm and homey and felt like the kind of place you'd raise kids. Not that I knew anything about that; my childhood wasn't exactly conventional.

I stuffed down that shitshow and perched on one of the stools at the breakfast counter while Ari went to the refrigerator. She didn't even ask if I wanted a beer, just grabbed one, uncapped it, and slid it across the marble to me.

"Thanks," I said. "So how was New York?"

"Amazing." Ari leaned back against the counter and let out a soft sigh. "I never wanted to leave."

"I hope you didn't tell Nic that." He wouldn't ever leave Verona. Not even for his wife. He was bound to this place. It was his legacy, his responsibility. One day, he would be the boss and the Family would look to him for leadership.

You didn't just walk away from that.

But Arianne knew that. She wouldn't be standing here with his ring on her finger if she didn't.

"You don't need to worry, Enzo, home will always be Verona." Her soft laughter made me bristle.

"That's not—"

"Hey." Nicco appeared, towel-drying his hair. "Happy New Year, man."

"Yeah, you too." I got up and we hugged. "Ari was just telling me she didn't want to leave the Big Apple."

He snagged her around the waist and pulled her slender body into his. When I'd first met Arianne, she was this meek girl unsure of her own shadow, but even I couldn't deny she had grown into her role as the Capizola heir… and now the Marchetti princess.

Everyone loved her. Uncle Toni; Matteo; Nicco's sister, Alessia. Ari slotted into our family as if she'd always been there.

And honestly, I still didn't really know how I felt about that.

Nicco loved her, I got it. I did. But he was going to be the boss. Arianne made him weak. He'd almost gone to war for her once. I didn't doubt he'd do it again.

No pussy was worth that, worth losing yourself.

"It was pretty fucking amazing." He tucked her into his chest, resting his chin on the crook of her shoulder. "But we'd never up and leave your cranky ass."

"Have you been talking to Matt?"

"What?" His brows furrowed.

"Nothing," I grumbled. They had a point. It wasn't like I was all rainbows and unicorns lately. But what did they expect after everything I thought I knew was blown to shreds with five little words?

*Your father is a traitor.*

Even now, weeks later, it was still hard to believe that Vincenzo Marchetti had betrayed his family.

The Family.

He'd broken the most cardinal rule of all, and there was punishment for it.

Death.

I could still hear the echo of the pistol firing, the soft

crunch of bone cracking and flesh squelching as the bullet implanted in his head.

The bullet fired from *my* piece.

I'd killed him. My own father. The only parent I'd ever known. The second he'd admitted murdering my aunt, I'd aimed for the kill shot and pulled the trigger.

And I didn't fucking miss.

I didn't regret it, not one fucking bit. You didn't betray the Family and get away with it.

But something like that, it changed you.

"E?" Nicco said, and I jerked out of the memory of my father's brain matter splattering all over the walls.

"You good?" he added, his brow pinched with concern.

"Yeah, nothing a little session at Uncle Mario's gym won't fix."

Arianne's eyes widened. "Not fighting?"

"I might get in the ring and burn off some steam." I wasn't a fighter, not like Nicco, but I wouldn't turn down the chance to go a few rounds with one of Mario's guys.

"Nicco," she whisper-hissed.

"He's a big boy, Bambolina. He can look after himself."

"Well, just so long as *you* don't get in the ring." She leveled him with a hard look.

"I promise."

My brow lifted. That was news to me. I knew Arianne didn't want Nicco fighting at L'Anello's, the club where the underground fight ring happened every weekend, but it was a part of him. You couldn't just switch off the blood thirst, the hunger. I knew that firsthand.

Memories of what I'd done that night didn't diminish over time, they only burrowed their way deeper, infecting my soul like poison.

Just then, the buzzer rang. The way all the blood drained from Arianne's face I knew without asking who it was.

"Crap, she's early." Guilt glittered in her eyes. "Is this going to be a problem?"

"Why the fuck would it be a problem?"

It was Nicco's turn to quirk a brow in my direction. Ari rolled her eyes and left us alone as she went to open the door.

"What?" I snapped.

"Nothing." Nicco searched my face for answers I didn't have.

I felt her before I saw her.

Nora Abato.

The only girl I'd ever let see past my stone-cold exterior.

And the one girl I couldn't ever get close to again.

"The view was amazing." Ari and Nora chatted as they came into the room. "God, Nor, it was perfect."

"Nora." Nicco welcomed her with open arms and they hugged. "It's good to see you."

"I hear you treated my bestie like a Princess."

"Queen," he corrected. "I treated her like a Queen." His eyes found Arianne and the two of them shared a longing look.

"Okay, okay, I know you're newlyweds, but knock it off," Nora let out a strangled laugh, "or I'll need to take a cold shower." Her eyes flicked to mine, but I immediately dropped my gaze, unwilling to acknowledge her.

"Wow, nice to see you too," she said thickly.

"We're going to head out," Nicco filled the beat of awkward silence. "Luis and Alexi will be right outside. Order whatever you want, I left my card on the nightstand." He cupped the back of Arianne's head and pulled her in for a kiss.

Nora's big doe eyes drilled holes into the side of my face, but I didn't look at her.

I couldn't.

If I looked at her, I'd remember, and if I remembered… well, it wouldn't end well for anyone.

My fist clenched against my thigh as I stood up. "I'll wait outside," I grumbled. Nicco was tongue deep in Arianne, and Nora was right there…

I tried to tell myself I didn't care. That the fact she'd found me in bed, hungover with some blonde draped over me like a cheap rug, didn't matter. We weren't anything to one another. I'd made no promises to her. It was just sex. Mind-blowing, hot as sin sex.

That's all it was.

Nora didn't say a word as I stalked out of the apartment and down the hall. I didn't stop until I crashed through the door and pulled out my smokes. It was a nasty habit, but it calmed me a little.

Two minutes later, Nicco found me. "You need to quit that shit," he grumbled.

I inhaled one last hit and dropped the butt, dragging it into the asphalt with my boot. "My car is down the street." He followed me, climbing into my Pontiac GTO without another word.

He was quiet.

Too fucking quiet.

And I knew he was gearing up to rail at me. Sliding into the driver's seat, I ran a hand through my hair.

"Are we going to talk about what happened?"

"Nope." I jammed the key in the ignition.

I wasn't entirely sure which part he wanted to talk about, but either way, it had been weeks. If I'd have wanted to talk, it would have happened by now.

I didn't want to talk. I wanted to forget.

"Enzo," Nicco sighed. My eyes slid to his. "Maybe if you just talked to her—"

"Not going to happen, cous. It is what it is. I would have only disappointed her in the end." Because I wasn't wired right. Because somewhere along the line, I'd got skipped when they were handing out all those happy fucking emotions.

Because deep down, I knew a woman would only bring me drama and distractions I didn't want or need.

"You had your reasons," he said.

"Nic, she found me in bed with some blonde, there's no coming back from that." I didn't even remember what happened that night. But I remembered Nora's face as she stood in the doorway.

My chest squeezed, but I ignored it. It was better this way.

She was too good for this world.

Too fucking good.

Nora believed everyone could be saved, that everyone wanted to be saved.

But I wasn't looking for redemption…

Because my soul already belonged to hell.

"NICCO, FIGLIO MIO." UNCLE TONI GRABBED MY COUSIN AND pulled him into a hug. Then he moved to me, gripping my shoulders and searching my face. "Lorenzo."

"What's up, Uncle Toni?"

"You haven't been around lately."

"I've been busy."

"Busy making a mess of our informants?"

Fuck.

"The stronzo deserved it."

"He did, but it wasn't your call to make, son."

I winced at the word.

I was nobody's son now.

I was twenty and my parents were dead. Both killed by me.

Exhaling a long, steady breath, I followed Nicco and his father into Uncle Toni's den. Matteo and his father, Uncle Michele, were already seated at the table.

This wasn't a casual meeting, it was business, and a trickle of anticipation ran through me. I needed something to do. Collecting pizzo, running jobs down in Providence, picking up the dirty work no one else wanted. I needed to keep busy.

"Lorenzo," Uncle Michele tapped the seat beside him, and I went to it. "Sit." He pulled it out, the legs scraping across the hardwood floor.

"What's up, old man?"

"How have you been? Your Aunt Marcella worries."

"I'm good," I said around a tight smile.

"We're here, Enzo." He squeezed my shoulder. "You're not alone."

"I know." Swallowing over the huge fucking lump in my throat, I ran a hand over my face.

"Niccolò," Uncle Toni said. "How was New York? How's that daughter-in-law of mine?"

"Ari is fine. We had a good time."

"A good time," Uncle Michele chuckled. "You think we

don't remember being newlyweds, kid? Me and your aunt went at it like—"

"Fuck's sake!" Matteo grumbled. "No one wants to hear about you and Mom, old man."

"It's about time you found yourself a good woman, Son. Your mother wants some grandbabies to fuss over."

Matteo almost choked on nothing. "B-babies? Jesus, Dad, I'm twenty."

"And we're not getting any younger, Matteo."

"Can you believe this shit?" he whispered to Nicco, who chuckled.

"I'm telling you now, Niccolò, don't be coming around to tell me Arianne is knocked up anytime soon. After everything that's happened the last few months, the last thing we need is a baby to contend with."

The mood in the room instantly sobered. Guilt washed over Uncle Toni, and Matteo sank further into his chair.

"Jesus," Nicco breathed, shooting me a wary glance.

"Enzo, I'm sorry, that was—"

"Relax, Uncle T, I'm fine. Shit happens, and he got what was coming to him. I'm only sorry I didn't figure it out sooner."

"No, son. Don't ever think that. What happened, it wasn't your fault, none of it."

All I could manage was a small nod.

"Anyway, I didn't call you all here to shoot the shit. We've got to figure out how to deal with our little problem in Providence." He steepled his fingers, exhaling a long breath.

"What happened with the rat?" Nicco asked. "Did he talk?"

"Ask E," Matteo said, and I pinned him with a hard look.

"Enzo?" Nicco demanded my attention.

"I may have gotten a little carried away when we were squeezing him for intel."

"How bad?" His jaw flexed.

"Broken jaw, smashed eye-socket, three broken ribs, and a couple of missing teeth," Matteo said grimly.

"Fuck, E."

"He's a rat."

"That we needed."

"Fuck that." I kicked my boot against the leg of the table.

"*Basta!*" Uncle Toni slammed his hand down on the table. "I'm changing things up a little. You serious about not going back to MU?"

"As a heart attack," I said.

"You're going to run with Gino and his crew."

"Gino?" Nicco barked. "But Enzo is on my crew."

"You need to focus on things here. On Arianne and your sister. I need you close, Niccolò."

"What does that have to do with moving Enzo to Gino's crew?"

"We're a few men short. Your Uncle Alonso called from Boston. He's dealing with the Diablos and needs some extra hands. I'm sending a few guys. It leaves us short. Things in VC are fairly stable right now. Roberto is playing nice. The shit with Mike Fascini is dead and buried. We can spare a man or two."

"I'm in," I said without hesitation. Gino's crew get their hands dirty. They didn't think first and act later, they handled shit when it needed to be handled.

"Enzo, cous, come on." Nicco's expression wavered. "It's always been the three of us."

"Things change." The second the words were out of my mouth, I regretted them. I didn't want to alienate him.

He was my cousin, my best friend, but I needed some space.

I needed to deal with this in my own way, in my own fucking time. I didn't need to be constantly around their concerned pity-filled stares.

"I need this," I grated out, hoping he would drop it.

To my relief, he did.

"You report to Gino now, okay?" Uncle Toni added. "As soon as he gets back from Providence, you're with him."

I nodded at Uncle Toni, feeling a lick of anticipation zip up my spine.

Gino Lupo and his crew were what the Family called enforcers, and I was all too willing to get my hands dirty.

"Good, it's done. You listen to G, follow his guidance, and you come back to us when you've worked through this shit, okay?"

"You got it, Boss."

"You'll be at Bella's birthday party though, right?" Matteo asked. "She'll kick your ass if you don't show."

"Like she could take me." Matteo's sister Arabella was a petite little thing with big blue eyes and a meek personality. "I'll be there." She was family. This wasn't about turning my back on them; it was about dealing with some of the crap running through my head.

The deceit.

The lies.

The betrayal.

Vincenzo Marchetti had been many things: cold, cruel, angry. But he'd always been nothing if not loyal. He'd lived, breathed, and bled for the Family, for Dominion.

Or at least, I'd thought he had.

Fuck.

It was like my head couldn't reconcile what my black dead heart already knew.

The restless energy inside me ignited into a firestorm. I needed a smoke. Some pot or a strong fucking drink. I felt like an addict tweaking for their next hit. I needed something —*anything*—to take the edge off.

"Breathe, son," Uncle Michele said in a hushed voice.

Nicco and his father were arguing about me. Nicco didn't want to let go; he didn't want me to get involved with the likes of Gino and his guys.

"Nic," I barked, my throat dry. "It's okay."

His head snapped up and his narrowed eyes found mine. "I don't like it, E. I don't like it one fucking bit."

"I know."

But it didn't matter because I needed this.

I needed it whether he liked it or not.

THE NEXT DAY I WAS WAITING OUTSIDE THE VERONA COUNTY Transitions Initiative, a local community center in Romany Square. Nicco had asked me to swing by and pick-up Arianne after she got finished volunteering. I'd wanted to tell him no, I wasn't a fucking babysitting service. But he was my best friend, and after Uncle Toni had dropped the bombshell that I was going to run with Gino and his guys, I figured it was the least I could do.

But when Nora appeared in the doorway, I knew I'd made a huge fucking mistake.

"Enzo?" Her eyes grew to saucers.

"What the fuck are you doing here?"

Hurt flashed in her eyes, but I really hadn't been expecting to find her here too.

"I decided to come help out," she said, pulling her chunky knit cardi closer together. "What are you doing here?"

"Nicco asked me to give Ari a ride home."

"Oh."

The air grew thick around us, energy crackling between us.

"That's nice of you."

I snorted. "Yeah, real nice."

"I know things are… strained between us," she lifted her chin a little, "but you don't have to be such an asshole about it." Her hand went to her mouth. "I'm sorry," sympathy glittered in her eyes, "that was uncalled for. I know you've been through a lot."

She might as well have slapped me upside the head.

Before I knew it, I'd closed the space between us. Nora jerked back, pressing herself against the wall. "Enzo, what are—"

"Hey, oh," Arianne appeared, and I immediately stepped back.

"Nicco couldn't make it and I didn't know…" My eyes flicked to Nora and her breath caught.

"Can you give Nora a ride too?"

"Doesn't look like I have a choice, does it?" I grumbled, taking off toward my car.

"I can call Luis," I heard Ari whisper. "We don't have to—"

"It's fine," Nora said.

Because that was Nora. Stubborn to a fault. Well, she was barking up the wrong fucking tree if she thought there was anything left to salvage between us. Because that shit was done.

The girls climbed into my car, Nora taking the back seat, thank fuck. I quickly realized though it wasn't anything but sweet torture, because every time I looked up, her face was right there. Taunting me. Reminding me of everything I could never have.

Things I didn't even want.

The air had been thick between us outside the VCTI, but it was toxic now.

No one spoke the short distance to Arianne and Nicco's apartment building. It was awkward as fuck, and I was counting the hours until I could get the fuck out of Verona.

When we finally rolled up outside of the building, Arianne turned to me and said, "Thank you. I'll see you at Arabella's party on the weekend?"

I nodded.

She glanced back at Nora, I'll call you later, okay?"

"Actually," Nora's eyes flicked to mine. "I think I'll wait for Luis, after all."

"Of course." Arianne climbed out and lifted the seat for her friend.

"I said I'd give you a ride," I gritted out, irritation vibrating inside me.

"I don't think that's a good idea, do you?" Her brow went up and before I could answer, she slipped out and slammed the door.

And I watched them walk away wondering why I didn't feel as relieved as fuck.

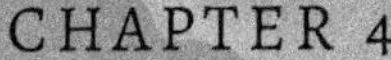

# CHAPTER 4

NORA

"Are you sure I look okay?" I fluffed my hair for the third time. My wild curls hung around my face, and my eyes were smoky and seductive. I'd even broken out my blood-red lipstick.

"Don't you think you're trying a little too hard?" Arianne eyed me through the mirror, and I frowned.

"I'm not trying to do anything other than look good."

"For Enzo," she quipped.

"No, not for Enzo. For myself." It was Arabella Bellatoni's sweet sixteen party, and it was set to be a big affair. The entire Marchetti family would be there. I wanted to look good. No, I wanted to look like a knockout. It had absolutely nothing to do with the brooding, arrogant guy that was avoiding me at every turn.

My stomach fluttered at the very thought of Enzo. He'd been such a jerk the other day and part of me hated him, hated the way he'd just written us off before we ever really got started… but the other part, the other part still wanted him, mistakes and all.

But I couldn't tell Ari that. She wouldn't understand. Nicco wasn't like his cousin. Nicco was loyal and protective and super possessive. Nicco loved with everything that he was. Fiercely. Deeply. Truly.

Something told me a guy like Enzo didn't know *how* to love.

The thought made my heart ache.

Everyone deserved a chance, a shot at something good. Something pure. Even the darkest of souls.

"Just promise me you'll be careful," Ari said. "After what happened with his father… Enzo is in a bad place. Nicco said —" She stopped herself.

Enzo's father had been killed in a collision right before the holidays. It came as a huge shock to everyone, and I couldn't even begin to imagine how he must be feeling. But he wouldn't even let me get close enough to ask.

"Mafia stuff?" I asked.

"Yeah, sorry." Guilt flashed in her eyes. "He couldn't tell me most of it, but Enzo isn't going to be around much."

"He isn't?" That got my attention.

"Nicco is worried, so whatever it is, must be bad."

"Enzo's a big boy, I'm sure he can handle himself." Except, I didn't really want to think about what handling himself meant. The illusion of a dark brooding bad boy was a hot fantasy, but the last few months had proved that reality and fantasy didn't always match up.

"Mrs. Marchetti, Miss Abato," Luis, Ari's personal body-guard, appeared. "The car is ready."

"Thank you, Luis. But please, stop calling me that."

"But it's your name, *Mrs. Marchetti*." I teased.

"It still doesn't feel real."

"Well, it is, babe. Enjoy it. It's not every day an eighteen-year-old girl meets her soul mate, marries him, and moves in together within… four months."

"God, when you say it like that it sounds really bad." Her cheeks pinked, and I fought a smile.

"Ari, who cares what it sounds like? You got your prince, babe. Your very own Prince of Hearts. Own that shit. Hell, I would."

"You know you'll find your prince one day, right?"

"I know." It wasn't like I wanted to settle down right now or anything. I was barely nineteen. I had three-and-a-half years of college left and a whole life to live. But I wanted what Ari and Nicco had. I wanted that special connection with someone, that bond.

"All set?" she asked, steering the subject to safer shores.

"As I'll ever be." I laced my arm through hers and we followed Luis out of the apartment.

"This will be fun," Ari whispered.

I didn't doubt it, but I also knew Enzo would be there… and that would be the sweetest kind of torture.

ANTONIO MARCHETTI HAD HIRED THE DIAMOND, A HIGH-END bar in Romany Square, for his niece's birthday party. I didn't know what I'd expected, but the pink and black balloons and streamers made it feel every bit a sweet sixteenth. Kids danced on the dance floor, weaving shapes with their arms, singing along to the latest hits while the adults watched on, chatting and drinking.

"Oh my God, look." I grabbed Ari's arm. "He's wearing a Fedora *and* suspenders."

"Nor!"

"What? I'm excited. It isn't everyday a girl gets to attend a mafia—"

She pressed a hand to my mouth. "Just breathe, please." Her eyes pleaded with me and I nodded.

"Sorry, I'm just… wow, okay. I'm chill."

She chuckled, but before she could answer, Nicco intercepted us.

"Bambolina," he breathed, letting his eyes drift slowly down her body. God, the way he looked at Arianne. Hungry. Possessive. As if she was the most beautiful woman on Earth.

She did look stunning though, in a sixties-style black dress with a layered skirt. I'd opted for something fitted and tight, a second skin of glitter and lace.

I felt sexy as hell, but no matter how good I felt, watching Nicco watch my best friend made me feel like I was wearing a burlap sack.

"I'm going to get a drink," I said, leaving them to it.

Ari called after me, but I continued weaving through the big round tables until I arrived at the sleek chrome bar.

"What can I get you?"

"The lady will take a vodka and cranberry," a smooth voice said.

I turned to meet Dane Marchetti's smirk. "Really?" My brow lifted with amusement.

"You look good, Nora."

"So do you." Nicco's cousin might have still been in high school, but there was no denying he had those strong Marchetti genes. Dark eyes and chiseled good looks, the ripped muscles, and tattoos. He was every bit as handsome as his cousins. But he was too young.

Shame. He would have been the perfect distraction from my thoughts tonight.

The bartender served my drink and fetched Dane a beer. He didn't bat an eyelid at his age, just handed it over with a smile.

"You gonna save me a dance later, dolcezza?"

"You're a real smoother talker, you know that?" My lips curved.

"You haven't seen nothing yet, baby."

"God, stop." Laughter bubbled in my chest as I jabbed my finger at his shoulder. "Do these lines actually work on the ladies?"

"Every single time."

"Color me impressed." I tucked a stray curl behind my ear before taking a sip of my drink. The vodka burned, but I liked the way it warmed my insides.

"I didn't know you were coming to town for Arabella's birthday." Dane and his family lived in Boston.

"I didn't know I could until the last minute. My old man has been keeping me on a tight leash after I—"

"Take a walk, kid," Enzo practically growled the words.

"Fuck you, E. I'm almost eighteen. I graduate in five months."

"Which makes you a kid still. I said take a wa—"

"I'll catch you later, Nora. Don't forget to save me a dance." Dane flashed me a wink before leaving me alone… with Enzo.

"Well, that was rude," I scolded him.

"What the fuck are you doing?" He glared down at me.

"Excuse me?"

"You heard me. He's my cousin. Are you really that desperate to snag your very own Marchetti that you'll stoop to Dane's level? He's still in high school."

"Are you done?" My body trembled with rage as I fisted my hands at my sides to stop myself from hitting him and making a scene.

I didn't know how he'd managed to signal the bartender and order a drink, but Enzo picked up his glass and knocked it back in one. Wiping his mouth with the back of his hand, he glowered at me once more. "Stay the fuck away from Dane, Nora. I mean it."

"Or what?" The words tumbled out.

He leaned down into my space, so close I could smell the spicy notes of his cologne. "Or you won't like what happens."

"Fuck you." I slammed my palms against his chest, smiling up at him. "Just because you made it perfectly clear *you* didn't want me, doesn't mean there aren't guys out there who do."

"Like Dane?" He scoffed. "He wouldn't know what to do with a woman like you if he tried."

Not girl.

Not chick.

*Woman.*

Why did I have to hone in on that, as if it was some kind of code for Enzo's repressed feelings toward me?

It wasn't.

The rational part of my brain knew that. It knew, and yet, the foolish part that believed in romance and fairytales and happily-ever-afters was eagerly waiting for his apology.

"Maybe I can show him the ropes, teach him a trick or two." I don't know who was more surprised at my words, me or Enzo. But the air turned thick around us, making it hard to breathe.

Enzo shook his head, running a hand through his thick dark hair. "Just stay the fuck away from my family," he snapped, and then he walked away.

Taking another small piece of my heart with him.

"WHAT'S WRONG?" ARI SAID THE SECOND SHE FOUND ME OVER by the buffet table. I'd made myself scarce after my conversation with Enzo. Not that it could really be called a conversation. No, that would involve actually talking to each other. Instead, he'd barked at me like I was his misbehaving puppy.

Asshole.

The more I stewed on it, the angrier I got. The constant flow of drinks didn't help.

"Nothing," I said, helping myself to another chip. "I'm fine."

"I'm fine usually means you're not fine." She gave me a pointed look. "I'm sorry I abandoned you. Nicco's family can be a little intense."

She said that like it was a bad thing, when I'd spent the last thirty minutes watching how happy she looked moving between Nicco's aunties.

"Please, I'm a big girl, I can take care of myself. Besides, Matteo and Dane keep checking in on me." Dane had repeatedly asked me to dance, but I'd declined. He was like a dog with a bone and I was worried if I threw him some scraps, he'd never leave me alone.

"Did something happen… with Enzo?"

"Like what?"

"I don't know, you tell me."

"Nothing happened." The lie felt all wrong as it rolled off

my tongue, but I didn't want Ari to worry, or put her in the middle of Nicco and his cousin.

Besides, nothing had happened. Not really.

Nothing I couldn't handle at least.

"There you are." Alessia appeared, her skin flushed. "What are you both doing hiding over here?"

"Not hiding. Just… observing."

"Well, stop, and come dance with me."

"Don't you want to enjoy the party with your friends?"

"They're not my friends, not really." Her smile fell. "It's different for Bella. Her brother isn't… you know? I mean, kids are still wary, but they don't completely avoid her like they do me."

"Fuck them," I said, draining my drink. "If they don't want to get to know you, that's their loss, Sia."

"You're right." She nodded. "So, you'll come dance?" Hope glittered in her eyes.

"Hell yeah. Ari?"

"You two go, I'm going to say hello to a couple more people."

My brows furrowed. "Sure, okay. But remember, it's a party. You're supposed to have fun."

I tried to ignore the pit in my stomach as Sia and I reached the dance floor. Bella spotted us and rushed over. "Nora, you came." She threw her arms around my neck.

"Uh, hey, birthday girl." I patted her back gently before forcing her to arm's length. "Are you drunk?"

"Ssh, if my dad finds out he'll lose his shit."

"Let me guess, Dane slipped you some drinks?"

"Yeah, right." She scoffed, still dancing. The bubblegum pink dress she wore looked killer with her dark raven hair and stilettos. "He wouldn't risk getting railed at by Matteo and our cousins."

"True story." Sia nodded.

"If your brother asks, I know nothing," I said around a tentative smile. "But please, for the love of God, don't drink anymore."

"Fine. Now dance." Bella grabbed my hand. "Dance!"

Their enthusiasm was infectious and soon the three of us were crowded by Alessia and Arabella's school friends and family, dancing like our lives depended on it.

"Oh my God, I love this one," the birthday girl yelled, pumping her fist in the air. Everyone laughed, watching as she and Sia moved into the middle of the crudely formed circle.

But the DJ slowed it right down on the next song, playing some sappy love song that had everyone pairing off. Nicco and Ari joined us. He scooped Arianne up into his arms while Matteo grabbed Arabella before any of the younger guys could make their move. Sia intercepted Dane and forced him to dance with her. Which left me... all alone.

My heart was heavy as I sank into the shadows and watched them. I liked to think of myself as a strong, independent woman. I was confident in my own skin; loved my curves and lack of filter, and my quirky t-shirt collection. But standing there, watching my best friend laugh and smile with her husband and his family, twisted something inside me.

I was happy for her, so freaking happy. But she was part of something bigger now. Her family was entwined with the Marchetti.

She was one of them.

An insider.

I always knew when Ari found her wings, she would soar,

but I'd never anticipated this. I was proud of her, so fucking proud. The way she handled the alpha men around her with nothing but grace and humility. She had them all eating out the palm of her hand, Antonio Marchetti included.

Arianne had this whole other life now, and honestly, I didn't know where I fit into that.

A server waltzed past with another tray of drinks and I snagged one, not bothering to inspect the contents as I drained the glass dry. The liquor coursed through my veins, making everything a little blurry. But I liked the sensation, hovering between being drunk and sober, when the edges of reality began to shimmer and shift into something else.

My eyes scanned the room, landing on Enzo. He stood immediately across from me, the sea of tables and bodies separating us. Our eyes connected and he trapped me there in his icy gaze.

Something had happened to him. Something *before* losing his father in the accident. It had made local news. Vincenzo Marchetti taken too soon from his family and friends. Arianne tried to tell me Enzo was just grieving, but it didn't explain the way he'd betrayed me with that skank.

I didn't know what had happened. I wasn't *allowed* to know. But I knew it was something bad. He wasn't the same Enzo I'd known a few months ago. Sure, he was still the quiet brooding mafioso, but he was different now.

He was cold and cruel.

It didn't stop me from crossing the room to him though. My body hummed with electricity with every step, the thread tethering us pulling taut and reeling me in.

When I finally reached him, he didn't chastise me or taunt me. Enzo grabbed my hand and pulled me away from the party, out of a staff exit and down a long, empty hall. I stumbled behind him, drunk on liquid courage and high on pure lust.

This was a bad idea.

The worst.

But I couldn't stop myself. I was under his thrall, completely at his mercy.

He grabbed a door handle at the end of the hall and pulled me inside. There wasn't even a chance to get my bearings before he was pushing me up against the wall and pinning me there, his big hand wrapped around my throat.

"You're playing with fire, Gattina." Enzo dipped his eyes to mine, searing me to the bone.

But I wasn't scared, not even a little bit.

"Yeah?" I smirked, loving how his eyes danced with torment. "Well, maybe I like the burn."

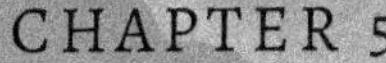

# CHAPTER 5

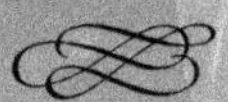

ENZO

She was under my skin.

I'd watched Nora all night. Watched as Matteo and Dane continually tried to lure her onto the dance floor with the promise of a good time. I knew Matt was probably doing it to piss me off, but Dane… that kid was too fucking self-absorbed to see past his own needs.

I knew she would be here. Arabella loved Nora. Sia too. I knew the root of their obsession with the girl with fire in her eyes and love in her heart.

Nora was good, too fucking good. But she was also strong, and unafraid to speak her mind, determined to go after the things she wanted.

And thank fuck, she still wanted me because the second my eyes landed on her tonight, I knew I had to have her again. I was a selfish bastard, concerned with only one thing, feeling her tight little body beneath me.

It probably meant something different to her. She probably thought it was my way of apologizing. It wasn't.

It was sex.

Nothing more, nothing less.

"Fuck, you're sexy." I clawed at the skirt on her dress, trying to find her pussy.

"And you're moving too slow," she hissed, grabbing my hand and guiding it to her damp panties. "God, yes," she cried as I rubbed her over the lacy material.

Of course, she was wearing lace. I smirked. Nora was good, but she was also as dirty as fuck. It's why I wanted a repeat. The sex had been mind-blowing. I could use that kind of tension reliever tonight.

Dipping my fingers into the lace, I curled two inside her wet heat, rolling my thumb over her clit.

"Enzo, God…" she breathed, her head rolling back against the wall with a *thud*.

"Guardami." I growled, squeezing her throat gently. It would be so easy to snap her neck, to watch the life drain from her hypnotic eyes.

Fuck, what was wrong with me?

I didn't want to kill Nora. I didn't even want to hurt her. But killing my old man, pulling that trigger and watching his brain splatter all over the wall, had flipped something inside me. Unleashed a darkness I wasn't sure I could contain.

"What is it?" she panted. "What's wrong?"

I hadn't even realized I'd pulled away until her voice pulled me from my thoughts. "Enzo?"

"Fuck," I grunted. "*Fuck!* This was a bad idea."

Nora scoffed, the sound so bitter and twisted it was like a punch to the gut. "You don't want me, is that it?"

My eyes narrowed. I needed to leave. I needed to get the

hell out of here before I did or said something I couldn't take back.

"Talk to me, E, please." Her expression softened, her bedroom eyes promising me things I had no right wanting. "I've been hoping we can talk. I'm so so sorry about your—"

I froze, red hot fury flooding me. "You shouldn't have come here with me." She flinched at my harsh tone. "Go back to the party, Nora." *Please, I'm begging you.*

"Seriously?" Her voice trembled. "You want me to go back out there and find another guy to keep me company? Dane was more than willing—"

I flew at her, grabbing her around the throat and pinning her to the wall. "Don't push me, Gattina."

"Why, what are you going to do? Hurt me? I'm shaking in my—"

I crashed my mouth down on Nora's, swallowing her sassy words. Stealing the very air from her lungs. She was fucking crazy, always pushing. Acting as if she didn't care about the way I treated her.

Why the fuck didn't she care?

She kissed me back with as much anger and frustration as I was drowning in, the two of us locked in a duel for dominance. Our tongues curled together, teeth nipping and lips sliding together with enough friction to start a wildfire.

"More," Nora rasped, fisting my shirt and erasing every sliver of space between us, until the hard lines of my body were pressed up against every soft curve she had.

Fuck, she felt good.

She wasn't supposed to feel this good.

"Use me," she gripped my jaw, raking her fingers over my scruff. "Use me, E. Take what you need."

She didn't know what she was asking. I wasn't the guy she knew *before*. I was different now. Changed by death.

Changed by *murder*.

Nora's hand went to my jeans and she popped the buttons like a pro. I didn't like to think about how she was so good at this stuff… I didn't like to think about her full stop. But she was there, in the back of my mind like a nightmare that I couldn't escape.

*It's just sex, that's all it can ever be.*

Her hand found its way into my jeans and she wrapped her fingers around my dick. "You want me," she teased, her lips peppering hot wet kisses all over my neck.

"I want what you can give me," I ground out, my hand flat against the wall as she pumped me harder. But Nora used my precarious position to her advantage and swung us around, so I was pressed up against the wall, completely at her mercy.

"What are you—"

She dropped to her knees and grinned up at me as she freed my dick. Fuck, she was beautiful.

Why did she have to be so fucking beautiful?

"Don't just look it at," I barked, the words rough against my throat. "Suck it."

Nora rolled her eyes at me before running her tongue over the tip. A sharp hiss escaped my lips as she took me into her mouth, hollowing her cheeks.

"Fuuuuck." The word reverberated in my chest as I tried to catch my breath. But she was too damn good at this, at making me forget my own goddamn name.

My fingers slid into her thick, silky curls, guiding her deeper over my length. Not that she needed any encouragement, Nora couldn't get enough of me. And don't even get me started on those little groans of pleasure vibrating from her pouty lips.

"Yeah, just like that." I relaxed against the wall, letting the sensations carry me away to somewhere else.

Her free hand curled around the back of my thigh, pulling me closer.

"Fuck, Gattina, I'm gonna… fuck." My chest heaved as blinding pleasure shot down my spine. Nora didn't miss a beat, swallowing me down like she'd been born to do it.

When she finally released me, her lust-drunk gaze lifted to mine. "Hmm." She grinned, dabbing the corner of her mouth with her thumb.

"Come here." I lifted Nora to her feet and slid my hand along the side of her neck, brushing my thumb over her pulse point. The air crackled between us, taunting me with all the things she wanted to give me that I would never allow myself to take.

Because this right here—stolen touches in the dark—would be all I could offer her. And no girl was cut out for that life.

Not even ones as strong as Nora.

My hand skated down her spine, fitting her body impossibly close to mine. There was something settling about feeling a woman's curves.

"How do you want me, Gattina? Slow and deep, or hard and fast?"

Nora's eyes glittered with desire, her skin flushed and breathing shallow.

"However I can get you," she whispered, her words like a poisoned arrow through my heart.

Because she meant it.

Nora meant every single fucking word.

My hand disappeared under her skirt, finding the soft flesh of her thighs, but Nora snagged my wrist. "No, E. I want you."

She pressed a single kiss to my lips and started walking backward, her fingers slowly hitching her skirt up around her waist. Stopping at a discarded table, Nora perched on the edge and crooked her finger at me. "Come get me," she drawled seductively.

I licked my lips, stalking toward her, imagining all the ways I wanted her. But none stood out more than Nora screaming my name as I fucked her into oblivion.

Loosening my tie, I pulled it free, snapping it between my hands. Nora's breath caught, her eyes wide as saucers.

"Do you trust me?"

"I..." She swallowed her last shred of rationality and nodded.

Looming down over her, I pressed one of my hands against her sternum and pushed her flat onto the table. Taking her hands in mine, I bound her wrists together and stretched them up over her head, securing the end of the tie to the underside of the table,

"Don't. Move," I demanded. "Move, and you won't like what happens."

I grabbed her panties and ripped the scraps of lace clean in two, stuffing them in my pocket. Nora writhed beneath me, and I tapped her thigh. "Behave."

Circling my fingers around my shaft, I pumped a couple of times, before dragging the tip of my dick through her wetness.

A violent shudder rolled through Nora as she cried out, "Condom. We need a condom."

Fuck.

I was two seconds away from slamming inside her and now she wanted to play it safe.

"Yeah," I said. "Okay." Pulling my wallet out, I retrieved a foil packet and ripped it open, rolling the latex over my hard on.

Once it was fully sheathed, I grabbed Nora's legs and slammed inside of her without warning. Her screams of pleasure echoed around the small room, boosting my adrenaline to epic proportions. She was so fucking tight, so fucking good.

I watched myself disappear into her hot little body, over and over, until sweat rolled down my back and her moans became background music.

"Enzo…"

My name on her lips was like music to my ears, and I folded my body over hers, running my nose along her jaw and kissing the corner of her mouth. "Tell me how it feels, Gattina."

"Good… it feels… God…" The words died on a throaty moan.

Nora's tits jiggled inside the cups of her dress as I rode her body fast and hard. I didn't want to stop. Her pussy had magical powers, blocking out all the noise in my head.

"More," she cried, arching her body into mine. My lips trailed down her neck, sucking hard on the skin at the base of her throat. It was a dick move, marking her, but I couldn't resist. Grazing the sensitive skin with my teeth, I reveled in Nora's pleasure-drenched whimpers.

She wanted me to mark her. To brand her and claim her. I would never understand what she saw in me.

My hand found its way back to her throat as I raced toward the edge.

"Let me touch you," she begged, lifting her hands. The tie came loose, and she reached for me. "Please."

I grabbed her wrists, slamming them back to the table. If she touched me, if she held me... I couldn't do it. This couldn't be about more than sex. A release. Two people using each other for a good time.

"No touching," I reminded her, rocking my hips at a slower, deeper pace. I was close, so fucking close.

"Fuck, Nora," I breathed, slipping a hand between our bodies and pinching her clit. Nora shattered, screaming my name into the shadows. It was enough to get me there and I came hard into the condom.

Dropping my head to Nora's collarbone, I dragged in a shaky breath.

"That was... wow." The awe in her voice was like a noose around my neck. But then she anchored her bound hands around the back of my neck, toying with the short hairs at the nape of my neck.

I went rigid, pulling back to look at her. "What the fuck are you doing?"

"What?" Her smile melted away, replaced with confusion.

"I told you not to touch me."

"Yeah, but I thought you meant—"

I yanked her arms back over my head and stood up, ripping off the condom and tying a knot in the end. Slinging it in the trash, I tucked myself back into my jeans and started inching away from her.

"Enzo?" Nora had lost some of her conviction and when I finally looked at her, wearing my kisses... my mark, dread snaked through me.

This was a huge fucking mistake.

"Are you at least going to untie me?" Disappointment glittered in her eyes.

Without a word, I untied Nora, jammed the tie in my pocket, and then made for the door.

"That's it, huh? That's all I'm worth to you. Some rough sex in the storage room?"

"Don't act like you didn't know what this was," I said coolly, my fingers trembling around the handle.

"You think I want more than you're willing to give me. I don't." She let out a resigned sigh, her expression neutral. "But a little respect would have been nice."

Even now, when I was being such an asshole, Nora managed to maintain her composure and grace.

She was a class act.

A strong, confident woman.

*Who deserves so much better than you.*

Nora ran a hand through her curls, taming them out of her face. Not once did she falter or glance away. She looked right into my eyes and demanded everything I couldn't give her.

Respect.

Apologies.

*Love.*

Fuck, what did I know about love?

I knew what I was supposed to feel, what I felt for my family and Dominion. I would take a bullet for my cousins, my aunties, and uncles. But I didn't know *how* to love, not the way a woman like Nora deserved.

"I can't do this," I grumbled.

"Do what? What is it you think I'm asking you to do? You ghosted me, Enzo. I was there. I waited for you to find me, to explain… but *you* walked away."

Shame burned through me like wildfire but there was no use dredging up the past. It had happened and although part of me felt like a total asshole for letting Nora find me in bed with that blonde, I knew it was for the best. She was getting too close, trying to soften my jagged edges, but a polished diamond was still sharp.

Nora had moved closer, her big doe eyes unwilling to let me escape. "You can talk to me…" She reached for me.

"Don't." It came out with such ferocity her hand fell away.

"I see." Nora stepped back. "You should go," she said quietly, her hand drifting to her collarbone.

"Yeah, I think you're right." I mentally imprinted the sight of her standing there to my memory. Who knew when I'd see her next. Once I started running for Gino's crew, life wouldn't be as smooth sailing as it was now. And Nora wasn't someone who would give you chance after chance. If I walked away now, there was every chance she would shut me out of her life for good.

But it was better than pulling her into my world, my fucked-up life.

Nora was better off without me.

No matter how much she believed she wanted me.

# CHAPTER 6

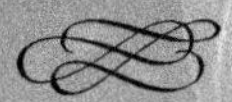

NORA

"There you are," Ari said as she reached me. "I've been looking everywhere for you."

"Sorry, I'm feeling a little funny. I think I'm going to call it a night."

"Already? But it's still early."

"Yeah," I replied around a tight smile. "I'm not feeling too great." The lie soured on my tongue, but she didn't need to know what I'd done.

"Do you need me to come—"

"No, I'll be fine." I hugged her. "You stay, enjoy the party. I'll call an Uber."

"Don't be silly, Luis will take you. He's around here somewhere."

He was. I'd spotted him standing watch at the main doors in and out of the room.

"Only if it's okay," I said, knowing she wouldn't let it drop.

"Come on." Ari took my hand and led me toward Luis.

"Mrs.—Arianne," he corrected himself, "Miss Abato, what can I do for you?"

"Can you give Nora a ride home? She's not feeling so good."

"I'm okay, just a little queasy."

"Of course." He nodded. "I'll have one of my men bring the car around front."

"Thanks, Luis, and make sure she gets into her apartment safely." Arianne shot me a bemused smile, and I rolled my eyes.

"I am quite capable of looking after myself."

"I know." She smiled. "But it would make me feel a whole lot better if I know Luis makes sure you're okay."

"What's going on?" Matteo swaggered over to us, beer in hand and collar loose. His smile was easy and his gaze slightly glassy.

Matteo Bellatoni was an adorable drunk.

"Nora is leaving."

"No!" He pouted. "You promised me a dance."

"Raincheck?" I chuckled.

"Everything's okay though, right?" Concern pinched his expression.

"Everything is fine." My smile felt weak, but it was all I could manage. Matteo cocked his head, frowning, and I knew he knew.

Maybe he didn't know everything… but he knew *something*. I needed to escape before the questions started.

"The car is almost ready," Luis announced, touching his hidden earpiece.

"Okay. I'll see you soon." I hugged Ari again. "Matteo, always a pleasure."

"Don't be a stranger," he said.

"You won't get rid of me that easily." I smirked.

Luis stepped aside to let me pass, but just as I was about to leave the room, I felt him.

Glancing over my shoulder, I saw Enzo standing in the shadows, watching me. A shudder rolled through me, remembering our moment in the storage room. I refused to label it as a mistake. How could something be a mistake when you wanted it so badly? And we had—we'd both wanted it.

Enzo just didn't want *me* enough.

With a defeated sigh, I let Luis guide me out of the bar and to the car waiting on the sidewalk. Another one of the Marchetti security detail exited the driver's side and came around to open the back door for me. I slid inside, relieved to be alone, concealed by the security glass and tinted windows.

I didn't cry. I wouldn't. But it hurt. It hurt so fucking much.

I wouldn't let Enzo Marchetti break my spirit though. I was better than that.

Stronger.

All I wanted was to be there for him. What hurt most was knowing I was good enough to fuck, but not good enough to have a conversation with.

*Damn you to hell, Enzo.*

Inhaling a sharp breath, I pressed my head against the cool glass, watching the city lights roll by until the streets became more familiar. By the time the car rolled to a stop outside La Stella, I wanted nothing more than to wash the night's events off me with a hot shower followed by a hot cocoa and my favorite fluffy pajamas.

Luis came around and opened the door. "Miss Abato."

"Thanks, Luis." I clutched my purse and headed for the door. But he followed.

"You don't need to come up," I said. "It's fine."

"Mrs. Marchetti—"

"Will kick your ass if she knows you're calling her *Mrs.* behind her back."

He cleared his throat. "Arianne."

My lips curved. "Fine. You may escort me inside. But then you're leaving. I'm fine. Everything is fine."

He gave me a pointed look, but I waved him off, going inside.

But when we reached my apartment, I came to an abrupt stop. "Luca?" My brows pinched.

"Oh, hey." He ran a hand through his hair, almost doing a double take when he saw my dress. "Wow, you look... wow."

"Uh, thanks." I flushed around a strangled chuckle. "What are you doing standing outside my apartment?"

"Funny story... I went down to take out the trash and got locked out of my apartment. I rang the super, but he isn't answering."

"You got locked—" I smothered the laughter building in my chest. "Easily done, I guess. Come on, you can come inside until the super answers."

"Miss Abato, I'm not sure that's—"

"You can leave now, Luis." My brow lifted, and he cussed under his breath.

"Very well, I'll be down the hall."

"Fine." I entered my apartment and invited Luca inside.

"Who was that?" he asked, following me to the kitchen.

"My best friend's bodyguard."

"Your best friend has a bodyguard? What is she? A celebrity or something."

*Or something.*

"My best friend is Arianne Capizola," I said. It was nothing he couldn't find out by Googling me. Ever since the wedding, Arianne's name had popped up in the press. Not to mention the fact she was an active member of Capizola Holdings board of directors now. Something like that got attention.

"Arianne Capizola? The Capizola heir… the same girl who married Niccolò Marchetti and brokered one of the biggest partnerships of Rhode Island's history?"

"That's the one." I offered him a beer.

"Holy shit… makes sense you'd live here I guess then." He took a long pull.

"Why's that?"

"This building belongs to Roberto Capizola." Luca shrugged. "The place is like Fort Knox."

"Especially when you're locking yourself out." I smirked, and he roared with laughter.

"Touché." Luca tipped the neck of his bottle toward me. "So where were you tonight?"

"At a party."

"Some party if you were home early."

"I didn't feel so good."

His expression fell. "Shit, Nora. I can go. Let me try the super one last time and I'll get out of your hair."

"Relax, I'm fine now." I let out a weary sigh. "Can you keep a secret?"

"I'm a closed book."

"I left because of a guy."

"Ah, I see." Sympathy shone in his eyes.

I don't know why I'd told him that, but it felt good getting it off my chest.

"Do you want to talk about him?"

"Not really. But I lied to everyone at the party about why I was leaving, so it feels good to tell someone the truth."

"Your secret's safe with me." A beat of silence followed as we both drank our beers. Then Luca said, "So, do you know them… the Marchetti?"

"Of course I know them, my best friend is married to one."

"And is it true, what they say about them?"

"I don't know, what do they say?"

His eyes crinkled with laughter. "I guess you'd have to kill me if you told me, huh?"

"Yup. So, I'd quit while you're ahead."

"I like you, Nora." The second the words spilled from his lips, the blood drained from Luca's face. "Shit, that came out all wrong. I just mean, it's refreshing to meet someone—a female such as yourself—who can just kick back and shoot the shit."

"Kick back and shoot the shit, huh? You make me sound like one of the guys."

"No, that's not what I mean at all. You just seem like a good person, Nora. Genuine. Funny… Gorgeous."

"Recovery accepted." I flashed him an amused smirk in an attempt to cover how off-guard he'd caught me. I wasn't used to guys being so honest with their feelings.

There had been a couple of guys since I started MU. But they were just sex. Sex and some casual conversation. One guy, Dan, had potential. But in the end, he didn't set my soul alight the way Enzo Marchetti did. So yeah, I'd had sex.

Good sex, bad sex, unmemorable sex. But there had only ever been one guy I'd wanted.

*Really* wanted.

And he was determined to push me away.

Luca's pocket began vibrating, cutting through the silence. "Hopefully that's the super and I can get out of your hair." He stood up and pulled out his cell. "Hello… yeah thanks, I'd appreciate it. Okay… See you in ten." He hung up. "He's on his way. I guess this is goodnight."

"Goodnight." I smiled, walking him to the door.

A strange sensation rolled through me as he slipped into the hall. It was nice talking to Luca. Easy, stimulating… nice. I didn't get any flirty or interested vibes from him. Even when he'd called me gorgeous it had felt more like a genuine compliment than a pickup line.

"I owe you," he said.

"You're new to town, right? Maybe I can show you where they keep the good beer… or coffee…"

"Yeah, I'd like that. I'm not exactly inundated with friends right now."

"Ouch."

"Whoa," guilt flashed in his eyes, "I clearly suck at making conversation tonight. I'd blame it on the beer, but that would only make me seem like a douchebag who can't hold his alcohol."

"It's fine. We can do coffee one day… as friends."

"You got it." He clicked his fingers in a totally dorky way that had me laughing. "Night, Nora."

"Night, Luca."

He took off across the hall, glancing back at the last second. "And Nora?"

"Yeah?"

"Whoever you were running from tonight, he's not worth it."

I closed the door and dropped my head to it with a thud. Luca was right, I knew he was.

But my heart?

My foolish fickle heart still wanted to fix the guy with darkness in his soul and pain in his eyes.

And despite all my better judgment, she was in no hurry to stop.

I DIDN'T EXPECT TO SEE ARI THE NEXT DAY, BUT THERE SHE was standing on my doorstep with a tray of coffee and a brown paper bag from my favorite coffee shop.

"This is a surprise," I said.

"Yeah, well, I felt like a bad friend after you left the party, so consider this a peace offering." She followed me into the kitchen.

"Babe, I already told you, I get it. You're married now. Things are going to change." My smile faltered.

"That's just it though. I don't want them to change. I mean, I love Nicco. God, I love him so much." A dreamy expression washed over her. "But I love you too. You're my best friend."

I snatched the brown paper bag open and pulled out a pastry. "And I'll always be your best friend. Especially, if you keep bringing me treats like this."

That earned me a small chuckle. "What really happened last night?"

My sugar high crashed and burned as I stuttered over the words. "Nothing happened."

"Nor, I'm not stupid. Enzo was extra grouchy after you left, and Matteo said he saw the two of you slip out of—"

"He's such a gossip," I grumbled under my breath.

"Do you want to talk about it?"

"There's nothing to say." My shoulders lifted in a small shrug.

"I don't believe that for a second." A beat passed as Ari searched my face for answers… answers I didn't have.

I couldn't explain why I felt drawn to Enzo, why I wanted to understand him, to fix him. Sure, he had that bad boy appeal, but it wasn't only that. I saw the torment in his eyes, felt his defenses ripple around him like a shield every time we were close. Enzo Marchetti was a complicated guy— layered and complex—and I wanted to strip back each layer and uncover the real him. The guy he didn't let anyone else see.

Even if I didn't like what I found.

"Did he tell you he won't be starting MU on Monday?"

My stomach sank as I tried to school my expression. He'd been inside me, fucking the very soul from my body, and he hadn't mentioned a goddamn thing.

"No," I steeled my spine. "He didn't… You knew?"

"Nicco only confirmed it last night." Sympathy shone in her eyes. "You know there's stuff he can't tell me."

"So that's it? He's just throwing away his entire college career?"

"Nora, you know that's not how it works."

"Nicco and Matteo?" I asked, knowing it was a stupid question. Nicco wouldn't leave Arianne, and Matteo… well, he was different. Something told me he wanted life to be as normal as possible.

But not Enzo.

He'd never really fit in at MU. It didn't make it any easier to hear though.

"What will he do instead? Wait, forget it. You can't answer that either."

She reached over and took my hand. "Because I don't know. If I did, I'd tell you."

"I guess that explains last night then," I murmured, trying hard to erase the images of last night from my head. Enzo's hand around my throat, his body riding mine.

"The two of you—"

I nodded. "It was goodbye." The thought hit me like a wrecking ball. Enzo hadn't dragged me to that storage room because he was jealous, although I didn't doubt that had a little to do with it. He'd done it because he wanted one last time with me.

That cold bastard.

He'd stoked the flames of hope in my chest while knowing he didn't have to see me every day around campus.

A wave of nausea rolled through me.

How foolish I'd been.

Enzo didn't care about me. He cared about what I could give him. A warm, willing body. My stubbornness had refused to accept that, because I felt the threads connecting us. And until this moment, part of me had truly believed that if I pulled hard enough, eventually, I'd find Enzo on the other end.

"Oh, Nor," Ari said, squeezing my hand.

"I'm fine." I shot her a weak smile, surprised to feel the dampness on my cheeks.

I rarely cried.

I was stronger than that.

But I was also only human and being wrong about Enzo cut deep.

"There's someone out there for you, I promise."

But what if I'd already found him?

What if I'd found the guy I was supposed to be with, and he refused to accept it?

What if he rejected me?

I guess I didn't need to wonder anymore.

My heart withered in my chest as reality crashed over me.

"Yeah, well, I think I need to focus on other things for a while." I stuffed the last bite of pastry into my mouth.

"I hate that he hurt you again."

"It's fine." My shoulders lifted in a half-hearted shrug.

"Nora, it's not fine. You deserve so much better. Enzo is… complicated. He doesn't know—"

"I really don't want to talk about this anymore. He's not coming back to school, so it's a moot point." I'd probably still see him occasionally at family events, but I could handle that. "Tell me about the party. Did Arabella enjoy it?"

"She did… until she got caught taking shots with Bailey and Dane. You should have seen Matteo, he lost it."

"Oh wow, I'm sorry I missed it." My lips curved.

"Everyone missed you."

I didn't believe that for a second, but I appreciated the sentiment.

"Bella and Sia made me promise we can all hang out soon, just the four of us."

"We totally should. We could have a girl's night. Face masks, manicures, champagne, a movie…"

"They'll love that. Sia is always talking about you. You're like the older, cooler sister she's never had."

"She loves you too."

"I know. But it's different. I'm her family now."

Her words stung. I knew Ari didn't mean them with any malicious intent, but there it was again. That word.

Family.

I had my mom, my dad, and my brother Gio. It's just the four of us. Three, if you count the fact that Gio was off at UPenn living out his dreams of going all the way to the NFL.

It had always been me and Arianne, the two of us against the world. But she had Nicco now. As the Capizola heir and the newly crowned Marchetti princess, she had a legion of men all willing to lay down their lives for her.

Enzo included.

He would take a bullet for his cousin's wife, protect her no matter what the costs. Because she was family now.

And me?

I was just the best friend worthy of sex…

But not good enough for his heart.

# CHAPTER 7

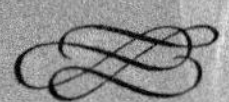

ENZO

"You look like shit," Matteo said, looking far too breezy for the morning after the night before.

I rubbed a hand over my head and down my face. "Is there juice?"

"Should be." He flicked his head to our refrigerator. Although he didn't stay here a lot anymore. He liked to be around for Arabella, so he usually crashed at their house.

But not last night.

Last night, I had hazy memories of him and Dane carrying me to one of the cars and shoving my drunk ass inside.

Fuck. I'd really hit the liquor hard after Nora left.

I went to open the refrigerator, but groaned in agony when a pain shot through my skull.

"Here," Matteo said. "You sit, and I'll get it."

Slumping onto one of the stools, I buried my face in my hands.

"Want to talk about it?" he asked.

"Nope."

"Good, I'll talk then, and you can listen. What the fuck are you doing, E?"

My head whipped up, another flash of pain ripping through me. Matteo smirked. "Serves you right for drinking your bodyweight in whisky."

"The juice?"

He handed me the carton and I drank straight from the box.

"That is so unhygienic."

"So don't drink it," I grumbled, wiping my mouth with the back of my hand. "Thanks… for getting me home."

"It was that or leave you there. She's really under your skin, huh?"

My eyes narrowed and his smirk only grew. "I don't know what the fuck you're talking about."

"Sure, you don't. So I didn't see the two of you slip out of the staff exit together?"

"Wasn't me."

"You're a terrible fucking liar. What I really want to know though, is what you did to her to make her leave?"

My chest tightened. It had been a dick move. Not the sex, the sex was great. But everything else had been an absolute shitshow.

"Fuck you, man," I hissed. "Fuck you."

"Nora is good people. You know that, right?"

"Seriously," my eyes shuttered as I inhaled a resigned sigh, "I'm not doing this."

"Okay, so you don't want to talk about Nora. Let's talk

about the fact you're dropping out of school to run with Gino and his crew. We both know what he and his guys get up to."

"Don't start, Matt, you sound like Nicco."

"He's worried. We both are. This isn't you, cous."

"Do you have any fucking idea what it's like?" A violent storm raged inside me. "I pulled the trigger, Matt. I pointed the gun at my old man's head and I. Pulled. The. Trigger. *Me.*" I inhaled a shuddering breath that I felt all the way to my dirty black soul. "So don't stand there and tell me running with Gino isn't me. Because from where I'm standing, I think it's exactly me." I leaped up, and the sound of the stool legs scraping the tiles filled our apartment.

"I'm sorry, okay?" He let out a thin breath. "I know it's hard—"

"Hard?" I sneered. "You don't have any fucking idea what it's like." His world hadn't been blown to shreds that night, not the same way mine had.

"Maybe you should talk—"

"I swear to fucking God, Matt, if you tell me to talk to someone, I'll—"

"Yeah, you're right. That's not the answer." He scrubbed his jaw. "But it's a damn sight better than selling your soul to the likes of Gino and his crew."

"I need this, cous," I said, the anger inside me abating slightly.

Trust Matteo to worm his way under my skin. I knew Nicco didn't approve, but he was less direct than our cousin. He believed in letting people arrive at their own decisions, and I was pretty certain that deep down, he knew what this meant to me.

I needed time away from Verona County. At least until I'd

finally slayed the demons that haunted my every waking thought.

"Just promise me you'll be careful. Something's coming. I can feel it." His expression darkened.

"Aunt Marcella giving you too much of that damn tea again?" She was as superstitious as they came.

"Don't you feel it?" He rubbed the back of his neck. "That shit with Johnny Morello… It was a warning."

"Nah," I said. "It's nothing. And even if it was, we'll deal with it."

"I hope you're right."

Matteo wasn't like me. He didn't revel in this life. Tolerated it? Sure, he had to. You didn't escape the Family. If you were born into it, you died in it. It was that simple. *La Famiglia prima di tutto*. The Family came first, always.

Ever since I was a kid, I'd wanted it. I'd wanted to do the Family's bidding. Back then, I'd wanted it so that I could be closer to my old man. I thought it would bond us, make him pleased. I thought if my father saw I was made for this life, he'd be proud.

Looking back, I'm not sure Vincenzo Marchetti was ever cut out to be a father. His parenting skills were lacking at best, but I'd never doubted his ability as a capo.

He was everything I'd ever wanted to be.

*Fearless.*

*Merciless.*

*Unwavering.*

But it was all a lie.

A sham.

He wasn't fearless. He was a fucking coward.

The blare of my cell phone cut through my thoughts and I dug it out of my pocket. "Yeah?" I barked.

"Enzo, son, it's me," Uncle Toni replied.

"What's up, Uncle T?"

"Change of plans. Gino is staying in Providence for a little longer. I want you to ride down there and meet him."

"Today?"

"The sooner the better."

"I'll leave right away."

"Good. I knew I could count on you." A beat passed. "And pack a bag, you could be gone a while."

"On it."

"Good, call me when you get there." He hung up and I pocketed my cell.

"You're leaving?" Matteo let out a long, steady breath.

"Gino needs me in Providence."

"Nicco isn't going to like this."

"Yeah, well, Nicco isn't calling the shots anymore." Not for me, at least.

"You don't have to do this, cous." Matteo smiled weakly. But not even one of his puppy dog smiles was going to change my mind.

"Yeah," I said, grimly. "I do."

PULLING OFF AT A REST STOP, I CUT THE ENGINE AND RAN A hand down my face. My cell phone had been blowing up since I left Verona less than an hour ago, and I knew the news had got back to my best friend.

I dialed Nicco's number and waited.

"What the fuck, Enzo?" he growled, the hostility in his voice making me bristle.

"I didn't want it to be a big deal. It's not like I'm leaving forever."

"You left without saying a fucking word." Hurt coated his words, making guilt snake through me.

"I need this," I said.

"And I need my best friend to talk to me. But I guess neither of us are getting what we want."

"Shit, Nic, I didn't do it to piss you off..."

"No, you knew if anyone could persuade you to stay, it was me."

"Maybe, yeah." My chest heaved as I expelled a long breath. "If it's any consolation, Matt gave me a pretty good talking to before I left."

"It doesn't," he snorted, "but I would have paid to hear that."

"You're worried, I get it. But you don't need to be. This is who I am."

"E, that's not—"

"We both know you're destined to call the shots and I'm destined to get my hands dirty. I've made my peace with it, you should too."

"Not like this though," he said quietly. "*Never* like this."

"Gino is good people. He'll look out for me."

"Damn right he will, or he'll have me to answer to."

"Hey, this thing with Morello," I said, "do you think we need to be worried?"

It wasn't uncommon for gangs or other organizations to try and make their presence known, especially in and around Providence. But the city had always been Marchetti territory. There was an MC, the Providence Phantoms, who rode out of their compound on the edge of the Woonasquatucket river, but they generally kept to themselves. Then there were the small-time dealers we let fly under the radar so long as they didn't start making waves. The Cruzers controlled all of the heavier narcotics coming in and out of Rhode Island, but we had a good thing going with Santiago Cruze, their top guy. The Family didn't usually get involved in narcotics, but it enjoyed a cut of the profits for letting Santiago and his guys operate out of Providence.

They had been the ones to hand over the rat when they'd gotten word that he'd been whispering Dominion business in a couple of guys ears. Guys no one recognized.

Outsiders.

The rat hadn't talked yet, and poor fucking Morello was lying in a hospital bed pissing through a tube.

"It could be nothing…" he said.

"Or it could be something."

"Yeah." Nicco let out a long sigh. "Just watch your back. Morello is a good guy, no enemies… an innocent."

I knew what he was saying. As far as we were aware, his only vice was being on the Family's books. An attack against him—random or otherwise—was an attack against us.

"Relax, I've got this."

"Yeah, that's what worries me." He scoffed.

"Don't you have husband duties to carry out?"

"Fuck you, cous, fuck you. One day some girl is gonna swoop in and knock you so hard on your ass you're not going to know what's hit you, and I'll be there to enjoy every second."

"I hate to disappoint you," I said, "but you're going to be waiting a long fucking time. I'm not cut out for that life."

"We'll see," Nicco grumbled under his breath.

"I need to get back on the road." I chose to ignore his comment. "I'll text you when I meet up with Gino."

"Make sure you do. I mean it, E. Just because you're running with his crew now, doesn't mean I don't want to be kept in the loop."

"Yeah, yeah, *boss*. I'll talk to you later."

"Stay safe."

"You too." I hung up, gunned the engine, and headed for the city, not stopping until I pulled up outside the address Uncle Toni had sent me.

It was some dive motel just outside the city, and Gino Lupo was leaning against the railing waiting for me.

"Enzo, my man," he said as I climbed out of the car, "long time no see." He approached me, thrusting out his hand.

I accepted it with a firm shake. "Gotta say, I wasn't expecting this. Not after—"

"What's the deal?" I cut him off. I didn't want to shoot the shit or dredge up what happened with my father. Everyone who needed to know the truth, knew about Vincenzo Marchetti's betrayal. And those that didn't, knew about his untimely death thanks to an oncoming truck and bad driving conditions.

Either way, he was gone.

Dead.

I didn't want to keep talking about a ghost.

"We got some intel that some outsiders have been sniffing around. Cruze gave us a name. Dominic Alejandro."

"Never heard of him."

"Tommy did a little digging and Alejandro has ties to a Mexican cartel in Connecticut. Rumor on the street is he's looking for somewhere to put down roots."

Tommy Gabini was the Family's investigator. There wasn't a secret he couldn't uncover, or a ruse he couldn't foil. He was the best, and so compensated heavily for his work.

"You tell Toni all this?"

"Of course. Why do you think he asked us to stay put? He wants us to feel Dominic out, and if necessary, handle him. But enough of that." He came around to my side and slung his arm around my shoulder. "Work can wait. Tonight, we induct you into our crew."

My brows furrowed. "Should I be worried?"

"You like liquor and pussy?" Gino grinned, revealing his gold tooth.

"Does a bear shit in the woods?" My mouth quirked.

"You're gonna fit right in, kid. Let's go."

I'D BEEN HERE BEFORE. DIMARCO'S WAS A HIGH-END STRIP club in the city owned by an arrogant asshole called Zander DiMarco. After he and Nicco almost got into it once last summer, Uncle Toni had given Uncle Michele responsibility over it.

Zander might have been a sleazy asshole known for getting a little handsy with his girls, but his club was a nice earner, one the Family wasn't prepared to lose. The décor was moody and seductive, crushed purple velvet curtains and a lot of chrome and glass. A runway jutted out from the stage, ending in the middle of the room where a pole was situated.

"Well, holy shit, Enzo Marchetti. Gino told me you'd be coming around." Zander swaggered over to us in his crisp white shirt and black slacks. His collar was open at the chest revealing a big gold medallion, and his hair was slicked back in that way guys with too much money and too few morals tended to wear it.

The guy was a grade A asshole, but I wasn't here to start anything. I was here to let off some steam before focusing on the task at hand.

"What'll it be, gentlemen?" He slung his arm over my shoulder, guiding us to a booth in the roped off VIP section. A couple of guys gave us the once over but soon dropped their gazes when they realized who we were.

I dropped down on the plush leather bench.

"I'll have one of my best girls come take your order. First round is on the house. Whatever you want… pussy, blow… dick…" His brow lifted with mild amusement. "I'll provide it." Zander snapped his fingers. "Gisele, get over here and keep my friends company." He glanced back at us. "Enjoy your evening, gentlemen."

The second he was out of earshot, I said, "I really don't like that guy."

"But the whisky is good, and the pussy is tight, my friend." Gino clapped me on the back. "Check out the redhead. Wouldn't mind me a little one on one time with her." He flicked his eyes over to the stage where one of Zander's girls was working the pole. She had legs for miles as she swung herself around it, performing some mesmerizing moves while her ample rack jiggled into the tiny little bra she wore.

"I'm more of a blonde hair, fake tits kind of man," one of Gino's guys said.

"Marc, you wouldn't know good pussy if it landed on your dick primed and ready to go."

"Fuck you, coglioni, fuck you." He flipped Gino off. "Hey, Enzo, back me up… redhead with a small handful, or blonde and busty?"

There had been a time I would have said blonde and busty. But all I saw now was a petite brunette with big doe eyes, pouty lips, and a smile that could bring a guy to his damn knees.

"My bad, man. If you like dick, that's all good—"

"Cazzo si," I tsked. "I like pussy as much as the next guy."

"Shit, bet you still can't believe Nicco went and got himself married?"

Thankfully, Gisele chose that exact moment to come and take our drink order. "What'll it be, gentlemen?" she said.

"Beers all round?" Gino answered.

"Nah, I'll take a whisky on the rocks. The top shelf stuff."

"Anything else?" She batted her eyelashes at me. She was exactly the kind of girl we'd just been discussing. Bottle blonde. Fake tits. Small waist and a pert, round ass. She had a body made for sin and lips made for sucking… and I didn't feel a damn thing.

Fuck.

I was broken. My dick protesting at the fact I'd drawn a line on anymore one on one time with Nora.

"Cat got your tongue or something?" Marc kicked my boot under the table, and I jerked out of my reverie.

"Huh, what?"

The guys chuckled, but I wasn't laughing. I was still stuck on the part where a hot girl was offering me so much more than just top shelf whisky, and I was too busy comparing her to the dark-haired girl I needed to get the fuck out of my system.

# CHAPTER 8

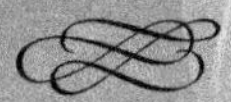

NORA

"Nora." Luca flashed me a blinding smile. "Fancy seeing you this morning." His eyes dipped to my chest, and I chuckled.

"No boo bees t-shirt today, sorry to disappoint." Heat flashed through me. Luca's gaze seemed innocent enough, but I was only human, and the guy was a snack.

"You're leaving for work?"

"I am." He nodded. "Walk you out?"

"Sure. Although if I don't get a move on, I'm going to be late."

Of course, the one morning I could have done with Maurice being around, he was taking a personal day. I usually enjoyed the walk to campus, but I was going to be late, on the first day of semester no less.

"I can give you a ride?" Luca said.

"For real? I don't want you to go out of your way."

"It's no problem, I'm going right past the college."

"Oh okay. Well, if you don't mind?"

"Nora," he chuckled, flashing me another blinding smile of his, "I wouldn't have offered if I minded. Come on. If we're quick, we can stop for coffee on the way."

We hurried out of the building and Luca led me to his car.

"A Mustang. Niiiiice."

"You know about cars?" His brow lifted as his hand paused on the door handle.

"I know a little. My dad and brother restored a 1966 Shelby Mustang before my brother left for college."

"My kind of people."

"Really? I didn't have you down as a supercar enthusiast."

"I'm a complex guy." Luca smirked, pulling the door open and motioning for me to get in.

"A gentleman too, it would seem."

"Oh, trust me, you haven't seen anything yet."

The slam of the door startled me as heat trickled through my veins. Luca was flirting with me—at least, I think he was.

When he climbed inside, he ran a hand through his thick, dark hair and flashed me another blinding smile. "Coffee? It'll be a five-minute detour."

"Sure, I have five minutes." I enjoyed his company, the easy banter, and those warm smiles.

Luca—

"What's your surname?" I blurted out, realizing I didn't know.

"Luca Bianco. And you are?"

"Nora." I smiled. "Nora Abato."

"Well, Nora Abato," he fired up the engine, "let's get you coffee and then to class."

LUCA INSISTED ON DRIVING ME TO THE PARKING LOT RIGHT beside my building. I'd arranged to meet Arianne and sure enough there she stood with Nicco and Matteo.

A deep frown crossed her expression as she made her way over to us.

"That's… the Capizola—"

"Arianne," I corrected Luca who looked a little starstruck.

Dejection flashed through me. It was silly. Arianne was somewhat of a local celebrity and I was no one. But I knew that starry-eyed look Luca was wearing. He was already bewitched by my best friend and they hadn't even officially met yet.

"Thanks for the ride," I said, trying to keep the hurt out of my voice. Shouldering the door, I climbed out, expecting Luca to stay put. Only, he didn't.

"Nora, what's going on?" Ari asked me.

"I was running late, so Luca gave me a ride," I said.

"Luca? The new neighbor."

"Hey," he joined us. "I'm Luca. Luca Bianco."

"And she's married." Nicco wrapped his arm around Arianne, moving her behind him ever so slightly.

"Whoa, man. I know, I was just… okay, that sounded all wrong. I apologize. I'm Luca." He thrust out his hand at Nicco. "Nora's new neighbor."

"You give all your neighbors a ride to class?" Matteo asked, and Nicco ignored his hand.

I shot them both a hard look, Luca let out a strained chuckle. "I can see I've got my work cut out for me. It's okay though, I like a challenge."

"And just what are your intentions for our… Nora".

"Matt," Ari scolded him.

"What? It's not like we aren't all thinking the same thing." He shrugged.

I wanted to be pissed at him, and part of me was. But I couldn't deny it felt nice witnessing his big brother routine. It made me feel like a part of their inner circle.

"You guys know I just moved into La Stella, right?" Luca's gaze flicked to mine and I gave him a weak smile.

"They know."

"So, I've been vetted."

"Okay, okay." I threw up my hands in exasperation. "This is just getting weird now. Luca offered to give me a ride because I was late for class and MU was on his route."

"Where do you work?" Nicco asked, still holding Ari protectively at his side.

"At VC Marketing Solutions."

He frowned. "Isn't that on the other side of the neighborhood?"

"What?" I looked up at Luca, feeling my cheeks heat. "You said it was on your way."

"I… uh, I may have told a tiny white lie."

"But why would you do that?" My brows knitted.

"I—"

The blare of Nicco's cell phone cut the air like a knife and I averted my gaze, feeling stripped bare sharing this strange moment with Luca… in front of my best friend, her overprotective husband, and his best friend.

Nicco barked into the phone before kissing Ari and stalking off to give himself some privacy.

"I should go." Luca touched my arm, startling me.

"Uh, yeah… sorry." My eyes flicked over to where Nicco

was shouting into his cell phone. "Thanks for the ride," I said, finally giving Luca attention.

"Anytime." He smiled. "It was nice to meet you all, even if slightly weird."

"You too," Ari said, but Matteo simply frowned.

He was especially grumpy today, which was weird, because the guy was usually a hoot.

I went to walk Luca back to his car, but he held up his hands. "I'll see you around, Nora."

With a wink, he jogged back to his car, climbed inside and drove off.

"I don't like him," Matteo said the second he was gone.

"Funny, I didn't ask." I poked my tongue out at him.

"So what's his deal?"

We began to walk toward the building, leaving Nicco on his call.

"Who Luca? He moved in across the hall."

"So he's interested?"

"Interested?" I balked. "I hardly know him."

"Matt, stop." Ari laced her arm through mine. "He seems… nice."

"But?" My narrowed gaze slid to hers.

"He's…"

"An outsider?" A derisive sigh escaped my lips. "You know, I'm not exactly part of the gang either."

"Nora, that's not—"

Just then, Nicco came back.

"Everything good?" Matteo asked.

"It will be."

The air turned thick with the dark cloud circling Nicco.

"What is it, what's wrong?" Ari asked.

Nicco glanced at me. "It's nothing."

"I see." My expression tightened, my stomach dropping. "How is Enzo by the way?"

"Fuck," Matteo hissed, but I'd already taken off toward the doors.

"Nora, wait." Arianne caught up with me. "He can't…"

"I know. But it doesn't change the fact I'll always be on the outside while you're…" I stopped myself. I wasn't being fair. Arianne hadn't asked to fall in love with a mafioso any more than I'd asked to fall for a guy who couldn't give me what I needed.

Just because she'd got her happy ending and I never would, wasn't reason to push her away.

"I'm sorry. I'm acting crazy," I said around a strained smile.

"You care about him."

"Yeah, well, it doesn't matter, does it? He left and didn't even think to tell me."

"Maybe it's time to move on. Enzo is going through some stuff…"

"You think I don't know that? I might not know everything, but I know…"

"He's gone, Nor. Enzo is gone, and from what I can tell, no one knows when he's coming back." She reached for my hand. "I'm sorry."

"It's fine." The words spilled from my lips with a heavy sigh. "I'm fine."

Ari nodded. "You're one of the strongest people I know."

Yeah. I'd thought so too.

But I wasn't so sure anymore.

After two hours of Intro to Sociology, I met Arianne in the food court for lunch. But as I approached the table where she sat with Nicco, I could tell everything was not fine.

"Hey, guys, what's up?"

"Oh, hey, I didn't see you there." Arianne smiled, but it didn't reach her eyes.

"Is everything okay?" I glanced between them.

"Yeah, it's fine," she said a little too quickly.

"If I interrupted, I can—" I thumbed to the direction I'd just come from.

"No, don't go. Nicco's just worried about Enzo."

"Bambolina." The word vibrated deep in his chest.

"She deserves to know. Besides, I'm not telling her anything, not really."

Sitting down, I inhaled a deep breath. "Where is he?"

"Out of town, on… business."

"I'm not an idiot, Nicco. I know what business means." My lips pursed. "Did something happen?" Fear snaked through me.

"I don't think so, but he hasn't called me in almost three days."

"Okay." My brows crinkled. "He's a big boy, I'm sure he can—"

"He's never gone that long without calling me."

"He's ignoring Nicco's calls." Arianne tucked herself into his side.

"Maybe he wants some space?"

"Yeah, that's what worries me." Nicco's jaw clenched as he stared off into the distance.

"He'll be okay though, right?" The words felt like ash on my tongue. "I mean, it's Enzo."

"Yeah, I'm sure he'll be fine."

"Has Matteo call—"

"Has Matteo what?" He appeared out of nowhere, dropping down on the bench beside me.

"Spoken to Enzo?" I asked.

"Hold up, she knows?" He frowned at Nicco.

"Nice, douchebag, real nice."

"Shit, I'm sorry." He grimaced, running a hand down his face. "I didn't… it came out wrong. I'm just surprised Nicco caved and told you."

"Matteo," Ari sighed, "you're not helping."

"Look, I get it. I'm an outsider. I'm not supposed to know this stuff. But Enzo is my… friend too." God, that word sounded so stupid. Enzo wasn't my friend.

"Friend, really?" Matteo's brow lifted. "Does E know about your *friendship*?"

"Just because he's gone, doesn't mean you have to replace him as the snarky asshole."

"I can see why he likes you."

"Matt!" Nicco snapped.

"Yeah, sorry. I'm just trying to keep things light. E is… he's E. He'll call when he's ready to call. If you're that worried, call Gino."

"Gino?" I asked.

"Shit, sorry." Matteo grimaced, rubbing his jaw. "Just how much are we telling them?"

"I think we're done here." Nicco gently nudged Ari off him and stood. "I'm heading to the gym." He stalked off toward the doors.

"The gym?" Ari said, leaping up, taking off after him.

"He's really that worried?" The knot in my stomach twisted.

"Don't look at me like that, Nora, you know I can't tell you anything."

"Right."

He let out a frustrated breath. "Enzo will be fine. He's just dealing with some stuff. He probably hasn't called because he's ass over elbow drunk and knee deep in pus—" I sucked in a sharp breath and he muttered, "Fuck, I'm sorry."

"For what? Telling me the truth?"

His eyes dropped and he cupped the back of his neck. When Matteo looked up again, his expression softened. "You were good for him, you know? And for what it's worth, I was rooting for you. But Enzo... he isn't like me or Nicco."

"So what you're saying is, he's a lost cause?"

"No, what I'm saying is... maybe you should focus on a guy that is emotionally available, like Luca."

"Luca?" I spluttered. "You think me and Luca—"

"Nora, he gave you a ride to class when he works a five-minute walk away from your building."

"Maybe he's just a nice guy?" I shrugged.

"Yeah, and maybe I'm the Easter Bunny."

"Hmm, I don't see it." My lips curved with amusement.

"Luca is nice... But he doesn't have that dark brooding vibe working for him."

"Oh, shut up. I'm not talking about this with you."

Awkward silence fell over us and then Matteo said, "I know this can't be easy for you. Watching Ari with Nicco. Being on the periphery to... everything."

"It is what it is. She's happy."

"They both are. But still, it sucks to want someone who doesn't feel the same."

His words weren't intended to be malicious, but it didn't stop them from cutting deep. I did want Enzo. I'd wanted him the first time I'd ever laid eyes on him. There was something in his haunted icy gaze that caught my interest. It had pulled me in, shackled me to him whether he wanted me or not.

"What do you know about unrequited feelings?" I teased.

It was a joke, but the second the words came out I saw the flash of hurt in Matteo's eyes.

"Matt?"

"Nothing." He gave me a tight smile. "You're right, I know nothing. But I know something about guys who give their neighbors a ride to class."

Laughter bubbled in my chest. This was the Matteo Bellatoni I knew and loved. Funny and warm. But something bothered me about his earlier mood. Something I realized probably had nothing to do with me, and everything to do with his best friend.

"He'll be okay, right?" I whispered, locking eyes on Matteo.

He let out a steady breath and clucked his tongue. "I hope so, Nora. I really fucking hope so."

"Hey Lucii," I said as I sat down in my Media and Society class.

"Hey, girl." She smiled, her bright blue eyes twinkling under the strip lighting. "Did you enjoy the holidays?"

"It was okay, I guess. I'd forgotten how much parents fuss."

"Tell me about it. My mom was constantly trying to feed me." We shared a chuckle. "I'm relieved to be back. I'd gotten used to the freedom."

"I feel you," I grumbled, thinking how suffocating it had been being back at the house. I loved my parents, loved them something fierce, but being back on the Capizola estate, at the cottage… it had made me realize how small our lives had been there. How sheltered.

"I heard about Arianne. I can't believe she's married… that's… wow."

"Yeah." I managed a weak smile. "But she's happy."

"Must be hard though, losing your best friend freshman year of college."

"It's not like that," I said, even though I could see why Lucii thought that. People were probably expecting to see the baby bump soon.

"Hey, a few of us are heading to Mercutio's tonight for happy hour. You should totally come."

"I…" I hesitated. After everything that had happened last semester, my social life had taken a backseat.

"Come on," she nudged my shoulder, "you know you want to."

"Yeah." A tentative smile spread over my lips. "Okay."

"Yay. It'll be fun. And there's always plenty of hot college guys and graduates hanging out." Her brows waggled suggestively. "I have your number still, so I'll text you with the details later. You're living in La Stella now, right?"

"Yeah."

"Oh my God, I would die to live there. Is it awesome? I bet it's awesome."

"It's pretty awesome." Something inside me twisted. I liked Lucii. We had a couple of classes together and she always made an effort to talk to me, but she didn't *know* me. Maybe it was time to rectify that though. My life was going to be different now Arianne was married. I needed to find my own way, I needed to make new friends and make a life for myself.

Because Enzo wasn't coming for me. He wasn't going to stride into the room and declare his feelings for me. And I was worth fighting for.

I was worth being the center of someone's world.

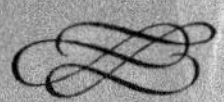

# CHAPTER 9

ENZO

"Tell me what I need to know." My fist crumpled against the guy's face, his sticky blood coating my hand. I'd left off the brass knuckles this time. I wanted to feel his bones crunch with every punch.

"I-I don't know nothing, Marchetti, I swear."

"That's what they all say until they're bleeding out like a pig, crying for their mama," Gino chuckled darkly. He was leaning against the door, twirling his Tanto blade in his hand.

"Look," I let out an exasperated sigh, clutching the guy by his collar, "we know you rented Dominic Alejandro a storage unit. Word on the street is that the Mexicans are looking to move into town. So just tell me what you know, and we can all be on our way."

"It's… it's not what you think, man. You've got it all wrong. Alejandro doesn't run with the Mexicans anymore, he's—"

I rammed my fist into his face again. He wasn't telling us anything useful. Maybe the fucker didn't know anything or maybe he was just trying to cover his tracks.

If Gino had his way, I knew there was probably zero chance of this coglioni walking out of here alive. Gino and his guys didn't leave loose ends. They cleaned up after themselves, always.

I could do it—I could be the one to drive Gino's blade through the guy's stomach and watch the life drain from his eyes—but a tiny part of me hesitated.

Death changed you.

I knew that from killing my father in cold blood. Every time your knife or pistol or even hands took a life, it took a part of you. And I knew if I walked this slippery slope with Gino's crew, there might not be any pieces of me left to return to Verona with.

But I needed this.

I needed to expel all the anger and betrayal swimming in my veins. I needed to feed the darkness swirling around me like a thundercloud.

I knew it was a slippery slope… but right now, I didn't care.

"Tell. Me. What. I. Need. To. Know." I punched him again, blood spraying into the air as he spat out a couple of teeth. His body slammed back into the chair, his eyes shuttering. Only this time, they didn't open again.

"Okay, Enzo, he's done for now." Gino approached me, laying a firm hand on my shoulder. "Go get cleaned up and get a drink. I'll handle it from here—"

"You don't need to do that, I can—"

"I said go. You've done enough, kid."

I bristled, baring my teeth. Gino noticed, smirking.

"You've still got a lot to learn about the world, Lorenzo. Take it from me, give too much of yourself too early, and you'll never get that shit back." Something passed over his mangled face. "Now go. I'll meet you at DiMarco's later."

DiMarco's had become our hangout the last few nights. The liquor flowed as freely as the pussy, and Zander was all too willing to indulge Gino and his men... and now, that invitation extended to myself.

I stormed away and grabbed a towel, wiping the blood off my hands. Then I snatched my jacket off the rack and shucked into it, before shouldering the door and spilling out into the dark alley.

My cell phone vibrated again, and this time, I dug it out of my pocket and checked the screen. It was hardly a surprise to see Nicco's name.

CALL ME.

TSKING, I TEXTED HIM BACK.

YOU NEED TO RELAX. I'M FINE. EVERYTHING IS FINE. I'LL CALL **when the job is done.**

MY CELL STARTED BLARING AWAY, MY BEST FRIEND'S NAME lighting up the screen. I hit decline and stuffed it back in my pocket. I didn't want to hear his concerns. I was here and Nicco was back in Verona, and right now, that's the way it needed to be.

My father had killed his mom in cold blood. He'd let Nicco and Alessia and Uncle Toni believe Aunt Lucia left because she couldn't hack being the boss' wife. That wasn't something I could just forget, and knowing Nicco the way I knew Nicco, it wasn't something he could just forget either.

Time and space would be good, for both of us.

Pulling out a smoke, I lit it up and dragged in a deep lungful, relishing the familiar burn. The motel was a stone's throw away from DiMarco's. I figured Gino picked it, so it was easier to fall into bed after a long night of top shelf liquor, high-end pussy, and shooting the shit. But I wondered if he had an ulterior motive.

Zander DiMarco was a showboater. He liked to flash his cash and his relationship with the Family. He was a friend to anyone who entered his bar as long as their wallet was fat, and their tastes expensive. Men wanted to be like Zander DiMarco, to soak up a good time. And when the good times rolled, people got complacent. They started talking about things they shouldn't.

I took off down the street toward the motel. My knuckles burned but I relished the sting. Pain reminded me I was alive, and for a little while, it abated the beast living inside me. I'd tear up the whole of Providence if it led me to whoever thought they could move in on Marchetti territory. Because nothing... *nothing* was more important to me than the Family. And after the shitshow with that traitorous son of a bitch I once called father, I needed to prove it more than ever.

If not to my Uncle Toni and the rest of the family... then to myself.

～

Gino and the guys met me at DiMarco's a little after eight. Guys crowded the stage, all looking to get a feel of the stripper working the pole. She was a hot little thing, legs for miles and curves in all the right places. But I wasn't feeling it, not tonight.

Not since Matteo had texted me earlier to say he'd bumped into Nora.

I hadn't replied. It wasn't like I had anything to say. Nora was nobody to me. Nothing. Yet, my fucking head hadn't quite got the memo because ever since seeing her name on my screen, I'd been grinding my teeth together like a junkie tweaking for their next hit.

My tight fist rubbed back and forth over my jean-clad thigh as I tried to focus on anything but her.

But it was fucking futile.

Nora Abato was under my skin, no matter how much I tried to claw her out.

"Yo, E," Marc said. "You look tense, my man. Why don't you grab a girl and head to one of the private rooms for a dance?" The sleazy fucker grinned.

"Nah, not tonight."

"That's not what you were saying the other night when you disappeared with Sherri," Dixon added, clapping me on the shoulder.

I shirked him off, barely able to remember the blonde I'd dragged into the restrooms and forced to her knees.

"Fuck you, coglioni."

"Leave the kid alone," Gino said, waving his guys off.

"Come on, boss, we're just goof—"

"Basta!" He slammed his hand down on the table. "Go grab a girl each and get the fuck out of here. Me and Enzo need to have a chat."

"Yeah, boss." Marc shot me an apologetic look. "Whatever you say." They left us alone and Gino ordered another round of drinks.

"You know, Enzo, I was a lot like you once." He relaxed back in the booth, his hard gaze fixed right on my face. "Full of anger and itching for a fight…"

"That's not—"

His hand cut through the air, silencing me. Gino arched a brow. "I get it. What went down with Vincenzo, that was some fucked up shit. But you've got to know, it's not on you."

"I should have known." I jammed my fingers into my hair and tugged the ends, the pit in my stomach carving deeper and deeper.

"The sins of our fathers do not lie on our shoulders. You need to remember that, kid." He smirked.

"Less of the *kid*, old man." I shot back around a wolfish grin of my own.

"Toni told me to take you under my wing, to let you work off some steam, but I won't let you lose yourself, Enzo. Just so we're clear, that's not gonna happen on my watch." His eyes bored into me as if he could see the very depths of my dark, twisted soul.

"I don't know how to let it go."

"You find a way, son. Drink it out of you, fuck it out of you, fight it out of you… you do what you need to do, and then you shake it off and lay that shit to rest, you hear me?"

With a reluctant nod, I downed the rest of my drink and stared out at the club. The rest of the guys were huddled over at the bar, chatting to a busty blonde. Gino and his guys didn't have roots. They didn't have women waiting at home or families wondering where they were and what they were doing. They lived for one thing and one thing only.

The Family.

They found honor and purpose in carrying out Uncle Toni's orders. They drank, fucked, and killed… much like my father had done.

Fuck.

He was infecting my every thought. No matter where my mind went, it all came back to him.

My jaw clenched as I itched for something—*someone*—to take my anger out on. Gino reached across the table, grabbing my wrist. "You need to let it go, son. That shit will eat you up until there's nothing left." He let out a steady breath. "Vincenzo was a traitor, and you took care of him."

My eyes shuttered as the lingering memory of the gunshot went off in my head. It was a sound I couldn't escape; every bang of a door or exhaust backfiring, I was back in that room, standing over my father's dead body.

My fist clenched against my thigh again and I ground out, "I need another drink."

"Sure thing. Then you grab the nearest piece of ass and go fuck some of that anger out of you. Best medicine there is." Gino nodded around a smug smile, as if he had all the fucking answers.

He'd done a lot of fucked up shit in his time. You didn't become the Family's number one enforcer without getting your hands bloody and your soul dirty. But I doubted that he'd killed the man who had given him life.

The waitress brought over another tray of drinks. "Courtesy of Zander," she purred, running a hand over my shoulder. Her thick lashes fluttered in my direction and Gino gave me another nod.

"Thanks," I said thickly, before removing her hand.

Gino tsked under his breath and the girl sauntered away

with dejection in her eyes. "If you're not going hit that, then don't mind if I do." He let out a hearty laugh, clambering from the booth.

"No way she'll want a shriveled dick like yours, *old man.*"

"You'd be surprised what this shriveled dick can do." He winked, taking off after the waitress.

I leaned back against the booth, letting out a heavy sigh. A bar like this was usually my kind of place. Good liquor and even better pussy. But everything was off.

My cell phone vibrated, and I dug it out of my pocket, half-expecting another text from Nicco.

It wasn't Nicco though.

It was Matteo.

HOPE YOU'RE STAYING OUT OF TROUBLE.

ROLLING MY EYES, I TEXTED HIM BACK A QUICK REPLY AND stuffed my cell phone in my pocket. I knew my cousins meant well, they always did, but this wasn't something a couple of texts and a few nights away from Verona was going to fix.

Downing my drink, I ran a hand over my jaw and stood, making my way to the restrooms. Gino was working his magic on the waitress, whispering into her ear as if she was the most beautiful girl he'd ever seen. Dirty old dog.

With a chuckle, I shouldered the door leading to the restrooms. But the sound of gentle sobs caught my attention, and I went left down the hall inside of the right.

"Hello?" I called, knocking on the door to the female bathroom.

"I, uh… I'll just be a minute."

I heard the faucet run, followed by the whirr of the hand dryer. I should have moved on, doubled back around and gone into the men's bathroom like I'd planned to. But curiosity got the better of me.

A few seconds later, the door creaked open and emerald eyes stared up at me. "Can I help you?"

"You were crying," I stated, backing up to give her room to step out into the hall.

"No, I wasn't." She steeled her expression and rolled out her shoulders.

My eyes narrowed. The faint mascara tracks down her cheeks weren't fooling me. But there was something else, a bruise blossoming along her cheek.

"Who did this to you?" I demanded, reaching for her.

"No one." She jerked back, letting her red hair fall around her face like a shield. "Excuse me, but I have to get back to work."

"You work here?" Anger zipped up my spine. If DiMarco was letting guys put their hands on his girls… fuck, I thought that shit had been dealt with last summer after he and Nicco got into it.

"I-I really have to go." She slipped around me and hurried down the hall.

"Fuck." My fist collided with the wall. I might have been a cold bastard, but I didn't tolerate violence toward women. Back when we were kids, I'd seen how much it had messed with Nicco's head watching his old man lose his temper one too many times with Aunt Lucia. He was a reformed man now, but it didn't change history.

I liked my women submissive, sure. But they were always more than willing to accommodate my rough touch.

My dick twitched behind my jeans, and I shook my head with mild laughter. At least one of us still had our priorities straight.

Because although I'd put space between me and Verona, there were some things you couldn't escape.

# CHAPTER 10

NORA

"What do you think?" Lucii yelled over the music.

"It's… loud." I grinned, slurping down my sugary cocktail. I was three drinks in and feeling all kinds of sexy. "Thanks for pushing me to come tonight."

"Anytime. We single girls have to stick together." She ran her tongue over her teeth. "My roommate Allie is already planning her wedding to her new beau. I swear, everyone around me is either going steady or already picking out furniture."

"Tell me about it," I murmured, swaying my hips to the beat.

"Shit, sorry." Lucii grimaced. "I didn't mean to rub salt in the wound."

"Relax, it's fine. Ari is happy, that's all that matters."

"God, of course. But married… wow." She downed the

rest of her drink and placed the glass on the nearest table. "It's freshman year of college. I want to live a little first. Sow my wild oats and experiment."

"Experiment?" A deep voice said. "Sign me up."

We both turned to greet the two guys staring at us with hunger in their eyes.

"I'm Isaac and this is my friend Nate."

"Lucii and that's Nora."

Isaac gave me a long, lingering look, letting his eyes fall down my body and back up. "Nice to meet you." The corner of his mouth tipped. He was tall, dark and handsome but looked far too preppy for my tastes.

"Can we get you girls a drink? Our friend Luca is at the bar."

"Luca?" I blurted because what were the chances?

But sure enough, when Isaac pointed at the bar, my new neighbor was standing there with his back to us.

"Wait a second. You're *boo bees Nora*?" A grin split Isaac's face and heat exploded in my cheeks.

"He told you about that?"

"About what?" Lucii asked, brows bunched with confusion.

"Luca, he's uh… he's my neighbor."

"He lives at La Stella too?"

"Sure does," I mumbled, suddenly feeling very over-dressed in the skintight little black dress and chunky heeled boots.

I looked hot. I just wasn't entirely sure I wanted Luca to see me like this. Especially not after telling his friends about my boo bees t-shirt.

I noticed Nate whispering to his friend. "I'll be right back," Isaac said, giving me a lingering look. There was something about his eyes that made a shiver skate down my spine. Like he was looking a little too hard. But then he took off, weaving his way through the crowd to Luca.

"We didn't tell him what we're drinking," Lucii added.

"You were drinking a Long Island Iced Tea," Nate arched a brow at her and then settled his dark gaze on mine. "And you're drinking a Strawberry Daiquiri."

"Okay, I don't know whether to be impressed or a little creeped out." She chuckled.

"I worked a semester in a cocktail bar."

"Gotcha." They shared a smile, but his eyes flicked back to mine. I ducked my head, taking another sip of my drink.

Lucii moved closer, chatting to him like they were old friends. But I remained a safe distance, dancing to the music and enjoying my drink. Soon, Luca and Isaac joined us.

"I realize how this looks," Luca said, sliding our tray of drinks onto the nearest table. "But I promise, I'm not stalking you."

"Glad to hear it." I smiled. "So how do you know Isaac and Nate?"

"Funny story, I met them at the gym."

"The gym?"

"Yup, and they took pity on me I guess."

"Lucky you."

"Yeah, I've been pretty lucky since I arrived in Verona." His eyes sparkled with things I wasn't sure I wanted to acknowledge. It had felt safe talking to him at my apartment. But this was different. We were in a bar late on a school night.

"So, wait a second, you told your new friends about my t-shirt?" I shot him a pointed look. "Why do I feel like the brunt of some locker room joke?"

"Nora, I would never…" Genuine hurt flashed over his handsome face. "Actually, I was telling them all about this pretty amazing girl who lives across the hall."

"Oh." My cheeks pinked as I struggled to meet his intense gaze. "I'm not sure what to say to that."

"You don't need to say anything. I get the impression the guy you told me about is still under your skin, so this isn't me making a move." He held up his hands in surrender.

My eyes lifted to his as my breath caught in my throat. "You're not—"

"Hey," Ari appeared out of nowhere.

"Ari? What the hell, babe?" I pulled her into a hug. "I thought you and Nicco had plans?" She'd told me as much when I'd mentioned my plans to her earlier.

"We did." She beamed. "But it feels like so long since we hung out. I hope you don't mind us crashing."

"Us?" My brows furrowed.

"Yeah, Nicco and Matteo are at the bar getting drinks."

"They are?" My stomach sank. I was so excited to have my best friend here, but Nicco and Matteo too… and Luca? Ugh. This was the last thing I'd wanted.

"Hey, Lucii." Arianne greeted her.

"Hey, I love your dress. You look so hot."

"Thanks. Luca, this is a surprise." She finally noticed the quiet guy beside me.

"Hey." He lifted his hand in a small wave. "It's good to see you again."

Ari's eyes flashed to mine, a hundred questions twinkling in her honey brown eyes. But in true Arianne Capizola fashion, she pressed her lips together in a tight smile and swallowed them. No doubt saving them for later, when we were alone.

"There you are." Nicco appeared, slipping his arm possessively around his wife. She smiled up at him in a way only a girl in love with a boy could. To watch them, the way they gravitated to one another, it made my heart soar and ache all at the same time.

They shared a lingering kiss and I heard Lucii let out a little sigh.

"God, I need to get laid," she added.

"I can definitely help with that," Nate said, shooting her a flirty wink.

"Dance with me?"

"It would be my pleasure."

Lucii grabbed his hand and pulled him toward the dance floor.

"Ah, do you want to…" Luca left the question hanging, but a voice chimed in, "If she's dancing with anyone, it'll be me."

I glanced over my shoulder to find Matteo grinning at me. "Behave," I chided.

"You owe me, Abato. Don't even try to deny it."

"Matt!" Nicco warned, but I refused to meet his stare.

Rolling my eyes, I ducked out of Matteo's hold and offered Luca an apologetic smile. This so wasn't how I saw the night going. I wanted to have fun. To relax and forget all about the Marchetti men, and I lumped Matteo in there, because although he was a Bellatoni by name, he was still one of them.

Trading my empty glass for my fresh drink, I slurped down a mouthful of the sugary sweet cocktail hyperaware of the fact they were all watching me: Luca, Matteo, Isaac, Arianne, and Nicco. I wasn't used to being in the limelight, and I wasn't sure I liked it.

Knocking back the rest of my drink, I inhaled a deep breath and said, "I'm going to dance."

Without waiting for their replies, I melted into the sea of bodies, trying to find Lucii and Nate. They were already pressed close, grinding on each other as they moved to the seductive tones of The Weeknd.

An arm wrapped around my waist from behind and I readied myself to scold Matteo, but when I spun around, I was met with Luca's cheeky grin. "One dance?" He pouted and I found myself grinning back.

"Fine, but just one. Seems like the neighborly thing to do."

Luca grabbed my hands and began weaving shapes in the air. The guy had moves, rolling and popping his hips in a way that had me licking my lips. "See something you like?" he teased.

"Less talking, more dancing, Casanova." I closed my eyes and let the music carry me away. This was what college was all about. Meeting cute guys and dancing in bars. Late nights, and early morning walks of shame back to your dorm room.

I wasn't supposed to be pining after a guy who would never take me out dancing or buy me flowers or make reservations at a fancy restaurant. I bet Luca would do all of those things. I mean, the guy had driven me to class when he worked right around the corner from our building.

My eyes fluttered open to Luca's heated stare as he watched me sway to the music. "You are so fucking beautiful." He grinned.

Just then someone barreled past us, knocking me into Luca. "Watch it, asshole," he shouted over the music, but the guy disappeared into the sea of bodies.

"Relax, I'm fine."

He ran his hands up my shoulders, holding me closer. "You sure?"

"Sure." I nodded. "But answer me this. How drunk are you right now?"

"I think you have me mistaken for someone else." He flashed me a goofy smile.

"You're so wasted." I batted his chest, freezing when I felt his muscles contract beneath my palm.

"Nora, I—"

"Take a walk, new guy." Matteo appeared. "The lady owes me a dance."

"The *lady* is kind of busy." I rolled my eyes and even over the music, I heard the two of them chuckle.

"She's all yours." Luca conceded, and I shot him a questioning look.

"The night's still young." He winked and headed back toward where Ari and Nicco were chatting with Isaac.

"You and me, Abato." Matteo crooked his finger. "Let's go."

He moved with ease, dancing literal circles around me. It wasn't the first time I'd seen Matteo Bellatoni strut his stuff and I soon found myself laughing along with him, letting him spin and twirl me until my feet burned and my cheeks hurt from all the smiling.

Of course, the DJ had to go and ruin it by switching to a slow song, but it didn't deter Matteo. He pulled me into his arms as if we were old friends. "How are you doing really?"

I eased back to meet his eyes. "I'm okay. Have you... have you spoken to him?"

I hated myself for asking, but I couldn't be anyone except the girl desperately concerned about a boy, no matter how hard she tried not to be.

Only Enzo wasn't a boy. He was a complicated, tortured soul. One that would drift into darker seas if he didn't have an anchor to guide him back to safer shores.

"He texted."

"He did?" Hope burrowed itself into my chest. "Is he okay? When will he be coming back? What did he say?"

"Whoa there, Nor. He's okay." His smile fell a little. "The rest… I don't know."

"What do you mean?"

Matteo slid a hand up my spine, holding me tighter as he rocked us to the sultry beat. "Enzo needs to work through some things."

"He lost his father, of course he's going to need time."

He tensed. It was only for a second, but I felt it all the same. "Matt?" My brows pinched. "What is it?"

"Nothing." He shook his head. "Let me enjoy this. It's been a while since I danced with a girl who wasn't my sister or cousin. You know, no one wants E to pull his head out of his ass and see what's right in front of him more than me."

"But?"

"I don't want you to be disappointed when it doesn't happen."

"You think I should move on." The words burned through me.

"I think… ah, fuck, Nor. I don't know what I think. Enzo needs someone like you. Strong willed, beautiful, so fucking smart."

"Easy there, I might start to think this is your attempt at seducing me."

"I know when to hedge my bets, and something tells me you, Nora Abato, would eat me alive in the sack." A playful smirk graced his rugged face.

"Want to know a secret?" He nodded and I added, "You're probably right."

The song faded out, the next one dropping a heavier beat. Matteo released me and ran a hand through his hair. He'd garnered quite the audience, girls standing in the wings, waiting to swoop in and bag themselves a bad boy with so much charm and swagger it practically oozed from his pores. But Matteo was a bad boy with a big heart. And I didn't doubt that one day, he would fall headfirst in love.

But it wasn't like that between us. I saw him as nothing more than a goofy older brother or cousin.

"Luca seems like a good guy. If you want to give him a chance, he gets my seal of approval."

"Didn't know I needed it, but thanks." I chuckled, trying to disguise the flash of hurt lancing my chest. Arianne had told me to move on, to not spend time waiting for Enzo to come around. But hearing it from his cousin, one of his best friends—and a guy I thought was rooting for me—well, it made my stomach sink into my toes.

Matteo thought Enzo was a lost cause too. I wanted to argue the point, but I knew these Marchetti men and it would be pointless.

Everyone had given up on there ever being an 'us.'

"Hey," Matteo added as we walked back to the others. "This is a good thing. Now you can give Luca a chance." He squeezed my shoulder in reassurance, but he might as well have been plunging a dagger in my heart.

Of all the people aware of mine and Enzo's short-lived relationship, I thought I could count on Matteo to fight with me.

But I guess he wasn't a gambling man, after all.

That or the odds were simply too stacked against me, and nobody liked betting on the losing team.

"I HAD FUUUUN TONIGHT." I LAID MY HEAD ON ARI'S SHOULDER as we waited for Luis to bring around their car.

"You're drunk." She eyed me with concern.

"Only a little bit. We should do this again, every month. Or every other weekend. I miss you, babe. I miss you so freakin' much."

"I miss you too." Guilt glittered in her eyes and I realized what a bitch I was being.

Ari deserved this. She deserved the fairytale love story and the happily ever after. She deserved nothing but good things.

"I'm so happy for you." I hugged her tight, pulling her out of Nicco's iron clad hold.

"Luis is here," he said.

"There you are." Lucii's voice pierced the air. If I was drunk, she was toasted. But we'd had fun. Luca, Nate, and Isaac had stuck around, and we'd all spent the night dancing and drinking and dancing some more. I couldn't remember the last time I'd had so much fun. Luca kept his distance, but I was enjoying myself too much to worry.

"We're getting pizza and heading back to my dorm… unless—"

"Afterparty at Luc's," Nate suggested.

"I… I mean I guess we can all go back to mine." His eyes landed on mine, but everything was a little blurry.

"Sounds like fun, but I'll have to bail," Isaac said. "Maybe next time." His eyes lingered on me for a second.

"Your loss, Isaac boy." Nate clapped him on the shoulder. "Let's roll. Nora, you might as well ride with us."

I glanced between Lucii and Ari. My best friend looked concerned, but she had nothing to worry about. I was fine. Better than fine. I was riding a wave of cocktail-induced bliss.

"I'll get a ride with these guys. You two go." I waved them off.

Matteo had left some time ago, something about his sister needing him at home. Ari had insisted on staying, so, of course, Nicco had stayed too.

Luis came around to open the door.

"Go," I said, when Ari hesitated.

"Bambolina, we should—"

"Yes, okay. Be safe," she said, leaning in to press a soft kiss to my cheek. "I'll call you tomorrow. And Nora," she grabbed my hand as I went to move away, "don't do anything you might regret."

Her words rattled inside my skull as I watched Nicco usher her into the car and climb in after her.

"Nora," Lucii's voice startled me and I spun around to greet my new friends. "Are we doing this or what?"

My eyes flicked to Luca and he gave me a timid smile. "We could always go to mine," I said.

"No." His gaze darkened. "I owe you."

ENZO

I stared at Matteo's name flashing on the screen. I'd silenced my cell phone a long time ago, sick of his incessant updates. He was at some bar with Nicco and Ari… and Nora. I knew he was trying to get a rise out of me.

"Here you go, gentlemen." A server slid a tray of drinks onto the table. "If you need anything else, just let me know." Her smoky eyes lingered on me, but I stared right through her. The persistent vibration of my cell was like an annoying itch I couldn't scratch.

Or an itch I knew I *shouldn't* scratch.

"You gonna get that?" Gino asked, motioning to my hand covering my cell.

I didn't want to. I needed to keep my distance. It was better… for everyone. *Especially her.*

It started ringing again and Gino chuckled. "If you don't get that, I will. And nobody will like how that ends."

"Yeah, yeah, keep your hair on, old man." I clambered from the booth and headed toward the emergency exit, hitting answer as I shouldered the door. "What?" I barked.

"Nice to hear your voice too," Matteo teased.

"What the fuck do you want?"

"Just to shoot the shit and see how my favorite cousin is doing. Since you've clearly forgotten how to use your cell."

"I texted."

"And I felt your reluctance in every word."

"Matt…"

"Yeah, yeah. I won't keep you. I just thought you'd like to know I left Nora at the bar… with Luca."

"Luca? Who the fuck is Luca?" My spine straightened.

"Luca is the guy who's going to swoop in and make Nora his unless you pull your head out your ass and do something about it."

"Matt, I've told you already—"

"You don't want her. Yeah, yeah, I got the memo when you fucked off to Providence. But you're making a mistake, cous. She cares about you, she cares… you just have to let her—"

"I'm not doing this with you. She's better off forgetting all about me." The words got stuck in my throat. "This Luca? He a good guy?" Because he already sounded like a fucking moron.

"Seems genuine. His rental application didn't flag anything."

"He lives in La Stella?"

"Yep, right across her hall."

Fuck.

"You saw his file?" I tried to keep my voice even.

"Not in person, no. But I had Maurice double check. No

one gets an apartment in La Stella without passing all the checks."

"Doesn't mean he's a decent guy though."

"He spent half the night staring at her with that look."

"What look?" My teeth ground together.

"You know, the starry-eyed look Nicco has whenever he's around Arianne."

"Fuck." It spilled out in a ragged breath before I could stop it.

"Exactly why I called," Matteo said.

"What do you want me to say? You know why I'm here. I need to get my head straight, I need to—"

"You need to learn to let people in, E. I know what happened with your old man messed you up, I get it, I do. But pushing us away, pushing her away, isn't the answer."

A loud bang drew my attention, and I dipped my hand into my jacket, feeling my fingers graze the butt of my pistol. I never went anywhere unarmed, an array of weapons strapped to my person. A Wharncliffe knife tucked into my boot, my brass knuckles, my pistol. I loved weapons almost as much as I loved my GTO. There was something comforting about knowing I could protect myself and the people I cared about. Besides, you never knew what enemies were lurking in the shadows.

Fuck.

I was starting to sound like him.

'Our enemies hide in plain sight, Enzo.' My father had once said to me. "They want to destroy what we have built and take it for their own. They want to see the Marchetti fall, to see the Family go up in smoke. Never forget that, figlio mio."

I'd always known my father would die for the Family. I just hadn't anticipated he would die a traitor.

Anger snaked through me, coiling around my chest with its sharp barbs as my fist clenched so tight my knuckles turned white.

He was still in my head… and I didn't know how the fuck to get him out.

"Cous?" Matteo's voice rattled through my skull.

"Yeah, I'm here."

"Just think about it…"

"Yeah."

But as I hung up, we both knew I wouldn't. Because sometimes to exorcise your demons, you had to become them.

∽

"WHAT THE—"

An incessant whirring sound pierced my skull, making me groan.

"Hmm, what is that?" A voice said, and I glanced over my shoulder to find a blonde sleeping naked beside me.

Fucking great.

After Matteo's call last night everything was a little hazy. There were drinks, a lot of them. As it neared closing time, Gino and the guys insisted on some of the girls joining us and we'd stayed at the bar getting drunker and hornier.

I had vague memories of the blonde being all over me. Loose lips and wandering hands. Despite the ringing in my ears and bass drum in my head, I felt pretty relaxed, so it wasn't hard to imagine what had happened when we'd eventually got back to my room.

"Are you going to answer that?" she groaned, pulling the sheet over her body.

I swung my legs over the edge and sat up, snatching up my cell. "Yeah?" I barked, not even checking the name.

"It's me," Gino sounded as rough as I felt, "we've got a problem."

"I'm listening."

"It's DiMarco's. There's been a break-in."

"A break-in?" Disbelief coated my words. "But we were only there like… five hours ago." It was barely six thirty.

"I know. Zander got a call from the local PD; they tripped the alarm. They're giving us time to get down there first and take a look."

"Yeah, I'm coming."

"Meet you downstairs in ten."

"Make it five," I said.

"What's wrong?" Blondie stared up at me with tired eyes.

"I've gotta go."

"Go? But it's early—"

"Duty calls." I started pulling on my pants and securing my weapons to my body.

"So it's true what they say about you." She pushed up on one elbow, flicking her hair off one shoulder.

"What do they say?"

"That you're dangerous."

A derisive snort crawled up my throat.

"So it's not… true?"

"What do you think?" I narrowed my eyes, shucking on my jacket. I remembered kissing her, running my hands over her tight little body. But I couldn't remember much after that.

Fuck. I'd been totally wasted.

"I'm thinking you should stay here and finish what you started last night," she damn near purred.

So we hadn't fucked then.

I didn't know whether to be relieved or disappointed.

She must have had her mouth on my dick though because most of the tension I'd felt talking to Matteo last night had dissipated. Even if the jealousy sat heavy in my chest, coiled around my heart like barbed wire.

"No can do, dolcezza, I gotta go. Stay though. Order room service. Take a shower." *But be gone when I get back.*

"You'll come back to me?"

"I don't think so, Blondie. This could take a while."

She pouted. "Well, if you want some company later, I could always leave my number."

"Yeah, you do that." I motioned to the notepad by the telephone. "I gotta go."

She flopped back with an exasperated breath, but I didn't wait around to hear her complaints. I'd stay away long enough to hope she was gone when I got back, and if she wasn't, I'd give it to her straight.

I wasn't interested in anything more than she gave me last night.

Gino was already waiting in reception. The grim expression on his face told me all I needed to know. He suspected Alejandro. Which meant whoever he was working with, or for, they were upping the ante and this time it was personal.

It couldn't have been a coincidence we were drinking at DiMarco's last night, right before it was hit.

They were watching us, taunting us... which changed everything.

"What's the plan?" I asked, noting it was just the two of us.

"We go check it out before the cops arrive. I already spoke

with Toni. We keep this between us for now, just you and me, okay?"

My brows furrowed. "What aren't you telling me?"

He gave me a sympathetic look and said, "Let's go."

DiMarco's was a mess. Whoever had been here had caused thousands of dollars worth of damage, smashing the mirrored walls and glass shelves housing Zander's impressive range of liquor. Chairs lay overturned and tables were at strange angles. It looked like a herd of wild animals had stormed right through the place.

"Jesus Christ." Glass crunched under Gino's boots as we made our way toward the back office. "Zander?" he called.

"In here." He sounded pissed.

We found him in his office, standing in the middle of the room with his back to us. "I think it's for you." His eyes caught mine over his shoulder.

"Say what?" I frowned.

"That." He jabbed his finger toward the far wall. I stepped closer, certain my eyes were deceiving me. But sure enough, there scrawled in blood red were the words, 'like father, like son.'

"This is what you wanted me to see?" I pinned Gino with a hard look.

"I wanted you to see it before we scrub it."

"Fuck." I ran a hand down my head and cupped my neck. This was bad, very fucking bad.

"You think this has something to do with my—" I hesitated, glancing at Zander.

"Seriously? My place just got fucking trashed because of yo—"

"Basta!" Gino hissed. "This is not Enzo's doing, and you'd do well to remember who he is."

"Yeah, yeah, my bad." Zander held up his hands in defense. "As long as the insurance covers it, it's all good."

Gino tsked, moving closer. "Give us the room for a second," he said with an air of authority.

"Come on, Gino, this is my fucking—"

"I said, give us the room."

"Yeah, whatever. I'll be out front." He took off, but Gino called after him, "And don't fucking touch anything."

"You good, kid?" He asked, the second Zander was gone.

"They know," I said, disbelief coating my words. "How the fuck do they know?"

Only a handful of people knew about my father's betrayal. In years gone by, if a man betrayed omertà, his death would be broadcast across the Family as a reminder of what happened to traitors. But times were different, and Uncle Toni tried to rule with respect instead of fear.

"They're clearly more connected than we first thought." He clapped me on the shoulder. "That or—"

"No, don't say it." My eyes finally tore away from the scrawl and slid to Gino. "Don't you fucking say it."

"We have to consider it, kid."

"My father." This could all be his doing.

Fuck.

My boot flew out connecting with the leg of the chair. Pain shot through my big toe and skittered up my leg but it barely registered.

"Better?"

"Not in the slightest."

"We'll get them, Enzo. Whoever is behind this, we'll get them. And when we do—"

"I put a bullet between their fucking eyes."

"Rein it in, kid. Harness all that anger and frustration, because something tells me you're gonna need it. Let's get this cleaned up before the cops get here. The last thing we need is them sticking their nose in where it doesn't belong."

Gino scanned the office before strolling toward Zander's drinks cabinet. He grabbed a wad of tissue paper out of the box and poured expensive whisky over it before moving to the mirror and scrubbing away all evidence of the message.

"Get rid of this." He thrust the soggy tissue paper at me. "I'll speak to Zander. You stay cool, okay? We came to assist Zander. That's all. I'm counting on you not to screw this up, kid."

Without a word, I crossed the room and slipped outside. Zander was hovering in the hall. His eyes collided with me and he blanched.

"Problem?" My brow rose. I wasn't afraid of these guys. They might have been older and wiser, but with the amount of anger and thirst for vengeance fueling me, I was deadlier.

"I don't even know where to start." His shady expression gave way to defeat. "This bar is my whole world."

"Let the cops do their job and then we'll send in someone to help you." Because no matter how irritating or shady somebody was, we looked after our own.

"Have you checked in on all the girls? Did everyone get home okay?"

"I can't get hold of Cait." His eyes dropped to the cell in his hand.

"Cait?" I hadn't heard that name in the last few days.

"She's my… she's one of my best girls. If you know what I'm saying." His lip curved with wicked intent.

God, I fucking hated this asshole.

"You want me to go check on her?"

"You'd do that?"

I shrugged. "Beats being here when the cops show up." Even if they sent over someone on our payroll, they still made me antsy.

"She lives on Jefferson Street, Park View Apartments. I just want to know she's okay."

My brows furrowed. "She someone to you?"

"Like I said, she's one of my best girls, and I protect my interests."

*I bet you do.* Sleazy motherfucker.

Growing up, once Nicco, Matteo, and I were given more responsibility in the Family, I'd always wondered why Uncle Toni aligned himself with guys like DiMarco. He was only out to line his own pocket. But Providence was Marchetti territory and it's just how business went. Plus, guys like DiMarco collected enemies like I collected shiny new sharp-edged toys to play with.

"I'll head over there and make sure she's okay."

Something flashed over his face, and his whole posture shifted. "Actually," he scrubbed his jaw, "I'm sure she's fine. I'll call her ag—"

"It's fine, I got it. I'll call as soon as I get over there and check it out." I regarded him for a second. DiMarco was usually the epitome of cool, calm, and collected, but he seemed a little ruffled and I couldn't work out if it was because of the break-in… or because of Cait.

"What's her full name?"

"Caitlin," he let out a derisive sigh. "Caitlin O'Connell."

"I'm on it. Tell Gino, I'll be back soon."

I didn't wait for his reply, walking straight out of the bar and into the brisk morning air. Dragging in a deep lungful, I gave myself a second before checking my maps app on my cell and taking off in the direction of Caitlin's apartment building.

Gino would probably kick my ass when I got back to DiMarco's, but I needed air. I needed space to fucking think after seeing that message scrawled on the wall. It wasn't done in blood, despite its red coloring. Fresh blood had this smell. A coppery metallic twang that permeated the air.

It was a smell you didn't ever forget.

Pulling out a smoke, I lit it up and inhaled a deep hit. Everyone was right, I needed to kick this habit. It made my skin stink, and my lungs burn… but I needed the routine. I needed to keep myself distracted. Because in the moments of silence, when everything was still, the memory of that night threatened to pull me under so far, I wouldn't ever make it back out in one piece.

I crossed the street and double checked the map. I was close. Caitlin lived around here somewhere. I'd been so desperate to get the fuck out of DiMarco's it hadn't occurred to me how odd it would seem, me turning up at a stranger's door. But I only needed proof she was okay, then I could take a slow walk back to the bar.

Stepping up to the buzzer, I pressed her number and waited. When no one answered, I pressed it again.

Still nothing.

Some guy slipped out of the building, so I waited for him to pass and then stuck my hand out to catch the door, ducking inside. I took two steps at a time until I arrived outside her apartment. I knocked on the door and waited.

Finally, I heard shuffling on the other side, and the door cracked open. "Can I help you?"

It was dark inside, her face cloaked in shadows, but her green eyes glittered up at me.

"DiMarco sent me," I said. "There was an incident at the bar."

"Incident?" She kept the door firmly in place, like a shield between us.

"Are you okay?" I asked. "Zander said you didn't answer his call for you to check-in."

"I… I should go. You can tell him I'm fine." She went to close the door, but my hand shot out, steadying it.

"Wait." There was something familiar about her. Gently, I pushed the door open further, forcing her to sidestep the damn thing.

"You."

Her breath hitched as she met my confused gaze. "Please," she begged. "Just tell him you saw me and that I'm fine."

My hand shot out, capturing her chin. I stared at her, my brows furrowed, and growled, "Tell me what the fuck happened."

# CHAPTER 12

NORA

"Morning," Luca said as I joined him at the breakfast counter.

"Why are you so fresh and awake and I'm… ugh, my head hurts."

He chuckled and shoved a glass of water and a couple of pain pills toward me. "Take these. It'll help."

He leaned back against the counter, watching me with those warm hazel eyes of his.

"Things got a little crazy, huh?"

"You could say that." After we'd gotten back to his apartment, Lucii had challenged the guys to beer pong. Only, Luca had no beer, so it became tequila pong. I'd crashed out after a couple of rounds and vaguely remembered someone carrying me into the guest bedroom.

"Thank you, for putting me to bed," I said.

"You remember that?" His brow arched.

"I remember… bits. I didn't do anything too embarrassing, did I?"

"I never kiss and tell." A faint smirk traced his lips.

"We didn't…" My cheeks burned.

"Relax," he chuckled, "you tried to kiss my face off, but I was the perfect gentleman."

"I did not," I gasped, and Luca's laughter only increased.

"You're teasing me." My brows furrowed, but relief seeped into me.

"I couldn't resist. Nothing happened. I don't take advantage of drunk girls. Even if they're as cute as you."

"Luca…"

"Nora…"

The air crackled with tension. I was ready to change the subject when Lucii breezed into the kitchen looking as fresh as a daisy.

"Why am I sitting here with a nest on my head," my hand went to my hair, trying to take the wild curls from my face, "and you two look like… like *that*."

"Good genes." Lucii shrugged, completely at home in a guy's kitchen. "Is there coffee?"

"I just made a fresh pot and I'm making pancakes."

"My hero." They shared a smile, and something twisted inside of me.

Luca wasn't mine… I had no right to feel jealous of their small interaction.

But did I want him to be mine?

That was the question I'd grappled with all night as we'd sat around until the early hours playing beer pong and listening to Nate regale us with stories of his college days.

"Where is Nate?" I asked her, because the last thing I

remembered was the two of them getting up close and personal on Luca's couch.

"He already left."

"Oh. Are you seeing him again?" I teased.

"Maybe." She shrugged.

"Well, before you leave, you can disinfect my couch." Luca gave her a pointed look and the three of us burst into laughter.

"It was a fun night. We should do it again. Although we might have to find a girl for Isaac next time. I kinda got the impression he didn't come because he didn't want to play fifth wheel."

"Fifth wheel?" The words spilled out, even though I knew exactly what she was getting at.

Luca cleared his throat and turned around to tend to the pancakes. Lucii shot me an amused look, but I ducked my head, nursing my glass of water.

"Good thing we don't have classes until late morning," I said. "I'm not sure I could handle it."

"Nothing giant sunglasses, a strong coffee, and some Advil won't fix." She grinned. "I'm going to use the bathroom."

"Can you remember where it is?" Luca asked, and she nodded.

"I think I'm just going to go…" I got up but the room span. My hand shot out to steady myself, but Luca was there, gripping my shoulders as he stared down at me with concern in his eyes.

"You good?"

"I… yeah, thank you."

"You know, I wanted to ask—"

"Your apartment is so—my bad, am I interrupting something?"

We both turned to meet Lucii's suggestive grin.

"Uh, no, I just felt a little lightheaded. I'm going to head back to my apartment though and take a shower. I'll see you in class later?"

"Sure thing."

"But I made pancakes." Luca frowned, but I was already backing away from him.

I smiled weakly. "Maybe another time."

I hurried down the hall into the guest bedroom and gathered up my purse, shoes, and cell phone and slipped out of Luca's apartment.

Last night had been fun... but something had changed between us. The invisible line between us blurring. I was attracted to him, that was a given. He was handsome, and sweet, and good.

But there was just one glaring issue.

He wasn't Enzo.

∾

"You should eat something," Ari said, concern lacing her words.

"I'm fine." I pushed the plate away from me and let out an exhausted sigh. "I'm just tired."

And classes so far today had been killer.

"You're burning the candle at both ends... you can't—"

"It was one night, babe. One night. Besides, it's freshman year. This is exactly what I'm supposed to be doing. Next year is for the hard work. This year is for partying and finding yourself."

"You did a pretty good job of finding yourself last night."

"Hey, what's that supposed to mean?" I didn't like the judgment in her tone.

Ari's expression softened. "I didn't mean it like that. I'm just worried about you. You're all alone in the apartment. Luca is—"

"He's good people, Ari. And he likes me. At least, I think he does. Is that so hard to believe?"

"Of course it isn't." She jerked back as if I'd slapped her. "Why would you even ask that?"

"I'm just grouchy."

"You mean hungover."

"Yeah, that too." My eyes fluttered closed. "Is it so wrong I let my hair down for a night?"

"Not at all. I just hope you're doing it for you and not to escape."

My eyes snapped open. "Say what?"

"I know you Nora. I'm your best friend. What happened with Enzo—"

"I think that ship has sailed, babe. He left."

He freaking left without uttering a word. I didn't ever imagine I was the kind of girl who could make a guy like Enzo stay... but a goodbye? That wasn't too much to ask.

"He did. And honestly, I want to say it's a good thing. But I can see you're hurting, and that makes you vulnerable."

"If you're worried about my honor, you needn't be. I lost my v-card in high school and it was completely unmemorable." I laughed, bitterly.

"Nora." Ari didn't join me. "I'm serious. Luca seems like a good guy. All I'm saying is if you jump into something with him, what happens when Enzo comes back?"

I suspected a whole lot of nothing. Whatever we had, or

might have had, was gone. I saw it when he walked away from me at Arabella's party.

"Can we talk about something else? This is hurting my head," I grumbled.

"Here, take this." She slung a box of pills across the table. Luis was watching us from his position at the doors leading in and out of the food court. Students came and went either not noticing him or accepting his presence without question. I guess that's what happened when you went to school with a local celebrity.

But Arianne wasn't a celebrity to me. She was my best friend. My ride or die. The only problem was, now she was Nicco's ride or die too.

"Hey," I said, shaking off my solemn mood. "Do you think the two of—"

"Ladies," Matteo leaped over the back of the couch I was perched on and dropped down beside me. "What's good for lunch?"

"You can have mine." I pushed my plate toward him.

"What's wrong with it?"

"Nothing," Ari said, "she's hungover." Nicco sat down beside her and immediately pulled her into a passionate kiss.

"Do you have to do that in public?" Tristan, Arianne's cousin, also joined us.

"She's my wife, Capizola. If I want to kiss her, I—"

"Okay," he snapped, "I'm sorry I asked. Hungover on a school day, Nor? How rebellious of you." Tristan smirked and I flipped him off.

There had been a time, not so long ago, that I didn't know what side Tristan stood on. He'd been best friends with Scott Fascini, the psychopath responsible for kidnapping me and going after Nicco and Arianne.

It was all water under the bridge now, but I saw the lingering tension between Nicco and Tristan. They had both taken on the role of her protector, and at one point, Tristan had tried to protect her from the one thing she'd needed more than anything.

Nicco.

"Countdown to graduation, Tris," I said. "Are you ready?"

"Is anyone ever ready?" He shrugged, popping a fry into his mouth.

"You still determined to take off for a year and travel?"

"If Mom and Uncle Roberto get their way, I'll be heading up a department at Capizola Holdings. But I feel like I need to spread my wings before I put down roots."

"We need you," Ari said. "I need you."

A low rumble came from Nicco.

"Relax, husband," she teased him, "I need you too."

"Gross, I think I just regurgitated some chili dog." Matteo grabbed my bottle of water. "Mind?"

"Go for it." I motioned for him to continue.

"So how did things go with Captain America?"

"Captain America?" My brows knitted.

"Yeah, Luca. He has that whole Chris Evans vibe working for him."

"Now that you mention it, he kind of does look like Captain America," Nicco added.

I held up my hand. "Can we please stop referring to him as Captain America?"

"They have a point, Nor." Arianne chuckled.

"Oh God, not you too."

"Who's Luca?" Tristan said, watching us with mild confusion.

"Just some guy who wants in Nora's pant—"

"Enough!" I smashed my hand over Matteo's mouth, drowning out his voice. "Luca is my new neighbor."

"Ah gotcha." He smirked.

"I give up. I'm going to hang out somewhere else." I grabbed my bag and got up. "Somewhere where my friends aren't complete assholes."

"Nora, babe, don't be like that," Matteo called after me. "We're only joking."

I flipped him off over my shoulder and kept walking. The truth was, I didn't want to deal with any of this right now. I didn't want to deal with my confusing feelings for Luca or my unrelenting feelings for Enzo.

What I wanted was quiet. My hungover brain couldn't handle much else.

Just as I reached the doors out of the food court, a hand snagged my arm.

"Nora, wait."

"I'm really not in the mood, babe." I stared at my best friend with pleading eyes.

"I know, and I'm sorry. I didn't mean to—"

"No, you did nothing wrong. I'm just... ugh, I'm so confused."

"Why don't we blow off classes this afternoon and have some girl's time?"

"Yeah?" My mood instantly lifted.

"Yeah. It's been too long."

"Ice cream, face masks, and Magic Mike?" I asked, hopeful.

"If that's what you want, then that's what we'll do." She tucked herself into my side and we walked out of the food court like that.

"The guys are sorry too."

"No one needs to be sorry." Any other day, I would have given them some snarky reply. But I wasn't feeling particularly snarky today.

"Everything's different now," I whispered, allowing myself a vulnerable moment.

"I know." Ari let out a soft sigh, gripping my arm tighter. "But you're still my best friend, Nor. Nothing will ever change that. I hope you know that."

"I know," I replied.

Because I did.

ARIANNE STAYED UNTIL SHE COULD NO LONGER KEEP HER EYES open. We'd gorged ourselves on ice cream and candy, drooling to the sexual revelation that was Channing Tatum and Alex Pettyfer.

Nicco sent Luis to pick her up, and I watched as he carried her down the hall, half-asleep. I closed my door and began cleaning up. This should have been our life together: movie nights and pamper sessions, sitting around gossiping about boys and classes.

But now she was married, and I was… pining after a guy who would never want me for more than what my body could give him.

A frustrated cry spilled from my lips as my chest heaved. I hated feeling like this. Weak and sorry for myself.

I wasn't weak.

I was a freaking firecracker.

I wasn't the kind of girl to sit around and wait for a guy to wake up and realize I was everything he needed.

I made things happen for myself. I took control of my own destiny.

And I refused to sit around and wait for Enzo Marchetti to pull his head out of his ass when there was another guy who saw me.

Luca saw me.

Without thinking, I marched out of my apartment and across the hall, banging on Luca's door.

"N-Nora?" He stared at me, wide-eyed, a towel wrapped firmly around his narrow waist. "Is something wrong?"

I didn't reply. Instead, I threw my arms around his neck and leaned up, crashing my mouth down on his.

"Whoa." His arm went around my waist as we stumbled back into his room, the door clicking shut behind us.

"Kiss me," I urged him, nervous energy zipping through my body. "I need for you to kiss me."

"Slow down…" He broke away, gazing down at me with concern. "Not that I'm complaining, because I'm not…"

"You don't want me?" I batted my eyelashes at him, liquid lust coursing through my veins.

I wanted this.

Needed it.

"Nora, you know I do."

"So, what's the problem?"

Because I could feel the evidence of his desire pressed up against my stomach.

"I don't want to be your rebound guy and I don't want you to do something you'll regret tomorrow."

His words were like a bucket of cold water and I pulled away, turning my back on him.

"You're hurting." It wasn't a question.

Luca stepped up behind me, running his hands up and down my shoulders. "Nora, look at me."

Slowly, I turned around, meeting his intense stare. "You are so fucking beautiful, and strong, and funny… I hate this guy, whoever he is, for making you doubt yourself." He pushed the messy curls from my face. "But if I have you, I'm going to want all of you. And I don't think you're ready for that." His thumb dropped to my mouth, lingering on the pillow of my bottom lip.

Energy pulsed around us, so thick I could almost taste it. I wanted him to kiss me. For the first time since I met Luca, I really *really* wanted him to kiss me.

So why didn't he?

"Luca?" His name fell from my lips in a whispered plea, but he didn't move.

He didn't do anything.

"This was clearly a mistake." Dejection burned through me as I tore out of his arms and retreated back toward the door.

"Nora, wait," he called, but my hand was already on the door handle. "Nora, please."

I spun around and met his apologetic gaze. "What, Luca? What is there left to say?"

He closed the distance between us until his hands gently cupped my face.

"I had a change of heart."

"What do you—"

His mouth captured mine in a bruising kiss.

Luca was kissing me.

He was kissing *me*.

And I was letting him.

# CHAPTER 13

ENZO

"I got a lead," Gino said the second I reached him.

It was a little after eight and we were at the restaurant beside the motel getting breakfast. The other patrons gave us a wide berth, but it wasn't anything I hadn't experienced before.

"About fucking time," I grumbled.

It had been six days since I left Verona. Six days of us chasing dead ends.

Whoever was orchestrating this whole thing knew how to stay off the grid.

The server brought over coffee and took our order. The second she turned her back, I said, "Before we get into what the hell we're going to do about this fucker, I need to ask you something."

"Go on."

"You ever seen Zander get violent with his girls?"

Gino's brow pinched. "He gets a bit handsy now and again but hurting them? Nah. He's all talk and no action that one."

I rubbed my jaw. "He asked me to go over and check on one of his girls. Caitlin O'Connell. But when I got over there, I recognized her. Found her crying in the bathroom at the club the other night."

"You think he's hurting her?"

"I don't know. She wouldn't tell me what happened. But if DiMarco is putting his hands on his girls… that shit don't fly with me."

He hissed between his teeth. "Word of advice, kid, don't get involved in another man's business. DiMarco is already a loose cannon. Don't give him a reason to cause a shitstorm we don't need right now. It was probably a John who got a little too enthusiastic."

I didn't like it. I didn't like it at all. But Gino was right. I was here to find out who was coming after the Family, not to get all up in Zander DiMarco's affairs. Besides, Caitlin had been unwilling to even let me inside her apartment, let alone interrogate her about what had happened. I'd left my number with her in case she needed anything, but I didn't expect to hear from her anytime soon.

"What's the plan?" I changed the subject.

"It's an address, an abandoned warehouse out by the river. The guy we worked over. I let him go."

"The fuck?" I gawked at him.

"Relax. Oldest trick in the book. Let a rat free and it'll lead you right back to its nest." He took a sip of his coffee. "I put a tracker on him and followed him out there. He met with another guy, but I didn't get a good look at him. Marc and Dixon have been staking out the place overnight. After our guy left, nobody else came or went."

"You think it's Alejandro?"

Gino nodded, and I clenched my fist against the table.

"When do we go?"

No one was supposed to know the truth about my father, especially not this asshole.

"Relax. Eat." Gino relaxed back in his chair. "It could be a long fucking day."

My skin vibrated with the need to find this motherfucker and get answers: who he was and what the fuck he hoped to achieve coming after the Family.

"Any word about Morello?" I asked Gino, trying to distract myself.

"He's out of the hospital. Won't be running any marathons for a while, but he'll be okay."

"That's good."

"Yeah, but listen, Enzo, we need to do this the right way. We need to find out what this fucker knows and what he plans on doing with it."

I nodded. "How are we doing this?"

"Just you and me initially. We'll stake the place out and bide our time until nightfall."

Which was about seven-and-a-half hours away.

Fuck. Today was going to drag like a bitch. But for as much as I wanted to end this thing, I also didn't want to risk him slipping through our fingers, so I would follow Gino's lead and wait.

"We end this thing tonight," he added. "Then you can get back to Verona and sink deep into your woman and let her absolve you of some of your sins."

"I don't have a woman," I argued.

"Kid, you might tell yourself that, but you ain't foolin' anyone. Seen that look in your eyes one too many times."

"I don't know what you're talking about."

He smirked. "Whatever you say, kid."

Just then, the server brought over our order and Gino dropped all talk of women to dig into his breakfast.

It didn't matter.

He was wrong.

I didn't have a woman.

Didn't want one, didn't need one.

I'd seen what the love of a good woman did to men like me. Made men. It distracted them. Rendered them weak. It blinded them with jealousy, pulling their loyalties in too many directions.

"Eat up, you're going to need your energy." Gino levelled me with a hard look. One that told me all I needed to know…

Tonight, we would finish this.

BY THE TIME THE SUN BEGAN TO SET OVER THE CITY SKYLINE, I was cold, hungry, and itching for a fight.

"I'm going to take a piss," I said, shouldering the door of my Pontiac.

"Make it quick. This asshole hasn't left the warehouse all day. He's gotta surface eventually."

Marc and Dixon had met us right at the spot this morning, informing us the guy was still inside. There had been no one coming or going all fucking day, which meant he was in there somewhere, biding his time the same way we were.

The brisk air stung my face as I went around the rear end

of the car and took a leak behind a tree. We'd survived the day on a few stale chips and cans of soda. Part of me wanted to say, 'fuck it' and storm the warehouse, but as Gino kept reminding me, it wasn't only my ass on the line. Uncle Toni wanted answers. He wanted to know who was messing with us and why. And Gino Lupo had a process.

One that included a lot of sitting around and talking about the fucking weather.

I wiped my hands down my jeans and got back in the car. Gino was peering through his binoculars.

"Anything?" I asked.

"The security light just came on. But I don't think—wait a second. Wait a—fuck, yeah, there's our guy." He shoved the lenses at me.

My heart beat hard in my chest as I focused on the guy in their line of sight. I didn't recognize him, but it was dark, and he was wearing all-black with a skull cap pulled over his head.

"We should move now," I said, eager to get this over with. But Gino's arm shot out in front of me.

"We wait. If he leaves, I want to get a look inside."

"And if he doesn't come back?"

"He will. It's his nest. They always come back."

We watched the guy climb into a beat-up truck and drive off.

"Okay, let's go. Stay behind me and don't fuck this up. This is recon only."

"Recon?" I sneered. "We've been sitting in my car all fucking day."

"What's wrong, kid? The life not as glamorous as you thought it would be?"

I hadn't really given it much thought. But I knew Gino and his guys got their hands dirty and I wanted in on the action.

"Let's go see what this pompinara is hiding." Gino pulled on some gloves before slipping out of the car and disappearing into the night.

I did the same, following him, sticking to the shadows. The warehouse was in a disused industrial area along the river. Its on-site security was long gone, leaving us to explore unnoticed.

Gino ushered me to the side of the building and mouthed, "We'll check for another way in."

I nodded, following him around the outer perimeter until we came across another door. It was secured with a padlock, but Gino produced some small bolt cutters from inside his leather jacket and made quick work of getting it off.

"Bingo," he whispered, gently cracking the door open. "Close it behind you and keep your eyes peeled."

"Got it."

Darkness consumed us as we entered a narrow passageway. Gino pulled out a flashlight and guided us deeper into the abandoned building. At the end there was a doorway leading into a vast open space.

"Anything?" I asked, growing impatient.

"Fuck, you need to see this." He disappeared inside and I followed.

"What the fuck?" My eyes went to the far wall. It was covered in newspaper cuttings, photographs, and string. Like one of those boards from a crime documentary.

"He's been watching us," I said, moving closer to the display. There were pictures of Morello outside his store.

DiMarco's and numerous other local businesses in and around Providence that had ties with the Family.

"This doesn't make any sense," I mumbled while Gino took photo after photo on his cell, probably to forward to Uncle Toni.

I reached out, ghosting my fingers over a recent photo of me, Nicco, and Matteo with Alessia. A chill ran down my spine. He wasn't just watching Providence; this fucker had been to Verona. He'd been watching *us*. There were other photos of Uncles Toni and Michele. A newspaper article reporting on Nicco and Arianne's wedding.

"Who the fuck is this asshole?"

Alejandro was supposed to be connected to the Mexican cartel in Connecticut. This didn't seem like their MO.

"Someone who knows too much," Gino said over my shoulder.

"But what's the endgame? It doesn't make any sense."

Morello and DiMarco's were business associates, they weren't legitimate Marchetti businesses. Why mess around with the small timers, when with all this intel, he could come right for the head of the snake?

"We're missing something here…" Gino mused.

But something caught my attention. It wasn't a sound so much as a smell.

"What is that?" I searched the immediate area, tracking the familiar scent. It was the same coppery twang I remembered from my childhood whenever my father and uncles took us hunting.

The unforgettable smell of death.

"We should call for backup," Gino said, but I was transfixed on finding the source of the pungent scent. With little natural light in the warehouse, I pulled out my cell phone to use the flashlight to guide my way. Old shelving was littered around the space, leaning against walls, and toppled over like a haphazard obstacle course. On the far wall there was a row of busted up lockers. I weaved through the mess aware of the sticky, squelchy sound underfoot.

"Gino," I called, and he came running, grinding to a halt when I dropped the beam and illuminated the pool of blood surrounding the lockers.

"Do you want to do the honors?" he asked me, and I leaned over, yanking open the first locker.

"Holy shit." The dead body toppled out, splatting over the floor in a spray of red mist.

"Fuck," Gino hissed. "That's Alejandro."

"Wha—"

Just then the clatter of footsteps sounded from somewhere behind us and we both glanced in that direction.

Someone else was in the warehouse.

Had the guy doubled back? Or had that been his intention all along?

The question evaporated as a figure came out of nowhere, knocking into me and sending me crashing to the bloody ground.

"Enzo," Gino roared as I tried to buck the guy off me. But with the blood acting as a lubricant, it was impossible to get any leverage.

"Surprise." He glared down at me, trapping my body between his and the cold ground beneath me.

"Get the fuck off me." I slammed my forehead into his nose, and he rolled away, grunting in agony. Gino leaned down and grabbed him by his collar, dragging him to his feet. But at the last second, I saw the glint of the blade.

"Gino, watch ou—"

The guy brought his hand high and jabbed it down in one fell swoop, the knife sliding into Gino's jugular like butter. All I could do was stand there and watch as dark-red blood spurted out of his neck.

"H-help me." He gurgled, clutching his neck with both hands, blood oozing down his gloved fingers, as the guy yanked his knife free and stepped away.

Gino staggered backward, swaying a little.

"Fuck, man." I rushed to his side, hardly able to believe what was happening. My hands went to cover his, trying to stem the blood. But it was everywhere seeping through over my gloves like a red river. "Tell me what to do? Tell me…"

"Don't let him e-escape." Gino's eyes went over my shoulder and I glanced back to the guy taking off toward the passageway.

"Go," he breathed with difficulty. The life was draining away from him before my very eyes.

"Fuck, FUCK!" I let out a guttural roar as Gino bled out in my arms.

"G-go." His eyes rolled.

I didn't want to leave him, but when I heard the rumble of an engine, I knew it was now or never.

"I'm sorry, man," I whispered, laying Gino down. He was unconscious now, blood still spurting out of his wound. "I'm so fucking sorry."

I ran out of the warehouse and to my car, ripping the door open and barreling inside. The truck was already on the move, but it was a rusted piece of shit that wouldn't out gun my baby.

Digging my cell from my jeans, I managed to dial Uncle Toni.

"Enzo, son? Thank fuck. Where are you?"

"Gino… he… he's…"

Fuck. There was so much blood.

"I'm sending back up. Just tell me where you are."

"I'm going after him." The words came out icy cold, detached from the bloodbath I'd just left. There would be time to mourn Gino, to raise a glass for him and pay our respects. But that time wasn't now.

"Lorenzo, listen to me. I want you to pull over and take a breath, son. We'll get this fucker, we will. But not tonight. Not like this."

"I can get him. I can—"

"*Vaffanculo!*" Uncle Toni roared. "I am not asking, Enzo. I am giving you a direct order. Pull the fuck over."

Before I could talk myself out of it, I hit disconnect and threw my cell into the center console. I needed to do this—I needed to know why he had all those photographs and newspaper cuttings of my family and friends. The need to know burned through me like acid and was the only thing spurring me on. That and blind rage.

I'd been around death, too much for a twenty-year-old guy. But I'd never watched the life drain, literally drain, right out of a friend before. A guy who had taken me under his wing without question.

I followed the truck, keeping a safe distance. He obviously hadn't noticed I'd given chase, making no effort to speed away. He'd taken the road out of Providence, joining the highway toward Verona. Nicco and Matteo blew up my cell phone, no doubt up to speed from Uncle Toni about what had gone down. I hoped that Marc and Dixon had gotten there in time to get help, but deep down in my gut, I knew Gino was gone.

There was too much blood. I was covered in the stuff. It

clung to my clothes like rainwater. The cloying scent only fueling my need for vengeance.

"I'm coming for you," I chanted to myself, driven only by rage. Part of me knew I should heed Uncle Toni's orders to step down, but I couldn't—I couldn't let this motherfucker escape. So I stayed on his ass, keeping the rusty-black truck in my line of sight.

But the guy didn't drive to Verona. He pulled off at a gas station about five miles out.

I made the turn and rolled into the forecourt, hiding between a couple of trucks parked up for the night. The guy climbed out of his truck, pulling on a black jacket over his hoodie. I couldn't see much of his face, hidden under a ball cap he'd obviously pulled on at some point on the drive here.

He disappeared inside and I waited.

My cell phone began blaring again and I finally grabbed it. "Yeah?"

"What the fuck, Enzo?" Nicco growled. "You were told to stand down."

"And let this fucker escape? He knows us, Nic. He fucking knows *us*. And he knows about—" The words died in my throat.

"I know… fuck, I know. But I don't like this. He's clearly dangerous."

I wanted to argue that so was I, but another truck rolled into the forecourt, blocking my line of sight to the store and the guy's truck.

"I need to go." I hung up, cussing the truck driver.

I had no choice now but to drive around the gas pumps to the small parking lot in front of the store if I wanted to keep an eye on his truck. I made the split decision and edged out my spot and slowly crawled the car around the forecourt.

But I was too fucking late, the truck already peeling out of the gas station and back onto the highway. I slammed my foot down on the gas and took off, the screech of tires filling the air. I wasn't about to lose this guy for anything.

I just hoped no one called the cops before I got to him.

# CHAPTER 14

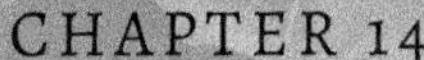

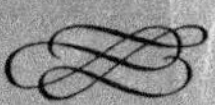

NORA

*I*'d just climbed into bed when a knock at my door rang out through the apartment.

God, I hoped it wasn't Luca. I wasn't ready to see him again yet, not after last night. I'd crept back into my apartment in the early hours of the morning after waking in his bed, his warm body tucked against mine.

My feelings for Luca were confusing. *I* was confused. So I'd taken a day off classes to spend time on some self-love. There wasn't much that a day of slumming around in lounge pants couldn't solve. I'd binge-watched some mindless TV, eaten my bodyweight in snacks, and enjoyed a homemade face mask, manicure, and pedicure. I felt shiny and new, even if my emotional state was still a mess.

Gingerly, I climbed out of bed and pulled an MU hoodie over my pajamas. It barely covered my legs, but it wasn't anything Luca or Maurice hadn't already seen.

But when I checked the peephole, my world imploded.

"Enzo?" I yanked open the door and stared at the guy who had left without so much as a word. "Oh my God, what happened?"

He was covered from head to toe in blood. A dark prince with death on his shoulder.

"Enzo?" I said again when he didn't reply. He just stood there, still and silent, his eyes soulless.

"Come on." I gently pulled him inside, noticing the way he flinched when I touched him. I ignored the pinch of dejection though. He was here and by the looks of him, he needed me.

I checked the hallway, noticing the splatters of blood. Crap.

"Wait right here," I said to Enzo as I went into my bedroom and retrieved my cell phone.

"Who are you—"

I held up my finger at Enzo, silencing him. "Maurice," I said the second he answered. "It's me."

"Miss Abato, what can I—"

"I need you at La Stella now, there's been a... Enzo is here."

"Lorenzo?"

"Yes."

"Is he okay?" Concern laced his words. "Are you safe?"

I smiled at that. If only he knew.

"Yes, I'm quite safe. Enzo won't hurt me." My eyes found Enzo's across the room, but his cloudy expression barely flinched. "You might want to bring some cleaning fluid and a fresh set of clothes."

Maurice sucked in a sharp breath. "I'll be right there.

Whatever you do, do not let Enzo leave. Not until I've spoken to Mr. Marchetti."

"Got it and thank you." I hung up, dropping my cell phone onto the sideboard.

Enzo tracked my every move as I slid the safety chain into place and went to the kitchen drawer and grabbed a trash bag.

"You should probably take those off and take a shower," I said. "Maurice is bringing you some clean clothes. There are towels and a robe in the bathroom. You can use whatever you need."

"Why are you doing this for me?" His lip twitched.

"The same reason you ended up on my doorstep and not anyone else's." I smiled weakly. "You know where the bathroom is. I'll give you some space."

Enzo stared at me intently, as if he was seeing me for the first time. I wanted to take that feeling and run with it, but I wasn't some naïve little girl. I knew from the state of him, whatever had gone down tonight wasn't good. And from his detached mood, I knew he was probably in shock.

For as much as I wanted to believe that Enzo being here changed things, I refused to let myself go there.

"You should go get cleaned up, you're a mess."

Blood caked his hands and face, smeared up his neck and soaked through his clothes. The sight was terrifying, but it didn't change the fact Enzo Marchetti was still one of the most beautiful men I'd ever laid eyes on.

He opened his mouth to speak but no words came… and that small flash of hope inside me flickered out.

*This doesn't change anything.* I had to remember that.

Enzo snatched up the bag and stalked off down the hall,

leaving a trail of bloody footprints. I wasn't even sure he was aware of just how blood-soaked he was.

I released a shaky breath and then set about cleaning up. When I was done, I threw the towel in the basin and braced myself against the counter. This was life with a mafioso. Blood-stained clothes and late night clean up jobs. Yet, the second I saw Enzo standing there on my doorstep, the only thing I wanted to do, was protect him. To pull him inside and comfort him.

What did that say about me if I was prepared to act first and ask questions later?

Across the hall was a good guy who wanted me. A good, honest man who could give me a secure, stable future. A man who would be there when I needed him.

Enzo wasn't that guy.

He dealt in dark deeds and secrets.

Yet, my heart beat harder for him than it ever had for another.

There was no explanation for that kind of connection. No rulebook for why some hearts entwined so deeply when others didn't.

It just was.

My cell phone started to vibrate, startling me from my reverie. "Hello?" I whispered.

"Nora, thank God. What happened? I heard Nicco tell Matteo that Enzo is at your place?"

"He just got here like five minutes ago."

"And?"

"It's bad, Ari… really bad. He was covered head to toe in blood and had this look in his eyes…" A violent shiver skated down my spine.

"You said *was* covered in blood?"

"He's taking a shower. I called Maurice, I didn't know what else to do."

"You did the right thing. Nicco is just talking to his father. Are you okay?"

"I guess… I mean, God, Ari…" The threads of my control slowly began to unravel as the weight of what was happening began to sink deep into my bones. "You didn't see how broken he looked."

"Do you want me to come over?"

"No!" I rushed out a little too hastily. "I just mean… it's Enzo. I don't think we should crowd him. I'm sure Nicco will know what to do."

In hindsight, I perhaps should have called him first, but Maurice was my personal bodyguard. He lived a three-minute walk away, and I knew he'd contact Nicco and Antonio Marchetti.

"Okay, text me if you need anything. And Nora…" She hesitated, and I knew I wasn't going to like her next words. "Be careful. It sounds like whatever happened was bad… Enzo will be hurting, he'll be confused. I don't want you to misread anything."

"Remember he doesn't want me, yep, I think I've got it," I said, unable to keep the bitterness out of my voice.

"Nora," she sighed. "That isn't what I meant."

"I'm fine, Ari. You don't have to worry about me. I'll text you later." I hung up before she could impart any more *advice* on me.

I wasn't stupid, I knew Enzo was running on autopilot right now. Trauma did that to people. But he'd still ended up at *my* apartment. I couldn't just completely ignore that.

I made us some hot chocolate while I waited for Maurice.

He showed up ten minutes later, armed with a duffel bag full of clothes for Enzo and cleaning fluid.

"Where is he?" he asked.

"Taking a shower."

"Good. When he's done, I want you to give him these and tell him to sit tight. The boss is coming straight here."

"Antonio Marchetti is coming here?"

Maurice ran a hand down his face. "He needs to speak with Enzo. You going to be okay? I can take you somewhere—"

"She stays."

I felt Enzo's deep graveled words all the way to the pit of my stomach.

"Got it." Maurice nodded. "There are fresh clothes in the bag. I'll handle the mess outside."

"Fuck," Enzo gritted out, standing there with just a white towel wrapped around his waist. Heat flowed through me like lava. "I didn't even think," he added.

"Relax, I got it. Just sit tight and wait for Toni to get here."

Enzo nodded, his eyes icy cold as they remained fixed on my face.

"I'll be right outside, Miss Abato."

"It's Nora," I called after him, letting out a sigh of frustration as he closed the door without correcting himself.

Silence echoed through the apartment as my eyes once again found Enzo. "I made us hot chocolate."

It had seemed like a good thing two minutes ago, but now I felt like a child offering the Big Bad Wolf a candy sucker.

"Thanks." Enzo let out a steady breath, his ink-covered abs contracting with the motion. "I should probably—" He picked up the bag.

"Yeah, okay." I swallowed, fire rising in my stomach like a tidal wave.

Enzo took off down the hall and disappeared into the guest bedroom. He'd been here before, but it seemed like a lifetime ago. When things were simpler, and we didn't have so much blood and destruction filling the cracks between us.

I grabbed my mug and got comfy on the couch. But I'd barely settled when there was another knock at the door.

Assuming it was Maurice, I placed down my drink and traipsed to the door, my heart doing another leap when I found Luca standing there.

"You're okay," he breathed, "thank fuck."

"L-Luca." I blinked. "What are you doing here?"

"I heard a commotion out in the hall and saw all the blood… what the hell—"

"You must be Luca."

Every cell in my body fired to life as Enzo stepped up behind me.

"Let me guess, you're the guy." Luca's gaze dropped to mine, a hundred questions there.

"Now is not a good time," I said, forcing my lips into a thin smile.

"Seriously?" Luca dropped his voice an octave. "You're going to do this after what happened last night?"

Enzo bristled behind me and I let out an exasperated breath. "You should go," I said firmly. "I'm okay, I promise. I'll explain everything tomorrow."

Luca's eyes narrowed, hurt flashing there. He lifted his dejected gaze to Enzo and electricity crackled between them.

"Luca, please…" I pulled at his arm. "I need you to go."

"Fine. But I'm right across the hall if you need me."

"I know, thank you," I mouthed, trying to silently convey that everything was okay.

But it wasn't.

I was literally stuck between the two men in my life.

Luca backed up slowly, reluctance etched into his expression. Running a brisk hand over his face, he spun on his heel and disappeared into his apartment. I closed the door with a soft sigh, turning to meet Enzo's hard glare.

"You fuck him?"

"You care?"

He made a clucking sound, pressing his lips into a thin line.

"You want a fight?" I let out a resigned sigh. "You won't find one here, not tonight." Barging past him, I went back to the couch and sat down.

Being around Enzo was always intense. He was like the sun, pulling everything else into its orbit. Except he wasn't the sun, not in the way most of us imagined the sun as a warm, inviting thing that made everything seem better.

He was something much worse.

Fiery, hot destruction.

Enzo grabbed his mug of hot chocolate and joined me, choosing the chair instead of the couch. I tried not to over-analyze why.

"Do you want to talk about what happened?" I asked.

"You know I can't. But for what it's worth, I am sorry I brought this to your door."

"So why did you?" I tucked my feet up onto the couch, noticing Enzo's dark eyes follow the line of my legs. A faint smirk traced his lips when I pulled the blanket off the back of the couch and covered myself.

"The truth?"

I nodded, my heart crashing wildly beneath my rib cage.

"I didn't even think. After I…" He inhaled a sharp breath. "I got in my car and just drove and ended up here. I know I shouldn't have come… fuck." His fist collided with the arm of my chair and I was relieved it was fabric and not wood.

"Antonio will be here soon."

"I'm sorry. I'm so fucking sorry, Gattina."

My breath caught at the pet name. He'd used it as an insult before, but this was different.

"So Luca… he seems nice." His expression darkened even more at the mention of my neighbor.

"He's a good guy."

"Is he treating you right?"

"We're not together, Enzo…"

"But you want to… be with him?"

*No, you stubborn asshole, I want to be with you.* I silenced the thoughts. If I pushed, Enzo would run. And he was here, talking to me for the first time in what felt like forever.

"It's not that simple."

"No," he let out a soft sigh, "I guess it isn't." Enzo sank into the chair, dropping his head back and closing his eyes. He was crashing. Whatever had happened tonight, the adrenaline was fizzling out.

I sat there, watching him. The clothes Maurice had brought over were dark gray sweats and a t-shirt that fit Enzo's big muscled framed like a second skin. It was rare to see him out of his jeans and black sweaters or shirts, but I wasn't complaining. Enzo could make a burlap sack look hot. He oozed sex appeal. From his electric blue eyes to the tattoos snaking up his arms and around his broad shoulders.

I wanted so badly to go to him, to trace the angles of his

jaw with my fingertips and take some of his pain for my own. But a loud knock at the door demanded my attention.

Enzo bolted upright and I smiled. "It's probably your uncle."

"Shit, yeah." He ran a hand through his damp hair.

"I'll get it and then give the two of you some space."

"Thanks."

I got up and went to the door, inhaling a calming breath before welcoming Antonio Marchetti, boss of the Marchetti crime family Dominion, into my apartment.

My home.

Totally not how I saw tonight ever going.

# CHAPTER 15

ENZO

*I* watched Nora disappear into her bedroom. I'd heard Maurice suggest she go someplace else, heard Uncle T mutter the same thing when she answered the door and invited him into her home. And I'd told him the same thing as I'd told Maurice. Nora stayed.

I'd already made a colossal fuck up by coming here. I wasn't about to put her at any more risk by sending her off somewhere I didn't have eyes on her.

No, it was better she was here, with me. Where I could keep her safe.

"Gino?" I asked, satisfied Nora was out of earshot.

"He's gone, son. I'm sorry."

"Fuck." I scrubbed my face, feeling the weight of Gino's death heavy on my shoulders.

"Don't do that," Uncle Toni said. "Don't carry this too. Gino knew the risks of the life. We all do. He died for this family and when the time is right, we will honor him into the afterlife. But first I need to know what the hell happened down there?"

"He sent you the photos?" Uncle Toni nodded and I continued. "Gino got a lead on a guy holed up at a warehouse in a disused industrial area along the river. We thought it was Dominic Alejandro. Marc and Dixon staked out the place overnight, we took over and spent the entire day watching. No one came or went." I grabbed one of the bottles of water Nora had left out for us.

She was fucking good at this stuff, so cool and composed. Most girls would have slammed the door in my face or called the cops when they saw all the blood. But not Nora. She was made of different stuff. Strong and sassy and so fucking selfless.

"Enzo, son... I know it's late, but I need to know everything."

Of course he did. There would need to be cleanup, a plan for the next steps. Uncle Toni would have guys out there within minutes of giving the order to look for the asshole toying with us.

"He finally left the warehouse, so Gino wanted to go check out his nest. We watched him drive away, made sure the coast was clear, and broke into the building. That's when we found the photos and the dead body."

"Bodies." Uncle Toni's expression turned grim. "Three in total. All stuffed in lockers."

"Gino said it was Alejandro."

"It looks likely."

"Do we know who the others are yet?"

"No, but I have guys working on it. Michele is already on his way to Providence."

"Is it safe?"

"He's taking precautions."

I nodded.

We were Marchetti. We didn't cower from our enemies. But when they had an inside edge, the rules were different, and everyone felt the pressure.

"He knows us, Uncle T. Like personally. When he attacked us, he said *surprise*." I'd forgotten until now or blocked it out. It had been a crazy couple of hours.

"He knows me. How is that even possible?" I stared at my uncle, hoping he had the answers I'd yet been able to find.

"I don't know, son. But I give you my word, we'll get to the bottom of this. What happened after he attacked Gino?"

"He took off. I gave chase until about five miles out of Verona. I lost him at a gas station." He must have taken the first exit and disappeared on the underpass. By the time I realized I'd lost him, it was too late, and I'd kept on driving.

"You should come home with me and—"

"Actually," my eyes flicked toward the hall, "I think I'm going to stay here."

He gave me a sharp nod and stood. "Niccolò is very fond of Miss Abato. Arianne too…" He left the words hanging. He didn't need to say it. It was only what everyone else thought —that Nora was too fucking good for a guy like me. But I couldn't leave her, not tonight. Not until I knew she was one hundred percent safe.

"I want round the clock security on this place," I said.

"It's already done." Uncle Toni waited for me to stand before pulling me in for a hug. "We have faced worse, Lorenzo. We will get to the bottom of this and Gino will be avenged, I swear to you. La Famiglia prima di tutto." He gripped my shoulder tight in promise. "Now go be with your woman. I have a woman of my own waiting for me at home."

His hearty chuckle filled Nora's apartment. It was good to see him finally admitting his feelings for Genevieve, his long-standing housekeeper.

After the truth came out about Aunt Lucia, we'd all expected him to spiral into a dark hole. But he hadn't.

I guess he was a better man than me.

"Try and get some rest."

Rest was the last thing on my mind. Earlier, on Nora's couch I had almost dropped off, but now… now I had restless energy zipping through me. I needed a drink or to fight or to…

Fuck.

I swallowed hard as I walked my uncle out of Nora's apartment.

"Maurice will be right outside and I'm posting two guys at the door. I'll call you when I know anything."

"Thanks," I said.

He disappeared down the hall and I closed the door, locking it and checking it twice. Then I padded into Nora's bathroom and retrieved all my weapons. My brass knuckles, two knives, and my pistol.

I wanted them all close by in case anything should happen.

Knocking on the bedroom door, I waited, but Nora didn't answer.

"Gattina?" I said, pushing the door open quietly and slipping inside. Nora was asleep, curled up on the bed.

The sight of her was like a lightning bolt to the chest. Without overthinking it, I dropped my weapons on the nightstand and stripped out of my clothes before pulling back the covers and climbing into bed behind her.

It was a bad idea.

The worst one I'd had in a while. But I needed to feel her soft curves against my body. To know she was safe in my arms.

Nora hadn't been in any of the photographs, but I didn't like the idea that this fucker knew about us, about Arianne. Because we all led back to Nora and she'd been through enough already.

When shit had got bad with Scott Fascini and Nora had been kidnapped, I'd been beside myself. He'd taken her right from under my nose. That kind of guilt didn't just evaporate. And I'd vowed to myself, no matter what did or didn't happen between us, that I would never let anything happen to her again.

That's why it had been so easy to walk away.

To protect her.

Not only from myself but also from the darkness of the world I inhabited.

Hooking my arm around her waist, I dragged Nora into the hard lines of my body. She murmured softly, snuggling closer. Wiggling her perfect round ass right against my crotch.

"You stayed," she whispered, her voice thick with sleep.

"Needed you, Gattina." I tucked my chin into the crook of her neck and breathed her in.

"Why do you call me that?"

"Because you're soft right here." My fingers dipped to Nora's navel and stroked her smooth skin.

"And…"

"And you have sharp claws when you need them. You protect those you care about fiercely."

"Keep going…" Her gentle laughter wrapped around me and made some of the tension in my muscles ebb away.

I'd forgotten how easy it was to just *be* with her. No bull-shit or pretenses. I don't know how she did it, but Nora disarmed me.

"Enzo?" She turned in my arms, staring up at me through her thick, dark lashes.

"We should get some sleep, it's late." And I'd already woken her once.

"I know there's a lot you can't tell me, and I get it. I do. But if you ever want to talk about anything, I'm here for you. I just want you to know that."

Fuck.

This girl.

This strong, brave, gutsy girl.

"I wish it were that simple," I said, plucking one of her stray curls between my fingers. "But this isn't a fairytale, Gattina."

"You think I don't know that? You think I don't know that you're not the hero of this story, but the villain?"

Her words slayed me. It was as if she'd opened up my chest and looked right into my fucking soul.

"Good and bad aren't two sides of a coin, Enzo. They're two ends of the same piece of string. We all have the capacity to be good just like we all have the capacity to be bad. A thief is a thief until he gives his wares to those less fortunate than himself. Then he becomes the hero of their story."

My lips curved. "It's a nice sentiment but—"

"No buts." She pressed a single kiss to my lips, her touch like fire, branding me to the bone.

"Just because someone makes bad choices doesn't mean they're inherently bad, just as someone who makes good choices isn't always inherently good. We're human, we all have imperfections and flaws.

"You say you're bad for me, but I think you'd go to great lengths to protect me. Even from yourself." She peered up at me, hesitating before she reached for me, gently stroking my jaw.

I snagged her wrist, holding her arm there. "Don't. I didn't stay for this." Although my body always had other ideas whenever she was around.

Nora nodded, withdrawing her hand. I didn't know whether to be disappointed or relieved, but I was bone weary and desperate to close my eyes and find peace.

"Goodnight, Enzo," she whispered, turning away from me. I dragged her body back to me and fitted us together once more.

"Goodnight, Gattina."

I tucked my face against Nora's soft skin and closed my eyes… letting her be my anchor for the night.

*"She didn't leave." My father wore a smug smirk as he spoke the words. "She found out what I'd done and threatened to tell you. Always so loyal," he said.*

*"You're telling me you killed my wife?" Uncle Toni trembled, anger rippling off him like a violent storm.*

*I couldn't believe what I was hearing. My father—my own fucking father was a traitor... and he'd killed my aunt, the boss' wife. What was this nightmare?*

*"I'll fucking gut you and feed you to the fish." Uncle Toni*

*stormed toward my father, but I ripped my pistol out of my jeans, pointed and fired the shot, blowing a hole right through the bastard's skull.*

*Everyone stared at me as if I'd lost my fucking mind. And maybe I had. Maybe this was all a sick, twisted nightmare I would wake up from any second.*

*"You good, son?" Uncle Toni was in front of me now, trying to peel the pistol from my hands.*

*"Better than him," I said, but it didn't sound like me.*

*"What do you want us to do with the body?" Uncle Michele asked.*

*"Burn him for all I care," I said, before spinning out of the room and stalking out of there. But as I reached the door, my father appeared, a hole right through his skull.*

*"You think just because I'm dead, I'm gone? I'll haunt you for the rest of your days, SON. You can kill me, burn me, and curse me..." His body began to go up in flames. "But I'm a part of you, Lorenzo. My blood runs through your veins. And you will never—"*

"Enzo, wake up. It's just a dream... it's just—"

Something touched me and my eyes snapped open right as my hand flew out and grabbed it.

"Enzo," someone cried. "It's me... it's only me."

"N-Nora?" I blinked, trying to figure out what the fuck was going on. My grip on her throat relaxed a little, but I didn't release her. Slowly, the memories from last night filtered into my mind.

*The warehouse...*

*Gino...*

*The blood... so much fucking blood...*

*Finding myself on Nora's doorstep...*

"Are you okay?"

"I think that ship has long sailed, Gattina," I ground out.

My thumb stroked her jaw and Nora smothered a moan. She liked a rough touch, being dominated, and in the past I'd been all too willing to oblige her. But something felt different between us now.

Something I didn't want to acknowledge.

"Did you fuck him?"

*Luca.* I scoffed. He looked like a pussy. Mooning after Nora with those puppy dog eyes. She didn't need an All-American boy next door; she needed a guy who knew how to handle her.

"Enzo, I thought we weren't going—"

"Did. You. Fuck. Him?"

Anger flashed in her eyes as she lifted her chin in defiance. Even with my hand wrapped around her throat, Nora wasn't scared. Turned on maybe, but never scared.

Jesus, this fucking girl.

If I had the capacity to ever love someone, it would be someone exactly like Nora. She was damn near perfect.

"And if I had? You pushed me away, Enzo. You did that. You really expect me to believe you haven't been fucking half of Verona?"

She wasn't angry, just resigned… and it fucking stung.

Because she was right.

Well, maybe not about the fucking part. But I hadn't been a saint. There had been other girls. Faceless girls I'd tried to lose myself in when the voices in my head got too loud.

"See… you're not so innocent. So don't come around here, acting like you care when we both know you don't care enough."

"They're not you." The words were out before I could stop them.

"Excuse me?"

"You heard me, Gattina." My hand slid around the back of her neck and anchored her to me. "They're never fucking you."

I hated it.

Hated the idea another guy had touched her, teased and tasted her. It brought out a primal need to thump my chest and roar her name.

Nora was mine.

Deep down, the caveman instincts buried inside me had claimed her long ago. But my head, my fucking head, knew it couldn't ever be.

This was as good as it got. Stolen touches in the dark. Whispered words in the night.

I didn't know how to love a girl like Nora. Not the way she deserved. I knew how to make her scream, to bring her body pleasure over and over again… but love?

What the fuck did a guy like me know about a thing like that?

"Enzo… we can't keep doing this." Nora touched her head to mine, inhaling a breath so deep I felt it down to the pit of my stomach.

"You make it quiet, Gattina. *You.*"

"Sometimes I wish I didn't." Her lips curved into a sad smile, the raw honesty in her words gutting me like a fish.

It wasn't fair to do this to her, not again. But I'd never claimed to be a good guy. I needed her. I needed to sink inside her warm, wet heat and chase away the demons that haunted my every waking thought.

She was strong.

So fucking strong. It would hurt when the sun came up and our masks slid back into place but for now, right here, I wanted to pretend that I wasn't the villain.

"Be with me, Gattina. Make it all go away." I ghosted my mouth over hers, feeling her shudder beneath my touch.

"You already have me," she whispered, and it was all the permission I needed.

In one swift motion, I rolled Nora underneath me, pinning her against the mattress with my hips. Her skin felt like heaven against mine. Soft and smooth and fucking alluring.

"Nemmeno immagini cosa ho intenzione di farti." Her lips parted as her breath caught. "I am going to fuck him right out of you, so you never forget who owns this pussy." My hand slipped between us, cupping her roughly.

But Nora didn't protest, she arched into my touch like the greedy little kitty I knew she was.

"You want this?" I slipped my fingers into her pajama shorts and teased her.

She pressed her lips together, nodding.

"Say it," I demanded. "You want it… say it."

"Y-yes." Nora gasped when I slowly pushed a finger inside her. "Yes, I want it. I want you, Enzo."

"I'm going to make you purr, Gattina." I kissed her jaw, trailing my tongue over the seam of her lips as I worked another finger inside her. "And then I'm going to make you come so hard you see stars."

# CHAPTER 16

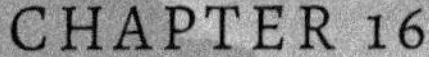

NORA

Kissing Enzo was like drowning. He stole the breath from my lungs and all thought from my mind. I melted into him as his tongue curled around mine in slow, expert licks. He didn't just kiss me—he devoured me.

I'd known the second I opened the door to him tonight, that this was inevitable. We couldn't be in the same vicinity without something happening between us.

We were magnets.

Drawn together by some invisible force.

But like magnets, we attracted *and* repelled, and I knew come morning, this moment would all be a distant memory. But I could live with that. Enzo needed me *right now*. He needed to lose himself in me. He needed me to chase away his demons and I would.

There wasn't much I wouldn't do for this complicated

guy. I knew Arianne wouldn't understand. Later, when the sun rose and she heard it in my voice or saw it in my eyes, I knew she wouldn't understand why I continually let Enzo back in.

Maybe part of myself didn't quite understand it either. But when we were together, in these rare moments of tender touches and desperate kisses, I felt at peace.

So I would give Enzo this, I would give myself this, but I was under no illusion that it meant anything more than this moment.

Enzo couldn't love me, couldn't love anyone, until he chose to a) believe himself worthy of love and b) believe himself capable of love. Whatever had happened in his past—and I'd gleaned snippets from his cousins—had done a real number on him. Nicco and Matteo had their sisters, they had a strong female influence, but not Enzo. He had himself and his father.

And now Vincenzo Marchetti was gone.

I couldn't imagine losing one parent, let alone two. Yet Enzo acted indifferent. I saw the cracks though. The rare moments when he chose to let his guard down, like right now.

Bringing my hands to his face, I took control of the kiss, pouring everything I felt into each brush of my lips, every flick of my tongue. I cared for this man. Deeply, truly, honestly. But I knew you couldn't make someone love you, and I wasn't sure Enzo would ever realize how good we could be together if he'd just open his stone-cold heart to the idea of there being something more between us.

"Fuck, you get me so hot," he drawled, dragging his mouth down the slope of my neck once more. His fingers pressed deep and slow, his thumb circling my clit with steady precision. Enzo knew how to touch me, how to make the waves of pleasure build inside me until I was panting his name.

My legs began to quiver, fire racing through my veins as he pushed me closer to the edge. "God, that feels so good," I breathed, running my nails down his back. A low groan rumbled in his chest and he nipped my bottom lip with his teeth, soothing the sting with his tongue.

"Come for me, Gattina, come all over my fingers."

His dirty words sent me flying off the edge, my body bowing into him as I cried his name.

Enzo crawled off me and stripped out of his boxers. He grabbed his wallet, retrieving a condom, and made quick work of ridding me of my pajamas.

Standing at the foot of the bed, he drank in the sight of me, pumping himself a couple of times. His was rock hard, the piercing in the tip of his dick glinting in the dark. I rubbed my thighs together in eager anticipation, I knew how good that felt rubbing inside me.

Enzo reached forward and wrapped a hand around my ankle, tugging me down the bed. My shriek of surprise filled the room. But then he was there, pressed right against my core, sliding himself through my wetness. It felt divine. Dirty and oh so good.

"Enzo…"

"Patience, Gattina." He pushed my legs wider, hooking them around his waist. Then inch by glorious inch, he rocked inside me. We both moaned, the intensity almost too much to bear.

"Fuck, you feel good." His eyes were blown with desire, dark and dangerous. But I wasn't scared. Enzo would never hurt me, not physically at least.

He pulled out slowly and slammed back inside, eliciting a breathy moan from my lips. His eyes were fixed on where our bodies were joined, and he watched with rapt fascination as he began fucking me hard and fast, as if he was exorcising his demons with every thrust. His thumb found my clit again, mirroring the pace of his hips. I reached for him, needing to feel his lips on mine, and Enzo came willingly, folding his big body over mine and kissing me like I was air, and he was drowning. His hand encircled my throat, pinning me in place to allow him complete control of my mouth, my body.

"So fucking beautiful." He went harder… faster… making the headboard crash against the wall, leaving no mistake as to what we were doing.

But I didn't care.

Nothing, *nothing* had ever felt better than this. Watching —*feeling*—a guy so untouchable as Enzo Marchetti lose control.

"Cazzo, come sei stretta," he purred against my lips, rocking into me with vigor. I could feel him everywhere. But that's what Enzo did whenever he was near—he consumed me. I knew I had it bad for this man. I knew if he asked me to be his, I would say yes in a heartbeat.

I also knew that he would never ask.

Which was why I couldn't keep doing this, not if I wanted to keep my sanity and my self-respect.

"What is it?" he asked, slowing his pace. "What's wrong?"

"Nothing." I forced a smile, curling my fingers in the hair at the nape of his neck and pulling him down to kiss me. "Make me shatter," I whispered.

His lips curved wickedly against mine. "It would be my honor."

No more words were spoken between us as Enzo showed me with his body what he would never tell me in words.

As I came, my body trembling around him, a rogue tear slipped down my cheek, knowing this was probably the last time I would ever be with him.

Our relationship wasn't made for the sunlight. It was nurtured in the dark, made strong only by the shadows and secrets that surrounded it. But come morning, they would turn to ash, and everything would go back to how it was before.

"Fuck, Nora... fuuuuck." Enzo stilled as he reached his own climax. Our bodies were slick with sweat and my lips were sore and swollen.

He pulled out and disappeared into my bathroom to get rid of the condom. I crawled into bed and pulled the covers up around my body. Enzo joined me seconds later, silent as he tucked his big body behind mine and laced his arm around my waist.

"Thank you." He kissed the nape of my neck and heavy silence filled the room.

*Thank you.*

Those words would forever haunt me.

I'd given Enzo a gift.

Something precious and coveted.

And he was grateful, I didn't doubt that, but that's all it was.

All it would ever be.

But right now, I was happy to let the lie continue.

I fell asleep wrapped in Enzo's arms believing he would never let me go.

∽

THE NEXT MORNING, I WAS AWAKE FIRST. I SLIPPED OUT OF BED and went to make coffee. After the intensity of last night, I needed some space.

I checked the hall, hardly surprised to find Maurice standing there. "Coffee?" I asked him, opening my door wide.

"I'll take one to go," he said around a thin smile.

"Suit yourself. Give me a minute." I made his coffee in a reusable cup and took it back into the hall.

"Thank you, Miss—" I shot him a hard look and he chuckled. "Nora."

"Better." The corner of my mouth tipped. "If you want another, you know where I am."

Maurice nodded and I went back inside. The apartment was still quiet, so I made myself a coffee and got a couple of biscuits from the tin and made myself comfortable on the couch.

My body ached in the best possible way, but I tried not to relive last night. Instead, I scrolled through my phone. I had a couple of texts from Lucii, inviting me to a party on the weekend. She'd asked Nate and thought I should invite Luca.

Ugh.

I texted her back that I would let her know my plans. I liked Lucii a lot, but I wasn't sure I wanted to make a thing out of going out with her, Nate, and Luca.

Draining my coffee, I went to make a fresh mug. I felt Enzo before I saw him.

"Morning," he said.

Turning slowly, I smiled. "Hey. There's fresh coffee or I have some juice in the refrigerator."

"Thanks." He went over and opened it, and I couldn't resist watching his ass in the snug gray sweatpants.

I got Enzo a glass and he poured himself some juice. "Listen, about last night—"

"Relax," I said, hating how awkward things already felt between us, "we don't have to do this."

"We don't?" He frowned.

"No. I know what last night was and it's fine."

"It is?"

"Yeah." I smiled again. "Do you want some breakfast? I was going to make pancakes."

"I could eat."

"Okay. I have class at ten, so I'll need to leave in like forty minutes."

"Shit, yeah. Maybe I should—"

"Stay. Eat. Something tells me you need it." My eyes dropped to his ridiculously shredded stomach, and it grumbled again.

"I am pretty hungry." His eyes flared, sending a bolt of heat through me. I inhaled a sharp breath.

"Do you miss it?" I asked, as I gathered all the ingredients.

"What's that?"

"School?"

"Nah, I never wanted to enroll at MU, but Uncle Toni thought it would be a good idea."

"So that's it? You'll just… work for your uncle now?" I peeked over at him, surprised to find him smirking at me.

"Yeah, I'll *work* for him."

"But Nicco and Matteo want something different?"

"Nicco won't leave Arianne's side. Especially not after what down with Fascini—"

Everything stopped as I was hit with an overwhelming wave of fear.

"Nora?"

"I'm fine." I brushed him off, forcing myself to take a deep breath. The nightmares had stopped a few weeks ago, but there were still moments when I was back there, tied to that chair with a gun pointed at my head.

"You sure you're—"

"Fine." My lips pursed. "I'm fine."

"You know I'll never forgive myself for what happened back then."

My brows furrowed. "It wasn't your fault. You didn't make Scott Fascini drug and kidnap me."

"I'm not only talking about that, Gattina." Something flashed in Enzo's eyes, but I didn't dare to latch onto it. He was feeling guilty, responsible… it didn't change anything.

"Feel free to use the shower while I make breakfast."

"Are you trying to get rid of me?" His eyes narrowed.

"What? No! I just thought—"

"Relax, Gattina." He stalked toward me and I jerked back.

"I should get moving if I want to make it to class on time."

Enzo stopped dead, letting out a steady breath. "I guess a quick shower couldn't hurt." He spun on his heel and took off down the hall, and I released the breath I'd been holding.

I don't know what I'd expected this morning, but it wasn't this. And it had thrown me for a loop.

Pouring the batter into a heated pan, I focused on the pancakes. By the time I'd made the first stack, Enzo returned, freshly showered and towel drying his hair.

"Smells good," he said, sitting at the breakfast counter.

"I have chocolate sauce or maple syrup." I pushed the plate toward him and retrieved the bottles from the cabinet.

"Thanks."

"Anytime."

Our eyes locked again, the strange current flowing

between us. Something was different, but I couldn't quite put my finger on what.

"So how are classes?"

I almost choked on my mouthful of food. Enzo was asking me about classes now? What strange universe had I woken up in?

"Don't look so surprised. It's only a question."

"Classes are good. It feels a little bit like starting over though, now Arianne and Nicco are practically joined at the hip."

"You noticed that, huh?"

"I mean, I get it. But college was supposed to be our adventure, and now it's not." I let out a tiny breath. "God, that sounds so selfish."

"No, it doesn't. You had plans together."

"Yeah. But I made a new friend. Well, not a new friend. I knew her already, but I think she has potential."

"Does this new friend have a name?"

"Lucii. She's in my Media and Society class. We went out the other night to a bar. It was fun." Enzo stiffened and I added, "What?"

"Will you be going out with her again?"

"She invited me to a party tomorrow night."

"Will there be guys at this party?"

"It's a party," I chuckled, "what do you think?"

Enzo didn't return my laughter. In fact, he didn't look pleased at all.

"Will Luca be there?"

"I don't know, maybe." I gave him a dismissive shrug. "I think Lucii has a thing for his friend."

"So you're going to see him again?"

Placing my fork down, I let out a frustrated sigh. "Does it

matter if I do?"

"He's not good enough for you."

"You don't even know him. Luca is a good guy, Enzo. I wouldn't have befriended him if he wasn't."

"Oh, come on, Gattina. Don't be so naïve. He doesn't want to be friends. He wants in your panties—"

"How dare you?" My voice shook with anger. "You don't want me, but you don't want anyone else to have me, is that it? Because I'll be honest, Enzo, that's bullshit, and you know it.

"You left. You fucked me and then you just left. Do you have any idea how that made me feel? Finding out from Ari that you were gone? That you thought so highly of me, I didn't even deserve a goodbye?"

"Shit, Nora, that's not…" he rubbed his jaw, "I—"

"No, Enzo. I'm talking, you're listening…" I jabbed my finger in his direction. "You turned up at *my* apartment. You came to me. And I did the only thing I know how when it comes to you, I let you in. But I can't keep doing it, Enzo. I won't. I have too much self-respect to be the girl sitting around waiting for the guy she wants to wake up and see what everyone else sees." I stood up and pushed the curls out of my face.

"One day a guy is going to come along and sweep me off my feet, and do you know what, he'll deserve me. He'll deserve me and when I give him my heart, he won't give it back. He'll keep it, he'll protect it… he'll cherish it. Because my heart is worthy, Enzo. *I'm* worthy."

He stared at me with a blank expression. I knew I'd probably caught him off guard, laying it all out for him, but I felt better.

Even if he had nothing to say to me.

Swallowing the hurt building inside me, I steeled my expression. "I'm going to take a shower. I think it would be a good idea if you're gone when I'm done."

"Nora…"

My fickle heart beat wildly in my chest as I waited….

And waited.

But Enzo's shoulders sank as he swallowed whatever he'd been about to say.

"Well, okay then. I think we're done here." I gave him a tight nod and walked away from him with my head held high…

Even if another part of my heart withered and died.

# CHAPTER 17

he urge to go after Nora was strong, but she was pissed, and I didn't want to make things any worse.

She hadn't even given me a chance to explain, to try to apologize. Instead, she'd dismissed me. Any other girl, and I would have been relieved to avoid any further awkward conversations. But Nora wasn't any girl.

Fuck, she had felt good under me last night. Chasing away my demons in a way that only she could. I'd come so damn hard, I'd seen stars. Which was pretty ironic considering I'd made a promise to make *her* see stars.

I flinched as her bedroom door slammed. Nora didn't want me here, that much was obvious, so I shoved another pancake in my mouth, drained my juice and set about collecting up my belongings.

Most of my weapons were still in her bedroom, so I

slipped inside and grabbed them. I could hear the waterfall from the shower, and couldn't help but picture her in there, naked, water kissing her smooth, olive skin. Fuck, what I wouldn't give to join her and lose myself for another half hour before life came crashing down around me again. But I liked my dick attached to my body and something told me if I even so much as tried to touch her, Nora would cut it right off.

The thought made me smirk. My Gattina could be a little firecracker when she wanted to be.

*Get a grip, asshole, she isn't yours.*

With one last look at the bathroom door, I hightailed it out of there, running straight into Maurice in the hall.

"Mr. Marchetti," he said in greeting.

"Do not leave her side," I ordered.

"The boss gave me strict orders to stay on her at all times."

Fuck. I didn't like the idea of her going to classes while this fucker was out there, taunting us. But I couldn't exactly tell her that, not before talking to Uncle Toni. And I'd seen nothing so far to suggest Nora was in harm's way. But being associated with the Family had been enough for him to go after Morello's store and DiMarco's bar.

"Change of plan," I said, making a snap decision. "She doesn't leave the apartment. Not until you hear from me."

"Miss Abato won't like that."

"She doesn't have to like it."

"What should I tell her?"

"I'm sure you'll think of something." I clapped him on the shoulder before taking off down the hall. I needed some fresh air and a smoke.

I'd hadn't even reached the front door when my cell started ringing.

"Yeah?"

"Where are you?" Nicco asked.

"Just leaving La Stella, why?"

"Darius got hit."

"Darius? Motherfucker." Darius was good people. A pawnbroker operating right out of Marchetti territory in La Riva, he cleaned money through his books for us occasionally. "What's the damage?"

"It's a mess." Nicco let out a low whistle.

"He's in Verona."

"Yep."

"Which means no one's safe." I was already doubling back around. "I'll bring Nora to your old man's house."

"We're already on our way."

I hung up, jogging up the stairs to Nora's apartment. Maurice was whispering into his earpiece. He gave me a terse nod as I walked straight inside.

"Enzo?" Nora was towel drying her hair as she forked a piece of pancake into her mouth. "What is it? What's wrong?"

"You need to come with me."

"What the hell are you talking about?" She scowled. "I'm not going anywhere with you, I have classes."

"Change of plans, Gattina. It isn't safe for you to be here right now."

"Safe? What the hell, Enzo? You weren't complaining last night when you were fucking me into—" She slammed her lips together and stared me down.

I arched a brow, fighting a smile. I loved this side of her… fucking loved her sass and smart mouth. But it wasn't a social visit, and we didn't have time to stand here and argue.

"Pack a bag. I don't know how long you'll be gone."

Her angry expression melted away. "It's really that serious?"

"We're not sure yet." I ran a hand down my face, letting out a heavy sigh. "But until we figure out how serious the threat is, I need you safe, okay?"

"Okay." She nodded, disappearing down the hall.

I stared after her. That had gone easier than I expected. Just then, there was a knock at the door.

"Yeah?" I called, assuming it was Maurice, but when he opened the door, I didn't expect to see Luca standing there as well.

"You," he said.

"Now's not a good time."

"I'm sorry, do you live here now?" He arched a brow. "I was hoping to talk to Nora."

"She's just—"

"It's fine, Enzo. I've got this." She dropped her bag at my feet and went to Luca pulling him into the hall.

Maurice shot me a bemused look right before he closed the door, and I flipped him off.

Silence echoed around Nora's apartment as she was out there in the hall, talking to him. Jealousy burned through my veins. I didn't like the idea of someone we barely knew out there with his hands on her. But Nora deserved her space and despite all my better judgment, I had to respect that.

Two minutes later, she came back inside.

"How is the lovely Luca?"

"Jealousy looks good on you." Her lips curved into a knowing smirk and I bristled.

"What did you tell him?"

"That I have to go away for a family emergency."

"Good, that'll buy us some time. Do you have everything?"

"I think so."

I nodded. "Let's go."

~

WE DIDN'T TAKE MY CAR. IT WAS TOO RISKY. I HAD MAURICE drive us to La Riva, with another security detail tailing behind us.

Nora was quiet on the ride there, texting somebody back and forth. I wanted to ask if it was Luca, to find out what was really going on between them, but I didn't.

It wouldn't change anything.

The most important thing right now was figuring out who this fucker was and bringing him down. Everything else could wait.

When we pulled up at Uncle Toni's house, everyone was already congregated. Arianne rushed over to Nora the second she climbed out of the black SUV.

"Thank God. I've been so worried."

"I'm fine," she said, hugging Ari back. "But I'll be a damn sight better when somebody tells me what the hell is going on." Her eyes went to mine, but Nicco called my name.

"Enzo." He welcomed me with open arms and the two of us hugged. "It's good to see you," he said. "Is she okay?"

"She's Nora," I said with a slight shrug and he chuckled.

"Nora, you're here," Alessia skipped out of the house with Bella in tow, but they both stopped in their tracks when another car rolled into the Marchetti driveway.

"What the fuck is he doing here?" I barked, watching Tristan Capizola climb out of the driver's side.

"I invited him," Nicco said, shooting me a warning look to play nice. "He's family now, and I want as many people looking out for the girls as possible."

He meant Arianne—he wanted as many people as possible looking out for Arianne. I couldn't blame him, but there had been a time when Tristan was the enemy.

I guess a lot had changed.

"I'm glad you called," he said, coming over to us. "Where do you want me?"

"You're with us. Luis," Nicco beckoned Ari's personal bodyguard over. "Take the girls into the living room and stay with them."

"Got it, boss."

My brow arched at that. Nicco wasn't the boss yet. But he sure sounded like the one in control. In fact, Uncle Toni wasn't anywhere to be seen.

"Come on," Nicco said, "let's go inside."

Of course. We needed to meet, to figure out how to deal with the new threat.

"Hey, Uncle T okay?" I asked Matteo as we filed in behind our cousin and Tristan.

"He said something about heartburn. Think Genevieve is trying to find him an antacid. I'm relieved as fuck you're back." He slung his arm around my neck. "Just promise me it's a permanent thing."

"Aww, did you miss me?" I tapped his face, shirking out from under his arm. "Has your old man checked in?"

"Called Uncle Toni right before you got here. He's okay. He's working with our guys in the local PD. But we're pretty sure after the shitshow at Darius' place, that your little friend followed you back to Verona."

Anger skittered down my spine. "Who the fuck is this

asshole?"

He grabbed my shoulder. "We'll figure it out, together."

I only hoped he was right…

Before anyone else got hurt.

~

We left the girls in the living room with Luis and headed for Uncle Toni's office. He was already seated at the head of the table, but he looked a little green around the gills.

"You good, Uncle T?" Matt asked.

"Got this damn acid reflux." He rubbed his chest vigorously. "Driving me up the wall."

"A gallon of milk," Tristan suggested. "Works for my mom every time."

"Well, it ain't working for me, son. Thanks for coming out here."

"Of course, anything to help."

I snorted at that.

"E," Nicco warned and I dropped into a chair, fixing my eyes right on the outsider.

Tristan Capizola wasn't one of us. Sure, he was Arianne's cousin, but being blood related didn't mean shit, my father was evidence of that.

"Enzo, knock it off," Uncle Toni added. "Tristan is our guest, and we will treat him as such. Michele found a bunch of stuff at the warehouse."

"What kind of stuff?"

"More photos, notes, a list of our businesses."

"Fuck," I hissed. "Anything else?"

"Yeah, but you're not going to like it."

"What?" Trepidation coursed through my veins.

"Your name came up a lot."

"It's personal," I said. Call it gut intuition or sixth sense, but I already knew this was somehow linked to me.

"Do you think it's related to Vincenzo?" Matteo asked, immediately realizing his mistake when Tristan said, "Vincenzo? What does he have to do with anything?"

My brow went up and he added, "Shit, man, that sounded insensitive. I was sorry to hear about his death."

I bristled, the temperature cooling in the room.

Nicco looked at me and then to his father. Antonio let out a long, steady breath as he rubbed a hand over his mouth.

"He's a part of this now. He should know the truth."

"What the fuck?" I balked, shooting up out of my seat. "You can't be serious."

"Lorenzo, you need to calm the fuck down."

"Come on, cous," Matteo added. "It sounds like we need all the help we can get right now."

Reluctantly, I sat back down.

"Vincenzo didn't die in a collision, he was killed."

"I see…" Tristan said. "Do I want to know who killed him?"

"Let's just say, he betrayed the Family and got what he deserved."

"No shit. You think the two are connected?"

"It's possible," Nicco replied.

"It's the most likely scenario," I said, conceding to the fact that Tristan was a part of this now, whether I liked it or not. "My father was promised power in return for betraying us. It's possible he might have been working with more people and with Mike Fascini serving jail time, the next in line has decided to try to get some kind of vengeance."

Something about the whole thing still didn't sit right with

me. I didn't recognize the guy at all… but the message scrawled across DiMarco's office wall, and then the way he'd said, 'surprise' when he'd knocked me down before attacking Gino… it was almost as if he knew me.

"I think you should lay low for a while," Uncle Toni said. "If this—"

"Fuck that. I want to get to this guy. I can't do that if I'm in hiding."

"Not in hiding. I want the girls with you. At the cabin."

"You're going to stick me on babysitting duty while there's some fucking psycho out there gunning for us? If I'm the target, use me as bait."

I would quite happily walk into the lion's den if it meant getting to look this fucker in the eye before I put a bullet through his skull.

"It isn't permanent. But if you go off the grid, it might smoke him out. He's in Verona County, we know that much. And now he's here, something tells me he won't be leaving until he finishes whatever it is he's started."

"But why hit Providence at all?" Nicco said.

"To lure me there."

"E, come on, that's a stretch. He wouldn't know you—"

"He would if he has been watching me."

I'd seen his display board with my own eyes. He'd been collecting intel, building a picture of our lives. If I was his main target, then it meant everyone around me was at risk.

Everyone including Nora.

"This is fucked up," Matteo breathed.

"I want you all to head up to the cabin for the weekend while we try to get a handle on this. I've locked down our most profitable businesses and given everyone else a warning. They know to keep an eye out. Let's give it twenty-four hours and see if he makes another move."

"And if he doesn't?" I asked, not liking this plan one bit.

"Then we'll cross that bridge when we get there."

Uncle Toni fixed his eyes on Nicco. "Liaise with Luis and his team about getting you all to the cabin and check in the moment you arrive there, okay?"

My cousin nodded. "What do we tell them?"

"It's Sia," Matt teased. "She's probably outside with a glass pressed to the wall as we speak."

"You're not wrong there, son. Just tell them as little as possible, but enough to keep them in line."

"Good luck with that, cous." Matteo clapped Nicco on the back.

"I... uh, where do you want me?" Tristan asked.

"You're with us." Nicco stood.

"This day just keeps getting better and better," I grumbled beneath my breath. Not only was I being exiled to the cabin with my annoying-as-hell cousins, my best friend and his wife, and Nora. But Capizola was also coming.

Fuck my life.

# CHAPTER 18

NORA

I'd been to the Marchetti cabin before. It was like a well-kept secret, nestled away in the dense forest of Blackstone Reserve. It was impossible to tell anyone the route given the fact we'd driven for a little over two hours for a journey that should have taken forty minutes tops. But I'd heard Nicco tell Luis they wanted to take the long route to make sure no one was following.

I was riding with Nicco, Arianne, and Enzo, and Arabella and Alessia were in another car with Matteo and Tristan.

That had caused some arguments. Nicco had wanted Tristan to ride with us and Enzo to ride with the girls. But Enzo had refused to budge. It would have been almost sweet if it wasn't for the fact we were being forced to spend the weekend at the cabin while Antonio and his men dealt with the *threat*.

The threat the guys refused to tell us much about. I was

pretty certain Nicco had given Arianne the lowdown. She was his wife and she had him wrapped around her little finger. But she was remaining tight-lipped, refusing to tell me anything.

So much for the sacred girl code of sisters before misters.

The SUV finally rolled to a stop. The sun was beginning to sink behind the tree line, the icy blast of wintry air a shock after the toasty warmth of the SUV.

Enzo offered me his hand, but I knocked it away, clambering out myself. I didn't need him suddenly acting like my protector when I'd managed just fine without him the last few weeks.

My cell vibrated and I moved away from the group, to read Luca's text.

LET ME KNOW YOU'RE OKAY, PLEASE.

HE WAS CONCERNED WHEN I SAID I HAD TO GO OUT OF TOWN for a family emergency. I wasn't sure he completely bought the lie, but I didn't have time to explain. Not that I could tell him anything.

I'M FINE. YOU DON'T NEED TO WORRY.

TOO LATE FOR THAT.

· · ·

I smiled. Luca was one of the good guys. Even after Enzo's sudden appearance in my life, he hadn't done the typical guy thing of getting pissed or jealous or walking away.

But Enzo's reappearance did complicate things because I didn't want to be unfair and lead Luca on. Which is exactly what I'd told him this morning.

"Hey, who is that?" Arianne came over and nudged my shoulder.

"Er, no one." I slipped my cell into my pocket.

"You're a terrible liar." She chuckled, lacing her arm through mine and guiding me toward the cabin. Enzo watched me like a hawk, but I refused to acknowledge him.

I'd been so determined to stand my ground with him this morning and then everything went to shit. Now I was stuck in close confines with him for the weekend.

We followed everyone inside, and Sia and Arabella immediately called dibs on their room.

"Me and Tristan can take the bunks," Matteo said, disappearing after the girls.

I glanced around to see Enzo's reaction, but he hadn't come inside yet.

"How are you holding up?" Tristan asked me.

"Okay, I guess. I'd prefer to be back at MU though."

"You and me both." He grimaced. "Is Enzo always so—"

"So what?"

"Nothing, man." Tristan slipped away with a sheepish expression.

"Where is everyone?" Enzo asked me, barely meeting my gaze.

"Gone to call dibs on their rooms."

His eyes narrowed as he did the math. "Let me guess. Nicco plans on sharing with Arianne?"

"I think they're already christening the bed."

I'd seen Nicco pull her into the first bedroom down the hall.

"But there aren't enough rooms."

"You're on the couch." Matteo appeared.

"The fuck, man?" He gawked. "We always share."

"You heard Uncle Toni, Tristan is our guest." He smirked. "We can't very well have *him* sleeping on the couch."

"It's fine," I said. "You can take the other bed in my room."

"Actually, you got the other king."

"Oh." My cheeks burned. "Well, I guess we can—"

"It's fine," Enzo gritted out, "I'll take the couch."

"Fine." I grabbed my bag off the floor and stomped down the hall. I'd thought that maybe we could be adults and put whatever was or wasn't between us aside, but I guess that was too much to ask. If Enzo wanted to sleep on the couch, then so be it.

Stubborn asshole.

The room was beautiful, just like the rest of the cabin. It was the perfect mix of rustic and modern. An ornately carved closet hugged the wall, beside it a matching dresser. The bed was the focal point on the opposite wall. I slung my bag down and perched on the edge of the bed.

A knock pulled me from my thoughts. "Come in," I called.

"Hey." Sia stuck her head around the door. "We wondered if you wanted to hang out?"

"Sure," I said, tapping the bed. Alessia slipped into the room, Arabella following close behind.

"What's the matter?" she asked.

"Nothing," I said.

"Is it Enzo? I saw the way he was watching you. Did something happen between the two of you?" Alessia's eyes were alight with anticipation.

I chuckled. "Take a breath there, Sia."

"Sorry." She blushed. "I just… Ugh, the two of you would be so good together."

"Right," Arabella agreed. "But Enzo is a total commitment-phobe."

"People change, Bella. Look at Nicco."

"Yeah, but what he and Ari have is rare. Like once in a lifetime."

Ouch.

I knew the youngest Marchetti didn't mean anything, but it didn't stop her words from stinging.

There was another knock and we all looked up at the door.

"Dare I enter?" Matteo appeared around the door, grinning.

"Girls only, get out, scemo." Bella grabbed a pillow and threw it at his head.

"Easy, Bel. I only wanted to let you know me and Enzo are heading out. We'll be back soon."

"Where are you going?" I asked.

"Boys stuff." He winked. "Nicco and Tristan will be here, and Luis and his guys are right outside."

"Be safe," Alessia said.

"Always." Matteo left, closing the door behind him.

"Where do you think they're going?" Bella frowned.

"Probably to check the perimeter."

"Isn't that what we have security for? So the guys don't have to do it?"

"They'll be okay." I offered Bella a reassuring smile.

"Nora's right. Enzo is a hard ass. He'll look out for Matteo."

"You seem awfully okay with all this," I said, and Alessia shrugged.

"It's all part and parcel of being a mafia princess."

"Mafia princess, huh?" My lips curved. "That does have a certain ring to it."

"God, Nora, don't encourage her." Bella rolled her eyes. "This isn't a game, Sia. Besides, you do realize you'll be a princess forever because Nicco and Uncle Antonio are never going to let you date?"

She flipped back against the cushions lined up on the bed. "Don't remind me. Anthony Aielio asked me out last week."

"He did? You never said anything." Hurt flashed across Bella's face.

"There wasn't much point. You're right, they'll never let me date."

"You have time," I said. "I remember guys in high school and—"

"Oh, Anthony isn't in high school. He graduated last year. His brother is in our class. Anthony helps their father run the family auto shop.

"So he's older."

"Only by a couple of years." She shrugged again.

"Trust me when I say, don't rush into something you might regret. Especially not with an older guy."

"How old were you... you know, when you lost your virginity?"

They both stared at me like I held the answers to the universe.

"Oh no you don't. I'm not going to give you sex advice, Nicco and Matteo will kill me."

"We won't tell them, promise."

Bella nodded, agreeing with her cousin. "You can trust us."

"Look, I get it. It's a confusing, scary, exciting time. But if I have one piece of advice, it's to wait and give yourself to someone who deserves you. You can't ever get your first time back."

"Penny Denver said it hurt her so bad she cried the entire time."

"Then he wasn't doing it right," I murmured.

"Have you and Enzo—"

"Nice try," my brow arched, "but I'm not doing this with the two of you. In fact, let's go see if Arianne has managed to detach herself from your brother's mouth. I don't know about you guys but I'm hungry."

I WAS HALFWAY THROUGH MAKING SPAGHETTI WHEN ENZO AND Matteo returned.

"Thank God." Bella shot up, making a beeline for her brother. My heart ached watching them. I knew that big brotherly affection firsthand, and although my brother Gio drove me up the wall, I missed him something fierce. But he was always destined for bigger things, for a life outside of Verona. Thanks to a full ride scholarship to UPenn, he was living his dream in Philadelphia, with hopes of going pro next year.

I discreetly glanced at Enzo. Hovering in the doorway, his big body ate up the space. His cheeks were flushed from the cold and it softened the sharp angles of his face. But when his icy gaze found mine, his expression darkened.

He was clearly as pleased to be stuck here as I was.

I turned around to tend to the spaghetti. It was my mom's recipe; the aromatic scent of garlic and herbs filling me with a strange sense of melancholy. I didn't want to worry my parents unnecessarily after what happened before, but the burning need to hear her voice coursed through me.

"Nor?" Arianne laid her hand on my arm, yanking me from my thoughts. "Are you okay?"

"Yeah, I'm fine. Find me some plates?"

"Of course."

I was hardly surprised Arianne knew her way around the kitchen. She had stayed here with Nicco before. Between us, we served the spaghetti, covering it with generous lashings of sauce. I sprinkled each plate with basil before calling everyone to the table. Nicco invited Luis to join us, but he declined, staying outside with the other security men.

"This looks great, Nora," Tristan said, helping me with the bread.

"I'm not just a pretty face, you know."

He chuckled, but it quickly died when Enzo scowled in our direction. "Ignore him," Matteo said. "He's just grouchy because he's gotta take the couch tonight."

"Listen, man, why don't you take my spot, and I can room with Nora. I'm sure she won't—"

Enzo's eyes narrowed to murderous slits as he glared at Tristan.

"I think that's a no, Capizola." Matteo snorted. "You're stuck with me, man, and E is stuck with—"

"*Matt.*" Nicco shot him a hard look and tension rippled around through the air.

"Fuck this," Enzo said, "I need a smoke." He spun around

and walked straight out of the cabin, letting the door slam shut behind him.

"Was it something I said?"

Bella grabbed her brother and yanked him down into the empty seat beside her. "You shouldn't push him, you know how he gets."

"He needs to—"

"Basta!" Nicco slammed his hand down on the table, making the silverware rattle. He let out an exasperated breath. "Can we just eat, please?"

"You don't need to tell me twice." Matteo began helping himself to bread and salad. But I wasn't feeling very hungry all of a sudden.

"Matt, you eat like a pig."

"But you love me, pulce." He roped his arm around Bella's neck and began to ruffle her hair.

"Get off of me, you big goofball." She shirked him off. "You are such a dork."

"I think it's cute," Ari said.

"You need me to come over there and ruffle your hair, cous?" Tristan asked her.

"Please don't." Nicco glowered.

"Relax, Marchetti. I'm only busting your balls. This is good, Nor. Just like my Nona used to make it."

"You're not hungry?" Ari caught my eye, and I shook my head, my gaze flicking to the door.

Tempers were bound to be frayed given the circumstances, but Enzo was so volatile, so angry all of the damn time. The fixer in me wanted to excuse myself and go check on him, but I knew he wouldn't thank me for it, so I forced myself to stay put.

"Can someone pass me the cheese, please?" Tristan asked,

and in their haste to help, Bella and Alessia knocked over the jug of water.

"Oops." Bella grimaced. "I'll grab some towels."

"Relax," Tristan said. "I've got it."

I wasn't the only one who noticed the girls track his every move as he went and fetched some paper towel.

"What the fuck is happening right now?" Matteo grumbled beneath his breath.

"I think Tristan has a fan club." I fought a smile, but Matteo looked anything but amused.

"Oh hell no." His hand flattened against the table.

"Relax, Matt," Ari said, "you can trust Tristan."

"It's not him I'm worried about." His eyes went to his sister and their cousin. "Don't get any silly ideas."

"God, Matteo, you're so freakin' embarrassing. He's like twenty."

"Twenty-two." Tristan corrected, rejoining us, clearly unaffected by his little fan club. "And Matteo is right. Don't get any ideas. I don't date high schoolers."

"Of course you fucking don't."

"Jesus," Nicco hissed. "Is it too much to ask to have a simple meal?"

"I know Uncle T thought it would be safer to bring the girls out to the cabin, but I'm thinking he didn't consider our safety." Matteo smirked, and Alessia and Bella both grabbed a handful of bread and threw it at him.

Tristan exploded with laughter while me and Ari tried our best not to join him. And Nicco…

Well, he looked like a guy with the weight of the world on his shoulders.

# CHAPTER 19

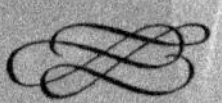

ENZO

*I* walked the perimeter of the cabin again. We'd been careful, covering our tracks once we left the highway, but it was better than standing still. Because when things were still, I was overcome with so much guilt and anger, I could barely breathe.

Nora made everything quiet. She made everything stop. Losing myself in her last night had been both a blessing and a curse. Every time she let me back in, another piece of me became hers. She'd never own my whole heart—that wasn't possible for something carved out of stone—but she owned enough jagged pieces of my soul for me to notice.

I never wanted this. I never wanted to tie myself to someone knowing that I couldn't ever be who they needed me to be. The Family came first, it would *always* come first. My loyalty, my life... my love, was reserved for Dominion, and Dominion alone.

But there was no denying that Nora Abato had buried herself under my skin. Like a slow acting poison, she was inside me. I cared whether she was safe. I cared who she was seeing and who she was spending time with. And I fucking cared that she was here.

Because of me.

Because this fucker somehow has ties to my old man. There were too many things that didn't quite add up yet, like why he'd started his campaign of destruction in Providence and not Verona. But the end game was the same. And the end game was all that mattered.

As my boots crunched against the ground, made hard from a cold winter, I pulled out my cell and dialed Uncle Michele.

"Enzo, son, what is it?"

"Any more news?" I asked, coming to a stop by a bench on the periphery of the woods.

"All leads ran dry. No prints, no address, no witnesses. This guy is a fucking ghost."

"Ghosts don't weigh two-hundred-and-fifty pounds, and I felt that fucker on top of me." Watched as he sank his blade into Gino's jugular.

Fuck.

He died… because of me.

And now this motherfucker was in Verona County. It was too close… too close to the people I cared about.

Too close to Nora.

Just the thought of him getting anywhere near her had me seething with anger.

"We'll get him, son. You took the girls to the cabin, right? They're safe."

"Yeah, they're here."

"So, let us focus on finding this asshole."

"I can't just sit here, doing nothing." It was fucking killing me.

"Shit, I know, kid. I know. But we'd all feel a helluva lot better knowing our girls have you around."

"Twenty-four hours. I'll stay twenty-four hours, but then I'm joining the hunt."

"You'll have to clear that with Toni, Lorenzo. You know the deal."

"Yeah." The boss's word was final. But I couldn't just stay here doing nothing. It was going to drive me in-fucking-sane.

The girls were inside, acting like this was a girl's weekend away. Not to mention the fact Nora was in there, and she was pissed. At me. At the fact I'd dragged her away from her life… from Luca.

Jesus, the guy was worse than a dog with a bone. Did she really like that good guy routine he had working for him?

"Fuck," I hissed, kicking the hard ground with my boot.

"You need to burn off some steam."

For a second I'd forgotten Uncle Michele was still on the line.

"Go for a run or something," he added.

*Or something.* I internally grumbled.

My eyes flickered back to the cabin.

"I'll call if there's any news," Uncle Michele said. "Keep our girls safe, Enzo. That's what we need you to do right now," he said. "Your pound of flesh will come."

We said goodbye and hung up.

My uncle was right, of course he was right. But I was

never very good at sitting around and waiting for the fight to come to us.

~

Eventually, I went back inside. I was fucking freezing, not to mention hungry.

"I left you a plate," Nora said. She was curled in one of the chairs, scrolling on her phone.

"Thanks."

Matteo caught my eye and silently asked if I was okay. I nodded, shucking out of my jacket and slinging it over the back of the couch.

"Watch it, asshole," Tristan said.

"Oops, my bad. I didn't see you there." My lips curved with smug satisfaction as I grabbed the plate Nora had left me and put it in the microwave.

"You okay?" Matteo joined me, perching at the breakfast counter.

"I'd rather not be here."

His expression fell and I sucked in a harsh breath. Of course Nora had chosen that exact moment to go to her room, walking straight past the kitchen area.

"Did she—"

"If the look on her face is anything to go by, then yeah, she did."

"Fuck." I scrubbed a hand over my jaw.

"What's happening with you two? I figured after last night you were *working out your differences*, but then today it's like you can't stand to be around one another?"

"We fucked," I said, checking the spaghetti. It was done, so I sat down opposite him and began digging in.

"Yeah, I kinda got that part, asshole. But what I don't understand is, how you even ended up there?"

"Welcome to my world. One minute I was chasing this fucker, the next I was outside her apartment covered in Gino's blood."

"Shit, man. I'm sorry." His teasing expression fell. "That had to be rough."

"It was fucked up, Matt. He just killed him… without a second thought."

"Who is this punk?"

"Whoever he is, we need to find him, and fast." Because my gut told me it was only the beginning.

"Where's Nic?" I shifted the subject to safer shores.

"Where do you think?" Matteo's eyes rolled. "They're still in the honeymoon phase."

"Lucky for him." My eyes flicked down the hall once more. "I met him," I added.

"Met who?"

"Who do you think? Luca." His name soured on my tongue.

"Oooh. And?"

"He's not the right guy for her."

"Is anyone?" His brow arched with amusement.

"Nora deserves…" I swallowed the words. What was I saying? She deserved a lot of things. Things I couldn't give her. So who was I to stand in her way and ruin her shot at happiness?

"Jesus, cous." Matteo got up. "You're a real fucking idiot sometimes." His hand landed on my shoulder as he passed me. "Enjoy the couch."

Matteo disappeared down the hall leaving me with… Tristan.

"What?" I barked at him as he peered over.

"Nothing. Nothing at all." He got up and took off down the hall too, leaving me all alone.

It was barely even nine-thirty, and everyone had fucked off to bed. I grabbed a beer from the refrigerator and finished up the meal Nora had made for everyone. Trust her to play mother hen. I didn't know why she had to do that, be so fucking good all of the time. My fist clenched around the fork.

By the time I was done, my mood had turned pitch black. I rinsed my plate and left it on the side, grabbed a bottle of whisky from the cabinet and the stack of blankets someone had left out, and made my way to the couch. It was a sectional big enough for two people to sleep on, but it wasn't a bed.

Fifteen minutes in, I was beginning to think I should have taken Nora up on her offer. But no good would come from being in the same room as her. She was pissed. And it was only making me even more pissed.

Fucking women.

My old man might have been a traitorous piece of shit, but he wasn't wrong about women. They were nothing but a distraction.

I didn't bother pouring myself a glass of whisky, just drank straight from the bottle. I would have killed for a blunt, but Nicco didn't like us doing that shit around the girls, and I wasn't a total asshole.

The sounds from whatever action movie was playing on the TV became white noise as the burn from the liquor flooded my senses. He was out there, plotting his next move, biding his time. And I was here, hiding like a pussy. Between Nicco,

Matteo, Tristan and the security team posted outside, the girls were safe. No one was going to get to them. I could go after him. It was a better use of my skill set being out there, hunting for him, than sitting here drinking my feelings because I couldn't get a hold on all the anger and guilt gnawing at my fucking soul.

I drained the whisky, letting it douse the fire inside me, replacing it with a simmering heat instead. My body slouched further into the couch, my thoughts becoming a jumbled mess of blood and death and destruction.

Until eventually, the darkness consumed me.

I woke with a start, my body caked in sweat.

"Fuck," I rasped, my throat as dry as the Sahara Desert. The open fire roared still, but someone must have turned up the thermostats because the place was like a furnace.

Slowly, I sat up, rubbing my head, trying to ease the pounding in my skull. My eyes landed on the empty bottle of whisky and I groaned. Not my best idea ever. But at least there had been no nightmares. And if there had, I couldn't fucking remember them.

I went in search of water, stripping out of my sweater and jeans as I went. I was half-tempted to go outside and cool off, but I knew if I took one step outside, whoever got the night shift would alert the rest of the team and then everyone would be awake.

So I decided against it, slipping into the bathroom at the end of the hall and splashing some cold water on my face. It wasn't so warm at this end of the cabin which made me think that maybe I had been having a nightmare after all. My skin was feverish, and my heart was racing like I'd just run a marathon.

"Fuck." I slammed my hand down on the counter, making the entire thing shake.

Just then, I heard footsteps in the hall. Shit. Someone was awake and I had no choice but to go out there and face them.

Washing my hands, I dried them on a towel before slipping out into the empty hall. Thank fuck. Whoever it was must have doubled back when they saw the bathroom in use.

I padded down the hall back into the living area, only to realize Nora was up and rummaging in the refrigerator. Staying in the shadows, I watched her for a second. Her hips swayed hypnotically as she leaned in, trying to locate whatever it was she wanted.

"Hungry?" I asked her and she almost jumped out of her skin.

"Oh my God," Nora breathed, clutching her chest, her thin pajama top doing little to conceal her perky tits. "You scared me half to death. What are you doing awake?"

"I could ask you the same thing, Gattina." I smirked.

"Please don't call me that."

My brows furrowed. "Is that how it is between us now?"

"How did you think it was going to be?" Nora lifted her chin in defiance. Usually, her sass turned me the fuck on, but after the night I'd had, it only fanned the flames of anger already raging in my stomach.

"Don't act like you didn't beg for it, la mia puttana."

Her palm collided against my cheek, pain ricocheting through my jaw. Nora gasped, stepping back, and I pressed forward, pinning her to the counter.

"You hit me." I rubbed my cheek, my blood boiling.

"You deserved it," she bit out. "I hate that you're hurting. I do. But I won't be your punching bag, Enzo. I deserve more than that."

I scoffed. "Like Luca?"

"I'm not doing this with you," she said, pressing her lips together and levelling me with a scathing look.

I didn't budge though, too worked up to just let her go. Part of me enjoyed this, craved the push and pull between us. It craved something else too, and before I knew it, I'd leaned in and run my nose along the curve of her neck.

"Fuck, Gattina, you smell delicious." My hips rolled against her, desperately seeking out her heat. Maybe I was still a little drunk or delirious from the nightmare because I couldn't think about anything except getting my hands on her sinful body.

"Enzo, don't do this." Her hands curled against my t-shirt. Even rough, her touch seared me to the bone.

"Are you telling me no, Gattina?" I leaned down, with every intention of letting my mouth ghost over Nora's lips, but she turned away at the last second, giving me her cheek instead.

Bitter laughter rumbled in my chest. I hated that she was defying me, pretending like she wasn't as hot for me as I was her, but Nora's defiance was like a red rag to a bull. I wanted to push her. To push and push until she snapped. Until she succumbed to the tension cracking between us.

"You can pretend I don't affect you, Gattina," I whispered against the shell of her ear, "but we both know if I slipped my hands in your itty-bitty little shorts, I'd find you soaking wet for me."

I heard the hitch of her breath, felt the shiver roll through her body. Nora was as wired as I was. Question was, was she going to give in to her baser instincts or was she going to continue her crusade to keep me out?

My hand slipped to her waist, stroking the sliver of skin there. Nora fought a moan, trying to pull away from me. But there was nowhere to go. I had her caged between the counter. Completely at my mercy. With Nora, nothing else— not the nightmares, or my old man, or the new fucker causing mayhem—could touch me. I was invincible. Untouchable. Nora made me feel like no one else ever had and although I didn't want to admit it, it was addictive.

*She* was addictive.

"Look at me, Gattina." I took hold of her chin and forced her face to mine. "Tell me you don't want me? Tell me you don't want me to drop to my knees and bury my face between your legs."

"That's all I am to you, isn't it?"

My brows drew together.

"A willing body. A hole to fuck when you need to work off some steam." Nora jabbed her finger in my chest. "You'll fuck me in the middle of the night when everyone's sleeping, but you'd rather sleep on the couch than share a room with me?"

What the fuck was she talking about?

What was happening right now had nothing to do with anything else. I was hungover and horny, and she was —furious.

Fuck.

She was silently seething at me and I'd completely misread the signs... because she was right, I hadn't fucking looked for them. I'd just assumed I could take what I needed from her the way I had before.

My hand dropped from her waist as I backed up and ran my fingers through my hair.

"What?" she sneered. "Nothing to say for yourself. Didn't think so. Now if you don't mind, get the hell out of my way." Shouldering past me, Nora disappeared into the shadows while I watched after her...

Wondering what the fuck had just happened.

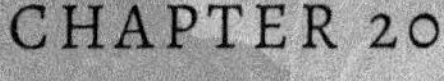

# CHAPTER 20

NORA

*I* barely slept.

After my run in with Enzo, my body had been too restless. He made me so angry. He'd barely said two words to me all day and then treated me like one of his whores. It hurt.

It hurt so damn much.

But that only amplified my anger because I was frustrated at myself for ever thinking I could reach him. For thinking that cold, cruel Enzo Marchetti would ever let his walls down long enough for me to crawl inside.

I could have let him touch me last night, let him take what he wanted right there up against the kitchen counter, but we weren't alone here. And it was one thing to give into him over and over in private…but in front of our friends and family?

I guess his opinion of me really was that low.

Willing myself out of bed, I pulled on a MU hoodie. It was chilly in the cabin, so I went in search of coffee and the roaring fire.

Enzo was already gone, but I'd expected nothing less. He'd spent most of yesterday gone too, as if he couldn't bear to be in the same room as me, and then, in the cover of darkness, acted as if he couldn't stay away.

I didn't want to live in the shadows. But Enzo was comfortable there. He preferred night over day, more at home in the darkness than the light.

As I turned on the coffee pot, my heart ached for him. But it quickly turned to stone when he appeared in the doorway and didn't even say good morning.

*Damn you, Enzo Marchetti.*

"Is there coffee?" Matteo appeared, his hair sticking up all in directions.

"Just making a fresh pot."

"You're too good to us," he said, heading straight to the couch and dive-bombing into the huge throw cushions. "How'd you sleep, cous?"

"How do you fucking think?" Enzo growled.

"I figured you'd pull your head out of your ass and go join Nora. But from your good mood this morning, I'm guessing that wasn't the case."

I peeked over at the two of them just in time to see Enzo flip Matteo the bird.

"Can you check if Luis and the guys want coffee?" I asked Enzo.

He narrowed his eyes. "Ask them yourself."

"Children," Matteo whistled. "What's with all this bad energy this morning?"

I stomped across the room and yanked open the door,

slipping out onto the porch. The thick layer of ice gave the whole place a winter wonderland vibe. It was so pretty I took a second to appreciate its beauty before calling Luis.

"Coffee?" I asked.

"That would be great, Miss Abato."

I rolled my eyes. No matter how many times I asked him and Maurice to call me Nora they still reverted back to my formal name.

When I went back inside, I found Enzo and Matteo in deep conversation. They both went quiet the second I closed the door and alerted them to my presence. But I ignored them, going straight for the coffee machine.

By the time I'd made enough coffee for Luis and his guys, Nicco and Arianne had joined us.

"You don't have to do all this," she said.

I shrugged. "Someone's gotta do it." Besides, keeping busy was a good distraction from throwing something at Enzo's head.

Asshole.

I stayed in the kitchen area, refusing to join the guys. Ari noticed and came over.

"What's wrong?" she whispered.

"Nothing." I sipped my coffee, letting the liquid warm me inside out.

"Did En—"

"Don't, Ari. Just don't." I let out an exasperated sigh.

Just then, my cell phone vibrated. I plucked it out of my pocket and smiled when I saw Luca's name.

"Your whole face lights up whenever he texts you." She observed.

"It isn't like that."

"But it could be…" Arianne left me with my thoughts

while she joined Nicco and the others. He pulled her onto his lap and wrapped a possessive arm around her waist, resting his chin in the crook of her shoulder. They looked so content, so happy.

My gaze collided with Enzo and time stood still. He had issues, I got it. I did. But I didn't really understand why he insisted on pushing everyone away. I didn't understand choosing loneliness.

It wasn't like Nicco had been looking for love either. He had responsibilities, a whole empire resting on his shoulders. Falling in love was the last thing he'd needed. But he couldn't resist destiny's plan. Arianne was made for him, and he for her. There was no escaping that, no matter how much he tried.

And now they were stronger than ever, and one day he would be the boss of the Marchetti Family and Arianne would sit at his side as his queen.

Love didn't make you weak, it made you strong. I truly believed that. It gave you something worth fighting for.

For the right person.

And therein lay the issue. Maybe I had to finally accept that me and Enzo weren't written in the stars. There was no happy ending for us. Because while I wanted all of Enzo, the good, the bad, and the downright ugly, the truth of the matter was, he didn't want all of me.

I felt tears well in my eyes and I averted my gaze, breaking the connection.

No one except him noticed as I slipped away and retreated to my room...

And of course, he let me go.

I'D JUST PULLED ON MY SWEATER AFTER A QUICK SHOWER, when a loud crash boomed through the cabin, followed by raised voices.

I rushed into the living room to find Enzo hunched over, bracing his hand, blood seeping from his knuckles.

"Oh my God, what happened?"

The girls, Sia and Bella, were huddled together on the couch, while Matteo stood between them and Enzo. Nicco was still in the chair, Ari curled in his lap, and Tristan was nowhere to be seen.

"What happened?" I asked, and everyone's head whipped up to me.

"Uncle Toni called," Matteo said. "It wasn't the news Enzo hoped for." His grimace told me all I needed to know.

"Somebody should clean that up." I motioned to Enzo's hand. "I'll find a first aid kit."

"It's nothing." Enzo protested.

Matteo whispered something to him, both of their eyes fixed on me.

"What?" I asked.

"Fuck this, I need some air." Enzo spun around and headed for the door, taking the air with him.

I stuffed down all the hurt and joined the others. "What happened?"

Matteo looked to Nicco and he let out a heavy sigh.

"Girls, go hang out in your room."

"Seriously?" Alessia hissed. "You're going to—"

"Alessia, do as I ask, please."

"Fine." She got up, pulling Bella with her. "But I'm not a kid anymore, Nicco. I know what you and my cousins do. I know what Daddy does. You don't have to protect me from this stuff."

"I will always protect you, sorella. Now go."

They took off down the hall.

"What did I miss?" Tristan appeared.

"I need you to do me a favor. Go keep the girls company."

"The girls?" He frowned. "You want me to babysit them?"

"No, I want you to make sure my sister stays put in her room. There's a difference."

"Fine, whatever." He stalked off after them.

"This is fun," Matteo said. "The whole family together. It's a shame Bailey didn't—"

"Bailey stays out of this," Nicco growled.

"Relax, cous. It was a joke. I was joking."

"Yeah, I know. I just don't want him anywhere near this."

My eyes flicked back and forth to the door Enzo just stormed out of.

"He'll be okay," Nicco said.

"Will he?"

Enzo had lashed out in front of his younger cousins. That seemed out of character, even for him.

"Are you going to tell us what's going on?" I looked at Arianne and she flinched. "You already know," I added, the weight of my words pressing down on my chest.

Nicco wasn't supposed to confide in Ari, not about everything. But she was his wife. The center of his universe.

"If I tell you this, it cannot leave this room."

"You don't trust me." Why did it hurt so much?

Enzo didn't trust me. Nicco didn't trust me. I was beginning to wonder if Arianne, the girl who knew me better than anyone, trusted me.

No, I knew she did. But her loyalties had shifted in the last few months. She was a part of a world I didn't inhabit now. A world I walked the periphery of, crossing in and out but never truly *knowing*.

"Someone is coming after the Family…"

"Okay… but what does that have to do with Enzo?"

Nicco and Matteo shared another look.

"Look, if you don't want to tell me this then—"

"Nor, it's not that," Ari sighed, rubbing her hand over Nicco's thigh. "It's complicated."

"Is Enzo in danger?" My stomach twisted. He wasn't one to shy away from a fight, I knew that. But I couldn't stand the thought of him being in the direct line of fire.

Nicco inhaled a sharp breath. "We think whoever is targeting us, has ties to Vincenzo."

"Enzo's father… but I don't understand." Vincenzo had been Antonio's second, his right-hand man. Why on Earth would—no.

*No!*

Matteo nodded slowly, his eyes filled with regret. "Vincenzo was a traitor."

"But… that doesn't make any sense. He died. He was in an accident and he—"

"There was no accident," Nicco said, thickly.

"You mean you killed him?" Because that's what the mafia did to traitors. They got rid of them.

An icy shudder rolled through me.

"I didn't kill him, Nora." Nicco looked right through me, and then he said two little words that shattered my heart.

"Enzo did."

～

"I STILL CAN'T BELIEVE IT," I SAID AS ME AND ARI LAY shoulder to shoulder on my bed.

"Yeah… when Nicco told me… I wanted to tell you. But it wasn't my story to tell."

"I understand. It explains so much."

Ari rolled onto her side and leaned on her fist. "Now you know why I've been so worried about you. Enzo isn't… he's in a dark place, Nor. Super dark. I'm not sure I want you around that."

"It doesn't matter now," I said, peering up at her.

"What do you mean?"

"I told him I'm done. I want more, Ari. I *deserve* more." But as I said the words, my heart shattered all over again.

Enzo only had his father growing up. A cold, vicious man by all accounts with a strong sense of loyalty to the Family. A man who shaped his son and his view of the world. A man who molded his son in his image…

"God, I can't imagine what Enzo must be feeling. No wonder he pushed me away."

"No, Nora, don't do that, don't excuse his behavior—"

"I'm not excusing it, but I get it. He killed his father, Ari." My voice cracked. "Enzo shot his father in cold blood. You don't just come back from something like that."

Her expression softened. "I know."

"It's why he left, isn't it?"

She nods. "Antonio wanted to give him time and space to deal with everything. But then this happened, and well, here we are."

"What a mess," I breathed, feeling my chest constrict.

Nicco had explained that the guy targeting them seemed to have a personal vendetta against Enzo, so they assumed it was someone connected to Vincenzo. Maybe a business partner or someone involved with the deal he cut with Mike Fascini to bring down the Marchetti empire.

Just then, male laughter filled the cabin.

"I wonder what they're doing."

"We could always go out there and see?" Ari suggested.

"Sure, okay." It felt like we'd been in here for hours, the sun long set over the tree line.

Matteo and Tristan had taken the girls for a walk earlier, but we'd declined. I wasn't feeling very sociable after Nicco had told me the truth about Enzo and his father.

I couldn't get it out of my head, couldn't even begin to imagine what Enzo was going through. It explained a lot. Why he pulled away suddenly, his deep-seated anger, his cruel words and cold demeanor. Enzo was carrying a burden most of us would never understand.

I followed Arianne into the living room to find the guys crowded around the table, playing poker. Enzo had obviously returned from wherever he'd been all day, but I forced myself not to look at him for fear that he would see the truth in my eyes.

I knew his darkest secrets now, and I knew he'd probably hate me for it.

But it didn't matter, because I didn't plan on telling him. Enzo obviously didn't want me to know... *or he would have told me.*

So I grabbed a chair and tucked myself between Tristan and Matteo so that I wouldn't be in his line of sight.

I was hardly surprised when Nicco pushed his chair back to accommodate Ari on his lap. They couldn't be in the same room without touching.

"Where are the girls?"

"Watching Rivervale or whatever it's called. You know, the one with the guy that wears that stupid hat. Bughead."

"You mean Riverdale?" I snickered. "And it's Jughead."

"Same thing." Matteo shrugged. "Enzo picked them up a bunch of snacks, it should keep them quiet for a while."

At just the mention of his name, my chest tightened.

"Are you playing, Nora?" Tristan asked as he shuffled the deck of cards.

"She doesn't want to play," Enzo said, and I bristled.

"What's the buy in?"

"One hundred dollars."

"Nor," Ari warned.

"Deal me in." I tapped the table.

"We don't have time to explain the rules to you, Abato."

Ouch.

Reducing me to my surname hurt but I refused to let Enzo chase me away. Arianne was my best friend and Tristan, Nicco, and Matteo were my friends by proxy. We had to find a way to be around each other.

"Are we playing Hold 'em, Omaha, or seven card stud?" I asked with a hint of smugness.

"Holy shit, Nora, I think I just came in my pants. You know poker?"

"I know a little bit." I shrugged, graciously accepting a stack of colored chips off Nicco.

"Straight up Texas Hold 'em, yeehaw," Matteo grinned. "But we like to spice things up with a little tequila." He grabbed a bottle off the floor and shook it in front of me. "Lose a hand and you gotta drink."

"Matt, I'm not sure that's a good idea," Arianne protested.

"Don't worry, *bambolina*," he smirked, "Nic won't drink

while you're here. But me and Tristan have some unsettled business."

"You do?" Ari asked. "That's news to me."

"Cocky fucker reckons he can drink me under the table."

"I'd put money on it." Tristan snorted.

"I've got twenty on Tristan."

"Seriously, Nora, you wound me." Matteo pouted at me, his huge puppy dog eyes almost too much to resist. But I stuck by my guns. "Sorry, Matt, but I've seen Tristan drink and you're going down."

"Oh, it's on, Capizola." He slapped his hand down on the table. "It's so on."

Matteo uncapped the tequila and poured us each a shot.

"Lose your hand, you drink. Fold, you drink. Go bust… drink. Got it?"

"Just deal the cards, already," Enzo grumbled. I could only just see his big hands from my position which given the stakes had just risen, was probably a good thing.

"Everyone in," Tristan asked, waiting for us to throw our chips in the pot. "Okay, let's play some poker."

# CHAPTER 21

ENZO

*N*ora was kicking our asses at poker.

I'd sucked in a sharp breath when she and Arianne had emerged from the bedroom and sat with us as if they had any business joining our game. But it had turned out she knew exactly what she was doing.

She'd played it cool to start with, folding on a number of early hands and taking tequila shot after tequila shot like a champ. Part of me wondered if she wanted to end up wasted. I wouldn't blame her if she did. The tension between us was so thick you could cut through it with a knife. Everyone felt it, glancing between us as we went head-to-head in yet another round.

I studied my cards, relieved I could barely see her around Matteo's frame. But as if he felt me staring, the fucker leaned back and gave me a clear view of Nora. Her brows were knitted in deep concentration, the soft lines of her face taut.

She was completely invested in the game, and I didn't think I'd ever seen anything so sexy as a girl who knew her way around a game of poker.

"Shit, man, she's going to wipe the floor with you." Matteo cackled, his head rolling slightly. We were almost a bottle and half of tequila in, between the four of us. Matteo and Tristan had lost the most rounds, with me coming in third. But Nora was tiny compared to the three of us, so every shot she took was at least two for us.

"How's it looking, Nor?" Arianne asked her. Nicco had bowed out three rounds in, unable to keep his hands off his wife. But they'd stayed to watch the show.

"It's okay." she pushed a stack of chips into the pot.

"Okay?" Matteo exploded with laughter. "Kick his ass, Nora. Fuck knows he deserves it."

A low growl rumbled in my chest as Tristan waited for me to make my play. "Call," I said confidently, matching her bet.

"Both players call." Tristan discarded the top card and slid off the next card, flipping it over and adding it to the table, followed by two more cards.

Silence echoed through the cabin as we checked our cards. I had a three of a kind. Nora's poker face gave nothing away as she glanced at me to the stack of chips and back to her cards.

"Bet," she said, pushing another stack of chips toward the pot.

I scrubbed a hand down my face. I needed to win this round. It wasn't about the money, it was about her. About not losing to her any more than I already had.

"I'm in," I said.

Tension crackled through the air as Matteo, Nicco, and

Arianne watched us duke it out.

Tristan took the next card and flipped it, adding it to the three on the table. "Seven of diamonds."

"Check," Nora said coolly.

"Raise." I called her bluff, trying to force her out of the game. Two-hundred and fifty bucks was a drop in the ocean to me, but to someone like Nora, it was money in her purse.

"Ooof," Matteo grunted.

"Can you shut the fuck up?"

"What? It's tense."

"Nora, the ball's in your court," Tristan said.

She studied her cards closely, her eyes flitting from her hand to the ones lined up on the table.

*Fold*, I wanted to hiss. *Just fold.*

"Call."

"Nora, are you sure? It's a lot of money." Arianne frowned, but Nora kept quiet, adding the right amount of chips to the pot.

"The turn," Tristan announced adding a fourth card.

Boom. I had four of a kind and the third highest hand a player could have. Logic told me she couldn't have a royal flush, given the lack of picture cards on the table, so she could only beat me with a straight flush. If the river card was a diamond it was a possibility, but what were the chances?

"What'll it be, Abato?" I said without thinking.

Her eyes snapped to mine, filled with an emotion I couldn't decipher. She looked hurt, but she also looked pissed as if I'd just kicked her puppy or something.

My brows furrowed. It was just a name. Shooting the shit over a game of poker. She'd insisted on sitting at the table with us. No one had made her play.

Her eyes narrowed, as she flicked her eyes to her cards

and back again.

"Call." The conviction in her voice rattled through my skull. She wasn't going to back down.

"You sure?" My brow lifted, and she craned her neck around Matteo to stare me right in the eyes.

"I said call."

"Have it your way." I matched her bet and waited for Tristan to flip the final card.

A sense of smugness washed over me as I eyed the ten of spades. She couldn't beat me. It was statistically impossible.

But Nora didn't chuck her cards. Instead, she pushed her remaining chips into the pot. "All in." Her eyes held a challenge, only I was no longer sure we were talking about the poker game.

"What's it going to be, Marchetti?" She threw my words back at me, and anger flared inside me.

No way she could beat me.

"Don't come crying to me when you lose, Gattina." I smirked. It shouldn't have felt so good to wipe the table with her, but after last night, the way she'd rejected me, I wanted her to hurt.

Her breath caught. I hadn't meant to say it. Not in front of everyone. But I was enjoying having her at my mercy, even if it wasn't in the way I really wanted.

"E," Nicco warned, but this wasn't between him and me. It was between me and the girl who had buried herself under my skin when I never wanted her there to begin with.

"Okay," Tristan said. "Show your hands."

Nora glanced at me, waiting.

"Four of a kind," I said, laying my cards out.

Her brows knitted for a second but then a slow smile spread over her face. "Looks like you'll be the one paying up,

Marchetti." She laid down her cards and I blinked in utter disbelief.

Four tens.

She'd pipped my four sevens. Fuck.

"And that, ladies and gentlemen, is how you play poker." Matteo was enjoying my downfall far too much.

"Fuck off." I grunted, pushing from the table.

"Ah, sore loser, cous?"

I flipped him off over my shoulder as I headed for the door. I needed a smoke. Or another bottle of whisky. Nora had schooled me in front of our friends, and I didn't like the feeling of once again being at her mercy.

Glancing back, I watched the others congratulate her as Tristan exchange the chips for one-hundred-dollar bills.

As if she felt me watching, Nora looked over her shoulder, our eyes colliding. I expected to see smug satisfaction in her big, round, doe eyes, but I found none.

Instead, she looked like the one who'd lost everything.

AFTER WALKING THE PERIMETER TO SOBER MYSELF UP AND REIN in my anger, I made my way back to the cabin. But right before I reached the door, my cell started vibrating.

"Uncle Toni?"

"How's it going up there?"

"It's… okay."

He chuckled. "The girls giving you a hard time?"

If only he knew.

"Anything?" I asked eagerly. After his call this morning to inform us that there had been no developments overnight, I was hoping they would have something by now.

"Nothing. Not even a sniff."

"Fuck."

"Just hang tight, son. He'll show."

"Maybe he's waiting for me to—"

"Lorenzo." He clucked his tongue. "Listen to me and listen good. I know you want in on this, but until we have no choice, I don't want you here, doing something you might later regret. Stay at the cabin. Leave the hunt to us."

"And if he doesn't show?"

"He will, son. They always do." He inhaled a long, steady breath. "You know, Enzo, your father—"

"Don't."

"You need to hear this, son. Your father, pezzo di merda, lost his way. He was blinded by greed and power. What happened with Vincenzo will haunt me forever because I was his brother. I should have seen the signs. *I* should have noticed. Me. That shit falls on my shoulders, Lorenzo. Not yours."

"It just makes no sense," I confessed. "He would have died for you."

"A wise man once said, 'greed makes a man foolish and blind, and makes him an easy prey for death.' Vincenzo knew what he was doing, and he paid the price. But I refuse to lose you to misplaced guilt, Lorenzo."

I scrubbed a hand over my face. He was right. I didn't want to pay for the sins of my father, but how did you escape his legacy when his DNA flowed through your veins?

"Go be with your cousins. I'll be in touch soon."

"Yeah, okay." I wanted to argue, but I knew there was no point. He was the boss as he'd so aptly pointed out more than once.

But when I stepped back into the cabin, I immediately regretted it.

"What the fuck?" I grumbled, watching as Nora danced with the girls, the three of them falling over each other and giggling hysterically.

"Guess who snuck a bottle of wine into their room." Matteo let out a strained breath. "Next time we need to lock that shit away."

"Oh relax, big brother." Bella poked her tongue out between her lips. "We're having fun. You should try it some time."

"Somebody make it stop." Matteo buried his face in his hands, but Nora strutted over to him and grabbed his hands.

"Bella's right, Matt, don't be such a spoilsport. We're stuck here... we may as well have some fuuuun." She staggered back and he leaped up, steadying her.

"You're halfway to being toasted." His eyes flicked to mine and I ground my teeth together, going to the kitchen. I was going to need something stronger than tequila to get through tonight.

The music went up a notch and the heavy beat of The Weeknd filled the cabin.

"I love this one," Sia yelled.

"Keep an eye on them," Nicco said as he pulled Arianne toward the hall leading to the bedrooms.

"Really? You want me to babysit while you two go fuck like newlyweds?"

Arianne winced at my harsh words.

"Just don't let them drink anymore," he said, cutting me with a hard look, "and make sure they drink a glass of water before bed. Oh, and make sure Tristan stays the fuck away from them."

"Tristan?" I balk. "What the fuck?"

"It would appear the girls have developed quite the crush on my cousin," Arianne explained.

"On *Tristan*?" Disbelief coated my words.

"Stranger things have happened." Nicco shook his head. "Just watch him."

"Nicco, Tristan would never—"

"Fine, watch them then. Just watch them. *All* of them. Nora included. She's drunk and she's hurting."

"Hurting? What the fuck are you—"

"One day you'll realize, E, and it'll probably be too damn late," he said, guiding his wife down the hall.

Nora was hurting?

She was the one who pushed me away last night, not the other way around. If anyone was supposed to feel dejected, it was me.

*You called her a whore.* I shut down the memory. I didn't mean it; it had just spilled out in the heat of the moment.

I watched her dancing with Matteo, the two of them laughing and joking. He was so fucking different to me. He found it easy; being around girls, charming them with his goofy smile and big heart. It didn't actually get him a lot of pussy. He was too picky when it came to who he let into his bed, but he could have had any girl who laid eyes on him.

Including Nora.

Fuck, they looked good together as he spun her around, reeling her in and then flinging her back out. Tristan watched on, sipping a beer and smiling at the two of them. Alessia and Bella were trying to replicate some girl band dance or something, which made me snort. They looked fucking ridiculous.

"You should come join us," Matteo called, and I flipped him off.

"Oh God," Bella cried suddenly, clutching her stomach. "I don't feel so good." She dashed toward the hall, Alessia hot on her heels.

"Don't throw up in the bedroom," she called after her cousin.

"Fuck's sake," Matteo ground out. "Looks like fun time is over." He stormed after his sister.

"I'm going to call it a night too, I think," Tristan said. He gave me a curt nod as he passed me on the way to the bedrooms.

Nora flopped down on the couch and grabbed her drink.

"Is that a good idea?" I asked, leaning against the wall.

"Do you care?"

My shoulders lifted in a small shrug. "Don't blame me tomorrow when you've got a hangover from hell."

"You're such a fucking hypocrite," she murmured, downing the drink in one.

I flinched at her cold tone.

"What, no comeback?"

My chest heaved as I stalked across the room to go outside for a smoke. She was drunk, and the last thing I wanted to do was get into it with an emotional, drunk girl.

But as I reached the door, she stood up and swayed on her feet.

"Whoa," she breathed.

"You good?" I fought a smirk as I went to go to her.

"I'm fine," she snapped, warding me off with her hand.

She wasn't fine. She was ass over elbow drunk. But I gave her space to pass me. Except she tripped on the corner of the rug and stumbled forward.

"Owwww," she cried, right as I caught her. "I've got it. I've got it." Nora glowered at me, her eyes cloudy and glittering with contempt.

I steadied her and stepped back. "Sure about that?"

She swayed gently on the spot. "I'm fine. At least, I will be when the room stops spinning." Burying her hands in her face, Nora began to topple again.

"Fuck," I grunted as I scooped her up, much to her displeasure.

"Put me down." She batted my chest. "I swear to God, Lorenzo Marchetti, put me down right this—*whoa*!" Her head rolled back as I stalked down the hall toward her room. I could hear Matteo berating Bella for getting drunk and puking everywhere. Thankfully, all was quiet from Nicco and Ari's room. Nobody needed to hear the two of them going at it.

Kicking the door open, I went inside and dropped Nora on the bed.

"Asshole," she hissed.

"I'll get you some water."

"I don't need any—" Her words rolled off my back as I left her to go and get her a glass of water and some Advil.

When I got back to her room, she was curled up in a ball, clutching a pillow.

"Nora?"

No answer.

I leaned over her and stroked the hair from her face. "Gattina?"

She murmured softly, snuggling the pillow tighter.

I lingered for a second, watching the gentle rise and fall of her chest and then I walked out of there...

Wishing I didn't have to.

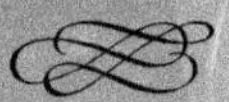

# CHAPTER 22

NORA

*I* woke with a brass band marching in my head.

"Ugh." Reaching out, I fumbled around to locate my cell phone and dragged it back to me.

It was a little after nine and I felt deathly. My mind was a hazy amateur movie of poker, tequila, and… *dancing*?

Huh?

That seemed a little odd, but I definitely remembered dancing with the girls and Matteo. I'd really hit the tequila hard after beating Enzo and winning the poker game. But it hadn't felt much like winning when he'd called me Gattina in front of everyone and then stormed from the cabin.

Damn him. He was such a stubborn asshole. Everyone could feel the tension between us. They'd spent the entire game glancing from him to me and back again, and it had become so much more than just a friendly game of poker. But in the end, Enzo did what Enzo always did.

He walked away.

And I did something out of the ordinary, I grabbed the half empty bottle of tequila, turned up the music, and decided to make the most of the situation.

Of course it had royally backfired.

My eyes fluttered closed as I tried to remember how I'd gotten to bed. And then it hit.

Enzo.

He'd carried me to bed.

Perfect.

Just perfect.

I clutched the pillow, groaning into the soft material. When I gingerly rolled onto my side, I frowned at the glass of water and box of pain pills. My lips curved a fraction. Maybe he wasn't a cold-hearted bastard after all.

I popped two tabs and swallowed them down. Tomorrow was Monday, and I wanted to go back to my life. To classes and some kind of normal. As far as I was aware, there had been no further attacks, so maybe whoever was targeting the Marchetti had given up. Or maybe they had it wrong. Maybe it wasn't related to Vincenzo at all.

A gentle knock at my door sounded like an explosion in my skull.

"Hello?" I groaned.

"It's me." Arianne slipped inside. "How are you feeling?"

"Like I drank my body weight in tequila."

"I hate to be the one to say it, but you did." She smiled but I found no judgment there. "He's really under your skin, isn't he?"

"What do you think?"

"Honestly?" Her brow lifted. "I think you're too good for him, Nora."

"It doesn't matter now anyway. He made his choice."

And it wasn't me.

"Do you think we can go home soon?"

I didn't want to spend a second longer here than necessary.

"Hopefully. Nicco is on the phone with his father right now."

"How are the girls?" I asked.

"Bella looks as green as you."

"Ouch."

"Matteo is still railing at her."

"At least I don't have to worry about Gio being around to lecture me."

Just then, my cell vibrated.

"Let me guess," Ari said as I checked it. "Luca?"

"Maybe." I smothered a smile as I read his text message.

WHEN ARE YOU COMING BACK? TURNS OUT OUR OTHER **neighbors are awfully boring.**

HOPEFULLY LATER TODAY.

DINNER AT MINE? I STILL OWE YOU...

"WHAT DOES HE WANT?" ARI ASKED, TRYING TO PEER OVER MY hands.

"He invited me for dinner."

"Like a date?"

"No, like two friends hanging out," I corrected her.

"Sounds like a date to me."

"He knows I'm not looking for anything serious right now."

"Just be careful, Nora. I know you probably want to get back at Enz—"

"That's not what this is, babe. Luca is a friend." And friends could have dinner, couldn't they?

ONLY IF I CAN HELP COOK?

I HIT SEND, AND HIS REPLY CAME STRAIGHT BACK.

DEAL. SEE YOU AROUND FIVE?

"TELL ME YOU DIDN'T JUST DO WHAT I THINK YOU DID." ARI frowned, concern shining in her eyes.

"What does it matter?"

"Even if we get to go home, you'll have round the clock security until Antonio is satisfied that the threat is gone."

"So?" I shrugged. "Maurice can protect me from outside Luca's apartment."

"And if Enzo finds out?"

"It's not a secret, babe. It isn't illegal to have dinner with a friend. Besides, he won't care."

"Because Enzo *not* caring has worked out so well for you in the past." She gave me a pointed look.

"What happened to *I'm too good for him?*"

"You are, but love doesn't always follow the rules. All I'm saying is don't push him too hard, because you might not like his response."

"There is nothing that guy can do to hurt me anymore than he already has," I confessed. But the second I said the words, I felt the lie coil around my heart.

There was another knock at the door, and Nicco stuck his head around it.

"What did he say?" Ari got up and went to him.

His eyes moved past her to mine, and just like that we were back to me being on the outside.

I pulled the covers around me and let out a frustrated sigh. "Can we go home or not?"

"Yeah, we're going home. But security will be increased, until we have a handle on this."

"Great, I'd better get used to Maurice following every time I go for a pee again then." In the days after my kidnapping, I'd had someone with me at all times. I couldn't move without Maurice or another security guy leaping into action. It was tiresome, not to mention suffocating. But that's what happened when you were Arianne Capizola's best friend and she was married to the Marchetti crime family's heir.

I didn't get kidnapped because *I* was important, I got taken because I was important to *her*.

It was the same now. No one wanted to hurt me directly, they wanted to hurt people close to the Family.

"We'll leave you to pack." Arianne shot me a sympathetic smile. Life wouldn't change for her. She'd stay at their well-guarded apartment in Romany Square with Nicco by her side. The girls would return home and be protected by their families, and me?

I'd go home to my apartment alone with Maurice for company.

∽

FORTY MINUTES LATER, AFTER A QUICK BREAKFAST, WE WERE packed into the SUVs heading back to Verona. Only this time, Tristan was riding with us in place of Enzo. Matteo said it was because tensions were high and Nicco wanted to know Enzo was with his sister should anything happen. But I knew every guy here and they would all take a bullet for Alessia Marchetti. Even Tristan. I'd seen the way he'd watched her this weekend. You couldn't help but be drawn to the Marchetti princess. She was kind and compassionate and she had this warmth that pulled you in whenever you were in her orbit. Tristan would never act on it; he was five years her senior and he knew Nicco would put a bullet through his skull if he so much as looked wrong at her. But I saw it. The longing in his eyes, the hunger. He was a hot-blooded male and in a couple of years she would be every guy's wet dream.

He caught my eye, frowning as if he could hear my thoughts. I smiled meekly and turned my attention to the tinted windows, watching the dense forest fade away in the distance.

My insides still felt a little tender, so I closed my eyes and let the hypnotic whir of the engine lull me to sleep.

It only felt like minutes later when Arianne gently shook my shoulder. "We're here Nora."

"Huh, what?" I blinked, wiping the drool from my mouth.

Tristan snorted and I flipped him off.

"We're at La Stella."

"We are?"

She nodded. "Want me to come—"

"No, Bambolina. Maurice and Alexi will stay with her."

"Fun," I mumbled. "I'll see you soon, okay?"

Arianne pulled me into a tight hug. "Be safe, and please do what Maurice says."

"Relax, I know the drill." I wasn't about to take any unnecessary risks, no matter how much I hated the idea of being under protective custody again.

The door opened and Maurice was there to guide me into the building. "It's good to see you again Miss—Nora." He gave me an apologetic smile.

"I wish I could say the same thing, Maurice, I really do." I trudged ahead of him, glancing around for the second SUV, but it was nowhere to be seen. They probably dropped the girls off at home first before doing whatever Matteo and Enzo planned on doing now they were back.

"Nicco explained that I am to be your full-time security detail again?"

"He did."

"They are happy for you to attend classes on Monday so long as I—"

"Yup, I got it." I waved him off, retrieving my key from my purse and unlocking my apartment. But at the last second, I stepped aside, letting him pass.

He withdrew his pistol and slipped inside. A minute later, he called, "all clear," and I went in.

I was getting another headache, so I went straight to the kitchen cabinet and pulled out a box of Advil and poured myself a glass of water. Dinner with Luca was at five. I had a few hours to recover.

"Maurice," I yelled, and he appeared. "I'm going back to bed. Please don't wake me unless absolutely necessary. This evening I'll be going across the hall to have dinner with Luca."

"Uh, Miss Abato… Nora," he corrected himself, "I'm not sure Mr. Marchetti would allow that."

"Nicco can go fuck himself."

"That's not—"

"Look, Luca was vetted. He's good people. He wouldn't live in the building if he wasn't. You can stand guard right outside or come in for all I care. But Maurice, I am going."

I stormed into my bedroom and slammed the door. I was being petulant, I knew that. But I was so annoyed. Annoyed that I was here alone, annoyed that Enzo lived up to his reputation as a cold-hearted bastard with no remorse, and most of all, I was annoyed at myself for being annoyed when he'd been through so much recently. Gah. My head was a jumble of thoughts and feelings and emotions I couldn't contain. I yanked off my sweater and shimmied out of my jeans, climbing into bed in just my tank top and panties, pulled the cover over my head and closed my eyes.

Maybe when I woke up this time, everything would be a damn sight better.

A girl could dream.

SOMEONE WAS IN THE ROOM WITH ME. I FELT THEM WATCHING me, a trickle of awareness making my hair stand on end. But when I finally opened my eyes, it was empty. I sat up and combed my fingers through my unruly curls.

"Maurice?" I called.

Nothing.

Odd.

I'd woken to the strangest sensation of being watched.

"Maurice?" I pushed off the covers and clambered out of bed and went into the living room.

"Nora?" He looked up from his newspaper. "What is it?"

"Were you just in my room?"

"No, why?"

"Huh." My finger found my lips and prodded. "I had the strangest dream. What time is it?"

"A little after three-thirty."

"I slept all day?"

"Hangovers will do that to you." He smirked and I rolled my eyes.

"I'm going to shower and get ready. Make yourself at home." Sarcasm laced my words, and his amused laughter followed me into the bathroom.

I took my time in the shower, washing away the last couple of days. There was no point in dwelling on what would never be. Arianne was right, Enzo was too lost to his demons to pull his head out of his ass long enough to see what was staring him in the face.

We were doomed from the start, and I had to accept it.

No matter how hard it was.

After finishing in the bathroom, I made my way back into my bedroom and checked my cell phone.

I HOPE YOU'RE HUNGRY.

I SMILED AT LUCA'S TEXT, MY STOMACH GRUMBLING IN appreciation. Now the nausea had passed, I could eat a small cow.

The black turtleneck sweater dress I picked molded to my shapely curves, but I didn't bother with shoes, choosing to go barefoot across the hall. This wasn't a date. It was two friends sharing a good meal and easy conversation. At least, as I knocked on Luca's door, my Maurice-shaped shadow behind me, that's what I hoped it would be.

The door swung open and Luca beamed. "You came."

"I said I would."

"Touché." He motioned for me to enter, but abruptly paused. "Is he joining us or—"

I glanced back at Maurice. "What'll it be, big guy?"

"I'll wait outside."

I nodded, shooting him an appreciative smile. I was safe with Luca. There was one door in and out, so unless the threat was going to scale the building and climb through Luca's balcony door, it was just the two of us.

"I hope everything was okay with your family?"

"It was fine, thank you. Crisis averted." I forced a smile, following him into the living room. The smell of garlic, parsley, and rich tomato sauce hit me, making my stomach growl.

"You're hungry?" An uncertain smirk played on his lips, to which I replied, "ravenous."

"And the bodyguard?"

"Just a precaution."

"Am I a threat now?"

"It isn't you they're worried about," I said, perching on a stool as he tended to the pan of pasta.

"Let me guess, you can't tell me."

"Honestly, I don't know much either." It was a white lie, but it was easier than the truth. "Being best friend's with Arianne Capizola comes with a certain set of complications."

"Is Enzo Marchetti one of them?"

My heart lurched into my throat. "You've been doing your research."

"I wanted to know who I'm up against, yeah."

"Luca, that's not—"

"Yeah, I know." He exhaled out a steady breath. "I was worried, so I did some Googling."

"You shouldn't have done that. If you want to know things about me, you should have asked."

"Would you have told me?" My lips pressed into a thin line and he added, "That's what I thought."'

"I came over here to get away from all that." I sighed.

"You can't blame me for being worried. There's something between us, Nora." His eyes bore into mine with so much intensity, I had to break the connection.

"Luca, don't do this, please. We agreed, friends only."

Silence ticked by, turning the air thick and suffocating. When he didn't answer, I got up. "Maybe this was a mistake."

"Wait," he rushed out. "I'm sorry. I didn't plan to make this awkward, I swear. I was going to play it cool, but then I saw you and everything got messed up in my head."

"Well, can you un-mess it so we can eat, because that smells so good and I'm really hungry." My stomach growled on cue.

"Deal. We eat, we talk, and we leave everything else at the door."

"That sounds perfect," I said. Because it did. Even if it was a temporary truce before Luca started fighting for me again. I knew he would. I saw the fierce determination in his eyes. But what I still didn't know…

Was, did I want him to?

## CHAPTER 23

ENZO

She was at Luca's eating his food in his fucking apartment. All because I was too fucked up to get my shit together and be the kind of guy she needed.

But I wasn't that guy.

I was never going to be that guy.

So what choice did I have but to let her go?

Grabbing the glass nearest to me, I launched it across the room, watching it smash against the wall, shattering into a thousand pieces.

Everything was a mess.

Nora was with Luca, giving him her smiles and sass and maybe if he was lucky, her sinful body. And I was stuck here, in my apartment, waiting for the call that the fucker toying with us had reared his ugly face again.

I didn't just want to destroy him, I wanted to break every

bone in his body and then spend my sweet time putting him back together so I could do it all over again.

I felt the weight of the knife strapped to my ankle, the pistol in its holster around my chest, and the brass knuckles tucked neatly in my inside pocket. I was a fighter primed for a fight... without an opponent. But the time would come, and when it did, that motherfucker was mine. I clenched my fist, feeling a lick of steely determination zip up my spine.

Just then, Matteo's voice rang out through the apartment. "Cous, you here?"

"Where else would I be?" I snapped.

"Thought you might be staking out La Stella. Trying to get a look at Nora and Luca." He strolled over to the refrigerator and grabbed two beers.

"Did you come here to bust my balls or to tell me we have a body to bury?"

"Someone's happy to see me." Matteo handed me a bottle and sat down on the chair opposite. "Actually, I came to stop you from doing something stupid. But I can see that's going well." He eyed the stained wall and pile of glass on the floor.

"I feel like I'm losing my fucking mind," I admitted. "All I can think about is my old man. His wicked fucking smirk as he confessed to killing Aunt Lucia. Then she's there... Nora... tangled up in the memories."

"Just admit it. You want her."

"Yeah, I fucking want her, she's—" Fuck. Nora was like no one else I'd ever met. But it didn't change anything. "I'm not cut out for that life."

"Who says? You? Because I gotta tell you, cous, you're not thinking straight lately."

I flipped him off. "Feel free to leave."

"And miss out on you sitting here like a lost puppy? No fucking chance. Besides, I'm here on official orders."

"You mean Nic's orders."

"Yeah." His expression fell. "He's worried."

My eyes rolled. "Because you're all fucking pussies. Ari has made him soft and you… you've always been soft."

"Seriously though, just go over there and tell her how you really feel. Kills two birds with one stone."

"How do you figure?"

"You get to protect her while boning—"

I grabbed a cushion and threw it at his head.

"What?" He caught it, chuckling. "You know I'm right. If you don't make a move soon, Luca will sweep in and—"

"She's better off without me." I tipped my head back and closed my eyes, swigging my beer.

"Whatever you say, man, but I want it noted that I think you're making a big fucking mistake."

"Noted." My eyes landed on his as I drained the rest of my beer and slammed it down on the table. "I think we're going to need something stronger."

THE BLARE OF MY CELL PHONE CUT THROUGH THE DARKNESS. I scrambled to find it, tapping the nightstand until my fingers grazed the smooth plastic.

"Yeah?" I grumbled, my head pounding.

"Mr. Marchetti, we've got a problem."

At the sound of Maurice's voice, I bolted upright. "What is it? Is she okay?"

"She's fine. But there's been an incident at La Stella, a package."

"A package?" I was already out of bed, pulling on my clothes, and arming myself with my favorite weapons.

"It was addressed to Nora."

Fuck.

*Fuck.*

My fist found the nearest wall. Pain exploded along my knuckles, but I barely felt it, red hot anger flooding every inch of me.

"What is it?"

"Well, that's the strange thing, sir." He sucked in a sharp breath. "It appears to be for you."

"I'm on my way."

"What should I tell Miss Abato?"

Shit, Nora. She was going to freak the fuck out.

"Nothing, don't wake her yet."

"That's the other thing, Mr. Marchetti," he hesitated.

"Go on…" My teeth ground together.

"She stayed over at her neighbor's, Mr. Bianco."

My stone heart plummeted into my toes.

She stayed over.

Did she fuck him? Let him touch her sinful curves and kiss her pouty lips?

Jealousy threatened to consume me as I imagined the two of them naked, bodies writhing and slick with sweat.

*Rein. It. The. Fuck. In.*

Just because she stayed over doesn't mean anything happened.

Who the fuck was I kidding? That's exactly what it meant.

I grabbed my keys. It was a little after midnight. The streets would be clear enough for me to drive, but I knew my cousins would kick my ass if they knew I'd driven over the limit.

"Yo, asshole," I banged on Matteo's door.

"Yeah?" he murmured.

"We need to go."

"Shit, now?" He sounded disoriented, but I knew it was from sleep and not liquor since he'd stopped after two beers while I'd kept going.

The door swung open revealing a half-naked Matteo. "Where?" He ran a hand down his face.

"Nora got a package at La Stella."

"Fuck. What's in it?"

"Maurice didn't give me the details over the phone. Just said he didn't think it was for Nora at all."

"If it's not for Nora then who—*oh shit.*"

"We need to go, now."

"Yeah, okay. Just let me grab some clothes."

Five minutes later, we were climbing into Matt's truck.

My leg bounced uncontrollably as we left Romany Square and made the short journey to University Hill.

"She'll be okay. Maurice and his team are there."

"Nora isn't there," I ground out.

"What do you mean, she isn't there?"

"She stayed over at Luca's."

"Shit, cous, that's rough. I'm sorry."

I felt his eyes on the side of my face, but I didn't meet his sympathetic gaze. "You and Nic were right all along," I muttered.

"I'm not following," he said.

"You told me she'd slip through my fingers."

"So fight for her. You're a Marchetti, E. Fighting's what we do."

My eyes flicked to his in a questioning expression.

"Oh, fuck you," he chuckled. "I can fight."

My brows hit my hairline as I smirked. "You fight like a girl."

"I'm a lover, not a fighter."

"Yeah, you are." But from where I was sitting, it didn't seem like such a bad thing to be. He wasn't harboring all the hate and bitterness I was. Sure, Uncle Michele wasn't a traitorous lying cunt, but I'd been like this *before*.

Angry.

Bitter.

Cold.

I was my father's son, and, deep down, I knew he was the reason I pushed Nora away. Not because of what I did but because of what I *was*.

A killer.

A cold blooded murderer.

A sinner.

She was too good, too fucking pure for this life. She deserved Prince Charming, not the villain.

She deserved someone like Luca. Someone who would be there and show up. Someone who wouldn't bring death and destruction and danger to her doorstep.

I scrubbed a hand down my face, wishing Matteo would step on it.

"So, if the parcel's for you, we have to assume he's watching you, or has, at the very least, done his homework."

"I don't give a shit about me."

"We can protect Nora."

"Not the point, Matt, and you know it." Nora was in this position because of me. Because whoever was fucking with us had some unfinished business all thanks to my father.

After what felt like a lifetime, Matteo finally pulled up

outside of La Stella. I leaped from the truck not giving a shit that I was out in the open. I had to get to her. Now.

But Maurice intercepted me before I even reached the stairs. "He left it at the main doors. Security called me when they noticed."

"They get any footage?" I glanced at the security cameras trained on the entrance to the building.

"Alexi is checking now."

"Good, let me know the second you hear. Where's the package?"

"Inside her apartment."

"She still with Luca?"

He nodded. "How do you want to proceed?"

"Show me the package."

I followed Maurice up to Nora's apartment. My eyes narrowed as I passed Luca's door. What I really wanted was to kick the fucking thing down and punish her for ever thinking she could pull that shit on me. But I knew better, and I knew Nora would only dig her heels in all the more if I went off at the deep end all because she'd done what I'd been doing week in and week out.

But those women meant nothing, they were a means to an end. Luca was different. He had boyfriend potential.

I forced myself to take a deep breath and follow Maurice into Nora's apartment.

"It's right over here." He led me to the breakfast counter.

The small box was nondescript except for a hand scrawled label with Nora's address on.

"Here." Maurice handed me a latex glove and I pulled it on, carefully opening the lid.

"What the fuck is that?" I peered inside, paling when I realized what I was staring at. "That's Gino's chain."

Now I could get a better look, I would recognize the heavy gold chain anywhere. The dried blood caked on the chain links confirmed it.

"Who is this motherfucker?" I hissed.

"What shall I do with it, sir?"

"Call our guys at local PD and have them run it for prints. Maybe we'll get lucky."

"I'll make sure it gets into the right hands."

"Thanks."

"And Miss Abato?"

"I'll deal with Nora."

Matteo appeared just then. "Well…"

"He sent me a souvenir."

The blood drained from his face. "Please tell me there were no body parts."

"Gino's blood encrusted gold chain."

"Fuck."

"Yeah. I'll be right back." I stormed past him, but Matteo caught my arm.

"Are you sure this is a good idea?"

"She needs to know."

And I needed her here, where I could keep my eye on her.

"She's going to be pissed." Matt grimaced.

"I can handle it." But as I said the words, I wasn't sure of anything anymore.

I was supposed to want to be out there, hunting him. Not resting until he was six feet under with a bullet hole through his skull. But all I could think about was getting Nora out of Luca's apartment and away from here, to somewhere safe. Somewhere the fucker couldn't walk right up to the door and leave her little packages.

"It's your death sentence," Matteo mumbled as I walked

away. It was almost one in the morning. They would be sleeping, hopefully not together because I wasn't ready to see that. It was bad enough collecting her from his apartment as it was.

I rapped my knuckles on the door and waited. When no one answered, I added a little force behind it.

"What the fuck are you doing?" Luca grimaced at the sight of me.

"I need to speak to Nora."

"She's sleeping. It's the middle of the fucking night."

"It's an emergency."

"An emergency? What kind of emergency?" He had the gall to stare me down. "Because from where I'm standing it looks like the guy who continually hurts her wants to hurt her again. Well, I got—"

"Enzo?"

Relief slammed into me, but then I saw what she was wearing and all the anger and jealousy I felt hit me like a tsunami.

"There's something we need to deal with," I said, barely able to look at her. Her long smooth legs peeking out from under a t-shirt.

*His fucking t-shirt.* Unless all of a sudden, she wore a man's size.

"I'll be across the hall," I said, spinning on my heel.

Luca started trying to comfort her, insisting she didn't need to follow my orders all the time. But I didn't stick around to hear the rest. Visions of her in his clothes were seared into the backs of my eyes.

And I hated it.

I hated it so fucking much.

But it wasn't the hatred that caught me off guard. It was

the regret. Thick, sludgy regret that slithered through me like a poisonous snake, coiling around my heart and threatening to squeeze the life right out of it.

I stormed back into her apartment and waited. Matteo didn't say a word, scrolling his phone, no doubt keeping Nicco in the loop.

A minute later, I felt her enter the room.

"What is it, what's wrong?" she asked.

"We've got a problem." I didn't meet her eyes.

"Enzo, look at me." I was powerless against her soft command, turning around to look at her. She was dressed, at least. "What. Happened?"

"Whoever is doing this… he knows you're here."

"*What?*"

"I'll just be…" Matteo left us alone.

"He must have been watching me, watching us." The words were like sandpaper against my throat. "He sent something to you… something for me."

"Oh my God." She wrapped her arms around herself and shivered. "H-he was here?"

"He didn't get inside the building, but he left the package at the front door."

"What was in it?"

"It doesn't matter."

"What was in it, Enzo?" She bit out, and I flinched.

"Gino's gold chain. The guy I was working with in Providence… the guy he… killed."

"Jesus," she breathed, and before I knew what was happening, she marched toward me and threw her arms around me. "I'm so sorry this is happening to you."

I stood there dumbfounded. I'd expected her to be angry, to scream and yell and blame me… I hadn't expected *this*.

"You can hug me back, you know," she chuckled softly, and I gingerly wrapped my arms around her, burying my face in the crook of her neck.

God, she felt good pressed up against me, holding me. I wanted to stay there forever, secreted away from all the shit circling me. But all too soon, she pulled away, tucking her wild curls behind her ear.

"Sorry," a slow blush spread up her neck and into her cheeks, "I just—"

"It's okay."

Something flashed in her eyes, but there was a knock at the door, and Maurice came inside. "We pulled the security footage."

"And?"

He grimaced. "You should probably come and take a look at it."

"Okay. Stay here with Nora. I need to call Nicco and Uncle Toni."

"Already handled."

"Thank you."

"The boss is sending more guys. We'll double security on both exits and put more guys outside Nora's—"

"Whoa, wait a second. You think he'll come back?" The blood drained from her face once more.

I wanted to reach out and touch her, comfort her the way she had comforted me. But I didn't know how. I didn't know…

"We can't take any risks," I said thickly. Glancing away so she wouldn't see the emotion in my eyes.

Jesus, he knew she lived here.

It changed everything.

"Maurice will stay right here with you okay?" I finally

went to her and cupped the back of her neck, staring down at her. "I'll be as quick as I can."

"Okay." She swallowed, but I saw the trust glitter in her eyes. After everything, Nora still trusted me to keep her safe.

Yet, it was knowing me, being someone important to me, that had put her in harm's way.

My hand lingered on her neck, the urge to kiss her so fucking overpowering that I immediately released her and stepped away.

She misread the action, hurt flashing in her eyes. "I'm going to get some coffee," she said. "Looks like it's going to be a long night."

I gave her a small nod…

And then I got the hell out of there.

# CHAPTER 24

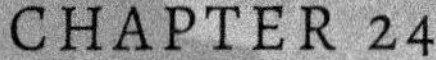

NORA

*I* made a fresh pot of coffee while we waited for Enzo to reappear.

Maurice made himself scarce, blending into the shadows in the corner of the living room. But Matteo didn't give me space. He perched at the counter, graciously accepting a mug of coffee from me.

"Nice t-shirt." His brow arched, and I let out a heavy sigh.

"It's not what you think."

"And what do you think I think?"

"Matt…"

"So, you're telling me, you didn't spend the night bumping uglies with your—"

A loud bang at the door startled us.

"What the hell?" Matteo mumbled.

"Stay back." Maurice withdrew his pistol. "I'll get it." But the second he checked the peephole; he holstered his gun. "It's Mr. Bianco."

"Jesus, the guy doesn't know when to quit, does he?"

I shot Matteo a scathing look. "Let him in, Maurice." Maurice glanced at Matteo and I let out an exasperated breath. "It's my apartment and unless I'm mistaken, I am not a prisoner here, so please answer the door for *Mr. Bianco*."

Maurice answered the door and stepped back.

"I'm sorry," Luca rushed out as I approached. "I know you told me to stay away, but I'm over there worrying, dreaming up all these crazy scenarios in my head, and I—"

"Luca, breathe." I chuckled but it came out strained. "I'm okay."

"I can see that." His cheeks burned. "Matteo." He gave him a stiff nod.

"I'd say it's good to see you again, but I'm loyal to my cousin so—"

"*Matt!*"

"What?" He shrugged. "You should probably wrap this up before Enzo comes back."

Fuck my life.

Why did this have to be happening?

All I'd wanted was to have dinner with a friend, and now I was stuck between a rock and a hard place again.

"Matteo's right, you should go," I said. "It's late and the crisis is averted. I'll talk to you tomorrow, okay?" I started to close the door, but Luca's hand flew out, stopping it.

"I suggest you back the fuck up." Enzo growled from down the hall. A shiver ran through me at the sheer anger in his voice. But there was something else there too, under the surface.

Something that sounded a lot like possessiveness.

"*Me?*" Luca balked. "If I recall correctly, it wasn't your apartment Nora spent the night at."

A gasp slipped from my lips, anger flooding. "You should go, Luca. Now!"

"Shit, Nora." He ran a hand down his face. "I didn't mean—"

"Just go. Maurice, please escort Luca back to his apartment." I stepped aside letting my bodyguard usher Luca away. His eyes pleaded with me, but I didn't concede. I was still too shocked he'd said that.

Enzo came closer, anger radiating off him. But he didn't berate me… he didn't say anything. Just stalked past me and disappeared into my apartment.

With a heavy heart, I followed him inside. Everything was such a mess, and this, it was my fault.

Enzo was discussing something with Maurice and Matteo. They looked over, but I disappeared into my bedroom, shedding the t-shirt Luca had let me borrow and pulling on my 'let's avocuddle' t-shirt and some pajama shorts.

When I went back into the living room, Matteo and Maurice were gone.

"Where is everyone?" I asked.

But Enzo didn't hear me, his dark gaze drinking in the sight of me. When his eyes landed on my t-shirt, an amused smirk tipped the corner of his mouth.

"What?"

"You are so fucking weird."

"Gee, thanks." I went over to the coffee machine, needing to distract myself from his intense stare.

I set about making a fresh pot and waited. I didn't feel him move behind me until his hands slid around my waist.

"Is it true?" he whispered, so quietly I almost missed it.

"Is what true?" I sucked in a harsh breath as he pulled me closer to his chest. His mouth dipped to my ear.

"Did you sleep with him, Gattina. Did you let him fuck you?"

"It doesn't matter," I said, my eyes fluttering closed as he breathed against the curve of my neck.

"It matters. You know it does."

"The last time I checked, you didn't want me." The words cut me deep.

"There isn't a single second of the day when I don't want you, Gattina. But it doesn't change the fact I *shouldn't* want you."

"Enzo." I tried to turn in his arms, but he had me caged against the counter.

"Just put me out of my misery and tell me..."

God, I wanted to tell him. I wanted to drive a knife through his heart the way he'd done so many times to me.

But I wasn't cruel and even now, I still didn't want to hurt him. Not when I knew he was dealing with so much.

"Enzo..." My voice cracked.

"It's okay, Gattina." His lips ghosted over my collarbone sending bolts of electricity zipping through me.

"I didn't sleep with him."

"What?"

"I went over to have dinner with him. There was wine. Too much wine. I spilled a glass all over me, so Luca gave me a clean t-shirt. I got embarrassed and a little upset. I didn't want to be alone, so he let me stay. We didn't—"

Enzo spun me in his arms. "You didn't fuck him?"

"I wanted to. I wanted to do it so much. I wanted to get back at you for hurting me. But I couldn't do it because no matter how much you don't want me to care, I do. I care, Lorenzo Marchetti." Tears pooled in the corners of my eyes as I slid my hands up his chest. "I care and I don't know how to stop." The first tear fell right as Enzo splayed his hand around my throat and kissed me. His lips were hard and bruising, every lick of his tongue steady and sure. He didn't just kiss me, he devoured me without hesitation.

"Fuck, Gattina," he rasped against my mouth. "I thought I'd lost you to him." Enzo grabbed my ass and lifted me slightly, grinding into me with impressive restraint.

My heart soared at his words, at the possessive way he held me, as if he would never let me go. I didn't want him to. I'd only ever wanted this. Us. Together.

"Never," I breathed. "He knows I'm yours. Only yours, Enzo."

He hoisted me higher, forcing my legs around his waist and walked me through the apartment until we were in my bedroom.

Liquid lust coursed through my body, I wanted him so much. But Enzo didn't kiss me again. Instead, he placed me on my feet and moved around my bed, pulling back the covers.

"Get in."

"But—"

"Get in the damn bed, Gattina." He smirked before yanking his sweater off. Heat flooded me as I traced the ink covering Enzo's body, every ridge and muscle. God, he was perfection.

He kicked off his boots and unbuttoned his jeans, pushing them over his hips and letting them pool at his feet. The thick outline of his erection didn't help the firestorm building in my stomach.

He climbed into bed and pulled me into his arms.

"Are you hugging me?"

"No," he said, "I'm avocuddling you."

A wide grin tugged at my mouth as I lifted my face to his. "Is this a dream? Did I bump my head and wake up in some alternate universe where bad boy Enzo Marchetti's got jokes?"

"Don't push it." His fingers attacked my waist, tickling and pinching, making me shriek.

"Okay, okay, I'm sorry… I won't mention it again." My laughter subsided, silence filling the space between us. "Are you okay?" I asked.

"Isn't that supposed to be my line?" Enzo swallowed thickly. "I am so fucking sorry to bring this to your door."

"What can I say, I'm a magnet for deranged murderous psychopaths." It was supposed to be a joke, but the second I said the words, I regretted them. "Enzo, I didn't mean—"

"I know what you meant." His fingers began stroking my skin, sending shivers skating up and down my skin. It was my turn to swallow. "Is this okay?" His voice crackled with lust.

I nodded, mesmerized by the way he looked at me. As if I was a precious stone, fragile and breakable.

His hand dropped to my thigh, hitching my leg over his hip. I leaned in to kiss him, but Enzo moved just out of reach, smirking. "I want to watch you," he said. "I want to see your eyes flutter and your cheeks flush when you come for me."

His hand moved higher along my thigh, stroking the skin there. Back and forth, back and forth, until he slid it between my legs and found my center. Hooking my panties aside, he pushed two fingers inside me, curling them deep while his thumb rolled over my clit in firm, lazy circles.

"God, that feels…" I pressed my lips together, trying to catch my breath. My eyes fluttered, but Enzo growled. "Look at me, Gattina. I need you to look at me."

He worked his fingers deeper… faster… touching some place inside me that made my toes curl and my stomach clench.

"Come sei bagnata. Mi fai impazzire."

My Italian was rusty, but I knew he was talking dirty to me.

"I want you," I breathed, clutching the sheet between my fingers as he took me higher and higher.

"Just let me do this for you." His eyes were almost black as he watched me slowly come undone, stroke by stroke.

"At least kiss me." It was a breathy plea as I arched into his hand, desperate for more.

"So fucking beautiful," he rasped, dipping his head and dragging his tongue along the column of my neck. His teeth nipped my jaw, chased with tiny kisses but Enzo didn't give me what I wanted. Instead, he teased me. Licking and sucking, tasting and touching. He trailed hot, wet kisses over my skin, burning me from the inside out, while his fingers worked me into a boneless, breathless mess.

"God, more…" I chanted like I was praying to some invisible deity. "More… I need—"

Finally, Enzo kissed me, hard and punishing, stealing the air from my lungs, as if he thought I might disappear at any moment and he wanted to imprint the taste of me on his lips forever.

My body began to tremble as intense waves of pleasure crashed over me.

"Come, Gattina," he whispered against my lips. "Come for me."

His name spilled from my lips.

*Enzo. Enzo. Enzo.*

He kissed me gently, drawing out every last drop of my orgasm. Then he lifted his fingers to his mouth and sucked them clean. "So fucking good."

My tummy clenched.

"I want to return the favor," I said, ready to shimmy down the bed and give him the best blow job of his life. But Enzo pulled me against his big, warm body and said, "Sleep, Gattina."

*Sleep?*

He wanted me to sleep, nearly naked and wrapped in his arms? It would be almost impossible, my body hyperaware of every place we were joined. Hip to hip, chest to chest, my lips pressed against the hollow of his neck, tasting his salty skin.

How could I possibly sleep when all I wanted to do was jump his bones?

But as he held me tight, a sense of peace washed over me, and I found myself drifting. I didn't want to. I wanted to capture every second of this moment because Enzo had a history of flipping the switch on me once the sun chased away the shadows. And I didn't want this to end.

I *never* wanted it to end.

I WOKE TO AN EMPTY BED. MY STOMACH SANK AS I SEARCHED for any signs of Enzo. His clothes no longer littered the floor, and his side of the bed was cold.

He'd been gone a while.

I wanted to be angry at him, but I was only angry at

myself. I should have known he would run. He'd been jealous, and jealousy made people act all kinds of crazy.

*You foolish, foolish girl.*

I let out a weary sigh. Enzo had been so different last night. So warm and tactile. He'd held me most of the night. I knew because I'd woken up at least three times. But the sun was up now, and like a ghost in the night, Enzo was gone.

My cell phone started to ring and I leaned over, snatching it off the nightstand, smiling at my best friend's name.

"Good morning," she said. "How are you?"

"Surprisingly, okay." *All thanks to a certain blue-eyed bad boy.*

"I can't believe it's happening again."

"Whoa, there. It isn't happening again. It was a package, Ari."

"It was a threat, Nor, and you need to take this more seriously. I've been talking to Nicco and we want you to come and stay with us."

"No," I said a little too hastily. "I mean, thank you, it's very kind of you to offer. But I'm not going to run, Ari. I won't do that." I couldn't explain it, but I didn't want to leave. This was my home. It had taken me long enough to feel safe here after what happened before, so I'd be damned if I let some asshole out for revenge chase me off again.

"Nora, just think about it. It isn't safe."

"I'm probably in the safest place I can be right now. Antonio has an army of guys here. No one is going to come or go without them knowing about it."

"When you put it like that… And Enzo is there, that makes me feel a lot better."

"Actually," I hesitated, "he left."

"He did? But Nicco just spoke to him and he said something about breakfast."

"He did?" Hope blossomed in my chest as I climbed out of bed. "Ari, I'm going to have to call you back." I hung up, and quickly pulled on my avocuddle t-shirt.

He left… Enzo left.

Didn't he?

But sure enough, when I opened the bedroom door, I found him cooking shirtless in my freaking kitchen.

Now I know I definitely died and went to heaven. I creeped up behind him, but Enzo sensed me, turning around right as I reached him. "Good morning," I said around the biggest smile.

"Good morning." His eyes dropped to my t-shirt, darting lower to my legs peeking out from under it. "While you eat your breakfast, I'm going to eat you."

His dirty words hit me right in the stomach.

"How long have you been awake?" I asked.

"A while. I don't sleep very well."

"Nightmares?"

He nodded, and I folded myself into his chest. Half of me expected him to pull away or reject me. But it was a morning of many surprises because Enzo wound his arms around my back and held me close.

"You stayed," I whispered.

"Yeah, Gattina," he looked down at me, eyes shining with possession. "I stayed."

# CHAPTER 25

ENZO

*I* watched her talking and laughing with Matteo over pancakes. It felt fucking weird, but something had shifted last night. Something I couldn't take back.

Something I didn't want to take back.

The second I'd heard Maurice's voice on the other end of the line, something had slammed into me. Fear that Nora was hurt. Fear that I'd never get to see her again, hold her again… kiss her again. It had ploughed through me like a wrecking ball.

It didn't matter that she was at Luca's, wearing his t-shirt and sleeping in his bed. Nora Abato was mine. Even when I hadn't wanted her to be, she was under my skin and on my mind.

Fuck. Admitting that still felt strange. But I was done fighting it. My number one priority now was finding this motherfucker and making sure he didn't come within an inch of Nora ever again.

The thought he'd been here, at her building, was enough to send me postal. I wanted to tear the fucker limb from limb.

"Are you going to stand there all morning?" Matt asked. "Or join us and eat?"

I pushed off the wall and went to them. Nora smiled up at me and my chest constricted. I guess this was what it felt like to be gone for a girl, all twisted up inside, wanting to make her happy, to see her smile, and soar... while wanting to shield her from anything and anyone who might try to hurt her.

"Are you sweating?" Matteo taunted and I flipped him off.

"It's hot in here."

"I hate to tell you, big guy," Nora shuffled closer, laying her head on my arm, "but it's not that warm." Her soft laughter was like music to my fucking ears.

Jesus, I was turning into a pussy already. I inwardly groaned. Matteo caught my eye and smirked, but I saw no malice there, only understanding.

He'd known. The fucker had known for a while now, and he'd been right.

I'd just been too unwilling to accept it.

"These are really good," Nora said, nibbling a pancake.

"You sound surprised, Gattina?" My brow quirked.

"A little." Her cheeks pinked and she looked so fucking adorable. I wanted to pounce on her and kiss the shit out of her syrupy sweet lips.

"You think just because he's a grumpy fucker with about as much charm as a cardboard cutout that he can't cook?" Matteo chuckled. "Then you would be sorely mistaken. My mom used to teach us. Said the only thing an Italian man needed to know in life was the art of cooking."

"She sounds like a wonderful woman."

"You met her at the wedding, no?" I asked her, immediately regretting it. "Shit, Nora, I didn't—"

"It's okay."

But it wasn't.

She'd been kidnapped after the wedding. Yanked right out of bed beside me and taken by Scott fucking Fascini. My fist clenched against my thigh, anger trickling through me like acid.

"Hey." Her hand covered mine. "I'm okay, Enzo. See." She took my hand and pressed it against her chest, right over her heart.

"You're in so much trouble, cous," Matteo howled with laughter and I flipped him off, keeping my focus on Nora.

"Yeah," I murmured. "I think you're right."

Nora frowned, but a knock at the door interrupted us.

"If that's your neighbor, I swear to God—"

"I'll go." She got up, but I beat her to it.

"Like hell you will." I grabbed my pistol off the counter and marched toward the door.

I heard Matteo mutter something about *letting me get it out of my system.* But disappointment washed over me when I saw Nicco and Arianne standing on the other side of the door.

"Expecting someone else?" he said, eyeing the gun in my hand.

"Don't ask," I grumbled, letting them in.

"You look different," Ari remarked, seeing straight through me.

"Nice to see you too." Closing the door, I followed them inside. Nora jumped up, running to hug Arianne.

"I'm so glad you're okay."

"I feel like we say that too much these days," Nora glanced at me and guilt shredded my insides. But she was in this life now. Whether I stood by her side or not, Nora was inextricably tied to the Family.

I realized that now. I realized why Nicco had refused to let Arianne go. Because whether he claimed her or not, she would forever be a target to his enemies just for the simple fact that she loved him.

The girls went to make everyone coffee while I sat with my cousins.

"Do I need to be worried about that?" His eyes flicked to Nora. She felt him staring and glanced over, smiling when her eyes collided with mine. "She's Arianne's best friend. If you break her heart—"

"It's not like that," I said, feeling myself grow tense. "I—"

"E has a serious case of heart eyes," Matteo said, but there was a strain to his words. "Isn't that right, cous?"

"Fuck off, cretino."

"So it's serious?"

I didn't like the way Nicco's brow furrowed. He doubted me. Probably hated the very idea of me anywhere near his wife's best friend. But at this point, I really didn't give a shit. Some crazy fucker had been within throwing distance of my woman, nothing Nicco did or didn't say would change the fact that I didn't plan on leaving her side unless it was to cut my enemy into tiny pieces.

"It's—"

"What are the three of you talking about?" The girls came over, placing our fresh coffees on the table.

"Nora and Enzo sitting in a tree, k-i-s—"

"If someone hands me my pistol, I can end this now," I joked.

"I think it's cute." Nora hovered since there was no room on the couch. I banded my arm around her waist and pulled her down on my lap. She smiled at me with so much emotion I felt winded.

Fuck, this girl.

*My* girl.

"So what do we know?" Nicco said.

"Fucker has a death wish," I mumbled, and Nora tensed above me.

"I won't ever pretend with you, Gattina," I whispered the words against the shell of her ear, unable to resist flicking my tongue over her skin. "This is me. I cuss too much, I enjoy making our enemies bleed, and I would die for any one of my family."

She turned into me, cupping my face. "I know who you are, Lorenzo Marchetti. I see you. I've always seen you."

"I really *really* want to fuck you right now."

Matteo snorted and I flipped him off again, while Nicco cleared his throat.

"Relax," I said, tucking her back into my chest. "I'm not going to do it right here."

"Tease," Nora quipped, and everyone laughed. Me included.

"This is nice," Ari said. "All we need now is to find Matteo a girl."

"You can leave me out of your little love fest." He got up and went to clean the breakfast plates. "I can handle my own sex life, thanks."

"You should try using it now and again then," I called after him. "Before it shrivels up and falls off."

Nora batted my chest. "Don't be so cruel."

I wrangled her into my arms and captured her lips in a hard kiss.

"Oh my God," Ari shrieked. "Look at them."

"Ugh." I grunted, dropping my face to Nora's shoulder. She chuckled, stroking her fingers through my hair. It felt so fucking good. My dick jumped to attention, desperate to be alone with her. Especially after last night, watching her come undone. It would have been easy to fuck her into oblivion, but I hadn't wanted to take advantage. The truth was, I needed a second to catch my breath, overwhelmed at all the new and fucking scary feelings I had wrecking me.

"I think it's cute."

I snorted. Cute and me weren't two words ever supposed to be in the same sentence. But that was Nora. Unapologetically honest. She didn't mince her words or hold back what she was feeling. She was the complete opposite of me in every way possible.

I gripped the back of her neck and touched my head to hers. "Why don't you give me and my cousins some space?"

"Anything you have to say, you can say it in front of us." Her brows knitted.

"I know and I'll tell you everything you need to know, I promise. But I really need to talk to them, and I would rather do it where I can keep my eye on you."

"Fine. Have you eaten?" she asked Arianne, who shook her head.

"We came straight here."

"Let's go make you some breakfast then." Nora stood up

and bent down to rake her fingers against my jaw, kissing me softly. "You get ten minutes."

"I only need five." I slapped her ass, relishing the little yelping sound she made. I'd have to see how many ways I could make her do that later, when we were alone and she was naked.

Nora led Arianne over to the kitchen and the two of them began getting ingredients out of the refrigerator.

"Matt's right, you've got it bad."

"Seriously, that's what you want to talk about?"

"Just take it slow. She's… and you're…"

"Yeah, I got the memo. She's too good for me." My eyes found her again. I'd never noticed it before—or I'd refused to notice it—but we were like magnets, always searching the other out across a room. Like right now, I felt the pull to her, the invisible thread tethering us.

"Tell me exactly what happened," Nicco's voice pulled me back to reality.

"The package was left outside the main entrance. Security picked it up and alerted Maurice. He called me. I watched the security footage and it's definitely him. He was kitted out in a black hoodie and he didn't make eye contact with the camera, but it was him."

"He didn't leave a note?"

"Nothing but Gino's bloodstained chain."

Nicco let out a thin breath.

"He's toying with me, Nic. Showing me he's got the upper hand. Who the fuck is this guy?"

"I don't know but we've got everyone working on this. You sent the package to the local PD?"

I nodded. "Maurice delivered it to our guys personally.

But they won't find any prints. This guy is a professional. He's a fucking ghost."

"We'll get him, I promise."

Something hit me. "Not that I don't appreciate you being here, because I do. But where's Uncle Toni?"

"He's sick." Nicco's expression fell.

Dread snaked through me. "How sick?"

"He says it's a bad case of heartburn, but—"

"You think it's something else."

His lips flattened into a grim line as he nodded. "Listen, I think Nora should move in with us until the worst is over. I can have Luis and Maurice on guard around the clock. The apartment has been modified with a state-of-the-art security system." He wasn't wrong. Their place was like Fort Knox.

But I didn't want Nora out of my sight, and somehow, I didn't think the invitation was for both of us.

"I already told Ari, I'm staying here," Nora called over.

"And I told her we should talk about it." Arianne pinned me with a hard look as if I had any sway over the choices Nora made.

"I can stay here with her," I said.

"Do you think that's a good idea?" Matteo reappeared.

"Where the fuck have you been?"

"To the bathroom, why?"

"Nora wants to stay here. I'm inclined to agree it's probably the safest option right now."

"He has a point, Nic," Matteo agreed. "There's security plus our guys, plus she has the friendly neighbor over the way who would jump in to defend her honor at any given chance."

A low growl rumbled in my chest, and Nicco shot me a strange look. "Do I need to be worried?" he asked.

"Not unless he comes knocking again to stir the pot."

I felt Nora staring at me and when I lifted my eyes to hers, she blushed. I was about two seconds away from telling everyone to get the hell out so I could make her blush all over, when Nicco's cell rang.

"Hello?" The color drained from his face. "Yeah, okay…. No, I understand. I'll be right there."

"What is it?" I asked, the second he hung up.

"It's my father," he exhaled a thin breath, "he collapsed."

Arianne rushed over to his side. "What happened?"

"I'm not sure yet. Genevieve said he was complaining all night of heartburn and this morning he just collapsed. They're on the way to the ER."

"Go," I said without hesitation. "We can handle this."

Nora ran her hand over my shoulder. "Enzo's right. Go be with him."

*Before it's too late.* I would never say the words, but I knew what losing Antonio would mean to Nicco. What it would mean for him.

For all of us.

"Okay, yeah. Fuck."

"Hey." Arianne pulled him into her arms, whispering softly, "We'll face it together. Always."

Nicco nodded. "Don't leave La Stella. Not until we know more. And be safe. All of you."

"We've got this. Go. And tell Uncle T we expect to see him up and busting balls soon." Matteo struggled to laugh, his face a picture of concern.

Arianne hugged Nora and we walked them to the door. Luis was waiting right outside with a somber expression on his face.

Fuck, this wasn't good. I scrubbed a hand down my face.

But then Nora was wrapping her arms around me and just for a second, everything felt okay again.

$$\sim$$

WE SPENT THE MORNING HANGING OUT AT NORA'S apartment. She did some studying while Matteo and I watched some gearhead show. It was an episode about restoring vintage Pontiacs, so I was pretty much in mindless TV heaven.

Nicco called to say Uncle Toni had suffered a heart attack, and he was in surgery. Not the phone call you wanted to ever get when the Family was being targeted by someone we couldn't get a hold on.

To say everyone was on edge was an understatement. But Nora took it in stride.

After an hour of studying, she came and sat with us. "Any word?" she asked, sliding her arm around my shoulder.

"Nothing." I planted a kiss on her cheek. "He's still in surgery."

"Surgery is good; it means they can fix him." She gave me a warm smile. "I was thinking, why don't we go out and get some fresh—"

"No." I barked. "No fucking way."

"Just hear me out." Her eyes narrowed with defiance. "We can all go, Maurice too. It's been a long morning and we're all getting a little stir crazy. It's the middle of the day, nothing is going to happen."

"I don't like it. Outside is an unknown factor. I can't control the surroundings. But in here, I can. I know exactly who is coming through that door." My eyes flicked over to the way in and out of her apartment.

"Okay," she let out a soft sigh, "it was just an idea."

I lifted her onto my lap and slid my arms around her waist. "I need to know you're safe, Gattina."

"I understand. But what if you don't find whoever is doing this?" She traced the line of my jaw with her fingers. "You can't keep me locked away in here forever. I have classes. I have a life, Enzo."

Fuck, she was right. But the thought of her stepping foot out of that door terrified me in a way I hadn't ever expected.

"Just give it some more time, please." I couldn't be worrying about her and Uncle Toni.

"Fine, a couple more days." Nora lowered her face to mine, sliding her lips against my mouth. I groaned, pulling her tighter. Matteo grumbled something about needing to check in with Maurice and left us to it.

"Maybe we should stop." She giggled, nudging her nose gently against mine.

I dived back in, kissing her hard. "He'll live. Besides, I've forgotten how good your pussy feels choking my dick."

"Enzo." She batted my chest, my name a breathless sigh on her lips. "You can't say stuff like that to me now I'm your —" Her eyes went wide with panic. "I didn't mean—"

"You're mine, Gattina. Label it, don't label it," I shrugged, "doesn't matter. I own your ass now and there isn't a single thing you can do about it."

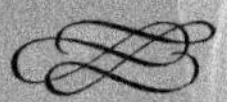

# CHAPTER 26

NORA

"Any news?" I asked Enzo as I made us lunch.

"He's out of surgery, thank fuck." He got up and made his way over to me, snagging me around the waist and pulling me back against his chest.

"Nicco must be going out of his mind." I glanced back at him.

"He'll pull through. Uncle T is made of strong stuff."

"And if he doesn't?" Enzo went rigid and I brushed my nose over his jaw. "Sorry, that was insensitive. I'm sure he'll be fine."

"He has to be, Gattina. Nicco isn't ready to become the boss."

I still couldn't believe Enzo's one-eighty. Not that I was complaining. I loved this side of him. Protective and possessive, it was everything I'd wanted. Everything I'd hoped for.

But there was still a little voice in the back of my mind whispering that Enzo was here out of obligation and guilt.

I didn't want to overanalyze, but I couldn't help it. If I'd have never stayed over at Luca's, and if the package had never been left outside La Stella, would I be here now, wrapped in Enzo's arms?

I liked to think we would have found our way back to one another eventually, but a small part of me knew circumstances played a helping hand in things.

"What is it?" Enzo whispered against my neck, his warm breath and the gentle strum of his fingers against my stomach made all my doubts disappear.

"I'm just thinking about Nicco."

"He'll be okay. Ari is with him; she'll keep him sane."

"How long do you think we'll have to stay here for?" I asked him, stirring the pan of boiling pasta.

"Until I know you're one-hundred percent safe."

"Nothing is ever certain," I said.

He stiffened again. "Yeah, well, until this fucker is in the ground, I want you where I can keep you safe."

A thrill went through me at his words. But for as much as I was enjoying having him all to myself, I didn't like the idea of hiding away forever.

I had classes. I had a life to get back to.

My cell vibrated and I slid it across the counter to read the incoming message.

"Is that—"

I quickly shielded it from Enzo, but it was too late.

"He's texting you?" Anger coated his words.

"He just wants to know I'm okay."

"I bet he does," Enzo grumbled, and I turned in his arms.

"Luca is… was a friend. He isn't just going to disappear because we're… doing this."

"It's cute you still can't say it." A slow smirk spread over Enzo's lips.

"No labels, remember?" If I labelled it, it would be real, and if it was real, it would be more painful if it all went wrong.

His eyes darkened as he dropped his head to mine. "I don't know how else to say it, Gattina, but you're mine. I know I don't deserve you. Fuck, I know that. But I have never felt more scared than I did when Maurice called."

Emotion balled in my throat as he pierced me with his icy-blue gaze. "Enzo, I—"

The blare of his cell cut through the room.

"You should get that," I said with a resigned sigh. "It could be Nicco."

He hesitated for a second then pulled away to dig out his cell phone.

"Yeah… thank fuck. Okay, she's fine… yeah, got it. Tell him I'm glad he's okay." He hung up and let out a long, steady breath. "Uncle Toni is okay, he's awake."

"That's great news." I launched myself at him, hugging him tight.

"Fuck, Gattina," he whispered. "I was scared there for a minute that he wasn't going to make it."

"It's okay." My hands slid to his face as I brushed my lips over his. "Everything is going to be okay."

I only hoped it was the truth.

∽

"GOD, ENZO, MORE," I BREATHED AS HIS TONGUE LAPPED AT MY core, taking me higher and higher.

"You taste so fucking good." He speared me with two fingers inside, curling them deep. My fingers tugged his hair, holding him in place as I arched into his mouth, desperate for more.

"My kitty is greedy," he purred, the words vibrating through me, tiny shocks of pleasure drenching my veins.

My 'tea Rex' t-shirt was bunched around my shoulders, giving Enzo the perfect opportunity to tease my breasts. His big hand plucked and squeezed, marking my flesh like he'd already marked my heart.

"Fuck, you taste good. I can't get enough."

His dirty words sent my orgasm crashing over me as I cried his name into the night.

He licked me clean, moaning with appreciation before rocking back on his haunches and gazing down at me.

"My turn?" I smirked, ready to sit up and wrap my lips around his monster dick. But his wicked grin turned my insides to molten lava.

"I'm not done with you yet." He grabbed my hips and flipped me onto my stomach, dragging my ass into the air, barely giving me time to catch my breath before his mouth latched onto me again, lapping at me like a man starved.

My body trembled, my knees buckling, but then he was there, the steel barbell through the tip of his dick brushing my sensitive, swollen skin.

"Fuck," I breathed, burying my head into the pillow.

"You're about to be fucked." His dark chuckle sent chills racing through me.

Enzo teased me a couple more times, sliding himself through my wetness and nudging my clit. But on the third time, he slammed inside me, making my body jolt forward. I pressed my hands into the mattress, steadying myself.

"Fuck, yeah, Gattina. Mi fai impazzire."

"More," I cried, lost to the sensations he stirred inside me.

"Your wish is my command." Enzo gave me everything, rocking into me over and over as his hands held my hips like he couldn't get enough. I'd have bruise marks tomorrow, but I didn't care. All I cared about was him using my body… *loving* my body in the way only he could. Because I was totally gone for this guy. Head over heels in lust with the guy with ice around his heart and hatred in his soul.

I didn't think it was possible to fall anymore, until he banded his arm around my waist and pulled me up, my back to his front. His hand slid to my throat and his lips went to my shoulder, kissing and sucking the damp skin there as he slowed his pace.

"Feel me, Gattina," he rasped. "Feel what you do to me."

"Enzo…" I panted, my body unraveling around him.

"Nothing… *nothing* will ever feel as good as this." His confession splintered me apart. "Yeah, that's it, Nora. Choke my dick… *fuck*." Enzo spilled inside of me, his teeth latching into my flesh as he broke the skin, soothing the sting with his tongue.

"Mine," he whispered. "Il mio."

The word slammed into me with renewed clarity.

I wasn't in lust with this complicated man.

I was head over heels in love with him.

"Nora?" He tilted my face to his and kissed me. "Is something wrong?"

"No." My lips curved with uncertainty as emotion swelled inside me. "Everything is perfect."

We cleaned up and climbed in bed. Enzo immediately

dragged me into the curve of his body. "We should get some sleep."

We didn't know what tomorrow would bring. Nobody did. But Antonio was awake, Enzo was here with me, and there had been no more threats. Still, I knew it was only the calm before the storm. But I truly felt like we could face what was coming as long as we stood together.

So when Enzo's cell phone started ringing again, fear trickled down my spine.

"Yeah?" He barked, keeping his arm wrapped firmly around my body. "Fuck, okay. Yeah, I'm coming."

"What is it?" My voice cracked the second he hung up.

"I need to go." He gently released me, climbed out of bed and started pulling on his clothes. "There's been another break-in."

"Where?"

"The VCTI."

"What?" I shot up and climbed out of bed. "But that doesn't make any sense. The VCTI isn't a Marchetti business." It was the center where Arianne volunteered. I'd helped out there a couple of times too.

"Nicco made a large donation to the center for her wedding present."

"Crap." Enzo was right. Arianne had been so excited. There was a press release and everything.

"But the VCTI helps people," I said, still unable to process what was happening. "Why would anyone—"

Enzo's expression darkened. "That's why I need to go, Gattina. This is on me. I should be there."

"But—"

Enzo cupped the back of my neck and smashed his lips to mine. It was a kiss to end all other kisses, a kiss that felt a lot like goodbye… but I refused to believe that. We were in a good place, we were.

"Promise me you'll come back to me," I said, winding my fingers into his t-shirt, my eyes fluttering closed with the weight of my words.

He tilted my face, staring intently at me. "I give you my word." Enzo kissed me again, softer this time, as if he was tracing the shape of my mouth and imprinting it to memory. "Come with me." He guided me into the living room and over to the couch as his fingers flew over his cell phone.

Seconds later, there was a knock at the door and Enzo let Maurice inside.

"You stay right here with her. Move another guy to this floor, but you stay right here until I get back."

"You have my word, Mr. Marchetti."

Enzo nodded. "I'll be back, I promise."

"Be safe." Emotion rushed up my throat, making my eyes sting. I didn't want him to go. I didn't want him to be in harm's way. And I didn't want him to have to hurt anyone, even if they deserved it. But this was what it meant to love a mafioso, to stand by their side. If I wanted to be with Enzo, I had to accept that.

He disappeared into the bedroom to retrieve his weapons, and I watched with strange fascination as he added them to his person. The deadly looking knife strapped to his ankle, a pistol holstered to his chest, and brass knuckles stuffed inside his jacket.

He was an armed soldier and it wasn't supposed to be such a turn on, but I couldn't help the heat pooling in my stomach at the sight of him.

"Promise me that no matter what happens you won't

leave this room unless Maurice says it is safe for you to do so."

"I-I promise." I gulped over the lump in my throat.

Another sharp nod and Enzo slipped out of my apartment leaving the room cold...

And my heart empty.

"Anything?" I asked for the hundredth time. Maurice shook his head. "It has only been thirty minutes."

Really?

It felt longer.

It felt like forever.

I hugged myself tighter, staring at the clock of the wall, willing it to move.

It was going to be a long night.

The vibration of my cell phone startled me from my reverie, and relief spread through me as I grabbed it off the coffee table hoping to see Enzo's name.

But it wasn't Enzo at all.

I know this is probably not a good time... but I'm kind of **in a bind and I don't have anyone else to call...**

"Nora?" Maurice asked and I held up my finger, calling Luca's number.

"Luca, what is it? What's wrong?"

"I... uh..." he sounded a little breathless. "So funny story, I decided to take a shower after drinking my body weight in tequila and I tripped—"

"Oh my God, are you okay?"

"I'll live but my face took the brunt and I have a pretty gruesome cut on my forehead… and I'm not very good with blood…" he trailed off.

"Luca?" I shrieked. "Okay, hold on… I'll—"

"Don't even think about it," Maurice shot up.

Crap. Yeah. Enzo would lose it if he knew I'd stepped foot out of the apartment, even if it was only to go across the hall.

"I'm going to send you help, okay? Maurice, he'll—"

"Need you," he breathed, and I didn't like how out of it he sounded.

"Maurice, go to Luca's, now!"

"Miss Ab—Nora, I had strict orders to stay—"

"I know, which is why I'm asking you to go and check on him." I gave him a pointed look. "If you don't, I will." Maurice hesitated and I let out an exasperated breath. "He's hurt, Maurice. Please just go over there and check on him. I'll lock the door behind you, I swear."

"Fine." He got up and moved to the door. "I'm going to radio downstairs and tell security you're here alone."

"Maurice, I'm not alone, you'll be right across the hall."

"Just stay put." From the furrow of his brows, I knew he wasn't happy about leaving me. But I couldn't just ignore Luca's plea for help. He slipped out of the door and I went and locked it.

What I really wanted was to check in with Enzo and make sure he was okay, but I didn't want to appear clingy.

To distract myself, I made myself a mug of hot cocoa with marshmallows. Despite the way I'd left things with Luca, I really did hope he was okay. I knew he probably felt like I'd led him on, and I guess I had. But I hadn't done it out of malicious intent. Luca was a good guy. He was easy to be around and he made me smile. But he didn't make my heart beat hard the way Enzo did.

A smile played on my lips just thinking about how over-protective and growly Enzo had been today. Some girls would have hated his alpha routine, but I loved it.

By the time I'd finished my hot cocoa I was growing increasingly worried about Luca. Maurice had been gone almost fifteen minutes.

I snatched up my cell phone and called Maurice, but it rang out.

God. What if it was worse than I thought? What if Luca needed medical attention?

I decided to call Luca. It rang out but then right before I hung up, he answered. "Nora?"

"Hey, are you okay?"

"I'm a little embarrassed, but yeah, Maurice fixed me up."

"He's still there?"

"No, he left a couple minutes ago. He isn't back with you?"

"No." Fear slithered up my spine as I went to the peephole and pressed my face to it. "I can't see him."

"Well, he can't have gone far. He was just right here."

"I'm going to call him again. I'll call you back in a second."

I dialed Maurice's number, but he didn't pick up. My heart raced as I mentally went through possibilities. He wouldn't have just up and left me. Not when Enzo had given me strict orders to stay put…

Maybe there was an imminent threat and he'd gone downstairs to deal with it.

Quickly, I called Luca back.

"Anything?" he asked.

"No, but I don't think it's safe here."

"For real? What—"

"I can't explain everything right now. I need to call Enzo."

"He's gone?"

"He had to… he went to deal with something."

"What have you gotten yourself into, Nora?" He trailed off.

"Please, don't. I didn't call to argue with you. I just want to find out where Maurice is."

"Let me help."

Chewing my bottom lip, I weighed up my options. Enzo was at least a twenty-minute ride away across town. Even if he picked up, he couldn't get here straight away. Calling the police wasn't an option, and Nicco was at the hospital with his dad.

"Fine," I said, making a snap decision.

"I'll come to you," he said.

"No, I'll come to you. Then we can figure out what to do." Maurice would probably appear by then, with an explanation for his sudden disappearance.

Changing into some lounge pants and a MU hoodie, I grabbed my keys and cell and made my way across to Luca's apartment.

The door was already open, so I pushed it open and called out, "Luca?" My heart raced in my chest as I slipped inside. "Lu—"

"Hey." He appeared, looking a little flushed.

"Are you okay?"

"I'm fine now. Well, apart from this." He motioned to his forehead. There was a small dressing above his brow.

"You're lucky," I said around a tentative smile. But Luca didn't return it, the air cooling around us.

"Did you call Enzo?" he asked, thinly.

"Not yet. But I should call him." I pulled out my cell phone, but something rang out in the apartment.

"Fuck," Luca muttered under his breath.

"Is something wrong?" I glanced around, drawn to the sound. There was something familiar about it. Something I couldn't quite—

"Is that Maurice's cell phone?" I asked, my blood turning to ice as I crossed Luca's apartment. "What the hell? *Maurice!*" I yelled.

He was crumpled up on the floor of Luca's bedroom floor, blood pouring from a thick gash in his head.

"What did you do?" I spun to face Luca, but he grabbed me from behind, yanking me backward. "What the hell—"

"I'm sorry, Nora." He jabbed me with something sharp. "I'm so fucking sorry." His voice was drowned out by the darkness consuming me.

"No," I screamed, but the words got stuck in my throat. *No!*

# CHAPTER 27

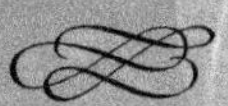

ENZO

Something was wrong. Maurice wasn't answering and I couldn't get hold of Nora.

I'd texted and called to reassure her I was okay, but that it was taking longer than planned at the VCTI because somebody had called the police, and they'd sent a rookie.

A rookie who wasn't on our payroll. So me and Matteo had to lie low while they did their thing.

Luckily for us, the center manager was a personal friend of Arianne's and Nicco's and had the foresight to leave out any mention of the package left for me. It was a bloodstained knife that I knew was coated in Gino's blood.

"Anything?" Matteo asked me as I checked my cell again.

"Nothing."

"Nora is probably sleeping," he said.

"Yeah." But it didn't explain why Maurice wasn't returning my calls.

Impatient, I called Alexi instead. But it only rang out.

"What the fuck is happening over there?"

"Try La Stella security." Matteo pulled out his cell and started dialing. "Fuck, it's ringing out."

"I gotta—"

"Yeah, go. I'll handle things here. Just be careful yeah?"

But that was like telling a fighter to take it easy in the ring. Trepidation coursed through me. If Nora was—

No, everything was fine.

It had to be.

The nervous energy zipping through me didn't abate though, as I floored my GTO back toward University Hill.

The second my car rolled to a stop outside the building, I knew what I hadn't wanted to believe.

I pulled out my cell and called Nicco.

"Enzo, what is it?" Sleep thickened his words.

"I'm sorry to call you, cous, but I need you, Nic. I need you at La Stella."

"Shit, yeah, okay. Talk me through what's happened."

Shouldering the door, I slipped inside. I should have passed at least two security guards by now. "Security is gone. I can't reach Maurice or Nora."

"Fuck," he breathed. "Okay, me and Luis are on our way with backup."

Icy cold fear trickled in my veins as I reached Nora's floor. It was silent save for the gentle hum of the strip lighting overhead. I crept close to Nora's apartment, silently praying that she was still inside, sleeping.

I gently tapped my knuckles against the door, waiting. "Come on, Gattina. Where the fuck are you?" I murmured to myself. Scrolling to her name, I hit call, hoping to hear it ring.

Nothing.

Fuck.

I dialed Maurice again. At first, it just rang out. But then I heard it, the faint familiar music of his ringtone. Moving closer to Luca's apartment, anger like I'd never known it swelled inside me.

They were at Bianco's?

What the fuck were they doing over there?

I knocked loudly, my body trembling with fury. If Luca had touched her, touched my Nora, I wouldn't be held responsible for my actions.

But no one answered.

"Yo, asshole, open up," I yelled, uncaring if I woke up the whole building. All kinds of scenarios ran through my head, but I needed to try and stay cool. "Luca!" I banged again. "Fuck this."

I pulled out my knife and wedged in into the door jamb, leveraging the door open enough to crash through the damn thing.

The apartment was empty. But I knew I'd heard Maurice's ringtone. Quickly, I dialed his number again and sure enough the noise rang out. I followed it through the apartment to a closed door.

I didn't want to open it, didn't want this nightmare to be real. Reaching for the handle, I slowly pushed it open. Maurice was laying there with a halo of dark-red blood surrounding his head.

"Fuck," I growled, dropping to my knees to check for his pulse.

He was unconscious, but I detected a faint pulse. Maurice needed medical attention and he needed it now, so I knew I had no choice but to call it in.

*"Fuck!"* I stood up and dragged a hand down my face, trying to figure out what the fuck to do. Luca was gone... Nora too. But I think I'd known the second I couldn't get a hold of her that something bad had happened.

The VCTI wasn't just another break-in, it was a diversion...

But Luca?

It didn't make any sense.

I sent an SOS message to Nicco and Matteo. They would both understand what it meant. If I didn't want another soldier to die right in front of me, I had to call nine-one-one. We'd have to worry about the consequences later.

I called it in, keeping the details as vague as possible. I needed to try to piece together what had happened here.

I needed to find Nora.

*Fuck. Nora...*

Pain ripped through me, and I staggered back against the wall. If she was hurt again... or worse...

I knew this could happen. I fucking knew and I still left her.

What the fuck was I thinking?

If anything happened to her...

I would never forgive myself.

NICCO AND MATTEO ARRIVED JUST AS THE EMTS WERE wheeling Maurice out of Luca's apartment.

"Fuck," Matteo breathed, his expression clouded with concern. "Is he going to be okay?"

"He's lost a lot of blood," I said, grimly.

"Mr. Marchetti," Philippi Dante, one of our friends from

the local PD approached us. "Do I need to be worried?" he asked quietly.

"We'll handle it."

"I already told them what I know," I said, shooting Dante a warning look.

"I think we've got everything for now. But I won't be able to bury it for long." He glanced around the room before leaning in. "You're going to have to give me something."

"Dante," Nicco said, "walk with me."

The two of them followed the EMTs out of the apartment deep in discussion, and I knew my cousin was probably trying to avoid a scene.

"What do we know?" Matteo asked the second they were gone.

"The security footage was cut about three hours ago. Right after I left."

"So what the hell was that at the VCTI?"

"A decoy."

"Fuck." He scrubbed his jaw. "And we think Luca took her? But he was vetted, man. I double checked his file myself."

"You did?" I jerked back. I knew he'd asked Maurice, but I didn't know he'd pulled Luca's file.

"Figured we should know who was hanging around your woman."

The words made my chest tighten.

"We'll get her back, Enzo," he said, laying a hand on my shoulder. "And our guys?"

"No sign of them."

"No way Bianco did this without help," Matteo said the words I'd been pondering ever since stepping foot into his apartment and finding Maurice bleeding out.

"I should have stayed away," I gritted out, fists clenched painfully at my sides. "I should have fucking stayed away from her."

"Come on, cous, don't do this. You couldn't have known Luca was involved. None of us could."

Before I could stop myself, my fist shot out and collided with the wall. Pain ripped through my knuckles, zipping up my wrist but I welcomed it. I'd welcome a whole lot more than that if it meant getting Nora back in one piece.

*I'm sorry, Gattina. I'm so fucking sorry.*

"Better?"

"No," I grunted. "But I will be when we find this mother-fucker and end him."

"I think we've got to assume he isn't working alone. He had to get Nora and our guys out of here somehow." His brows crinkled but then his eyes widened. "We checked La Stella's security feed, but we didn't check La Luna."

"Shit, you're right." La Luna was Roberto's second building in University Hill, the one across the street with line of sight to its sister building.

Matteo pulled out his cell. "Tristan, yeah, sorry to call so late… We need a favor. Can you call security over at La Luna and tell them we're gonna need to take a look at their security feeds for the last two hours." He gave me a sharp nod. "Appreciate it, man. And yeah, we will."

"He's going to hook us up."

"What's that?" Nicco came back inside, alone this time.

"Tristan is going to call the security guys over at La Luna and have them pull the security footage of the last two hours. Whoever helped Luca had to have a vehicle which means we should be able to see something."

He nodded, his eyes narrowing at me. "You good?"

"What do you think?"

"We'll get her back."

"We have to." Because anything else wasn't an option.

"We will. Nora isn't the target—"

"No, she's the fucking bait." I stormed out of there, needing air.

Crashing through the main doors, I pulled out a smoke, and waited for my cousins to join me, knowing they would be right behind me.

Sure enough, a minute later, they spilled out onto the quiet sidewalk.

"Should we call my dad?" Matteo asked. After my father, Uncle Michele stepped up as Antonio's second. So with Uncle Toni out of action in the hospital, all decisions were supposed to go through Uncle Michele. But time was against us.

"You can update him, but we do this with or without him. I'm not waiting." The words vibrated deep in the pit of my stomach. "That fucker has Nora, he has my woman."

And I intended on her getting her back, consequences be damned.

We walked the short distance to La Luna in thick silence. One of Roberto's guys met us at the door.

"Mr. Capizola called ahead. Please, follow me."

"Have you pulled the footage?"

"We have, and you'll want to see this." He guided us to the security office.

Another guy looked up from the screen. "A black van left the underground parking lot about forty-five minutes ago. Drove right on out. Looked to be in a rush too."

"Fuck." My fist slammed against the table, making the computers screens rattle and shake.

"Relax." Nicco pulled me back, moving around me to get a closer look. He pulled out his phone and scrolled through his contacts. "Tommy, sorry for the late-night call. I need you to run some plates for us. I suspect they're fake or cloned but see what you can find." He started reeling off the license plates. When he was done, he hung up. "Where do you lose them?"

"Right here." The guy pointed to one of the grids on the screen. "The police department might be able to track him on their cameras though."

"Thanks, we appreciate it." Nicco went to walk away but I stalled closer to the monitor.

"Wait. When did we see the van arrive?"

"We didn't run the footage that far back, but we can look."

"Do it."

"What are you thinking?" Nicco asked me.

"Something still doesn't add up." We'd found nothing. Not even a speck of blood. It was as if they were never there. "We've all met Bianco. He might be hiding something but he's not capable of this. He's just the puppet."

I'd met the guy toying with us, been right up close and personal with him. It definitely wasn't Luca, so what was the connection?

"He's working with whoever is coming after us," Nicco said.

"That's my bet." I nodded, my jaw working overtime as I tried to piece together the puzzle. We were still missing something.

"Did Luca—Stop," I yelled, my eyes fixating on Luca and a couple of guys entering the building. "When was that?"

"Yesterday afternoon. A little after one." My eyes

narrowed, watching as security stopped them to interrogate Luca about his friends.

"Wait, freeze it and zoom in. Motherfuck—"

"That's Nate and Isaac, Luca's friends," Matteo cut me off. "We met them the other night at the bar."

The ground went from under me. "That's the guy." I jabbed my finger at the grainy image.

"Who, Isaac? No way! We both met him, he seemed legit."

"I'm telling you, that's the fucking guy. Fuck." I blew out a steady breath. "I need to know everything you know about that guy, stat." Adrenaline pumped through me, blood roaring in my eyes. I was staring right at him. The guy responsible for killing Gino, the guy who had left the package for me at La Stella and the VCTI. The guy I knew without doubt had taken Nora.

"I don't know anything about him," Matteo said around a tight expression. "His friend Nate hooked up with Nora's friend Lucii."

"Arianne knows her." Nicco pulled his cell out to call his wife. It was the middle of the night, but I had no doubt that Arianne would be glued to her phone waiting for any word from Nicco.

He disappeared out of the room. "I can't believe it. We were right there at the club with him. He seemed… normal."

"This isn't on you, Matt. The fucker is toying with us." It was a game. Some sick, twisted game.

Just then, Nicco came back into the room. "I've got Lucii's name. Tommy is going to do his thing and dig up her number."

"Good, that's good." Matteo shot me a concerned look.

"I'm okay." I lied. Anger had infiltrated every inch of me,

coursing through my veins like wildfire. But it wasn't only anger I felt. The bitter sting of regret coiled around my heart.

This was all my fault.

No one could take that away from me.

We left La Luna and walked the short distance back to La Stella, piling into Matteo's truck.

"We need that number," I ground out, my leg bouncing uncontrollably.

"Tommy will come through," Nicco said.

"He'd better."

Because we had nothing else to go on. No clues. No leads. Just a name and a face.

And the hope that my cousins were right—that Nora wasn't the endgame.

I was.

# CHAPTER 28

NORA

My eyes flickered open to faulty strip lighting. It made it difficult to focus, the constant flicker. Dim then glare. Dim then glare. A brass band beat loudly in my skull, making me groan in agony.

Where the hell was I?

And why couldn't I move?

Panic raced up my spine as I slowly found my senses. I couldn't move because my hands were bound behind my back and my ankles bound together, secured to the chair I was seated on.

"What the—" The icy fingers of fear wrapped around my throat, stealing the words. "Hello," I managed to choke out. "Someone help me." Straining against the restraints, another wave of panic crashed over me.

This wasn't happening, not again.

*Breathe*, I silently urged myself, *just breathe*. Somehow, I managed to calm myself, trying to focus on the things I could control, like my bodily functions. I might have been bound, but I still had my sight and hearing and my sense of smell. A groan sounded over to my right and my eyes strained against the poor lighting.

"Luca?" I gasped. He was slumped in the corner, hands bound in front of his body. "Luca, can you hear me?"

"N-Nora?" His eyes were heavy-lidded. "I'm sorry… so fucking… sorry." He started to fall out of consciousness.

"Luca, stay with me, please… stay with me."

"Hurts… it hurts." His eyes fluttered open.

"What happened?"

The last thing I remembered was Luca jabbing me with a needle… and Maurice—

"Oh God," my voice cracked, "what did you do?"

"I had no choice… he… he—"

"Well, well, you're awake." A figure stepped into the room and confusion welled inside me.

"Isaac?" My eyes grew to saucers.

"Surprise!" He smirked deviously.

"But… I-I don't understand…"

"You're not supposed to, baby. This is between me and your boyfriend."

"My—*what?*"

It didn't make sense. Isaac was Luca's friend. He wasn't the guy doing this.

He couldn't be.

"You… why?"

"Why?" He stalked toward me, crouching to my eye level. "Now there's the million-dollar question, isn't it?" Reaching out, he ran his knuckles down my cheek. Luca groaned to my right, but I didn't look over at him.

"It was all you?"

"The Family's enforcer, the break-ins, and my personal favorite, the VCTI. I've been a busy guy."

"But why?"

"Nah-ah, baby." He beeped my nose. "We'll get to that when your boyfriend arrives. Assuming he figures it out." Isaac winked at me, but my head was too busy swimming with confusion.

What the hell was happening?

Isaac wasn't the guy coming after the Marchetti, he couldn't be. He was just a regular guy who worked out at the same gym as Luca.

Except he wasn't.

Because I was tied to a chair and Luca was on the floor, slumped against the wall and barely conscious.

"What do you want?" I shrieked, fear drenching my words. My hands and feet strained against their bindings, but it was futile. They were too tight, the cable ties cutting into my skin.

"Please, just let us go."

"Aww, now I know you're not one of those girls... a damsel in distress. From what I've seen you like it rough."

Bile crawled up my throat and I swallowed hard, breathing through my nose. He'd been watching me... watching me with Enzo.

Who the hell was this guy?

"Do you like cold-blooded killers, baby?" He pulled a knife out from behind his back. "Do you like a little pain?"

My breath caught in my throat as he pushed the tip of the blade against my clavicle. Featherlight, Isaac traced the knife over my skin, following the hollow of my collarbone.

"Please," it was a ragged plea as I tried not to move even a millimeter.

"How I'd love to slice you open and see what you're really made of." There was a wicked glint in his eye, an honesty that made my stomach wash with fear. "But the fun is only just getting started."

A chill ran down my spine at the threat in his voice.

"Enzo won't let you get away with this," I spat, letting my emotions get the better of me.

"Oh, baby," he flashed me a wolfish grin, before standing, "I'm counting on it."

ISAAC LEFT US AFTER THAT. LEFT US COLD AND ALONE AND scared. Luca was in and out of consciousness. I couldn't see any blood or contusions, but the flickering strip lighting made it difficult to see right into the darkened corners of the room.

"Luca, are you awake?" I whispered, every muscle in my body heavy and sore. I had no idea how long we'd been here. It could have been a couple of hours, it could have been an entire day. Time was nothing. But for every minute that passed, my hope faded.

What if Enzo didn't come?

What if he and his family couldn't find us?

Couldn't find me.

*What if he did?*

I wasn't foolish, I knew this would only affirm Enzo's resistance to be with me. He would take one look at me tied to this chair, dehydrated and confused, and vow to never put me in this situation again.

So as much as I wanted him to appear in the doorway, to come and save us, part of me—the naïve part of me that was just a girl in love with a guy—didn't want it to be him. Because I knew what it meant…

And I knew it was the end of us before we'd even really gotten started.

Emotion rushed up my throat, stinging the backs of my eyes. I was a good person, or at least, I tried to be. I took my vitamins and gave to charity and helped old ladies across the street. I tried to treat people the way I hoped to be treated, kind and with compassion. I often saw past people's walls and didn't judge someone for the lifestyle they chose. But I knew that bad things happened to good people all the time. So even though I was scared and hurting, I didn't have the capacity to blame Enzo or his family for this. The same way I hadn't blamed Nicco and Arianne when Scott Fascini took me.

A strangled laugh spilled from my lips. What were the chances that I would find myself here again? I guess when you kept company with the mafia, anything was possible.

I sucked in a shaky breath. Enzo would find us, he would. I could imagine him now, on a rampage through Verona, burning buildings to the ground and ploughing through anyone who dared to stand in his way. His anger was always there, under the surface, only made worse since his father's death.

God. I'd never gotten the chance to tell him how sorry I was for what he'd had to do. I hadn't wanted him to pull away, not when he was finally letting me in, so I'd kept his secret. I would *always* keep his secret if it meant protecting what we shared. But one day, I'd hoped he would tell me. I'd hoped he would share with me his secrets and pain.

The lights flickered overhead, plunging the room once more into total darkness.

"Luca?" I called, fear sitting heavy in the pit of my stomach. "Luca?"

"H-here…" It was a faint groan. "I'm here."

His voice, although pained, settled something inside me. I knew Luca had a hand in taking me, but I didn't want him to die. I wanted him to survive this thing and then explain to me what the hell had happened.

"Hold on," I croaked, my throat dry and sore. "You have to hold on. Enzo will come."

But as I said the words, all I could think was, he was walking right into a trap.

TIME LOST ALL MEANING. AT SOME POINT, LUCA HAD SLIPPED under and hadn't resurfaced. Silent tears rolled down my cheeks. If he didn't get medical help soon, he might never wake up.

"Isaac," I yelled. "ISAAC!"

He appeared in the door like the reaper sent to claim my soul. But he didn't look concerned, he looked… excited.

"Showtime," he rasped, stalking toward me with a knife. He grabbed my hands and slid right through the third cable tie binding the tie around each wrist. Then he worked on setting my ankles free.

"Try anything and I'll gut you like a fish," he snarled. "Your boyfriend is here now, so it makes no difference to me whether you make it out of this alive or in a body bag."

An icy shudder rolled through me. This wasn't the Isaac I'd met at the bar. That guy was cool and aloof, but he wasn't cruel. But then, I remembered I had felt something a little off about him. As if he watched me a little too closely. Honestly, I'd just thought he wanted me.

The idea seemed preposterous now, seeing as he was dragging me down a long hall with a seven-inch blade pressed to the small of my back.

He yanked me into another room, one with windows. Sunlight poured inside, tinged pinkish orange. Sunset. Jesus. I'd been here hours. Enzo would be going out of his mind.

We waited in silence. Isaac was skittish, his eyes darting to and from the window as he kept his knife at my back and his other hand on my shoulder. Then the door in front of me opened and my heart lurched into my throat.

Enzo.

His eyes were wild, anger burning in his icy depths. His jaw was clenched painfully tight and his fists pressed at his sides. He looked murderous. But when his eyes shifted to mine, his whole expression softened.

He was here.

Enzo had come for me.

"Took you long enough," Isaac spat the words, slowly inching us back.

Enzo stepped forward and Isaac whipped the knife around my front, pressing it against my throat. "I wouldn't do that if I were you."

Enzo's hands shot up as he stalled. "This isn't about Nora. It's about you and me, Vinnie."

"Oooh, you're good." He chuckled darkly. "You're really fucking good. How'd you find out?"

"One of our guys is a dab hand at uncovering secrets."

"Tommy Gabini? Should have guessed. He said he was one of the best."

"Who said?" Enzo frowned and I knew my expression matched his. They weren't making any sense.

"Oh, come on, Lorenzo. Surely, you've figured it out by now. Or did the infamous Tommy Gabini fail to uncover the biggest secret of all?"

Enzo started inching closer again, but Isaac moved us deeper into the room. They were dancing around each other with me right in the middle, the sharp edge of the blade so close to my skin I could feel the coolness of it.

I swallowed hard. Enzo caught the small movement, and his eyes went to mine. Dark eyes full of regret and apology. I wanted to tell him to stop, to reassure him that he didn't have to carry this burden alone. But I couldn't speak. I could barely breathe for fear of my skin slicing open against the knife's edge.

My body trembled violently.

"She's shaking," Isaac said. "Trembling like an animal about to meet its bloody end. Do you think he felt it too? The claws of death coming to reap his soul?"

"Vincenzo Marchetti was a traitor and a murderer."

I was still missing something. Something Enzo had apparently figured out.

Isaac wasn't called Isaac at all. His name was Vinnie.

Vinnie.

*Vinnie.*

Vincenzo…

No.

*No!*

It wasn't possible… and yet…

"You're wrong, *brother*. Our father was a great man who deserved so much more than being Antonio's right-hand man. Vincenzo had the stomach to get the job done. He—"

"What the fuck did you just say?" The blood had completely drained from Enzo's face.

"You heard me, Lorenzo. Guess you weren't the apple of your father's eye, after all."

Oh God.

Realization flickered across Enzo's face.

A brother.

He had a brother.

A brother Vincenzo had kept from him, kept from everyone if this family reunion was anything to go by.

*Oh, Enzo.*

"You're lying". Enzo's voice shook with anger.

"Am I? Our father told me all about you, brother. All that rage inside you, the blood thirst, the desire to drown in darkness. He had high, high hopes for you… but like always, you were a bitter disappointment." The temperature cooled in the room as the two brothers faced off against each other.

"And then, you killed him. You chose Antonio, the Family, over your own flesh and blood, you fucking piece of shit."

"What do you want, Vinnie? You want vengeance, is that it? You want your pound of flesh? Then come and get it. I'm right here." Enzo opened his arms to the side, goading my captor.

"You think I want to kill you?" His dark laughter snaked through me, coiled around my heart like barbed wire. "I don't want to kill you… yet. First, I want you to watch as I destroy the thing you love most in the world."

My blood turned to ice at his words, but I couldn't move, I couldn't do anything.

"I'm going to ruin her and you're going to stand here and watch."

"Touch her and I'll—"

"You'll what? Kill me. I'd like to see you try while I have a knife pressed to your girlfriend's throat."

Tears streamed down my face. I wanted to be strong. I wanted to be the kind of woman who laughed in the face of danger. But the reality was, my world was splintering apart right in front of me.

I wanted to live. I wanted to graduate college and decide what to do with my life, maybe travel before settling down. I wanted to get married, a big over the top wedding with all my friends and family, and then I wanted a life with the guy I loved more than anything.

I wanted that… I wanted it so much.

But Vinnie had taken that from me. The second he'd made Luca kidnap me, he'd ruined my future. Because I knew Enzo, and I knew he wouldn't ever forgive himself for this.

My eyes settled on his rugged face. He couldn't even meet my eyes, focused solely on his psychopathic brother.

"This is between me and you, just let her go."

"And give up the opportunity to destroy your world the way you destroyed mine? Our father was everything to me… *everything* and you took him from me."

"She isn't anyone to me," Enzo said with so much sincerity my heart cracked wide open. "She's just good pussy, that's all."

"Ohhh, hear that, baby." Vinnie pressed his mouth to my ear. "He's good. So good I almost believed him."

"It's the truth. If our father taught me anything, it was to never let a woman into my life. Nora isn't my woman, Vinnie, she's just a piece of ass I like to lose myself in occasionally."

His words cut like tiny blades across my heart, ripping open old scars and forming new ones.

"Liar. She's yours… whether you're man enough to admit it or not. She's yours and I'm going to fucking destroy her."

Enzo finally gave me his eyes and what I saw there gutted me. He didn't know how to end this. Not with us both walking away alive.

I screwed my eyes shut, trying to push down the tidal wave of emotion battering my insides.

"Time's up, brother," he sneered. "Say goodbye to your heart."

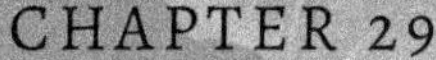

# CHAPTER 29

ENZO

He was going to kill her.

This motherfucker was going to kill the only girl I'd ever loved.

And I did.

I loved Nora.

Maybe not in a conventional way, but she owned my heart… and I think deep down she'd taken mine the first time I'd ever laid eyes on her.

Nora wasn't like most girls. She was strong and selfless and sassy, unapologetic and feisty. She went after what she wanted with zero fucks given.

And she'd wanted me.

Nora Abato had seen past all my darkness and found the sliver of light buried deep inside my soul.

A mistake she was going to die for.

Fuck.

Vinnie yanked her over to a table and folded her over it, dropping his free hand to his belt buckle. My blood turned to molten lava as I watched him claw at her lounge pants, pulling them down enough to reveal her ass.

"Don't," my voice didn't sound like my own as I stepped forward.

"Make a move and I'll end her." He still had the blade pressed right to her throat. Her big brown eyes silently pleaded with me, but I was paralyzed, watching as he grasped his dick and slowly fed it into her.

Nora's cries filled the room, cracking my chest wide open.

"NO!" I yelled. "Please…"

"God, she's tight," Vinnie grinned at me as he thrust into her over and over. "I can see why you fell hard for this pussy. Fuck me, she's squeezing my dick so tight."

His fingers gripped her hips tightly, making pain flare in her eyes, but my strong, brave girl didn't flinch. She took it all while I stood there powerless to do anything else but watch.

Fuck.

*FUCK!*

A violent storm raged inside of me. I wanted to tear this fucker limb from limb, to rip his heart from his chest and watch the life drain from his eyes. But I was powerless. If I tried to shoot him—and I had a fucking perfect aim—he could still hurt Nora, or worse.

I couldn't take that risk. I had to wait until he was distracted.

His grunts of exertion filled the room as he pounded into her. Bile rushed up my throat, but I forced it down. It was my fault Nora was in this position. The least I could do was be there with her in this living nightmare.

Her eyes remained locked on mine, tears dripping down her face.

"Now," the word formed on her lips and at first, I didn't understand, but then realization slammed into me.

In his vigor to hurt her, to ruin her, Vinnie had let his hand at her throat relax, enough for the knife to drop away from her throat a little.

It was risky, but it was now or never.

"Do it," she mouthed. "Do it."

"Fuck yeah, take it, bitch. Take it like a good little whore."

I slowly reached into my jacket and grasped the butt of my pistol. My heart crashed against my rib cage, blood roaring in my ears, as I whipped it out. "Hey, brother?" I called and Vinnie looked up, fear stunning him. The shot rang out through the room, reverberating through me. "Tell our father to go fuck himself."

Vinnie collapsed in a heap and Nora scrambled away, tripping over his body. I rushed to her side and pulled her into my arms. "I've got you, Gattina. I've got you."

"Oh my God." She clawed at my sweater. "Is he—"

"He's dead." It was a kill shot and I hadn't missed. "It's over…" The words felt like ash on my tongue. Because Nora should never have been in the middle of this in the first place.

"Enzo?" Voices rang out in the building and Nora flinched, pressing herself closer.

"Relax, Gattina, it's just Nicco and Matteo."

"It is?" Her body melted against mine, the adrenaline leaving her and shock kicking in. I gently pulled her to her feet and straightened out her clothes. Nora was like a rag doll in my arms as I picked her up, cradling her against my chest.

"In here," I yelled back.

They burst through the door seconds later, a string of expletives leaving their lips as they took in the sight before me.

"Is she—"

I shook my head. Nora was barely conscious. "I need you to take her," I said to Matteo. "Take her to Arianne and call the doctor."

"How bad?" He gently eased Nora into his arms.

"Bad." My eyes shuttered as anger drenched my veins.

"Fuck. Yeah, okay. Backup is on its way."

I gave my cousin a sharp nod, and he turned to leave, but Nora murmured my name. "Ssh, Gattina." I gently stroked her face. "You're safe now. I promise."

"S-stay with me."

"I've got to take care of some things here, but I'll be there soon. Matteo and Arianne will be with you. Luis too."

"M-Maurice?"

Nicco shook his head and I swallowed the truth. "He's okay." The lie soured on my tongue, but she'd had enough to deal with for one day.

"Go," I said to Matteo, watching as he carried her out and away from me. From this absolute clusterfuck.

"What the fuck happened?" Nicco asked.

"He raped her… he fucking—" I grabbed the nearest chair and launched it across the room, kicking the one next to it. Pain skittered through my foot, but it wasn't enough. I wanted to destroy everything in eyesight.

"E, breathe. You need to bre—"

"He was my *brother*."

"W-what?"

I nodded. "Vincenzo Marchetti's long lost bastard child. By the sounds of it, he and daddy dearest were pretty tight."

"But how—

"Your guess is as good as mine. He knew everything, Nicco. He knew about Nora, about me… what I did. It was all about revenge."

"Fuck." Nicco stalked over to Vinnie's dead body and kicked his leg. "He tell you anything else?"

"Doesn't matter. He's gone now and I hope he rots in hell with our father."

"There's no sign of Bianco."

Just then, a knocking sound filtered down the hall.

"What is that?" I said, drawing my pistol again as we moved through the abandoned building on the outskirts of La Riva. All this time, Vinnie was holed up right on our doorstep.

After Lucii had given us Nate's number. He'd pointed us in the direction of Isaac's apartment. We'd found a copy of a rental agreement for an industrial unit alongside the river. It was almost too easy. Now I was beginning to wonder if it wasn't just another clue, all part of his game.

It didn't matter now, he was gone. And Nora and I were still here.

Fuck. Nora.

"Hey." Nicco gripped my shoulder and then moved ahead of me.

"H-help," a voice said, and we followed the moans into a small room at the back of the building.

"Stay alert," he ordered, and I raised my pistol into the air, taking aim should any more surprises jump out on us.

But when Nicco pushed the door open, I dropped my weapon, my mouth hanging wide open.

Because there in the corner of the room, half-conscious and bound was Luca.

~

IT TURNED OUT LUCA WASN'T AN ACCOMPLICE. ISAAC HAD blackmailed him with threats of going after his ex in Pawtucket. Much like me and my family, he knew things about her. Her address, her place of work. It was enough to spook Luca into doing his bidding, and for as much as I wanted to put a bullet through his brains for ever putting Nora in danger, part of me got it. Because there wasn't much I wouldn't do for the girl I loved either.

Fuck, it felt weird admitting that.

But it was the least of my problems as I pulled up outside Nicco and Arianne's building.

Thanks to mine and Nicco's handiwork, the emergency services were attending to an anonymously reported blaze on the outskirts of La Riva. Soon, there wouldn't be anything left of Vinnie to find. We'd need to figure out a story to tell Lucii and Nate, but that could wait until morning.

Right now, there was only one place I needed to be.

Arianne greeted me at the door.

"Enzo, thank God." She pulled me into her arms and hugged me tight. "I've been so worried." Ari released me with an awkward smile.

"Thanks," I clipped out. "How is she?"

Her expression fell. "She's sleeping right now. Doc checked her over, took some blood, and gave her some pain pills."

I sucked in a harsh breath. "Can I—"

"Of course. She was asking for you the whole time."

My chest squeezed.

Nicco had gone to the hospital with Luca. We needed to get his story straight and he knew I wasn't levelheaded enough to do it.

"Can I get you anything?" Ari asked me as I followed her into the apartment.

"No, I'm good."

I wasn't.

I felt like I'd woken from a nightmare, unsure of what was real and what wasn't.

"I'll give the two of you some space, but if you need anything…"

I nodded. It was all I could manage. As I walked the short distance to their guest bedroom, my heart was in my throat. I'd watched that fucker rape her. Heard his moans of pleasure, witnessed her tears as he broke her.

How the fuck was I supposed to go in there and hold her?

I didn't know how to do this, to be the hero who comes to save the day.

"She'd want you to go to her," Ari said, and I glanced back to find her watching me.

"This is all my fault."

"You know she won't blame you. Isaac… I mean Vinnie," sympathy shone in her eyes, "made his choices. It's the only thing we can control, Enzo. How we choose to respond to something. That's what counts. So you can walk away and prove to her and everyone else that you don't deserve her, or you can be the guy we know you can be, and go in there and just be with her."

"You're different, you know."

"Love changes you," she said with conviction. "I know you think it makes you weak, but it doesn't. Love makes you strong, Enzo. It gives you something worth fighting for."

"I'm glad Nicco has you."

"And I'm glad Nora has you," she said. "I'm trusting you with her heart, don't let me down."

Too stunned for words, I slipped into the bedroom. Nora was curled up on her side, in a fitful sleep. She whimpered and I wanted to go back to that building and kill my brother all over again.

Fuck.

My brother.

It was going to take some time to wrap my head around that. But until Tommy dug around to unearth my father's secrets, I knew answers would have to wait.

"N-no," Nora cried, and I rushed to her side.

"Ssh, Gattina. I'm here. I'm right here."

"E-Enzo?" Her eyes flickered open. "You're here."

"I'm here."

That settled her and she slipped under again. I quickly removed all my weapons and stripped down to my boxer briefs and climbed in beside her. Even in her sleep, Nora gravitated to me, nestling her body in the curve of mine. Slipping an arm around her, I closed my eyes and focused on the sound of her breathing.

And before long, fell into a dreamless sleep.

WHEN I WOKE UP, IT WAS TO DARK BROWN EYES STARING at me.

"Hey." She smiled weakly. The usual fire in her eyes had

dimmed and her skin was pale. And fuck, if it wasn't a stark reminder of what had happened.

"Hey," I replied over the lump in my throat. "How are you feeling?"

"Like I was kidnapped by a psycho… again."

Heavy silence filled the space between us.

"I am so fucking sorry, Gattina. I keep thinking that if I'd have just—"

"Don't." Nora pressed her finger to my lips. "Nothing you say or do will ever make me think any of this was your fault, so I'm asking you… no, I'm telling you, don't." She pinned me with a hard look. "Maurice, is he—"

I couldn't lie to her, not now. Earlier in the building had been different. But Nora was safe now.

She was here, and she was safe.

*But it's too late. He already ruined her.*

"He didn't make it."

"God, no…" Her pained sobs were like a knife to the heart.

"I'm so sorry, I'm so fucking sorry." My hand curved around the back of Nora's neck, anchoring her to me while she broke apart.

"I can't believe he's gone," she murmured through the deluge of tears.

Panic had me in a chokehold. I didn't know how to do this, to be who she needed. Not when I was the source of her pain and anguish.

Nora cried and cried. She cried until there were no tears left to cry and her breathing slowed. When I was certain she was asleep, I slipped out of the bed and pulled on my clothes.

It was early, a little after six, but I found Nicco sitting at the breakfast counter, nursing a coffee.

"Couldn't sleep?" I asked, joining him.

"Figured someone should keep an eye on you."

"I told her about Maurice. I had to."

"I know."

"How do you do it, Nic? How do you live with yourself knowing that you've pulled her into our world?"

"You just do. Love isn't fair. It doesn't play by the rules, E. It's emotional warfare and Arianne conquered me. She fucking slayed me until I knew I would never be able to let her go." He took a long sip of coffee. "So now I spend my days not worrying about what our love will cost, but how to protect it."

"You're a better man than me," I murmured. "I don't think I'll ever be able to forget watching him—" A lump got stuck in my throat.

"You need to focus on Nora. She's going to need you over the coming days." He levelled me with a dark look. "She needs you, Enzo."

I heard his words, felt them attack my heart like bullets.

Nora needed me.

But it was me who had gotten her into this mess.

*Me* who had put her in the firing line.

Vinnie wanted to make me pay for killing our father. He wanted to take something from me, the way I'd taken it from him.

I leaped up. "I need to get some air."

Nicco let out a heavy sigh. "I'm begging you, don't do this."

"I'll be back," I said, but I could tell from his grim expression he didn't believe me.

As I grabbed my keys and walked out of his apartment, I wasn't sure I believed me either.

# CHAPTER 30

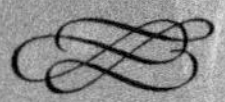

NORA

"*N*ora," Arianne peeked her face around the door. "I brought you something to eat."

"I'm not hungry," I said.

"Oh, Nor. You've got to eat." She left the plate on the dresser and came over to me.

"I had some crackers this morning."

"It isn't enough."

"I just can't, babe." I felt too sick. It wasn't a physical side effect like a stomach flu, it was something much worse.

It was a symptom of my broken heart.

It was two days since I'd woken up in Nicco and Arianne's guest room, cold and alone.

Enzo had left.

He'd left me.

And although he climbed into bed with me every night

after he thought I'd fallen to sleep, I knew he was trying to find the words I didn't know he'd ever manage to say.

We were done.

Tears pooled into the corners of my eyes as I croaked, "How is he?"

"He's… okay."

"You're a terrible liar." A weak smile played on my lips.

"He comes back every night. He just needs time."

Yeah, and I needed him.

I needed him so damn much.

Something inside felt broken, inexplicably altered. Arianne had tried to get me to talk about it, but I wasn't ready.

So I spent my days in bed, watching mindless TV, waiting for Enzo to slide in behind me and draw me into his arms. Because despite the fact he was slowly shredding my heart apart, being close to him was the only time that peace found me.

I could still vividly remember Vinnie rutting into me, his fingers digging into my hips and his dirty words lashing my insides.

"I hate this," I cried. "I fucking hate this."

I wasn't weak.

I was Nora goddamn Abato. I didn't want to let some psychopath like Vinnie break my spirit. But I got it now. I understood what it was like to have your dignity torn to shreds, to have your body used, and your soul stained.

Because that's what it was, a stain on my soul I wasn't sure I would ever forget.

"Nora, you know I—"

"Don't. Please, babe, just don't." I wasn't there yet. I wasn't ready to hear her words of encouragement and reassurance, even though she knew what I was going through.

"Okay. But I just want you to know, whenever you're ready to talk about it, I'm here." She gently squeezed my hand.

"Thanks. I'd feel better if he was here, and not out there doing whatever he's doing," I confessed.

"Nora, you know how he gets. Enzo had a full plate with the stuff with his father but throw in this revelation about Vinnie and you getting hurt…" She let out a small sigh. "It's going to take time."

"I just wish he'd talk to me."

I'd been so sure he would walk away the second he found me, but he hadn't. Sure, he wasn't around during daylight, but he came back to me every night. I knew the fact he came in darkness and left before sunlight wasn't exactly conventional, but nothing about us ever had been.

I pulled the cushion closer, taking comfort in its soft fluffy casing. Arianne leaned over and brushed the stray hairs from my face. "I hate to see you like this. Why don't you come and watch some TV in the living room? It's just the two of us. Nicco is… out."

Code word for Nicco was trying to talk Enzo off a ledge somewhere.

"Maybe later." I closed my eyes and tried to shut it all out. The pain I felt every time I thought of that day, the heartache I felt thinking of Enzo, the utter despair I felt about the future.

"This isn't you, Nora." Concern coated Arianne's words. "I know you're hurting, and I know you need time, but don't let this break you. You're so strong."

"I think I'm going to sleep now," I whispered, refusing to look at her.

"Okay, you know where I am if you need me."

But it wasn't Arianne I needed.

It was Enzo.

And he'd left me.

COOL HANDS SLIPPED OVER MY HIPS AND DRAGGED MY BODY backward. My eyes fluttered open as Enzo got comfortable behind me. The digital clock on the nightstand read a little after one. His lips hovered against the nape of my neck, whispering Italian words I couldn't quite distinguish, save for one phrase.

Perdonami.

*Forgive me.*

I don't know how I knew, but I knew this was the last time he would climb into bed with me. Deep down in my soul, I knew this was goodbye.

Tears stung my eyes as my body began to tremble.

"Nora?" It was a whispered slur, a faint trace of liquor on his breath.

Of course he'd been out drinking. Because that's what guys like Enzo did. They drank and fought and fucked their problems away.

*Damn you, Enzo.*

The silence was deafening, the distance between us cavernous.

His breathing slowed and I knew he was falling to sleep. But I couldn't do it. I couldn't pretend for a second longer.

"Were you even going to tell me?" I whispered. "Or were you going to slip out as if you were never here?"

"You're awake." He tensed behind me.

"You didn't answer my question."

"I… Fuck, I don't know what to say."

I turned in his arms, staring up at him. "You can't even look at me, can you?"

"Fuck, Gattina, that's not what this is." His eyes glittered in the dark, darting around my face, but never fully meeting my eyes.

"So what is it? Because I've spent the last two days in hell, waiting for you to come to me… and you didn't."

"I tried…"

"But you couldn't." I let out a resigned sigh.

"I'm so fucking sorry, Gattina."

"Yeah, me too." The words shattered my heart. But it was only what I already knew.

Enzo had given up.

He was so lost to his own demons that he couldn't see what was staring him in the eyes. I didn't want to beg, I wouldn't.

I had too much self-respect for that.

I wanted to be someone's sun. The center of someone's universe. Instead, I was a burden. And now I was tarnished.

Broken.

"I think you should leave," my voice shook.

"Nora, please don't do this."

"I've given you everything." Tears dripped down my cheeks. "But it still isn't good enough…" *I'm not good enough.*

"It isn't you, Gattina. You have to know that." Enzo cupped my face, running his thumb along the line of my jaw.

He touched me like I was fragile glass, about to shatter at any second.

The irony of the sentiment wasn't lost on me.

"You are so fucking good, so fucking strong. You deserve someone who can protect you, someone who will keep you safe. I'm not that guy, Nora." Regret clouded his eyes. "I don't know how to be that guy."

*Try,* I wanted to scream. *Just try.*

But I didn't want Enzo to try for me, I wanted him to try because *he* wanted to.

Enzo wasn't done though. He closed the distance between us, letting his mouth ghost over mine. "I'm going to go away for a while."

"W-what?" Panic flooded my veins.

He nodded. "I think it's best we get some distance. I need to deal with shit, and it'll be easier on you if I'm not around all the time."

"When will you leave?" He was ripping my heart out of my chest cavity and he was too blinded by anger to see it.

"As soon as Uncle Toni is home, which should be a couple of days."

"I see." Ice began freezing around my heart.

"For what it's worth, I am sorry. The last thing I ever wanted was for you to get hurt. You deserve the world, Gattina, and one day, you'll find someone worthy of you."

Enzo sealed his mouth over mine, kissing me slow and deep, tracing the shape of my lips with his tongue. I kissed him back, imprinting the taste of him, the slight scratch of his stubble against my skin, the way his tongue expertly curled around my own. For as much as I hated him in this moment, I never wanted to forget him.

I never wanted to forget that for a small moment in time, Enzo Marchetti had been mine.

"Go," tears trickled down my lips, "go, before I ask you to stay." I kissed him harder, never wanting to let go.

But eventually I broke away, inhaling a ragged breath. "You know you can keep running from life, Enzo, but one day, you're going to look back and realize you had everything, and you tossed it away, and you'll have to live with that."

He climbed out of bed and pulled on his clothes. Without another word, he went to the door, lingering for a second. In another life he would have declared his undying love for me.

In another life, he would have stayed.

But this wasn't a fairy tale.

And Enzo wasn't the hero.

IT TOOK ME ANOTHER FOUR DAYS UNTIL I FINALLY LEFT NICCO and Arianne's guest room. My body had finally begun to heal, but my heart... that would take a while longer. You didn't just forget about someone like Enzo. But Ari was right, I couldn't let this—or him—break me.

So I showered, pulled on some clean clothes, and joined Nicco and Arianne for breakfast.

"This is a surprise," my best friend said.

"I figured it's time to enter the real world again." My shoulders lifted in a small shrug.

"I'll get you a plate." Nicco got up.

"I think I'm going to start classes up on Monday."

"I think that sounds like a great idea."

"Here," Nicco offered me a plate. "If you need anything, you only have to ask."

"Actually, I was hoping you might take me to Maurice's grave." I hadn't attended the funeral. I couldn't.

"Of course. Just say when."

"Thank you." A smile traced my lips. "How's your father?"

"He's finding being on bed rest hard. I think Genevieve is ready to throw in the towel."

"She loves him." Ari gazed up at him. "She'll stick by him because that's what you do when you lov—gosh, me and my big mouth."

"You don't need to do that, babe. It's okay. I'm okay."

I didn't ask about Enzo. It was dangerous territory for me. But I knew he had left Verona since Antonio was home.

I locked down my unresolved feelings about him and tried to force down some pancakes.

"If it's okay, I'd like to stay here, just a few more days."

"Actually," Ari said, laying her hand on Nicco's hand. "We've been talking, and we'd like you to move in here."

"Ari, that's kind and all, but I can't—"

"Hear me out," she added. "We don't mean live with us, but there's an apartment up for rent right down the hall."

"There is?"

She nodded. "It's only a one bed but we checked it out and think it would be per—"

"Yes," I rushed out, relief seeping into me. "If you're sure you don't mind, I would actually love that." I wasn't sure I could return to La Stella without Maurice. It would be a permanent reminder of what had happened. Not to mention that I wasn't ready to see Luca. He'd been texting me, but it was still too raw. Part of me was relieved to discover he was moving back to Pawtucket.

Nicco had filled me in on the truth; explained how Vinnie blackmailed Luca to do his bidding. But it didn't diminish the fact that he'd drugged and kidnapped me. I could forgive eventually, but I would never ever forget.

"Of course. We'll take care of everything. You can stay here until it's ready."

"Thank you."

"We just want you to be happy, Nor, and to feel safe."

"I'll get there." Heartache wasn't something you could get over. You had to feel it, embrace it. You had to go through it to get to the other side. But every day, I was beginning to feel a little more of the old me push to the surface. I was a fighter. A survivor. And I would get through this. A sense of resolve washed over me, and I tipped my head to the ceiling, inhaling deeply.

I was going to be okay.

My heart would forever carry the scars of Enzo, but it was slowly piecing itself back together. Because I was resilient.

I was strong.

And I would get through this.

It was Saturday night and Matteo and Alessia had come over to hang out at the apartment. The rental wasn't going to be ready for another week, so I planned to stay with Nicco and Ari until it was.

"Don't start without me," I said, getting up. "I need to pee and then I'm going to make a fresh bowl of popcorn."

We were halfway through a movie marathon, and surprisingly, I was having fun. It was the first day I felt like myself. My cheeks hurt from all the laughter and smiling but it felt so damn good.

It didn't stop the hole in my heart aching, but I was here and I was okay, and that was enough.

It had to be.

After washing my hands, I dried them on the towel and slipped back into the hall, but the low rumble of hushed voices gave me pause.

"Should tell her."

"No, she's been doing better. Knowing will only confuse her," Ari said.

"I think she should know," Alessia added. "She's in love with him. It isn't fair to keep it—"

"Keep what from me?" I stepped into the room taking the air with me.

"Fuck," Matteo grumbled, while Arianne looked as guilty as sin.

"What aren't you telling me?"

"Enzo isn't—"

"*Matt!*" Nicco shook his head. "It doesn't matter, Nora. It won't change anything, and Ari is right, you've been doing so well. Don't let—"

"Will someone please just tell me what's going on?"

"Enzo didn't leave," Sia blurted out.

Nicco buried his face in his hand with a heavy groan.

"Guess the cat's out of the bag." Matteo smiled weakly.

"What do you mean, he didn't leave? He said—"

"We know, Nor." Arianne stood up and came to me. "But he couldn't do it. He couldn't leave."

"W-why couldn't he do it?"

"Why do you think?"

Pain lashed my insides. "Where is he then?" I cried.

Because he hadn't been around and no one so much as mentioned him around me.

Nicco made a derisive noise in the back of his throat.

"He's in a bad place, Nor." Ari took my hand. "It's better you don't—"

"He really didn't leave?" It wasn't supposed to matter. Part of me knew it didn't. But the other part clung onto Alessia's words, letting them grow into something else entirely.

He stayed.

He stayed… *for me?*

But he was still punishing himself.

"I need to see him." The words spilled from my lips without thought.

"Nor, I don't think that's a good idea."

"You're probably right, but I need to see him, babe." There was still so much left unsaid between us. Things I should have told him. Things I should have made him hear.

"Arianne is right, now is probably not—"

"Will you help me?" I asked Matteo.

"Oh, come on, Nora, don't put me in this position."

"Weren't you the one who said not to give up?"

"Fuck," he muttered. "I really need to learn not to open my big mouth."

"Will you help me or not?"

He ran a hand down his face and blew out a steady breath. "I will. But I warn you now." His expression dropped, making my chest constrict. "You might not like what you find."

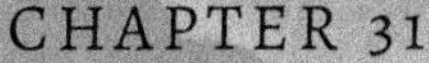

# CHAPTER 31

ENZO

"I'll have another one." I slammed my glass down on the bar, and the bartender, a guy named Billy, shook his head.

"I should cut you off."

"But we both know you won't." My brow arched and he shrugged.

"Suit yourself man, but you're going to feel like an ass when I have to call Matteo or Nicco to drag your drunk ass out of here."

Here was L'Anello's. It was Saturday and the bar was crammed full of people looking for a good time. But I wasn't here for anything other than to find solace at the bottom of a glass.

It had been days since I'd seen her.

I couldn't even think about Nora without a huge pit carving through my stomach.

I should have left. I should have gotten in my car and driven far, far away from Verona County. But when it came down to it, I couldn't do it.

I needed to be here, just in case she needed me. Just in case—

Fuck!

My fist curled against the sleek chrome counter. Nora didn't need me. She probably hated me. I didn't blame her. I was a fucking mess.

After the shitshow with Vinnie, I'd spent a couple of nights avoiding her in the day only to sneak into her bed at night to hold her. I think I'd always known she wasn't really sleeping, but I hadn't wanted to talk, and she seemed content in lying there in silence.

I knew it couldn't last though. She would eventually want answers, answers I didn't have. So I'd taken the coward's way out.

And now I felt like a boat adrift without an anchor. Because that's what Nora was to me, my anchor. She was my North fucking Star in dark, dismal skies, and I'd walked away.

Again.

I could imagine my old man and my brother looking down on me, reveling in my misery. I'd killed them both, exterminated them like the vermin they were, but somehow, I was the one still here suffering.

I just needed it to stop. I needed them to get the fuck out of my head.

"Hey, Enzo." A brunette stepped into my line of sight, laying her hand on my thigh. "You're looking good."

For a second, I had to blink through the liquor haze clouding my thoughts. It wasn't Nora, I knew that. But if I squinted a little and didn't focus too hard, she bore some resemblance.

"You look lonely, you should buy me a drink and I'll keep you company." She batted her eyelashes, smirking suggestively.

"Not tonight." I removed her hand from my thigh. "Take a walk."

She pouted, twirling a finger around a lock of hair. It was longer than Nora's, and a lighter shade of brown.

Upon closer inspection she wasn't anything like my Gattina.

Her pet name on my tongue slayed me. I hadn't even spoken the word, but it was right there. Taunting me. Reminding me of everything I wanted and could never have.

"Another." I flagged Billy down, ignoring the girl. Eventually, she took off, moving onto the next available guy.

"Not your type?" he asked.

"Nah."

"More of a blonde and fake tits kinda guy?"

"Something like that."

Or at least, I used to be. Until Nora had swept in and blown everything I thought I knew to shreds.

"I need to piss." I drained my fresh drink in one and wiped my mouth with the back of my hand. The second I stood though, the room spun.

"Whoa, there, Enzo, take it easy."

"I'm good." I waved him off, stalking across the crowded room to the bar. Guys stopped to greet me, and girls tried to get my attention, but I didn't feel like socializing.

In fact, it was a bad fucking idea that I was here in the first place. But it beat being back at my apartment, alone and miserable, wondering what Nora was doing, and whether she missed me as much as I missed her.

Fuck, I missed her.

I missed her smile and sass and those stupid fucking t-shirts she liked to wear.

I just missed *her*.

But I wasn't good for her. I'd proved that one too many times.

I managed to stumble my way to the restrooms, staggering into a stall to do my thing. When I was done, I washed my hands. My reflection stared back at me. The dark circles around my eyes were haunting.

*His* eyes.

My fist flew out before I could stop it, colliding with the glass. It shattered, slicing open my knuckles.

"Fuck." Blood dripped down my hand and I grabbed a bunch of paper towels out of the dispenser and wrapped it around the cut, trying to stem the flow.

A couple of guys burst into the bathroom, took one look at me and immediately backtracked. Everything was still spinning as I staggered out of there.

"Oh my God, Enzo," the girl from a second ago came rushing over. "What did you do?"

"Doesn't matter," I grunted, trying to shake her off. But she wrapped her hand around my arm in a vice grip and steered me back toward the bar.

"Whisky on the rocks." She signaled Billy. "And a bucket of ice and a first aid kit."

"I'm fine."

"You're getting blood everywhere." Her eyes went to the wet soggy paper towel stained red.

Billy came back with her order. "You might want to do

this somewhere a little quieter," he suggested.

"Good thinking. Come on." She tugged me back through the crowd, slipping into a door marked 'private.' A security guy nodded at me, or maybe he was nodding at her. Everything was starting to get really fucked up in my head. But then she was pulling me into a small room with a crushed velvet couch. "Sit," she ordered.

"What's your name?" I slurred as I dropped onto the plush couch.

"Natalia. Now let me look at your hand." Gently unwrapping my hand, she flinched. "You made quite a mess of this."

I could see double. Two of her, two of my hand. Her features blurred together and for a second, I saw Nora.

My Nora.

*My Gattina.*

"Nora," I mumbled as she cleaned up my cuts, dressing it in a bandage from the first aid kit.

"There," she said. "All better."

"Don't talk," I snapped.

When she talked, I remembered she wasn't Nora. And I really fucking wanted her to be Nora.

"No?" Her eyes darkened as she licked her lips. "What did you want to do then?" Slowly, Natalia lowered herself onto my lap, straddling my hips. She wrapped her slender fingers around my neck and lowered her face to mine. "I can think of a few things that don't involve talking."

Her lips brushed mine, and for a second I was with Nora, kissing Nora.

"Get your slutty hands off him."

"Nora?" I blinked over at the little firecracker in the doorway, glaring at me as if I'd just—

*"Nora?"*

Fuck. I was tripping. Nora wasn't here. She was at Nicco and Ari's apartment.

But then the girl was yanked off my lap, her shrieks filling the air.

"I said get the hell off him." The Nora apparition grabbed a fistful of the girl's hair and started dragging her toward the door while I sat there, barely clinging onto consciousness.

My hand throbbed as blood started seeping through the bandage.

"What the fuck did you do?"

"Matteo?" I balked as he materialized in front of me. I was definitely tripping. Whatever Billy had plied me with was some strong shit.

"You're a fucking mess," he said, throwing a bottle of water at me. "I honestly don't know why she keeps fighting for you." His eyes went to where Nora was standing.

Nora was here too?

What the fuck was going on?

"Give us some space", she said to my cousin who had moved into the room, smirking at me as if he was enjoying the show.

"You sure? Maybe this should wait."

"I don't think it can. Please…"

"Fine, but I'll be right outside." He pinned me with a serious look. "Don't fuck anything else up. This is your last shot."

Last shot?

What the fuck was he talking about? I hadn't asked him to bring Nora here.

Matteo slipped out of the room, closing the door. The door was like a gunshot to my already racing heart.

"You should drink that," she said, eyeing the water in my

hand. I uncapped it and guzzled the contents down, letting the ice-cold liquid temper some of the fire inside me.

"Did you fuck her?" Nora approached me. She didn't sound angry, she sounded disappointed… resigned, and it cut deep.

It cut really fucking deep.

She didn't come close, just stood there in front of me. Out of reach. Always fucking out of reach. Contempt rolling off her in thick angry waves.

I swallowed hard. "You think I…"

"Well, did you?"

"No, Gattina, I didn't fuck her." I released a thin breath. Fucking her hadn't even crossed my mind, even when I'd thought she was Nora.

Because deep down, I knew. I knew her face was all wrong and her voice was all shrill. Even if my glassy eyes had betrayed me, my heart knew.

It would always fucking know.

"You're hurt," she said, glancing at my hand.

"It's nothing. Had a little run in with a mirror."

"What are you doing, Enzo? You said you were leaving, you said—"

"Yeah, well, I said a lot of things I didn't mean." My eyes narrowed.

Nora being here was sobering. I felt the liquor coursing through my veins evaporate until I could see every blemish on her skin, the way her lips trembled as she stared me down.

It was her.

It was always fucking her.

I dragged a hand over my face.

"I wanted to kill her."

"E-excuse me?" I spat out.

"For touching you. For *kissing* you," Nora seethed. "I wanted to drag her off you and rip out her heart. But you're not mine anymore," she inhaled a sharp breath, "maybe you never were." Nora took two steps toward me, my heart beating so fucking hard I thought it was going to explode.

"But that doesn't mean you shouldn't hear the words. It doesn't mean that just because you think you're unworthy of love that you should never experience it." She came to a stop in front of me, and gently cupped my face forcing me to look up at her. But she didn't need to force me to do anything, I couldn't take my eyes off her.

Nora was so fucking beautiful it hurt.

"I love you, Enzo Marchetti. I think I've loved you for a while. You think you're a dark soul with a faulty heart. But you're so much more than that. We all need darkness to shine. And you make me light up like no one else ever has. I'm not asking you for anything you don't want to give, but I am asking you to try to at least see what I see. What Nicco and Matteo, and Alessia, and Arianne see.

"You are a good person, Enzo. You care about your family, you would die for them. And I know that your father messed you up. I know he starved you of love until you began to believe you weren't worthy of it. And I know what you had to do to him. But none of it, not a single thing, changes the fact that you are worthy. And I love you, Enzo. I love you."

Speechless.

I was fucking speechless.

It was like she'd taken every insecurity I'd had as a child and plucked it from my soul.

She knew.

She knew about my father, about what I'd done.

I don't know why I was surprised. Nicco couldn't hold his own shit where Arianne was concerned. It went against everything we were to tell outsiders about Family business. But Arianne wasn't an outsider. She was half of his fucking heart, his woman… his Queen.

She was as much a part of this now as he was.

Could it really be that simple?

Could love really conquer all?

"I-I don't know what to say." Dejection flared in her eyes. But everything was coming at me a mile a minute, slamming into me with such force I couldn't sort through the jumbled thoughts to give her a response she deserved.

"That's okay. You have a lot to think about. But you need to know that you don't have to do this anymore. You don't have to escape to bars to try to drown out your feelings. You don't have to fight or fuck your way to peace. I can be that for you. I can be the person you turn to when it gets too much. I can be your shoulder, your willing body… even your punching bag—"

"Gattina, I would never—"

"Ssh, I know." She smiled, pressing a finger to my lips, her touch burning me inside out. "I meant an emotional punching bag. I'll be all of those for you because I love you. I love you so fucking much, Enzo, and I wouldn't be the girl I am if I never told you that."

"I—"

"You have a lot to think on," she cut me off. "But know if you go near another girl again, I won't be held responsible for my actions." Her brow lifted, and laughter rumbled in my chest.

Fuck, this girl.

She was everything.

Every-fucking-thing.

"I love you, Enzo." She gently pulled her finger away, replacing it with her soft lips. "But I won't spend my life chasing you. This is it… your last chance. The question is are you brave enough to take a leap of faith?"

# CHAPTER 32

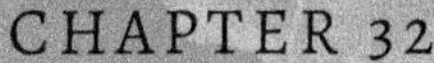

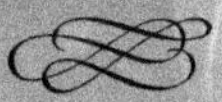

NORA

Four days after I'd stormed into L'Anello's and found Enzo with some whore draped all over him, I still hadn't heard from him.

I'd left him that night with nothing more than a soft kiss and an ultimatum.

A small part of me—the hopeless romantic, the girl who wanted her very own love story—had thought he would chase me down the second I left and declare his endless love for me. But of course, he hadn't. Because this wasn't a fairy tale and Enzo wasn't your average guy.

So I waited.

I didn't let it distract me from pressing forward with my life though. I resumed classes, saw my friends, and threw myself back into life *before* Enzo Marchetti.

As the days went by, so too did the quiet hope that he

would eventually show. But I didn't let it crush me this time, I couldn't.

I'd bared my soul to Enzo, confessed every single thing he made me feel. What he chose to do with it... well, that was on him.

I walked the short distance to the main campus parking lot. Nicco and Ari were picking me up as they wanted to show me my new apartment. It was almost ready, and I was looking forward to a fresh start.

They'd both been so supportive. Giving me space when I needed it and keeping me company when I didn't want to be alone. I owed them big time. Only yesterday, they had both accompanied me to visit Maurice's grave. I'd sat at his headstone, in my boo bees t-shirt, talking nonsense, just like old times.

The other five security guards had also been killed at the hands of Vinnie, but I didn't *know* them, not the way I'd known my personal bodyguard.

When I arrived at the parking lot, there was no sign of Nicco's car though. He usually rode his motorbike, but that wasn't practical when you were chauffeuring around your wife and her best friend, so he'd caved and bought a brand new car.

A couple of seconds later, Matteo's truck appeared.

"This is a surprise," I said as he climbed out. "Why aren't you in class?"

"Secret mafia stuff." He winked.

"Haha, very funny." He liked to give me shit about my strange fascination with the Family. But it wasn't every day you got to meet and hang out with real life mafiosi.

"Nicco and Ari got held up. But I was in the area, so I said I'd swing by and give you a ride."

"Well, thank you." I beamed at him, accepting his help into the truck.

Matteo got in and fired up the ignition, the engine rumbling to life. "All set?" he asked and there was something in his eyes.

"What are you up to?" I asked, thinly.

"Who, me? Nothing. Not a damn thing." An amused smirk tipped the corner of his mouth.

It was a look I knew well.

A look that told me Matteo was up to something.

WE DIDN'T MAKE IT TO NICCO AND ARIANNE'S APARTMENT. Instead, he pulled up in front of the apartment he shared with Enzo.

"Erm, Matteo, what are we doing here?" My heart picked up speed.

"It's just a pit stop. I need to grab some things."

"Some things?" My brow lifted.

"Yeah, come on, I don't bite. And Enzo is out."

"Oh." I hadn't even noticed his car wasn't in the parking lot.

"I can stay here—"

"Don't be silly. It's my apartment too. Besides, I need you to come and help me with this."

His façade was a lot more convincing than it had been back at MU.

"Fine." I let out a soft sigh. "But I'm not lifting anything heavy."

"Deal."

Matteo came around and got the door. He was such a romantic at heart, so different to his cousin.

My heart lurched into my throat, but I ignored it. It had been four days and there had been no sign of Enzo. I had to accept that maybe my declaration wasn't enough.

"You know," Matteo said as we entered their building. "What you did at the bar, that was pretty badass."

"Yeah, but it didn't change anything." A sigh of resignation escaped my lips.

"Maybe not. But you fought for it, you fought for *him*, Nora. And I think that's a pretty incredible thing."

I nodded over the giant lump in my throat.

I hadn't been here since the morning I'd found Enzo in bed with some busty blonde. The memories gave me pause as we reached the door. But Matteo was right there, to steer me inside.

The second we stepped inside though, I realized Matteo had played me.

Enzo shot up off the couch. "Hi," he said.

"Hi. What is this?" I glanced around at Matteo and guilt twinkled in his eyes.

"Don't hate me." He grinned. "I'm just gonna—" He slipped out of the apartment and closed the door behind him.

"How have you been?" Enzo asked, his eyes darting around mine.

He was nervous.

Big bad Enzo Marchetti was nervous.

"I'm okay. You?"

He rubbed his jaw. "About what happened, at the bar... I swear to God, nothing happened with me and that woman. I was drunk and she was trying to—"

"You don't need to explain. I got a front row seat to what she was trying, remember?"

He flinched, his silence deafening.

"What am I doing here, Enzo?"

"I wanted to talk," he said.

"That would involve actually talking." My lips curved wryly.

"This doesn't come easy for me. I've never had to—"

"I know."

"Fuck. Maybe it'll just be easier if I show you." He offered me his hand, and I took it. Because it was Enzo, and I'd never been able to tell him no.

He pulled me into his arms, staring down at me with such intensity I felt winded.

"After you left L'Anello's, I wanted to come after you. I wanted to chase you so fucking bad. But I knew I needed to figure out what I wanted… I mean, I want you. I've always wanted you, Nora. That isn't the issue here, just so we're clear."

"I know."

"I didn't want to let you down again. Not when you deserve so much…"

Enzo took my hand and led me into his bedroom. At first, I didn't notice anything. But then I saw it.

I saw the perfume on his dresser, the avocuddle t-shirt draped over the back of his chair. I spotted the magazine on the nightstand, and the scarf hanging over the back of his door.

"W-what is this?" Confusion crinkled my brows.

"I know you're supposed to be moving into the apartment in Nicco's building. But what if you moved in… here?"

"You want me to move in? But—"

"I want you, Nora." Enzo snagged a hand around my waist and pulled me into his chest, my back to his front. "I want you in my bed, I want your face to be the first thing I see when I wake up, I want to know you're safe. Always."

"I-I don't know what to say." My heart was a band of wild horses galloping inside my chest.

He wanted me to move in.

Stone-hearted, commitment-phobe Enzo Marchetti wanted to live with me.

I was speechless.

Completely and utterly speechless.

"Nora?" he asked, turning me in his arms, concern glittering in his eyes.

"You'll have to get a mattress. I can't… not after you…"

"Already done."

"You bought me a mattress?"

"And this…" He plucked something out of his back pocket and took my hand, placing the key in my palm.

"You got me a key."

"To *our* apartment. If you want it, that is…"

Tears clung to my lashes as I nodded. "I want it. I really, really want it."

"Thank fuck." He blushed. He actually blushed. "Because I already moved in all your stuff."

"What?" I spluttered.

"I had a little help, but it was my idea." A smug smirk tugged at his mouth.

"I can't believe you did that."

"Well, you see, there's this girl. She's kind of a badass… she's sexy and sassy and so fucking selfless. She taught me some things…"

"Oh yeah, like what?"

"She taught me that it's okay to hurt, that it's okay to live with your pain. But she also taught me that it's okay to accept help, to admit that you can't do it alone. She taught me that just because you've never known the love of a parent doesn't mean you won't ever know love for yourself. Because I do, Gattina. I fucking love you. I love your heart and your strength. I love your body and your pure soul. I even love those fucking ridiculous t-shirts you wear."

"You love me?" My heart was fit to burst at his words. It was everything I'd ever wanted.

"Mi sono innamorato di te."

"I think you should show me," I said around a smug grin.

Enzo scooped me up in his arms and carried me over to the bed. "Your wish is my command il mio cuore."

Our story wasn't perfect.

It was messy and raw and painful, but it was also real. It was ours and nobody could ever take that away from us.

Sometimes you had to go through the darkness to get to the light…

And I wouldn't change a single thing.

Enzo lay me down on the bed and hovered over me. "I can't believe I almost lost you." He stared at me like he was seeing me for the first time.

"I'm right here." I leaned up to kiss him, letting my lips slide softly against his. He buried his hand in my hair, stroking the slope of my neck as he kissed me deeper.

"Is this okay?"

I nodded, locking my hands around his neck and pulling him closer. "I love you," I whispered, and I felt him shiver at my words.

It was a heady feeling, to know that I could bring this

man to his knees. But I wouldn't ever take his love for granted or wield it as a weapon.

"I want to touch you, Gattina..." He let the words hang between us. I knew what he was asking me, and the truth was, I didn't know how I felt about being with him so soon after his brother's vicious attack.

I wanted Enzo, that wasn't the problem, but I knew I still hadn't dealt with everything that had happened.

"I... I think I'm ready." My voice cracked, betraying me.

"We'll take it slow." He climbed off me, before shedding his clothes. Then he reached for my hand, tugging me gently.

Enzo handled me softer than he ever had, taking his sweet time to undress me. His fingers followed the curve of my waist, gliding up my spine as he drew me into his warm body. "I need you, Nora. I will always need you. But I need to know that you're safe more."

"Kiss me," I said.

He dipped his head, capturing my lips in a bruising kiss. His tongue curled around mine, slow and unhurried, tasting and teasing while his fingers stroked a blazing path across my skin.

"So fucking beautiful," he hummed against my skin.

"I love this side of you," I murmured overwhelmed with how good he was making me feel.

"Yeah? Well don't tell anyone. I have a rep to protect." Enzo smirked, before guiding me back onto the bed. But this time, he climbed beside me and pulled me close into his body.

"What are you doing?" I asked.

"I figure we should probably talk."

"You want to talk? *Now*? Who are you and what have you done with the Enzo Marchetti I know and love?"

"Gattina," his icy gaze pinned me to the spot. "We need to talk about this."

"I know." I expelled a small breath.

How did you talk about something you wanted to pretend had never happened?

Enzo was there… he watched as his brother—

A garbled sob spilled from my lips.

"I'm here," Enzo said. "I'm right here and I will never let anyone hurt you again. I swear to God, Nora." Fierce possessiveness clung to his words.

My fingers clawed at his chest, needing to get closer as I broke in his arms. Enzo didn't try to shush me or talk to me, he just held me. Held me until the tears subsided and my breathing slowed.

"What happened," he said, gently nudging his nose against mine, "I need you to know it changes nothing for me. Not a damn thing, okay?"

I nodded. "I just hate that you saw it… that it will always be there, between us."

"It doesn't have to be. We can choose to look forward and not back. Someone once said to me, all I needed to do was take a leap of faith. Well, I'm asking you to do the same. Take a leap on me, Gattina… *with* me, and I'll always catch you. I promise."

"You're good at this, you know."

"That's where you're wrong. I'm not good at this… you are. You make me want to try, Nora. You make me want to be a better man." Enzo kissed me, stroking his thumb over my cheek. This, lying here with him, was like a salve to my bruised soul.

"I can't promise I'll always get it right," he went on, "but I promise to spend every second of every day trying to be worthy."

"You don't need to try," I whispered, stealing a chaste kiss. "You already are."

Enzo sucked in a sharp breath and I loved that, again, I'd shocked him with my raw honesty.

But everyone deserved to be loved.

And I would spend every second of every day showing *him* that.

# EPILOGUE

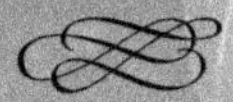

NORA

"I see it," I pressed my face against the window of Enzo's GTO as we approached the city. New York's skyline lit up the distance and excitement buzzed inside me.

"I can't wait to explore."

"Explore?" Enzo grumbled, sliding his hand along my knee. "I can't wait to get you naked."

A shiver rolled down my spine. "You were inside me less than six hours ago."

"Six hours too long."

Soft laughter bubbled in my chest.

Enzo was insatiable… and I loved it.

At first, after he finally gave into his feelings for me, I was worried things would be too intense after what happened with his brother. But Enzo had been patient with me. He hadn't pushed or demanded anything of me I couldn't give.

He'd been the perfect gentleman, and then when I was finally ready to be with him, he'd loved me in the way only he could.

His fingers walked higher, disappearing under my skirt. I clapped my hand down on his. "Oh no you don't, you're driving."

"And you're sexy."

I poked my tongue between my teeth. "Patience. Are you going to tell me where we're staying yet?" Enzo had planned our entire weekend from start to finish, and I couldn't wait to enjoy some time away with him, just the two of us.

Since Enzo had given me a key to his apartment, we'd been inseparable. He drove me to classes each morning and picked me up at the end of every day. Antonio was still on strict orders from the doctor to take it easy, so Nicco was taking a more hands-on approach in the Family. I knew Arianne worried, but we'd both made our choice and the Marchetti were part of our lives now, and I wouldn't have wanted it any other way.

My parents and brother hadn't taken the news so well. My father knew all about the hot-headed Marchetti boy with a cold exterior and black soul. But I was an adult, and I was happy. So freaking happy. Besides, I knew Enzo would win them over eventually.

He'd softened somewhat. Not with everyone. But it was there, peeking through the surface. He let Alessia and Arabella come over for girl's night and let me fill his apartment with girly shit, including my array of humorous t-shirts.

Enzo welcomed me into his life as if I was always supposed to be there, and I couldn't explain it, but we just worked.

"It's a shame Arianne and Nicco couldn't come," I said.

Originally, the four of us were going to make the trip to celebrate Ari's birthday. But with Antonio still recovering, they decided to stay behind. Things were quiet since Vinnie, but I knew it wouldn't always be like that. There would be more threats and attacks, more lies and secrets. This was the life I'd chosen though, and I knew without doubt Enzo would always protect me.

"God, it's so beautiful." We were driving right into the thick of the city. I'd never felt more small or insignificant than with New York's high rises looming over us. I cranked the window and stuck my head outside, letting out a shriek of excitement as the cool air rushed over my face. When I ducked back inside, Enzo was frowning over at me.

"You're fucking crazy."

"But you love me."

"Yeah, I do." A smirk played on his lips.

"Are we almost there?"

"Patience, Gattina." He chuckled. It was fast becoming one of my favorite sounds. It didn't happen very often, but whenever it did, it completely melted my insides.

"Can you at least tell me *something*?" I knew he had plans, he'd spent enough time colluding with Nicco and Ari. "Please?" I batted my eyelashes for good measure.

"I can tell you one thing…" It was a heated whisper. "I'm going to fuck you so hard tonight you see stars."

"Enzo, that's not a thing," I tried to sound disappointed. But the truth was… I really hoped he did.

ENZO

"What do you think?" I leaned against the doorjamb, watching Nora's reaction as she took in our suite.

"Are you sure this is our room?"

My bank account was pretty sure. But the fifteen hundred dollar a night price tag was worth every penny to see her speechless.

Pushing off the jamb, I stalked toward her. "It's ours for three whole nights. Imagine all the ways I can make you scream up here." My mind was already full of ideas.

I always wanted Nora. The truth was, I couldn't get enough of her. She'd fast become my newest addiction and she was all too willing to let me indulge.

The guys busted my balls about it all the time. But I didn't give a fuck. Nora was the better half of my soul and I was so fucking grateful to have her in my life.

Sweeping the hair off her face, I dipped my head and pressed a single kiss to her collarbone.

"Mmm," a moan slipped from her lips.

"We should check out the view." I'd specifically booked a room at The NYC Skyline for its amazing view of the city. Nora had been obsessed with coming here ever since Nicco brought Arianne for their honeymoon. She wanted to do the whole tourist thing and visit all the sights.

I just wanted to do her.

My hands clamped on her hips as I guided her over to the enormous window giving us a panoramic view of the iconic skyline.

"Wow," she murmured, relaxing back into my arms.

Skimming her waist with my hands, I glided them down

her back and over the curve of her ass, dipping underneath her sexy as fuck skirt.

"Enzo," she warned, but she was here, she'd gotten her wish. Now, it was time for me to get mine.

"Hands on the glass, Gattina, and don't move." I dropped to my knees and pushed her skirt up her waist to find the waistband on her panties and gently ease them down her hips. I couldn't resist raking my teeth over the soft curve of her ass, and she moaned again.

"You are so bad."

It was like being outside, the vast glass panels bringing the city inside. But no one could see us up here. Even if they could, I wouldn't have stopped.

I needed her.

I needed Nora in a way I couldn't fully describe.

Deeply.

Wholly.

Viscerally.

She was the calm to my temper, the light to my dark. She was my anchor, my reason, and I was determined to make this weekend memorable, for more than one reason.

Unable to wait a second longer, I dived in, licking her like a man starved. Nora gasped, a string of expletives falling from her lips as I pushed two digits deep inside her and worked her with my tongue while pumping my fingers in and out.

"God… that is… *God!*" Her knees buckled, but I banded my arm around her waist and held her still. She was at my mercy, about to be wrecked by my touch.

"You taste like heaven," I speared my tongue inside her, rolling my thumb over her clit in perfect synchrony.

"Jesus, Lorenzo... it's..." The words died as she moaned over and over, the sounds of her pleasure filling the room.

I wanted the whole fucking place to hear her, to know that this woman belonged to me.

Only ever me.

My love for Nora was borderline obsessive. I drove her to classes every day, returned later to pick her up. If she wanted to hang out with Lucii and her other girlfriends, I usually put one of our guys on them and had him constantly check-in. I'd almost lost her, and I didn't plan on that ever happening again. So yeah, I was a little over the top, but Nora didn't seem to mind. In fact, I think my Gattina secretly liked it.

Her back bowed as she rocked against me, desperate for more, desperate for what only I could give her. "I'm so close..." Raw lust drenched her words. But I had no plans to make her come yet. I wanted her desperate for me.

Boneless.

Breathless.

*Mine.*

I curved my fingers and rubbed, quickly withdrawing them when I felt her body begin to coil tight.

"Enzo, what the hell?" She glared down at me over her shoulder.

"Patience, Gattina." I smirked.

Standing, I snapped my belt and pushed my jeans open enough to free my dick. I was rock hard and ready to sink deep inside her. "Hands on the glass," I ordered when she tried to turn and reach for me.

Nora giggled. "You're bossy."

"And you're a brat." Stepping up behind her, I wrapped a hand around her throat bringing my mouth to the side of her neck. "Tell me what you want."

"You, Enzo. Only ever you."

"Right answer." I nipped her skin as I folded my body over hers and slammed inside of her. "You're mine, Gattina. Mine."

And I would spend forever showing her.

NORA

We spent the next day sightseeing. Enzo grudgingly let me drag him through Times Square. We took silly selfies in the M&M's store and posed with the Hard Rock Café giant guitar. He was patient and slightly amused by how excited I was. Then we headed to Central Park and Enzo had completely surprised me by suggesting we take one of the horse-drawn carriages. It was so romantic, cuddled up beside my dark and brooding bad boy as we explored the gorgeous landscape.

We had dinner reservations later, but Enzo was keeping quiet about the details.

"Well, do I need to dress up or go casual?" I asked.

"Maybe avoid the t-shirts, yeah?" His eyes dropped to my 'Ah! the element of surprise' shirt.

"There's nothing wrong with my t-shirt." I pouted. It looked killer teamed with my skirt, stockings, boots, and brand-new leather jacket. It had been a gift from Enzo. He said his badass girlfriend needed a badass jacket.

I loved it.

"You'd look better with it tied around your wrists while I —" He leaned in, whispering all the dirty things he wanted to do to me. My soft laughter filled the air as we walked the scenic route back to our hotel.

"You'll need to wear something warm."

I nestled into his side and grinned up at him. "But I have you to keep me warm."

Enzo raked his teeth over my earlobe sending bolts of pleasure rippling through me. "Maybe I should cancel our reservations tonight and eat you instead."

"You are so bad."

His lips curved in a smug smirk. "Oh, you don't know the half of it."

"Holy shit, for real?" I stared up at Edge, the highest outside sky deck in the Western Hemisphere. I'd wanted so badly to get tickets, but when I'd looked into it, it was fully booked.

"But how?"

"I have my ways."

It was late. We'd gotten back to the hotel suite and spent hours wrapped up in each other. Enzo didn't seem in a rush to make our dinner reservations and I was all too happy to enjoy him and our ridiculously swanky suite.

My stomach grumbled. "Maybe we should have grabbed something to eat first."

"Don't you trust me?"

Oh, I did. But I was pretty sure Edge didn't serve food.

We rode the elevator to the hundredth floor. It was so fast there wasn't even time to fool around, but Enzo couldn't resist smacking my ass as I stepped out ahead of him.

"Mr. Marchetti, Miss Abato, welcome to Edge." A host in a three-piece black suit greeted us.

I glanced at Enzo and he smirked.

"We are very honored you chose to dine with us tonight."

"Dine?" I mouthed at my smug looking boyfriend.

"I told you to trust me."

The host led us into the observation room where a server was waiting with a tray of champagne. "Welcome to Edge," she said.

"Thank you." My heart fluttered wildly in my chest. I was used to being with Enzo now. He and his family were well-known all over Rhode Island. But New York? I hadn't expected such treatment.

"We have the place all to ourselves?" I whispered to Enzo, quickly realizing we were the only people not in uniform.

"Just you and me, Gattina. Come on." His hand slipped to the small of my back urging me closer to the huge glass window. The view was incredible; so much so I inhaled a sharp breath.

"It's something, huh?" The host said.

"It really is." I couldn't stop smiling. This was so freaking romantic, and so out of character for my brooding bad boy.

"Dinner will be served shortly. We thought you might like to take in the view first."

"That would be great," I said. "Thank you."

He led us to the doors leading onto the observation deck. Enzo took my hand and moved ahead of me, leading me to the Eastern point. He pulled me around to his front and banded his arms around my waist, dropping his chin on my shoulder as we stared at the city lights. "What do you think?"

"I love it, thank you."

"I knew how badly you wanted to come up here, so I made a few calls."

"I can't believe you did all this for me. It's perfect." A ball of emotion lodged in my throat.

"There isn't much I wouldn't do you for you, Gattina, you

know that, right?"

"I know."

"I may not always be able to tell you what I'm feeling or thinking, but I'll always try, Nora. I want you to know that."

Silence drifted over us as we enjoyed the moment.

"What are you thinking right now?" I eventually whispered.

"I'm thinking that one day, I'll bring you back here and ask you to be mine forever."

My heart raced wildly in my chest as I imagined him on one knee before me. I wanted that one day.

God, I wanted it so much.

"What are you thinking?" Enzo ran his lips along my jaw before stealing a kiss.

"I'm thinking that one day," I tilted my face and kissed him back. "I'll say yes."


MATTEO

"So how was the Big Apple? Did you manage to do any sightseeing?"

"Fuck off." Enzo grumbled.

"What? It's a legit question." I chuckled. "Let me guess, you did nothing but sightseeing... Nora was so pumped about the trip."

"She was pumped... a lot." The smug fucker smirked, and I shook my head.

"Did you just make a joke? Fuck, man, I'm going to need to check for your balls because that girl has you all—"

"We saw the sights. I made her come twice on the trip to Ellis Island."

I almost choked on my own breath. "I bet the other

passengers loved that."

"Hired a private boat."

"Of course you did."

"If it's good enough for Nic." He shrugged.

"I'm happy for you, man, you two deserved to come out on top." Silence settled between us.

We were in my truck on the way to Providence to see Zander DiMarco. Things were still tense after his bar got hit by Enzo's half-brother. Zander wanted out, but you didn't get out of a deal with the Family. It didn't work like that. And he needed a little reminder of that fact.

Since Enzo had spent time up there with Gino, Nicco had asked us to go try and broker some peace. I wasn't sure Enzo was the man for the job, but he didn't seem to care, all too happy to follow orders and get the job done.

"She's good for you," I said.

He was softer around the edges, we all saw it. He was still Enzo—the love of a good woman didn't change that—but he was different.

My chest tightened, but I stuffed those memories down. It had been months and months since I'd spent one amazing night with a red-haired, green-eyed angel. Caitlin. If that was even her real name.

We'd been in Providence and there had been a bad storm. I'd stumbled across a girl being threatened in a dark alley… and well, one thing led to another and I'd spent the night at her place. It was the best sex I'd ever had. But when I'd finally plucked up the courage to drive back down there and track her down, she was gone.

And I went back to my life without the Irish beauty who had marked my soul.

Enzo's cell phone started ringing, but he took one look at

the number and ignored it.

"Who is that?"

"Beats me." He shrugged.

It immediately started ringing again.

"Maybe you should answer it. It could be important."

He plucked the thing out of the center console and barked, "Yeah?"

I smirked. He was such a grumpy asshole still. I guess there were some things the love of a good woman couldn't change.

"What? Yeah, okay. We're on our way." He hung up and grumbled, "Fuck."

"What is it?"

"When I was down here with Gino, I helped one of Zander's girls out. I think that fucker was hurting her."

"What?"

"Yeah, I don't know for sure what went down. But I gave her my number in case she ever needed help."

"That was her?"

"No, that was the hospital."

"Fuck," I breathed. "Is she okay?"

"They didn't say much, but she specifically asked for me."

"She's at Providence General?"

"No, she's at County in Pawtucket. So we're going to have to make a detour."

"Sure, man. Whatever you need." If there was one thing I hated, it was men who beat women.

THIRTY MINUTES LATER, WE ARRIVED AT THE HOSPITAL. A nurse directed us to the correct bay and Enzo went off to chat with another nurse. The place was a hive of activity as staff came and went, treating patients. I'd never much liked these places because they usually ended in bad news.

"She's down here." Enzo beckoned me over and we went down another hall. "Bay five." He grabbed the curtain and slipped inside.

"You came," a voice said.

"Yeah, I brought a friend with me. Is it okay if he—"

"Sure, I guess."

I went inside the small bay and my heart damn near exploded in my chest.

"You."

"I-I don't understand," I croaked, feeling myself grow hot all over.

"Wait, a minute," Enzo frowned. "You two know each other? But how?"

He was drilling holes into my face, but I couldn't take my eyes off the woman lying in bed. Her face was littered with bruises and she had finger marks around her neck.

"Matteo?" Enzo gripped my shoulder as my knees went weak.

"*Caitlin?*" The word barely got out over the lump in my throat.

It was her.

The girl from that night.

She was one of Zander's girls?

A stripper?

It couldn't be.

Yet, Enzo knew her. He'd helped her. And she'd called him.

What the fuck was going on?

# PLAYLIST

Broken – Isack Danielson
You Should Be Sad – Halsey
Heartless – Dermot Kennedy
Heartless – The Weeknd
Ludens – Bring Me the Horizon
Throne – Bring Me the Horizon
I'm Ready – Sam Smith, Demi Levato
Mad At You – Noah Cyrus, Gallant
End of All Days – Thirty Second to Mars
Scars – James Bay
Life's A Mess – Juice WRLD ft. Halsey
Die For Me – Post Malone ft. Halsey, Future
Someone to You – BANNNERS
I Have Questions – Camila Cabello
Lie to Me – Five Seconds of Summer, Julia Michaels
Hurts Like Hell – Fleurie
Sacrifice – Black Atlas ft. Jessie Reyez
Exile – Taylor Swift ft. Bon Iver
Wrong Direction – Hailee Steinfield

Fire on Fire – Sam Smith

Stone – Jaymes Young

Hurricane – Thirty Seconds to Mars

Still Don't Know My Name – Labrinth

Prisoner – Miley Cyrus ft. Dua Lipa

Out of This World – Bush

Heaven – Julia Michaels

Secret Love Song – Little Mix ft. Jason Derulo

# AUTHOR'S NOTE

Oh Enzo, my dark and dangerous mafioso.

I always knew this couple would break… and break me they did. I hope you enjoyed their push and pull as much as I enjoyed writing it.

As always, a huge thank you to my team – for keeping me sane, now more than ever. To Darlene and Athena for proofreading the story at the drop of a hat. To my promo team and my readers / spoiler groups – your enthusiasm and support for my characters and stories makes it all worthwhile. To Give Me Books for always organizing yet another book promotion.

And finally, to the bloggers, reviewers, and bookstagrammers who continue to support me, without you I wouldn't get to do this, so thank you. THANK YOU!

I can't wait to bring you more stories in the Verona Legacy world.

Until next time,
L A xo

# ABOUT THE AUTHOR

**Angsty. Edgy. Addictive Romance**

Author of mature young adult and new adult novels, L A is happiest writing the kind of books she loves to read: addictive stories full of teenage angst, tension, twists and turns.

Home is a small town in the middle of England where she currently juggles being a full-time writer with being a mother/referee to two little people. In her spare time (and when she's not camped out in front of the laptop) you'll most likely find L A immersed in a book, escaping the chaos that is life.

L A loves connecting with readers.

The best places to find her are:
www.lacotton.com